Sam Holden is the pen name of an author and
journalist. He lives in Wiltshire with his wife and two
children. His *Hapless Househusband* novels are partially
based on his experience of (briefly) swapping roles with
his wife.

Praise for Sam Holden

'A very very funny and often touching account of
one man's struggle to try and run Planet Home. This
book should be compulsory reading for every bloke
who wonders what his wife is making all that fuss about
– and for every woman who has wanted to kill that
bloke.' *Allison Pearson*

'This book actually made me laugh out loud and I
stayed up way past my bedtime to finish it! A funny
and different take on parenthood, well paced, with
believable characters and perceptive insight into the
chaos that often surrounds young children.'
My Weekly

'It is a hilarious read and so true to life, it should be
compulsory reading for all husbands.'
www.bettybookmark.co.uk

'Laugh out loud' *The Sun*

Also available by Sam Holden

Diary of a Hapless Househusband

Growing Pains of a Hapless Househusband

Sam Holden

arrow books

Published by Arrow Books 2008

2 4 6 8 10 9 7 5 3 1

First published in Great Britain in 2008 by
Arrow Books
Random House, 20 Vauxhall Bridge Road,
London SW1V 2SA

www.rbooks.co.uk

Addresses for companies within The Random House Group Limited can be
found at: www.randomhouse.co.uk/offices.htm

The Random House Group Limited Reg. No. 954009

A CIP catalogue record for this book
is available from the British Library

ISBN 9780099518075

The Random House Group Limited supports The Forest Stewardship
Council (FSC), the leading international forest certification organisation. All our
titles that are printed on Greenpeace approved FSC certified paper carry the
FSC logo. Our paper procurement policy can be found at
www.rbooks.co.uk/environment

Typeset by SX Composing DTP, Rayleigh, Essex
Printed in the UK by CPI Bookmarque, Croydon, CR0 4TD

This book is for

SAMANTHA DE MELLO, TAMSIN EVANS,
CARLA FILMER, RACHEL HOLLAND &
KATHERINE MASSEY

Tuesday 25 December
5.30 a.m.

Oh frabjous day, callooh, callay, it's Christmas. Glad tidings of joy etc. etc. And what a fun day it's going to be. The highlight will undoubtedly be Sally's mother, who I haven't seen since Easter last year. That, I recall, was something of a disaster, culminating in Jane and Derek, Sally's parents, hotfooting it out in a huff. Sally has made me promise to behave, but it will be difficult. Although it ought to be no harder than a regular Sunday lunch, cooking Christmas lunch is always uniquely stressful. Perhaps I've been too ambitious with the menu, but my God there's a lot to do between now and two o'clock. The only reason why I'm up so damn early is because I'm so wired about it, and not because I'm doing what my mother did. She would put the turkey in the oven at this sort of time in order for it to be perfectly desiccated by lunch. You could take a mouthful of breast, and feel all the moisture in your body drain. By the time you'd had your fourth mouthful, you needed to be reconstituted as if you were powdered human being.

1

I suspect I'd be a lot more chilled if it had been a vintage year, but it really hasn't. This time last year, things were looking so good. We had a fat pile of dosh in the bank, thanks to Sir Roger + Sally's job going well + me actually doing all right as a househusband = life couldn't be much better. Last Christmas was brilliant (and not just because of the lack of Jane and Derek), and when I twiddled the snapped wishbone over my head, I wished that our family would always be as happy as it was then.

So much for bloody wishbones. Cursebones, more like. Thanks to one defective immersion heater and an insurance policy that covered us for everything barring defective immersion heaters, the money went as quickly as the flood that greeted us when we returned from two weeks in Portugal. There was not one part of the house that the water hadn't permeated, and we considered knocking it down and starting again. All our stuff – books, clothes, electrical equipment, pictures, you name it – was ruined. It took six months to sort out the mess, and even now, the house still has an unwholesome air of damp, while our bank account is now completely arid.

Peter and Daisy took it badly, not least because we ended up living in a succession of B & Bs, friends' houses and rented houses, none of which were ideal. They missed our house, their toys (most of which are now in landfill), and were all too aware that Mummy and Daddy weren't exactly in the best of moods. As a result, I indulged them, and gave in to their every whim. This was a mistake, a big mistake. By the time we got back home a few weeks ago, Peter and Daisy had become the most spoiled, whiny children imaginable. They're so bad that they'll soon need ASBOs. Daisy has developed a violent streak, and insists on biting and scratching her brother whenever she can. Peter, meanwhile, is ludicrously demanding, and if he doesn't get what he wants he goes into full tantrum mode, rolling around on the floor, kicking and screaming etc. I was going to take him to a psychiatrist until my mother told me I was the same – 'typical Holden man'. On reflection, perhaps Peter's similarity to me *is* a reason for going to a psychiatrist.

I'm also worried about Sally. Ever since the Great Flood, she's become somewhat taciturn. She's also had a few problems at work, some of which she can tell me about, and some that she can't – wretched secrecy! The ones she can tell me include being passed over for promotion and having her department 'downsized', and I can only speculate as to the others. There was a point in April when she was terribly upset about something, and all she could say was that it was too easy to forget that her job involved people's lives. I asked her if somebody had died, and she said that it was 'somebodies', and even though it wasn't her fault, she still felt responsible. Until that point, I thought there was something glamorous about Sally 'working for the Government', but now I just think that it's a nasty little business for nasty little people (not her of course). I want her out of it, and I've told her as much. But what will we do for money?

Right, I must get on. Christmas Day! Hooray! Fuck, I feel festive.

6.00 a.m.

Have just discovered that we have no turkey. Turkey is still at the butcher's, from where I should have picked it up yesterday afternoon. This is a major disaster. Almost worse than the Great Flood. Why didn't the bloody butcher phone me? What was the point of him taking down my number when I ordered it? Fuckityfuckpoo. All we have is a 4lb chicken in the freezer. That will have to do. And God knows what Jane is going to say. Perhaps I should roast her instead. Unpleasant image of mother-in-law stuffed with chestnut stuffing. Still, there's enough meat on her to keep us going for weeks.

10.00 p.m.

I don't know whether that's merely the worst Christmas Day I've ever had, or the worst Christmas Day anybody in the world has ever had, including Dean Martin, who actually died on Christmas Day. What will have to suffice for the moment is a list of what went wrong:

1. The lack of turkey, as mentioned. Sally wanted to kill me, but I mollified her by saying that was a picnic compared to what I wanted to do to myself.
2. Daisy bit Peter so hard at breakfast that she

actually drew blood. The poor little chap now has deep sororal indentations on his right forearm. Naturally, it took Peter some two hours to recover. Daisy was shut in her bedroom, which made her apoplectic. Sally disapproves of such punishment, but I said that as I was cooking, I was in charge. 'Do you want to shut me in the bedroom as well?' she asked. Not a bad idea, I replied.

3. Ensuing row with Sally. Slammed doors, car engine started, ran out and begged her to stay, she said she was only driving off to clear her head. She's been doing a lot of this recently.

4. Phone call from contrite Sally 10 minutes later informing me she'd had a puncture on the main road and could I pick her up? Bundle children into other car and collect her. Spend 30 seconds attempting to loosen the wheel nuts before admitting failure. Get back home, and call the breakdown people. Line engaged. Decide that I will call back later. Car is far enough off the road.

5. Arrival of Jane and Derek. Instant bollocking for not removing Jane's coat quickly enough. Want to tell her that I would more readily remove her head.

6. Everything OK(ish) until LUNCH, at which Jane was livid at the lack of turkey. I tried to bullshit my way out of it by saying that I didn't really approve of the way that turkeys are reared, to which Jane responded that this was another

example of the 'pathetic sensitivity' that my generation showed to animals. 'It's free-range this, organic that – what's the world coming to?' Cue row between Jane and me about animal husbandry, which was only terminated by Jane announcing that her 'turkey substitute' was raw. Did I eat everything raw, even chicken? She would contract 'salamanella', how could I feed this to her?

7. Jane was right. I chucked the whole chicken into the microwave (much to her disgust – 'We'll get nucleated') which resulted in it being utterly dried out and tasteless.

8. Daisy and Peter behaved atrociously during lunch, which naturally earned much opprobrium from Jane. 'So much for the "househusband" experiment.' It's hard to quantify quite how rude Jane really is. At least Derek just sat and got quietly pissed. I expect he does that most meals. I decided to copy him, which wasn't a great idea.

9. 'Couldn't you have put something a little more generous than 10 p's in the Christmas pudding?'

10. 'Why aren't you standing up for the Queen?'

11. 'We decided not to give you a present this year. We helped you enough after the flood.'

12. 'Do you have the receipt?'

13. 'Don't these children ever behave?'

14. 'It's a pity the rain's so bad, otherwise you could take them for a walk.'

15. At 5.30 a knock on the door. Two policemen,

grim faces, which caused instant sobriety. 'Are you Samuel James Holden?' Heart went thumpity-thump, brain went fuckity-fuck. What could it be? 'Are you the keeper of a green Citroën estate, registration number . . .' Turned out the car wasn't far enough off the road, as a juggernaut had clipped it, which in turn caused it to swerve into the other lane, narrowly avoiding a minibus full of disabled children, but not avoiding the bank, into which the lorry (which apparently contained turkeys – I could have grabbed one!) ploughed, blocking both lanes and thus causing a massive tailback. Turns out I'm being charged with 'leaving a vehicle in a place of endangerment', for which Sally was so apologetic, for which I felt livid, and Jane accused me of being a criminal.

16. After that, I drank a lot more.
17. I don't remember Jane and Derek leaving.
18. I now feel hung-over and dried out, like the chicken.

Roll on the New Year. Happy Bloody Christmas.

Tuesday 1 January

Not exactly a great New Year's Eve last night, largely owing to the fact that I spent it on my own. Sally was called up to the office at 5 o'clock in the afternoon – some flare-up in Ktyteklhdfistan or somewhere – and she didn't get back until 7 this evening. As a result spent the whole day trying to fend off Peter and Daisy's pleadings for their mummy, while doing my best to entertain them. By the time Sally got home, I was ready to vent my spleen, but she looked so knackered, that I thought it would be dreadfully unfair. Instead, I poured her a large gin and tonic and put a slutty supermarket pizza in the oven and we sat down to watch a DVD (all of which we were supposed to do last night).

Predictably, Sally fell asleep just as the *opening* credits began to roll, and so I half-carried her upstairs and tucked her into bed. She murmured something appreciative and then she fell back asleep before I turned off the light. Gave up on the film, and instead sat down to write this.

I really wish Sally would give up her job. I know that it's an impossibility, but there MUST be something else she could do. Even just to move departments to something less taxing would help, but she'd see that as a sign of failure, which I suppose would be fair enough. It might help if I do more consultancy work for Sir Roger, but the more work I do, the less I am able to look after the children, which means hiring a nanny, which is not exactly the point of me being at home to raise them. At least not in Sally's book. And that's a very strict book.

After the disaster that was Christmas, and the non-event that has been New Year, I don't feel good about this year at all.

Friday 4 January

I should have been a soothsayer. My old company has been taken over by Minto Fellowes (what sort of name is that for a firm of management consultants?) which means great news for the partners – I'm guessing a cool £3–5 million each – but not great news for Sam Holden. In fact, utterly crap news: 'Unfortunately, Minto Fellowes operates a strict non-outsourceable operation, which means that your freelance contract will now terminate at the end of February.' That was pretty much it, no apology, no regret. I tried calling Sir Roger, but he was in Antigua apparently. For the next month. Wanker. After all I've done for him. If it weren't for me discovering that those bastards Chris and David were trying to run down the company before taking it over, he wouldn't have had a firm to sell, and now he's tanning his man boobs on some exclusive beach with his latest bimbo.

At bathtime, I got Daisy and Peter to stick up some of their rubber letters on to the tiles to form the sentence 'Sir Roger is a treacherous bastard', and then took a picture of them pulling faces next to it. (I wanted to put something a lot ruder, but I thought explaining what the words 'tosser' and 'fuckwit' meant was somewhat inappropriate for a four-year-old boy and a two-year-old girl.) I then emailed the result to my old work buddy Clive, but the email bounced back.

Broke the bad news to Sally when she got back. I nearly didn't, as she looked drained, but worked on the principle that there was no good time to tell her.

'What are we going to do?' she said.

'Well, we've got your income still. It's not as though we're broke.'

'But we were hoping that your consultancy would bring in enough to cover some school fees.'

'I know, I know,' I said, 'and I'll find some more consultancy work.'

An arched Sally eyebrow appeared over a bloodshot eye.

'Really?'

'Really. Honestly, it'll be fine.'

'Oh God, please don't say "it'll be fine".'

'But it will be, I mean it.'

'You always say that as well.'

We stood in silence until Sally turned and opened the fridge. A small jug of off cream fell out and smashed on to the floor, severely splattering her shoes, which I immediately noticed were suede. I watched Sally's shoulders slump. Normally, she would have had a bit of a fit – I'm pretty sure these are currently (or were) her most favoured footwear – but instead she just turned round with a resigned expression and slipped the shoes off, examined them, and then put them in the bin.

'But, but,' I stammered. 'They'll be fine, won't they?'

Sally shook her head and returned to the fridge.

'Is there anything to actually eat in here?'

'Plenty,' I said.

She withdrew a rubbery leek.

'Well, not that, obviously.'

Next came a bowl with something slightly blue in it.

God knows what it was, but it followed the shoes, along with several other foodstuffs that were either past their sell-by dates, too colourful or not colourful enough.

'What were you planning to cook us this evening?'

I picked up the phone.

'Fancy a takeaway?' I asked boyishly. 'Chinese? Curry? Pizza?'

'I think I'm going to have a bath and go to bed.'

Sunday 6 January

In the end, the weekend wasn't too bad. We had Nigel and Clare round for lunch today, and even though we barely spoke to each other as we attempted to feed and police the five children, it was good to see old friends, and really great to see that the children got on so well. Both Peter and Daisy, barring the odd minor tantrum, were the perfect little hosts, and shared all their toys, which was nothing short of a miracle.

What wasn't so great was the news that Nigel has been promoted, which now means they can send their bunch to the oh-so-swanky private primary school, and they're also looking to buy a new house. Naturally, I pretended to be delighted for him, but if I'm being honest, I can only be genuinely happy at friends' success if I'm also doing well. Is this just me? I don't think so. Surely it's human nature. At least I hope it is. However, I think I've got a bit too much of whatever it is, as I find my heart also leaps when I hear that a friend has failed. I suspect this makes me a very bad person, but I hope not.

In truth, I want my friends and I all to be equally rich and successful. This evening I told Sally that if I won £5 million on the lottery, I'd give each of our good friends £250,000 so they wouldn't feel so jealous.

'But you should be giving them that money because you were generous and wanted to share your luck,' she said.

'Not at all,' I replied. 'I'd be giving them the money as a sort of bribe to stop them hating me.'

'But that's awful.'

'I don't think so. Besides, I doubt they'd worry about my motive. I wouldn't if someone gave me a quarter of a million quid.'

'Do all men think like this?'

'Yes,' I said confidently. 'It's a nasty place inside the male head.'

Sally grimaced.

'Charming,' she said. 'So basically you think that men hate all men richer than them?'

'Yup.'

'And you only really like the ones who are poorer than you?'

I thought about this.

'Um, yes.'

'In that case,' she said, 'you'd better start looking for some new friends.'

Sally's logic was unpalatably brutal. I am easily the poorest of my friends, but the whole point of me becoming a househusband was that such things didn't matter. However, they still do. I wish I could just find some sort of middle ground between being Total New Dad and Incredibly Rich Dad. The only ground I'm in is some sort of swamp. I feel like sending Sir Roger one of the crappy postcards of the local church and writing 'Wish You Were Here' on it, with an arrow pointing to the graveyard.

Just before I came up, Sally reminded me that we have dinner with her sister Victoria next Friday. This is fine, as Victoria is a lot poorer than us, so I like her immensely despite her pothead vocab. Her boyfriend Rick is some sort of 'landscape designer', who is indeed extremely poor, so I think he may have to become my new best friend.

Tuesday 8 January

Whatever is happening in Ktyteklhdfistan is getting worse. Not that I can possibly know what is actually happening there, because places like Ktyteklhdfistan never appear on the news. (I doubt that they ever did.) However, what I do know is that Sally is working increasingly late, and when she gets home, she bashes away furiously on her laptop. She seems muted and distant. I've never known her like this. She also looks somewhat tired, and I even thought I spotted a grey hair in amongst her normally shampoo-advert-like long brown tresses.

When I ask her what the matter is, all she can say is that things in Ktyteklhdfistan are pretty bad and there's a lot to sort out. She can't be more specific, which is infuriating.

'Surely you can tell me something?' I asked this evening.

She shook her head as she drained her third glass of wine. (Another worrying development – she's beginning to drink as much as me.)

'Not even a little bit?'

'Nope.'

'Is the world going to end? Have they got nukes?'

Worryingly, Sally paused.

'Put it this way,' she sighed. 'The country is a fucking mess. That's about the politest way I can put it.'

(Oh dear. Swearing like me as well.)

I felt a little helpless. After all, there was not a lot I could say or do.

'I know,' I said eventually.

'What?'

'Perhaps they need some management consultants.'

Sally looked at me, wide-eyed.

'Are you being serious?'

'Of course not!' I lied.

Thursday 10 January

I'm ruing my latest 'it'll be fine'. There is no consultancy work out there, not even for me, the great whistleblower who saved Sir Roger's august firm of Musker Walsh and Sloss (Consultants) Ltd. I am feeling increasingly bitter about this, perhaps more so than when I lost my job.

I'm also feeling a bit guilty that I've taken this out on

Peter and Daisy. After picking up Peter from school and Daisy from playgroup, the rest of the day was a bit of a washout. Literally, because it was raining, and metaphorically because everything I attempted to do with them felt half-hearted. They picked up on my mood immediately, and as a result, they were bolshy. Example: painting. Normally they love painting, but today they showed a marked reluctance.

'Painting's boring,' said Peter after I had plonked the paints and brushes bad-temperedly down in front of him on the kitchen table.

'But you like painting.'

'No I don't.'

Peter's reluctance was copied by Daisy, who shook her head and went 'no' each time I tried to put a paintbrush in her hand. Normally she is good for a squiggle or two, but today she just flung the paintbrush to the floor. I then told her this was naughty, and she burst into tears.

'Mummy!' she kept crying.

'Mummy's at work,' I shouted.

'I want my mummy!' started Peter.

Gritted teeth.

'Mummy is not here,' I said slowly.

Cue large shouting match which saw me leave them alone in the kitchen while I read the paper in the living room. Or rather, I pretended to read the paper as all I could concentrate on was the ceaseless bellyaching.

'Just get on and paint!' I shouted, knowing that this

would only infuriate them, but by now I was feeling bloody-minded.

'Mummy!'

'I don't want to do painting!'

'Mummy!'

And so on. All because I had started them off badly. It was my fault, I knew it, but I find it impossible to hide my mood from them. Perhaps I should be more professional, and not take my problems to 'work', but they should realise that Daddy is human as well, even if not a particularly brilliant one. Later, partly out of guilt, but more because I actually wanted to, I gave them both some huge cuddles on the sofa, and order was restored.

My whole life is stretching in front of me, and from here it looks like something Daisy would have painted had she been willing – a bloody mess, a meaningless bunch of squiggles and splodges that add up to very little, but something which other people must be polite about. I'll be able to see it in my friends' eyes, the same look that I give Daisy and Peter when I admire their artwork. And there'll be the same words as well – the over enthusiastic 'well dones' and 'good for yous'. But the big difference between the children and me is that they're proud of what they do. I just pretend to be.

Oh God. This is all getting self-pitying and revolting. Dinner at Victoria's tomorrow night – there had better not be any rich people there.

Sunday 13 January

Dinner at Victoria's was so much better than I expected. So so much better. In fact, potentially life-changing. I must do my best not to get too excited. But I can't help it, and I doubt anybody would be able to keep calm in my circumstances. I've gone from the equivalent of *nul points* to the cusp of Eurovision greatness in just a few days, and if this thing pays off, boy will it pay off.

Anyway, to begin at the beginning. The assembled looked pretty much as I had feared – absurd facial hair, clothes too young for the bodies therein – but there was one of them towards whom I immediately gravitated. Despite having those standard 'I'm alternative, me' rectangular glasses, and an inexcusable ponytail (I really thought ponytails had been collectively shorn in about 1997), he looked a little more bright-eyed and less stoned than the rest of Victoria's friends.

It turned out he was called Dom Simons, and he was a TV producer. (I should have guessed.) Normally, I have little time for people in the media. Most of them are full of crap, and think they know exactly how the world works with their glib categorisations and zeitgeisty spiel, and sure enough, Dom seemed no exception. Also, like most media people, he believed that his voice was the only one worth listening to, and he spent the first ten minutes telling me all about himself. Still, he was entertaining enough, and beneath the self-puffery there seemed to beat the heart of a genuinely intelligent and interesting bloke.

Eventually, he asked me what I did. I'm always tempted to lie at this point, because saying 'I'm a house-husband' sounds so wet. In fact, I've practised saying it so many times, I feel like an actor who's been asked to play James Bond, and is hung up on how to say, 'The name's Bond, James Bond.' I've tried saying it in a sort of macho way, but that just sounds pathetic. On this occasion, I just kind of blurted out:

'ActuallyI'mahousehusband.'

'What was that?'

'A househusband. You know, I stay at home and look after the children.'

Dom's eyes bulged roundly behind his rectangular frames.

'Wow,' he said. 'That's awesome.'

'Awesome? Well, if you think nappies are awesome, think again.'

Dom's glasses slipped down his nose a little. He looked genuinely 100 per cent surprised.

'How . . . but how . . . how did it happen? I mean did you choose to do this? Or what?'

'Well it's quite simple. I got sacked. And then my wife decided that she would go back to work, because her job was more interesting, and she thought in these days of sexual equality there was no reason why she shouldn't be the breadwinner.'

I was aware, even as I was saying all this, that I had said it a thousand times before.

Another wow from Dominic, and then: 'So what did you do before then?'

This is getting increasingly common. When I tell most blokes that I'm a househusband, they find it so beyond their ken that they then ask what I used to do.

'I was a management consultant.'

'OK,' said Dom, manfully struggling to work out what to say next. 'And, um, how did you find that?' he asked.

'To tell the truth I enjoyed it.'

'D'you miss it?'

I chewed this over along with a stale crisp. Victoria's crisps are always stale. Why is that?

'I miss the office life,' I said. 'I don't miss the politics. I suppose what I miss most of all is making some sort of professional impact. You know, with management consultancy, you're actually going to a firm, and within a few weeks you've made them more profitable, and you've really made a huge difference.'

'I thought you lot just sacked people.'

I waggled my finger in a vaguely schoolmasterly way.

'Aha! A common misconception,' I replied playfully, although in truth I was a little narked. It's so unfair that everybody thinks that management consultants just sack people in order to make companies look profitable. When we went to some big insurance firm down in Poole, I remember recommending that they should actually employ more people. I told all this to Dom, who seemed to take it on board. Well, he sorted of nodded a bit, before asking me whether I still kept my hand in.

'I do a bit of consultancy from time to time,' I said sheepishly. 'Good for staying in the loop, that sort of thing.'

More absent-minded nodding. I could tell that I was beginning to bore him. (This is something else that seems to be happening more often. Either I really have got more boring, or I have always been boring, and am now far more sensitive.) My next conversational gambit was therefore born out of desperation.

'But you know what?' I asked. 'I think I'd make the subject of a great TV programme.'

This time Dom's eyes popped open so widely that they actually went beyond his frames, making it look as though he had two Tube logos stuck on his face.

'You?' he spluttered on his mulled wine.

'Why not? You know, a real-life documentary of a househusband. The trials and tribulations of an ordinary bloke stuck in a woman's job.'

More bulging. It was hardly surprising – the idea was not exactly well thought out, and had only been voiced in order to make conversation.

'Well, it's, um, very *interesting*,' said Dom.

'You think so?'

'Yesssss,' he said convincingly. 'But I think it needs another element, you know, a celebrity or something.'

A celebrity. Why did it always have to be a celebrity? What right do celebrities have to lecture us? The other night I caught the end of some female comedian presenting a programme on the British Empire. What did she know about it? Precisely nothing. About as much as my old history tutor knows about situation comedy. In fact, probably less than that. And then, in the midst of my seethe about celebs, a brainwave.

'Why not a programme about me trying to bring up my children according to the techniques of management consultancy?'

'What?'

Excitedly, I told Dom all about the Holden Childcare Programme, and how I had attempted to raise Daisy and Peter using it.

'Did it work?' Dom asked.

'Er, no,' I admitted sheepishly. 'So perhaps the idea isn't really a flyer after all.'

'Well, that doesn't technically matter,' said Dom.

'What doesn't?'

'Whether it worked or not.'

'Why not?'

'Well, truth should never get in the way of good factual entertainment.'

Now it was the turn of my eyes to bulge.

'I thought that only applied to travel writing.'

Dom laughed a little.

'You know all those makeover programmes?'

'Sort of.'

(I didn't want to admit that I knew them a little too well. They're on when I cook dinner.)

'The ones in which they make a new you, or a new house, all that crap.'

'Yes, I know.'

'Well, they're a load of shit.'

'Really?'

'Yup, completely made up.'

'How can you be so sure?' I asked.

21

'I make the bloody things.'

My turn to splutter on mulled wine.

'Really?'

'Yup.'

Dom then gave me a list of the programmes he had made, most of which I had either heard of, or had indeed watched.

'Remember the one where that old bag had a tummy tuck?'

'Sure,' I replied. 'That was incredible – she looked so much better.'

'Well, she refused to have the surgery.'

'But I thought I saw her being operated on.'

'Stock footage.'

'But she *looked* thinner. I mean, her tummy had disappeared.'

'We just Photoshopped it out.'

'You can do that?'

Dom smiled, perhaps a little smugly.

'We can do *anything*.'

'But isn't that just, well, you know, *lying*?' I asked.

'I guess so. But we're giving the punters what they want.'

I was shocked. And I also felt a little naïve.

'But don't the participants complain?' I asked.

'No,' said Dom, adjusting his glasses. 'We make them sign non-disclosure agreements, so if they moan, we sue the fuck off them.'

Christ, I thought, the man was amoral. He would have made a great management consultant. Before I could say anything, Dom continued.

'So that's why it doesn't matter whether your management consultancy childcare works or not.'

Dom emptied his glass and then smiled a little.

'I'm warming to the idea, you know,' he said.

'Well, I was only joking, I mean, I wasn't seriously suggesting . . .'

'No, I think it's got some mileage. "Business" is sexy at the moment, and I like the way this combines that with home life.'

'You do?'

Dom paused.

'I've got it!' he said. 'We get you to go around and management-consult problem children. You know, in you go with your "sound business practices" and pie charts and what have you, and by the end of the week the children are good as gold and eat their greens etc.'

Now I was warming to the idea.

'We could call it something like *Wonderhubby*,' I said.

Dom laughed and then invited me to give him five, which I did, somewhat awkwardly, as I am the least 'street' person you could meet, with the exception of Dom.

'*Wonderhubby*! I like it!'

'Thanks,' I said. In fact, I rather liked it as well.

The one person who didn't like it AT ALL was Sally. I told her about my conversation with Dom in the car on the way home, and she was dismissive.

'Yes darling, I can quite see you as a TV superstar.'

The sarcasm tore through my drunken gaiety.

'I know you think it's just a silly idea,' I said, 'but honestly, Dom's serious. He's asked me to give him a bell on Monday to arrange a meeting.'

'You are joking.'

'Not at all.'

Sally half-sighed, half-yawned.

'I know what you're thinking,' she said. 'You're thinking that in a year's time you'll have made zillions of pounds, and you'll be enjoying worldwide fame, and then I can give up work and then we can live happily ever after off the proceeds of your lucrative TV career.'

'Exactly,' I said, determined that being unashamedly optimistic was the best policy. 'Just you wait.'

'Oh I will.'

I wish Sally wasn't quite so negative about my ideas. I admit, not all of them come to something, but when they do, they work out really well. I can't be bothered to list them all right now, but there are plenty.

Monday 14 January
Left a message with Dom this morning. Didn't get a reply. I expect he's incredibly busy. Most people in TV are.

Tuesday 15 January
Left two messages with Dom, and then sent an email – I guessed his address from his company's website. No replies. When Sally got in (late) she asked me whether

I had heard anything. I was tempted to lie, but couldn't do so because a) I'm thoroughly decent and trustworthy and don't lie to my wife (often) and b) she'd see through me if I did.

'What did I tell you?' she said. 'It was just one of those drunken dinner-party conversations.'

'But this was before we got drunk,' I pleaded. 'This was one of those rare sober dinner-party conversations. In fact, it was before we had any dinner at all. Honestly, Sally, he really liked the idea.'

'*Wonderhubby*? Are you sure he wasn't winding you up?'

'The name was my idea.'

An arched Sally eyebrow.

'How's work?' I asked, changing the subject. 'Is the world going to explode?'

'Who knows?' she replied, before pouring herself a large glass of wine.

Her tone sounded in no way light-hearted.

'And frankly,' she continued, 'who cares?'

This smacked slightly of self-pity and I told her so.

'I'm sorry, I'm not being much fun, I know.'

'No need to apologise,' I said. 'Everybody goes through crap stages at work.'

We hugged and then kissed and then went to bed with the rest of the bottle of wine.

Thursday 17 January

Still nothing from that ponytailed tosser. Sally was right, it was just one of those conversations. I now feel utterly let down and rather sheepish. Mooted the idea of finding another TV producer to Sally over a (late) dinner, and she looked unimpressed.

'Sweetheart,' she said, 'don't you think this bloke Dom may have just been making conversation with you?'

I chewed it over, along with my slightly-too-tough pork chop. (Why can I never cook pork just right? I must have some porcine blind spot.)

'No, I don't think so,' I replied, genuinely worried that Sally might have been right. By now, I was imagining what I could do with a pair of scissors and Dom's ponytail.

'Anyway, I think you should concentrate on getting some more consultancy work,' Sally said.

She was right. That's the thing about Sally – she usually is. And, even when she's right, my pig-headedness won't allow me to acknowledge it.

'Just you see,' I said.

Sally rolled her eyes backward. We dropped the conversation.

Wednesday 23 January

Oh my God. I can't believe she's back – Emily the Jodhpur Mum; Emily of the voracious threesome-with-two-Greek-fishermen-in-a-beach-hut; Emily who tried to instigate some swinging with Sally and me; divorced Emily who had fled the village. This morning, when I dropped Peter and Daisy at school, I caught a glimpse of *those* jodhpur-clad legs and derrière from the other end of the high street. Just to confirm, I rang her at lunchtime, and she answered. I put the phone down immediately, thanking God that I had remembered to withhold my number.

I mean, it's not that I fancy Emily, it's just that life is so much less complicated without her around. Clearly, after THAT evening last summer, in which Emily tried to jump into both our pants, Sally despises her. However, that was never an issue, because when she and Jim got divorced, it was Emily and the children who moved out of the village. But now she's here, and one of these days, I'll bump into her. I can just see myself coming over all 'osh–gosh' and sweaty and nervous. Idiot.

However, even though I know she's trouble, Emily is good fun, and Peter and Thomas (her youngest) used to get on really well. Frankly, I could do with some good company, and Emily is certainly that. After all, how many other people round here open up a bottle of wine at eleven in the morning?

I don't think I'll tell Sally. At least not yet. We've sort of been here before, I know, and I should learn from my previous mistakes. But, as it is, Sally's got enough on her plate at work, and I don't want her being distracted by thoughts of her husband and the village vamp having cute 'playdates' together.

Still nothing from Dom. Have just sent one last email, risking what feeble amount of dignity I have left.

Thursday 24 January

Well, I was right. I did come over all sweaty and nervous. Was it because she was wearing her jodhpurs? Or was it because I couldn't shake out of my head the image of her being spit-roasted by Pavlos and Kyriacou? Or, yet again, was it the memory of her rubbing herself against me at that dinner? Whatever it was, I stammered and spluttered like a teenager, or rather, like I used to when I was a teenager – i.e., a LOT. In fact, I think I actually went 'osh–gosh' when she said her absurdly flirtatious 'well, hello' outside the school gate.

'Hi,' I then managed to say, my voice making me the lead chorister I never was. 'So, are you, um, you know, back here?'

Emily grinned. Not a great grin to be honest, a bit gummy, but nevertheless, still quite saucy.

'No,' she replied, 'this is just a ghost.'

I looked gormlessly at her.

'Ha ha,' I eventually sort-of-laughed when my dim brain eventually clicked into gear.

'He's grown,' she said, looking down at my midriff.

Jesus, I thought, right here, right now, at 9.05 outside the school gate. Now she was divorced, she was even more insatiable. I wasn't aware that 'he' had in fact grown, and I started to curse my priapism. I remained muted in shock.

'It's amazing how fast they grow,' Emily continued as she looked down. 'I bet the girls just love him!'

She then knelt down, the fabric of her jodhpurs

stretching tightly over her frankly pretty damn perfect legs.

'Really Emily, I um . . .' I stammered.

'Can I give him a kiss?' she said.

Moments before winning the fool of the year award, it occurred to me that she wasn't talking about my groin. To my utter relief, she was talking about Peter, who was standing silently by my side, sucking his thumb.

'Of course you can!' I said in a falsetto.

Emily proceeded to give Peter a large hug and a smacker on the cheek, and she then did the same to Daisy, who chuckled appreciatively from her buggy.

'Say hello to Emily Peter,' I said, forcing his thumb out of his mouth.

'Hello to Emily Peter,' he said.

'Do you want to come round and play?' she asked him. 'Thomas has missed you.'

'Yes,' said Peter.

'Yes *please*,' I said to Peter, who had already shoved his thumb back in his mouth.

Emily stood up.

'And how about his daddy? Would he like to come round and play soon?'

Sometimes I am amazed at my self-control. Today, however, was not one of those times.

'Well, um, yes. When?'

'Tomorrow morning?'

'Er, OK!'

I feel such a rat. And I'm certainly not going to tell Sally. I feel like an adulterer, but so long as I don't do anything (which I won't), then my conscience should be clear. There's no point in telling her, because it will only upset her. So, in a way, it's a kindness.

I still feel like a rat, though.

Friday 25 January

This time, much to my disappointment (and slight relief) Emily did not offer me a glass of wine when I turned up with Daisy at 11 o'clock (no playgroup on Fridays, which is probably just as well – Daisy makes a great 'shield'). Instead, it was instant coffee and a packet of bourbons. ('Sorry, since the divorce I can't afford real coffee, and I'm not the type of hausfrau who bakes her own biscuits.') Leaving Daisy to play with some of Thomas's Transformers and Power Rangers, Emily and I sat down and we caught up with each other's news. She told me that the divorce had been hideous, but quick, and Jim had done the decent thing and let her keep the house, although she had to pay him rent for his 50 per cent. Jim was now living up in London, and already had a new girlfriend, called Emily coincidentally. ('At least when he moans out my name in a moment of passion, he won't be caught out.') I then told Emily about the Great Flood, and how work for me had dried up.

'That's awful,' she said, leaning forward, one hand stretched out as if to touch my knee. Thankfully, I was too far away for any such flirtatious contact, and I kept it that way.

'I know,' I replied. 'Bit of a bummer.'

'That's an understatement! So what are you going to do?'

I shrugged my shoulders in a slightly dejected fashion.

'Dunno,' I said, sounding like a teenage loser.

'Can you do some freelancing?'

'I could, but there's not a lot of work about.'

I was desperate to tell her about *Wonderhubby*, but I suspected she would just laugh at me. For a while, we kind of marked time with talk about children and news about the locals – all pretty anodyne stuff, which we were clearly both finding a little dull. It felt like – and I really hope it wasn't – the sort of vapid meaningless conversation you have with someone before you kiss them for the first time. You both know what's in the air, and you both know that you should be doing something else with your mouths rather than talking, but neither of you have yet found the guts to just get on with it. Of course, vapid meaningless conversation can occur without any sexual chemistry, and it would be an error to stick your tongue down the throat of every woman who was a crap conversationalist. I have made this error on several occasions.

So, out of desperation, I decided to bring up *Wonderhubby*, largely because I had run out of things to say. I told Emily all about how the programme would work, etc. She just smirked the whole way through my 'pitch'.

'So what do you think?' I asked. 'Your face tells me that you think it's a load of crap.'

'Quite the opposite,' she replied.

'Really? I suspect you're only saying that to humour me.'

Emily shook her head, and the gesture looked sincere. Her eyes opened wide, strengthening the impression of truthfulness. (I get the feeling that Emily in fact does a lot of lying.)

'Not at all!' she said. 'I really like the idea, I really do. It's so much better than half the crap that gets on the TV these days.'

'You really think so? Honestly?'

'Absolutely. After all, you've got nothing to lose, have you?'

I didn't know whether I should be insulted by this, so I decided not to be.

'Quite,' I replied.

'One thing,' said Emily.

'Yes?'

'Will Sally be up for appearing in it?'

'What do you mean?'

'Well, obviously, if you're going to present yourself as the perfect househusband, you're going to need to show how blissfully happy you are as a family, you know, show the viewers the benchmark which they should be aiming towards.'

There was a trace of bitterness in the way Emily said 'blissfully'. But she had a point – Sally would have to be involved. And, if I know my wife well enough, it's the last thing she'd want to do.

'I'm sure she'd be absolutely fine with it,' I said.

'Really?'

'Of course. Anyway, we're getting ahead of ourselves here! After all, I'm just a bloke sitting in a village in the middle of England with a crackpot idea for a TV programme and a TV producer who won't return his emails. There must be hundreds of people like me.'

I couldn't believe how sensible I was sounding. It was as if Emily's enthusiasm had forced me to become more realistic. Now I know how Sally feels when she talks to me. No wonder she sometimes calls me Tigger.

I'd prefer 'tiger', frankly.

Sunday 27 January

Went to Sally's parents for lunch today. I had caved in to Sally's insistence that it was unrealistic that I would never see them again, and that soon the children would ask questions, and there would never be a good time to see them so why not now, etc. etc. Jane was on her typically acidulous form, and carried on dropping hints about my lack of employment. Despite Sally's protestations that looking after the children and running the house was a form of employment, Jane persisted in her usual tirade. Still, she can be witty, much to my annoyance. While we were getting to the end of the roast chicken, Jane and Peter pulled the wishbone. Jane won, and judging by her technique, she certainly cheated.

She then made a great palaver of waving the bone over her head and mumbling silently.

'What are you wishing for?' I asked.

'I can't tell you that, Sam,' she replied. 'Don't you know how it works?'

'How what works?'

Jane tutted.

'If you tell someone what you're wishing for, then it will never come true.'

'Oh.'

(How come I have never heard this before? Is it just me?)

Jane put the bone down on her plate.

'So then,' I continued, 'do you think it will come true?'

She fixed me with her Margaret-Thatcher-like stare.

'Well, you're still here, aren't you?'

I smirked sarcastically back at her, frustrated at my inability to think of a witty response quickly enough. Jane smirked too, in a repellently smug sort of way, like a poisonous nine-year-old girl who has eaten the last sweet in the packet and is crowing about it. I wanted to ram the wishbone down her throat, shouting, 'Wish on that, bitchface!' but instead I just asked if I might have another roast potato.

'Certainly not,' Jane replied. 'Those are for the dog.'

I know my place.

Tuesday 29 January

I don't believe it. At 15.56 I received an email from Dom. When it arrived, my heart fluttered, and when I read it, it fluttered even more.

Sam
Sorry not to have replied to your (many!) calls and
emails. Been megafrantic editing a doc on fat
people. Still crazee about *Wonderhubby*. When can
you come in and discuss? How about Thursday?
And can you bring the kids? Would be good to show
my colleagues how effective you are as a dad!
Cheers
Dom

The first thing I did was to email Dom right back, to say
that Thursday at 12 would be perfect. The second thing
I did was to forward the email to Sally, with a mildly
triumphant, 'See? Not just a drunken dinner-party
conversation.'

After a few minutes the following pinged back:

Darling
He sounds like a complete berk. Not entirely keen
on children missing school/playgroup to go to some
TV studio, but you must do what you must do. How
are P & D? Hope you managed to get them some
air this afternoon – weather's been glorious, at least
it has in London. I won't need a big supper as ate
well at lunch.
Love you
Sxxxxxxxxxxxxxxxxxx

There was something maddeningly dismissive about
Sally's tone, but what really stuck in my craw was the

reminder of my domestic responsibilities. I knew the subtext perfectly well – 'don't you go getting any ideas, young man' – and so that evening, over our light supper, I had it out with her.

'You really don't like this *Wonderhubby* thing, do you?'

Sally put down her fork and studied the particularly fine mushroom omelette I had made.

'To be honest, I was rather hoping it would go away.'

'Why?'

'Because I think it will come to nothing, and you will have wasted a load of time and effort.'

'How can you know that?'

'I can't, but if I were to place a bet . . .'

'I wish you weren't so negative the whole time.'

'I'm not!' Sally snapped. 'You always accuse me of being negative. Just because I'm not like you, and just because I don't jump in feet first at every opportunity, doesn't mean I'm negative.'

I didn't reply. I thought she was wrong, but I had somehow lost the will to argue. I got up and slid the rest of my omelette into the bin.

'Look,' Sally said. 'I'm sorry, it's just that I can't quite share your enthusiasm. It's not as if this bloke Dom emailed you the next day, is it?'

'He was *busy*.'

Sally waved that one away.

'We're all busy,' she said.

'Well, not everyone thinks it's a crap idea.'

'Oh yes? Like who?'

'Well, Emily for one.'

Pin drop silence.

I couldn't believe what I had said. Of all the names I could have come up with, I said HERS. Fool, Holden, you sodding fool.

'*Emily?*'

'That's right, Emily,' I said, trying to sound calm about it. 'She's moved back to the village. Jim's moved to London and she's renting 50 per cent of the house off him. I think it's a very good way of doing things . . .'

'And when did you see her?'

'At the school gates. We chatted a bit, caught up on news, you know.'

'And you told her about your TV idea at the school gates?'

Crunch time. Did I mention that I had been round to Emily's house? Well, I had nothing to hide, and if I did hide it, then Sally would be bound to find out, and when she did, she would assume I was hiding something far worse than I actually was, so in the end, I thought it better not to keep things hidden. Phew.

'She invited me round for coffee last week.'

'You kept that quiet.'

'Didn't think it worth mentioning.'

'Is that right?'

'Well, I also thought you might get jealous, and I didn't want that.'

'How very thoughtful,' said Sally. 'But I rather thought you were the jealous one.'

Immediately my mind flashed back to over a year ago,

when I obsessively chased Sally through the streets of London while she was ensconced in the back of a car with ex-beau-cum-close-confidant-and-colleague-who-I-now-know-is-gay Nick.

'We can all get jealous,' I replied.

Sally sighed.

'I'm not being jealous Sam, I'm just being protective. The last time we went to her house, she tried to have sex with you, and kept saying how good-looking you were. You do remember that, don't you?'

'Just a bit.'

'So it shouldn't surprise you that I might not like the idea of you going round there.'

'Which is why I didn't tell you.'

'Wrong, Sam. Which is why you shouldn't have gone round there in the first place.'

'Are you telling me who I should and shouldn't see during my days?'

'No! But we know what Emily is like, and by seeing her you're playing with fire.'

'I can keep her under control.'

'You can, can you?'

I was genuinely angry by now.

'Look – I have no interest in Emily. I don't fancy her, she's not my type. If she still fancies me, then that's her problem, isn't it? But she's good company, and heavens above, I could do with some adult conversation during the day.'

'There are plenty of other people you can see.'

'Like who?'

Sally named some names, names of people that I have no interest in seeing. I dismissed them all as either being too boring, or women who clearly didn't like the idea of a man 'invading' their female-only world of coffee mornings and lunchtime quiche.

'Well, you do what you want, Sam, you always do.'

'Now you're making me sound like some selfish twat, riding roughshod over your feelings.'

'You said it.'

With that, Sally went upstairs and shut herself in the bathroom. When we went to bed, there was a sort of polite kiss goodnight, a kiss that engendered more frostiness than had we not bothered.

Wednesday 30 January

I spent much of today preparing for tomorrow's meeting. I have to confess that I am more than a little nervous. The last time I did something like this was back at work, although we used to have weeks – if not months – to prepare an important pitch. And not only that, we had secretaries and researchers and all manner of other support staff. Instead, I have Peter and Daisy, who are crap at PowerPoint. Nevertheless, I think I've managed to cobble something together that will be both convincing and 'sexy'. (I think that's a word these TV people use a lot.)

Both children have been on particularly revolting form today, especially Daisy. At lunchtime she refused to eat her tomatoes, and kept trying to get down from the table. Under normal circumstances, the slack dad that I am, I would have let her toddle off, convincing myself that a few chunks of ham and bread constituted a healthy lunch. However, today I decided that I would put my foot down, in a pathetic attempt to exert some discipline before tomorrow's meeting.

'Don't want them!' she announced. (I think this is the only sentence Daisy knows.)

'But you like tomatoes,' I insisted.

'Don't want them!'

'Come on, Daisy, you must eat your fruit! Otherwise you won't become a big strong girl.'

(I briefly wondered how much she actually wanted to become a big strong girl.)

'Don't want them!'

I picked up half a cherry tomato and held it near her mouth.

'Come on Daisy – just eat this one and the ones on your plate and then you can get down.'

'DON'T WANT IT!' (A slight variation. Her language is definitely improving.)

She started struggling to get down from her chair, but I forced her to sit. This thwarting of her 'great escape' served to only make her more furious, and soon she started to scream, the prelude to a full-on Daisy tantrum. Still, I tried to play it cool, which went against my entire nature.

'Come on Daisy. Just. One. Little. Tomato.'

Had she screamed any louder or higher, then I swear the light bulbs would have burst. She was turning the same colour as the food I was trying to feed her, and she was writhing in her chair like a dervish.

'DOWN!' she kept screaming. 'DOWN! GET DOWN!'

'No Daisy! You stay here until you finish your lunch!'

By now my voice was beginning to rise, partly because I was getting angry, but more crucially because I wanted to drown out her tantrum. For the next two minutes, our screaming increased to the point that I was sure the neighbours would call the police. What could I do? I was determined not to let her get down, and I was doubly determined that she was going to finish her food.

Options included:

1) Walk away and let her stew. This would have been hopeless, as she can scream for hours, and that would have driven me insane.

2) Force the food into her mouth. Clearly too dangerous.

3) Continue yelling. Tempting, but traumatic.

4) Give her a smack on the bottom. Hmmmmm. Corporal punishment. Tricky one. I once smacked Peter on the bottom, and although it had the desired effect, I've regretted it ever since. But right then, I came closer than I've been in ages to giving Daisy a smack. While she carried on screaming, writhing and doing the full 'terrible two' tantrum, I caught sight of the two of us reflected in the kitchen window. I looked so big next to her, and she so small and defenceless, that

it made me realise that it would be a complete abuse of my physical superiority.

5) Sit there and ignore it. I've tried that tactic before, but it doesn't work. Her will is too strong, and mine is too weak.

6) Pour a glass of water over her. Extremely appealing – would shock her but not harm her. Show her that I was very cross. Only downside was that it might be humiliating, but by then I was beyond such niceties, so this was the option I plumped for.

At first, I thought the tactic backfired. Although I gently sploshed only a finger of water on the top of her head, she screamed even louder, a feat I didn't think was possible.

'Eat your tomatoes, Daisy!' I growled.

I stood poised with the glass.

'Otherwise I'll pour more water on you!'

'NO!'

Whereupon she grabbed all the remaining tomato halves and shoved them in her mouth as though she hadn't eaten in a month. She chewed them messily, and the seeds splurged all the way down her white top, but I couldn't care. The tactic had worked! I decided immediately that I would include it as part of my *Wonderhubby* pitch.

While her temper subsided, I confess that I felt sorry for the little thing, and I gave her the most enormous hug, and told her that Daddy was so happy that she had eaten her food, and that she was a good girl. She sniffled and sobbed for quite a few minutes, which almost made me sniffle and sob as well. Had I been cruel to her? I don't know, but what I do know is that I haven't told Sally what I did. I expect housewives don't confess all their errors to their husbands, so I don't see why I should be any different.

Anyway, big day tomorrow, very big day. I think I know what I'm going to say, but what the hell, I can just make it up as I go along. After all, that's all they do on TV anyway.

Thursday 31 January

It would have been so much easier without the children. Everything always is. (In fact, being a househusband without children would be the best job in the world, although it wouldn't actually be called a job, it would be called 'unemployed'.) Peter and Daisy behaved atrociously. The worst ever. It would have made so much more sense to have left them at school/ playgroup, but in my boundless confidence, I thought they would prove to be great examples of the Holden Childcare Programme (not that it really exists).

The first mistake was taking the train, which, naturally, was overcrowded and delayed. I had wanted to sit at a table, but none were available, so the three of us had to cram into two seats which made those found on a budget airline look like armchairs in a country house hotel.

For two minutes – perhaps three – this was fine. Daisy

and Peter coloured in their respective colouring-in books – Spider-Man for Peter, Little Mermaid for Daisy – and I even had the opportunity to briefly wonder what sort of offspring Spidey and Ariel would have in the event of their getting it together. And then the trolley came, containing all the crap you never ate unless you were on a train.

'Daddy, can I have a crisp?' asked Peter.

'Crisp! Crisp! Crisp!' chanted Daisy excitedly, bouncing up and down on my lap.

'No you can't,' I replied. 'It's not lunchtime.'

They simultaneously let out the sort of whine that attracted the attention of everyone in earshot, which in this instance meant the entire carriage. I was aware of some fairly disapproving scrutiny, and I was determined to show the world how excellent a father I was by not caving in.

'Ah, ah,' I went, holding up an admonishing finger. 'No whining.'

'But I want a crisp!' said Peter.

'I'm hungry,' said Daisy.

(Incidentally, Daisy's two-year-old speech is never quite as fluent as this diary makes out. 'I'm hungry' was more like 'I ungee', but for the sake of future generations of Holdens – should there be any reading this – I feel that it is best to translate Daisy's highly individual version of English.)

'In that case you can have an apple,' I said, reaching inside the daybag.

I fumbled in its dark interior, smugly congratulating

myself on being Captain Efficient. Before we left, I had sliced up said fruit and put it in a Tupperware container, along with some water biscuits. Very healthy. Very keen. Very perfect dad. Very out of character.

However, there was one small problem. I couldn't find the container.

'But I want a crisp!'

'Crisp! Crisp! Crisp!'

I looked up from the bag, catching the eye of the trolley bloke, who was pouring warmish water into a cup for the middle-aged woman across the aisle. He looked at me, no doubt wondering whether I was going to give in.

'Crisp! Crisp!'

I rummaged in the bag again, noting that I had usefully brought their swimming costumes and some towels. Bugger. Completely the wrong bag. Not just no apple and no biscuits, but no water bottles, nappies, or anything else that might actually be of some use.

'Crisp!'

'Daisy, stop it!' I barked.

'Would you like anything, sir?' asked the trolley bloke.

'I'd like a crisp!' Peter informed him.

'He wasn't talking to you,' I said.

'Cheese and onion,' said Peter, almost admirably oblivious to his father.

'Or do you have salt and vinegar?' he asked.

'Peter!' I hissed.

'Crisp! Crisp! Crisp!' Daisy chanted.

I was desperate for a coffee, but I decided that it would be unfair if I ordered something and the children didn't, so I shook my head.

'No thanks,' I said through gritted teeth. 'We're fine.'

Trolley bloke trundled off, much to the annoyance of Peter and Daisy.

'It's not fair!' moaned Peter.

Daisy started to bellow.

'Ungee! Ungee!'

'Well, it's not my fault you didn't eat enough breakfast.'

The middle-aged woman looked at me with an expression that suggested that it was my fault. I just stared back at her with axe-murderer eyes and she looked back down at what passed for tea on our train line.

I decided the only way to distract my now apoplectic children was to resume the colouring, but to no avail. They weren't going to be bought off so easily. Instead, they continued to moan about the lack of crisps, which was not just infuriating, but highly embarrassing. The 'tuts' from our fellow passengers were about as regular as the text-message bleeps emanating from the teenage girls behind us, and equally annoying.

And then Daisy went mysteriously quiet. A look of fierce concentration came across her face, and she then looked as though she was having some moment of epiphany.

'Daddy,' she smiled. 'I done a poo.'

I didn't need telling, and within seconds, neither did teenage girls or middle-aged woman. The former were giggling, and the latter gave me another foul stare. I closed my eyes, and tried to think Zen thoughts. Here we were, ten minutes into a seventy-minute journey, and I had a son who was noisily bleating for junk food, a daughter who had just created a small brown Krakatoa in her pants, and a carriage full of pissed-off people. Needless to say, nothing in the Holden Childcare Programme can prepare a parent for such a situation, so I did the decent thing – and bought three packets of crisps. When Peter moaned that there was no cheese and onion, I told him he could get off at the next stop and stay there. He looked terrified – for the first time ever, he seemed to have believed one of my threats.

The Daisy nappy situation was sorted when we arrived in London, although the only nappies stocked in the chemist at the station were not to Daisy's high standards. However, her bleating may have had more to do with the fact that I had to change her on the floor of one of the cubicles in the Gents. Normally I try to use the disabled lavatory in these circumstances, but, as usual, it was locked, and there was no one around who had a key.

After we emerged, I felt ready to go home. The last thing I wanted to do was to give a presentation, but I steeled myself, and thought of the riches and fame as I tried to hail a cab. Miraculously, we arrived at the TV company at 12.05, just five minutes late, and I thanked my all-too-rare good judgement that I hadn't plumped for the train an hour later, which, if one were travelling without children, would have left plenty of time.

The reception area was just as I expected – all marble and steel, with a brace of flatscreens showing the company's output, and another showing some rolling news channel. Perched behind some swanky iMac sat a studenty-looking girl, with red-dyed hair and a pierced nose, without both of which she might have been quite attractive.

'Hello,' she smiled. 'Can I help you?'

'Hi – we're here to see Dom Simons. Sam Holden at twelve o'clock.'

Studenty-girl looked at her iMac and frowned.

'What was the name again?'

'Sam Holden.'

(How hard a name is it to remember?)

'To see Dom?'

'Thassright.'

'Hmm . . . hold on, I'll give him a call. I'm sure everything's fine, but it just doesn't seem to be on the screen.'

I briefly closed my eyes. If the fucker had forgotten, I would kill him, I really would. I listened to Studenty-girl explain the situation, and then I could make out an 'oh shit' down the line. So he had forgotten, the bugger. I sort of collapsed my shoulders and felt pathetically small. Not a great start to one's stellar TV career. I made eyes at Studenty-girl that I wanted to talk to him, but she held up her hand while she listened to Dom.

'OK,' she said, eventually. 'I'll ask him to wait.'

She put the phone down.

'Wait till when?' I asked curtly.

She grimaced, sympathising with the situation.

'Until 12.45. Is that OK?'

'Not really.'

'I'm sorry.'

I tried to calm myself down. More Zen thoughts were required. (I really need to take up meditation one of these days. I always think it's for goatee-wearers, but perhaps it should be mandatory for all those who look after children.)

'There's a café just round the corner, you could go there. It's quite nice.'

We did go there. It wasn't nice, at least it wasn't for me. It wasn't a café, but a caff, which are sometimes all right, but this one was really dreadful and had that unmistakable *aire de chip fat rancide*. The children, on the other hand, loved it, as it only served the beige food of which they are so fond – chips, bread, egg – which they munched away on very happily.

As we walked back, Daisy fell asleep in her buggy, and Peter became ratty, demanding that he watch TV etc., and wondering where Necky was. (Necky is our unimaginative name for his teddy giraffe.) I told him that Necky had to stay at home in case he got lost, which caused more whingeing from him, and more shortening of my temper.

An apologetic Dom was waiting for us in the reception.

'I'm so sorry,' he said, his eyes doing that bulging Tube-station-logo thing again, and he sounded as if he meant it.

'Perfectly all right,' I said breezily as we shook hands. I wished I had the balls to give him a bollocking, but you can only give bollockings from positions of strength, and my balls aren't big enough (yet) to make me feel strong.

'Bit of a cock-up by my secretary,' he said.

That old one.

'Typical,' I replied, rolling my eyes in faux-empathetic exasperation.

'Anyway, let's go upstairs and meet the team and you can give us a little presentation of how you see it, and then we can have a powwow.'

I gulped inwardly as I wheeled Daisy to the bottom of the stairs, where I indicated that Dom might help me carry her up in her buggy.

'So sorry, of course. No kids of my own!'

'Can we go home now?' asked Peter as we climbed the stairs.

'Not now,' I hissed.

'But I'm tired,' he moaned and then started to lie down.

'C'mon, get up!'

I paused, and Daisy and her buggy sort of hovered dangerously in mid-air halfway up the stairs.

'I said, get up!'

Peter pretended that he had fallen asleep, a trick that he is employing far too frequently these days.

'If you don't get up, I shall leave you there!'

This time, he somehow knew my threat was empty.

'Peter!'

I glanced at Dom, who was clearly uncomfortable, not just at the lack of discipline, but also at the somewhat precarious position he found himself in.

'PETER!'

No move, the little sod.

'All right, you stay there while I get Daisy up the stairs.'

Dom and I manhandled Sleeping Beauty and her buggy to the top, where we set her down gently, but evidently not gently enough for madame. She woke up, looked around and started squealing 'Mummy!' at the top of her voice.

'It's OK Daisy,' I pleaded. 'Daddy's here.'

'Mummy!'

I closed my eyes, wishing all this away. Here I was, supposedly about to set myself up as the perfect dad, the Wonderhubby, and I couldn't get my own children up a flight of stairs without one of them having a tantrum, and the other one having a strop. (There is a subtle difference between the two – some 80 decibels.) The only place I wanted to be right there and then was on a sunlit golf course with Nigel, looking forward to a few sly pints afterwards.

'I'm sorry about this,' I said to Dom, 'they're, um, not normally this bad.'

Dom nodded unconvincingly. I left Daisy with him and went back down to pick up Peter, who moaned as I half-dragged, half-carried him up. Daisy's noise didn't abate, and as we approached the main open-plan office, about a dozen sets of eyes looked up from their iMacs to see 75 per cent of the Holden family burst in. I pulled a sort of comedy grimace.

'You'd better come in here,' said Dom, indicating his office. There was a slightly tetchy note in his voice, which made me think that he too would rather be on his equivalent of a golf course. He steered us in, and then shut the door. Peter and Daisy were still moaning and stropping, although the volume had decreased.

'I want to watch TV!' Peter demanded.

In the corner of the office was a massive flatscreen.

'TV! TV! TV!' chanted Daisy, whose little face lit up at the prospect.

I looked at Dom.

'Can you get CBeebies on that?'

Dom picked up the remote control.

'We can probably get Iranian CBeebies on this.'

In a few seconds the children were muted, sitting on a huge leather sofa, sucking their thumbs and watching *Bob the Builder*.

'Phew!' I said.

Dom just raised his eyebrows.

'Perhaps we should have the meeting somewhere else.'

'It seems wrong to kick you out of your office.'

'Not at all – I think it's for the best.'

I picked up my laptop bag and Dom showed me into a conference room. There was a projector into which I plugged my laptop, and within a few minutes I started to flick through my presentation. By the time Dom came back with a couple of colleagues the screen was showing my first slide, which read '*Wonderhubby* – Applying the Strategies of Management Consultancy to the Challenges of the 21st Century Domestic Environment'.

'Snappy stuff!' said Dom as he sat down.

'This is Emma,' he continued, 'and this too is Emma.'

'Hi,' said the Emmas in unison.

'This Emma is head of programme development,' Dom explained, 'and this Emma is head of programme acquisition.'

'Is there a difference?' I asked, slightly too aggressively.

'A huge amount,' said the Emmas. In unison. No kidding.

'Anyway,' said Dom, folding his arms. 'Tell us all about *Wonderhubby*. It's caused quite a stir, I can tell you.'

The Emmas nodded. Bollocks, I thought.

'Really?' I went.

'Really.'

I coughed. I strained my ears, listening for any nonsense coming from Dom's office, but at this stage, the TV was still working its magic. Oh, how I love the television. The best invention ever. If the stuff on it was any better, I'd be happy to leave them in front of it all day.

'Well, if it's OK with you,' I began, 'I'd like to give you a small presentation, outlining how I see the project, and its core aims and targets, and then fleshing out its narrative.'

The Emmas let out a slight giggle.

'What's the matter?' I asked.

'Nothing.'

'Um,' went Dom, slightly hesitant, 'you don't need to, er, talk like a management consultant to us. Save it for the programme.'

'Oh,' I said, unaware that I was in full consultant mode. The thing was, it was all coming back far too easily, all those 'bullshit bingo' words and phrases that to management consultants are meat and drink, or rather carnivorous consumable and digestible fluid.

'No problem,' I continued, a little unsure of what to say next. Try and talk like a human being, I said to myself, which would be hard when I considered what was coming on the next slide.

I clicked the mouse. Up it came. A whole load of crap that I had written the day before. This one was headlined 'Aims', and featured a load of bullet-pointed sub-headings.

- Workplace/Domestic Synthesis
- Cross-Comparison of Strategic Performance Tools
- The Contrasting Dynamic of Humour-Based Scenarios
- Entertainment Yield
- Optimising Childcare Solution Packages
- Personality-driven Focus and Acquisition

I took a deep breath. Would they go for it, I wondered? What were they thinking? The faces of Dom and the Emmas told me all I needed to know. Their lips were all sort of puffed out, trying to contain 'church laugh'.

'I know you think this is funny,' I said, 'But I assure you this is all workaday stuff for us management consultants.'

'Gosh,' said Development Emma.

'OK,' said Acquisition Emma.

'Keep going,' said Dom, 'I love it.'

'You do?'

'I think it's great. It's the type of bullsh— I mean, the type of approach that will make the programme, um, fresh and entertaining.'

'You think so?'

'Oh yes.'

Encouraged, I continued. I spoke in general terms for the first five minutes, outlining how successful I had been in adapting my skills as a consultant to the home, and how it had reaped such enormous rewards in terms of the children's behaviour and their development. I just had to hope that the frequent raised eyebrows were signs of encouragement rather than of cynicism.

'My approach,' I said, 'will be in four stages. First, qualitative and quantitative evaluation. I will enter into the clients' homes, and establish where the problems lie. Secondly, I shall process-consult them, and draw up a framework in which we can go forward together. The third stage will be rollout-stroke-implementation, and this will clearly be the crux of the programme. The fourth and final stage will be appraisal and re-evaluation, in which we employ some of the same functions in stage one in order to establish quantitative and qualitative performance differentials . . .'

Dom cleared his throat.

'Yes?' I asked.

'Um, doesn't this just, um . . .'

He was struggling to be polite.

'. . . um, mean that you're going to go there, tell them what to do, and then leave, come back, and see how they've done?'

I chewed over his words. I thought a bold response was called for.

'Yes,' I said. 'In essence.'

'So all management consultancy really is, is telling people what to do.'

More chewing.

'Not quite that simple.'

Now it was Acquisition Emma's turn to pipe up.

'What I don't get,' she said, 'is how this is different from any of the other nanny-style remake programmes.'

I was ready for this.

'Aha, I'm glad you asked me this.'

'You are?'

'Yes. Because there's an enormous difference. Huge. Massive. A gulf, even. As big as the Gulf of Finland.'

'Finland?'

'Yes. I went there for a stag weekend, and it's a very big gulf. Very big indeed.'

'OK,' said Acquisition Emma, cautiously.

'A big difference,' I said.

'Which is?' asked Dom.

'Methodology. Implementation. Solution processes.'

'Can you be a little more precise?' asked Development Emma.

'Of course,' I said.

A brief silence while I wracked my rusty brain. The problem about being a househusband for so long is that I'm sure part of my brain has gone numb, atrophied.

'I shall be using all the techniques of management consultancy in the home, and that's the crucial difference.'

'But what techniques are they exactly?' asked Dom. 'I mean, what if a child is not eating his food? What would be the management-consultant approach as opposed to the normal approach?'

I briefly thought back to the water debacle with Daisy, and tried to expunge it from my mind.

'Well,' I started, 'as one would do in a management consultancy environment, we would seek to establish the cause for non-take-up. This could be for any number of reasons – pricing, inadequate marketing, little perceived need for the goods or service and so on . . .'

'Sorry to interrupt,' interrupted Development Emma. 'We are talking about food here.'

'I was coming to that,' I said, narrowing my eyes, trying to look hard. She didn't look that intimidated, to be honest.

'Anyway, I was saying, there could be any number of reasons, so the first thing to do is to evaluate what they might be, and then implement a range of solutions that will facilitate a take-up of the goods or service – in this case, say, baked beans. Is that clear?'

'Um . . .'

'Er . . .'

'But . . .'

'Good!' I said, clapping my hands together, 'I'm glad you're still with me!'

For the next few minutes I worked my way through the rest of the slides, talking as quickly as I could just in case Peter and Daisy suddenly decided that watching TV wasn't the best activity in the world. By the time I had finished, Dom and the Emmas were sitting there motionless. They must have been impressed.

'So, what do you think?' I asked.

'It's different,' said the Emmas, in unison again.

'That's the idea.'

Dom made a funny sort of frown.

'I'm still not clear on the tone of the programme,' he said. 'I mean, would we play this for laughs, or would it be deadly serious?'

'Deadly serious, I would have thought.'

'Hmmm.'

'I mean, these will be real children,' I said, 'real families we will be dealing with. We can't just take the piss.'

'Hmmm.'

Dom was being annoyingly non-committal with his 'hmmms'.

There was a knock on the door, and in walked a

somewhat frazzled-looking middle-aged woman who had the air 'sensible person' sprayed all over her. She looked at me with an expression of dread on her face.

'Er, Sam?'

'Yes.'

'Your children, they're um, well, you'd better come and see.'

I raced out the door, trying to look calm. What had they done? Vandalised the office? Urinated against Dom's desk? Puked on the carpet? Scribbled on the walls?

The answer was all of the above. I noticed the puke first, then the graffiti, followed by the pee, before my eyes rested on a lamp that had fallen over 'all by itself Daddy' and smashed into the enormous billion-pound flatscreen.

I didn't know where to begin. I thought about scooping them up and running out the door, but that was clearly not an option. Behind me, the Emmas gasped and Dom let out a dry chuckle.

'You know what I think,' he said. 'We should definitely make a programme.'

I turned round.

'You're joking,' I said, looking into his eyes to gauge some sort of irony.

'No,' he replied sincerely. 'I think TV is ready for the Holden Children Programme.'

'Well, not your TV,' I said, my somewhat feeble witticism masking my discombobulation. Did he REALLY want to make *Wonderhubby*?

To tell the truth, on the journey home (predictably hellish) I grew even more confused. I couldn't work out whether Dom was taking the piss, and whether I was going to be one of those people who was abused by the TV, misrepresented, etc. But as soon as I think about the potential dosh (minus the cost of one expensive television) all those thoughts are dispelled.

Will discuss with Sally over the weekend. I think I know what she'll think.

Sunday 3 February

My suspicions were right. Sally thinks it's a crap idea. It was clear she didn't really want to talk about it, so I dropped the subject, which I thought was rather mature of me, or perhaps indicated that we've now been married long enough to know what's worth discussing, and what's not.

Monday 4 February

Email from Dom, outlining the structure of the show – pretty much as I had explained, so some of my presentation must have gone in. It appears that he is being genuine. I still can't quite believe his enthusiasm. However, he wrote that just because they'd bought into it, it didn't mean that the TV stations would. They pitched hundreds of ideas per year, and only a handful got made, so I wasn't to get my hopes up.

Still, I can't help but think of fame and fortune. I'm

doing my best to mask my excitement from Sally, not least because she is having an even more crap time at work. Every time she gets home, she seems even more exhausted than she did the night before. This evening she looked terrible (not so terrible as to look unfanciable, but just really really tired).

As we ate supper, I asked her what the matter was. She gave that familiar I-can't-tell-you sigh.

'I know it's all Top Secret,' I said as I carved into our (perfectly cooked) lamb chops, 'but it seems as though you're carrying the weight of the world on your shoulders.'

At that, Sally's shoulders literally fell, and she sighed again.

'Is everybody at work like you?' I asked.

'How do you mean?'

'You know – tired.'

'Pretty much. But more just us in Central Asia.'

'I know you don't want to tell me, but I can only assume that something nasty's brewing, and I'll also assume that it's terrorists with dirty bombs or nukes or something and that you're doing your best to stop it. And I know this sounds silly, but it really does seem to be getting you down, getting you down to the extent that you almost seem depressed.'

Sally shook her head as she put down her knife and fork. The lamb chop – again, I must stress, perfectly cooked – remained largely untouched.

'I don't think I'm depressed,' she argued. 'But it is very stressful. I obviously can't say whether you're right or not, but if we fuck things up, then a lot of people could get hurt in a very nasty way. And it's up to us and the Americans to stop it all happening. And part of the problem is that the Americans think we've fucked up, and we think they've fucked up, and so there's a lot of crap flying around between us, crap that's getting in the way of us doing our fucking jobs and stopping what it is we're trying to stop.'

I'd never heard Sally so uncouth. I rather liked it.

'And is your neck on the line if it all goes wrong?'

I briefly marvelled at my mixed metaphor.

'In a way, it doesn't matter about my neck,' she replied. 'Small beer compared to what would have happened if things had got to the stage where my neck was for the chop.'

'How much longer is this going to go on for?'

'I have no idea,' she said.

She got up, went to the fridge, and extracted a bottle of Chablis.

'How long is a piece of string, huh?' I asked.

'Exactly.'

She rummaged around the drawer for the corkscrew and then proceeded to cut the foil around the top of the bottle. I watched her, inwardly remarking that it was always me who opened wine, probably because I'm more of a dipso. Sally's lack of practice soon became evident.

'Here,' I said, 'let me do it.'

'I can bloody do it myself,' she snapped.

'OK, OK.'

She couldn't, because the cork broke in half as she half-wrenched, half-twisted it out the bottle.

'Fuck!'

'It doesn't matter,' I said, 'it's perfectly salvageable.'

She handed the bottle to me.

'You see,' she said, 'I'm shit at everything.'

'That's not true. You can't extrapolate any supposed inadequacies from the dodgy cork on a bottle of Chablis.'

'It's symbolic.'

'No it's not,' I insisted. 'You'll be believing in astrology next.'

'Perhaps I should,' she said, and then a smile crossed her face. In a few seconds, the evening newspaper had been extracted from her handbag and she was flicking through for the horoscopes.

'Here we go,' she said. 'Taurus. That's me. "Although you have been having some work troubles recently, the rise of Saturn in your constellation will mean they will soon come to an end. In the meantime, you must ensure that you keep a calm head, and show others that your strong will and determination can see you through bad times as well as good."'

Sally looked up, triumphantly.

'Wow,' I went. 'Pretty accurate for a load of dross.'

'I'll say. Perhaps there's something in it after all.'

I snorted.

'All right,' said Sally, 'let's read Leo then.'

I sighed. I HATE astrology, hate the infantile moronic illogical turdy basis of it all, despise the very

63

notion that if the moon can have an effect on the sea, then it's not unreasonable to think that the planets and stars might have some effect on us humans, as aren't we 90 per cent made of water blah blah. Honestly, what a load of crap. Listen people, the moon has an effect on tides because of the changes in its gravitational pull on the earth's surface. There's no possible way that the stars can affect the human body in the same – or any – way.

'Leo,' Sally began. ' "This is a time for going ahead with new projects. The Moon in Uranus [I think that's what she said] means a time of great creation and productivity. Now would be a great opportunity to take a risk and just go for it. With the right drive and energy, you have a great chance of succeeding." '

'Aha,' I went. 'This augurs well for *Wonderhubby*.'

'Oh God,' said Sally. 'Not that.'

'Look,' I said, triumphantly tapping the newspaper with my fork, 'it's in the stars.'

'But I thought you thought this was all bollocks.'

'Nope,' I said. 'I think it's brilliant.'

And, much to my later disgust, I realised that I wasn't being entirely sarcastic.

Wednesday 6 February

I think the children must have picked up on my good mood engendered by imminent fame and fortune. After school today, Peter asked why I kept dancing around the kitchen when I was cooking their supper.

'It's because I'm very happy,' I said.

'Yes, but why are you dancing?'

'Because when you're happy, you sometimes feel like dancing.'

A quick frown, and then: 'Do people feel like dancing when they are sad?'

Now it was my turn for a quick frown.

'Probably not.'

'Do you get sad daddy?'

'Sometimes, but at the moment, I'm very happy.'

'Why?'

'Because Daddy may be making a TV programme.'

'A TV programme! What about? Soldiers?'

'No, about being a Daddy.'

Peter's crest fell.

'Oh.'

'But you and Daisy can be in it as well.'

'On TV? Can we be on TV?'

'Yes!'

'TV! TV!' Peter chanted.

'TV! TV!' Daisy chorused.

'Can we watch TV?' asked Peter.

''An 'e 'otch TV?' echoed Daisy.

'No,' I said.

A collective whine until I bought them off with the promise of TV after supper. It occurs to me that Sally may not want the children on the TV programme. And now I'm worrying about whether Sally might want to be on it. Chances of that: 0.05 percent. I shall need to tread carefully, and certainly won't mention it until the programme is in the bag. If it is in the bag.

Sunday 10 February

Last night, after a perfectly lovely day *en famille*, Sally and I had the most enormous row about *WonderHubby*. (Notice how I now give it a capital H midword – looks more trendy, I think.) So much for reaching that stage of marriage in which we know what not to discuss.

It came about because at bathtime Peter kept banging on about how Daddy was going to be on TV, and although I tried to calm him down, it was obvious to Sally that it had been a topic of conversation between the children and me. By the time we had finished processing Peter and Daisy, and had tucked them up etc., I could see Sally was looking thoroughly hacked off, and when we got down to the kitchen I decided to have it out with her.

'You really don't want me to do it, do you?'

'What?'

'The *WonderHubby* programme.'

'I didn't think it was necessarily happening,' she said. 'I thought it was going to be pitched to the TV channels first.'

'Yes, but Dom thinks there's a good chance of a pilot being commissioned.'

'Does he now?'

'Yes.'

'And will you be paid for this pilot?'

'I don't know,' I replied, expressing genuine ignorance. 'I assume they'll bung me something, because the TV company needs a budget to actually make the thing.'

'How much money do you think they will "bung" you?'

'I have no idea.'

A Sally sigh.

'I don't want to rain on your parade . . .' she began.

'Yes you do,' I interrupted. 'You always do whenever I have these ideas.'

'But Sam, your ideas are often a little, you know, off the wall. Remember how you wanted to be a fireman?'

Flashback to my Near Death Experience on the ladder, when I had flirted with the idea of becoming a volunteer fireman the year before last, despite my fear of heights. A shudder.

'Yes I do. But I gave it a go, and it didn't work. All I'm saying is that I want to give this a go. And, if it doesn't work, I've tried it, and it's out of my system. But, if it does work, then great, it means some money, perhaps a lot of money.'

'But Sam, I don't see you as a TV personality. I'm sorry, I just can't see it working at all. And if you want my honest opinion, then I'd say the whole thing is a waste of time, and it's stopping you getting on and trying to find some proper part-time work that you can fit in around the children. Come on Sam, that's not so unreasonable.'

I rubbed my eyes, trying to wish away the whole conversation.

'There is barely any work out there,' I said.

'You haven't looked!'

'I have.'

'When?'

'When?' I replied. 'When you've been at work! When do you think? But there's nothing there – eff all. So what am I supposed to do? What do you want me to do? Sell jam? Join the W fucking I?'

'Of course not! I just want you to try to do something that is realistic and, more importantly, will bring us in some regular money. This *WonderHubby* thing is such a long shot and so unstable, I don't think we've got the luxury of you taking a punt like that.'

'It's not taking a punt. All I'm doing is giving it a go. Taking a punt suggests that we're losing something if it doesn't work. We won't be. We've got everything to gain.'

Sally sat at the kitchen table and flicked through an old colour supplement. But I could tell she wasn't really concentrating on it, she was merely collecting her thoughts. In the meantime, I helped myself to a beer, offered her something to drink, got the 'glass of white wine' I was expecting, and gave it to her. All very civil.

'My other worry is that it does work,' said Sally.

'Oh great,' I went. 'Fucked if it fails, buggered if it works.'

'Think about it, Sam, how will you be able to look after Peter and Daisy if you're off filming your exciting TV show? Have you thought about that?'

I hadn't.

'Of course I have,' I said.

'And?'

'And what?'

'And what will you do with them while you're management-consulting all those oh-so-grateful families? Leave them with a nanny?'

'No,' I said. 'I thought I'd leave them with the Gruffalo.'

'Don't be flippant.'

'I'm not. Of course I'd leave them with a nanny! Who else did you expect I'd leave them with?'

Sally held up her hands to stop me.

'I always thought,' she said, in a tone of great forced calm, 'that the whole point of the way we were doing things was that we didn't have to have a nanny, and that we believed the only people who should be bringing up the children were us, and not some stranger from God Knows Where.'

'I know that – but this would only be temporary when I'm on location.'

' "When I'm on location",' Sally scoffed. 'Aren't we Mr TV all of a sudden?'

'What else am I supposed to say?'

Sally shrugged. She took a large slug of her wine.

'Anyway,' she said, 'can't you see the irony of it all? You'll be telling the world what a great dad you are, and while you do so, you'll be leaving the children with a complete stranger.'

'Not necessarily,' I said.

'What do you mean?'

'You could look after them.'

'Me? How?'

'If the programme got commissioned, we'd have enough money for you to be able to give up work.'

Sally looked at me, just looked at me so witheringly, so contemptuously.

'Give up work? You really think I'd chuck in my career – and my responsibility to the people I work for – just because you're on some TV show?'

'I thought you'd be dying to give it up,' I said. 'It's not as though you're having a ball, is it?'

'That's not the point, Sam!'

'What is the point then?'

'My job is important!'

'And so would be my TV programme!'

'Really? As important as saving lives?'

'Sally Holden – she saves the world.'

'Fuck off,' said Sally, 'you're being juvenile.'

'And you're being self-important.'

'No I am not.'

And with that, she left the room and went upstairs, where she watched TV in the spare bedroom, refusing offers of supper, drinks or rapprochement.

Today has been frosty, to say the least. Our Sunday-night shag is not looking that likely.

Tuesday 12 February

At least SOMEONE likes my putative TV programme,

but it's not someone I can really hold up as a cold and neutral observer. Yup, it's Emily. Despite my attempts to avoid her, she spotted me at the school gate after I had dropped off Peter and Daisy, and instantly detected I was looking somewhat down.

'Hello? What's this?'

'What's what?'

'You've got a face longer than the horse I'm about to ride.'

I couldn't help but smirk at Emily's risqué simile. And, true to cheap-porn-mag form, she was wearing jodhpurs, which meant that I went into the normal gauche unsuave form that I adopt when presented with a woman thus dressed.

'Um . . . have I? Er . . . no, quite fine thanks. You know, weather's a bit shit. Think I must have SAD or something.'

'SAD?'

'Seasonal affective disorder.'

'Right,' said Emily, utterly unconvinced.

'Just need a holiday or something,' I said.

'Right,' she said again. 'Or a drink. Why not come round for an early lunch after you've picked Daisy up?'

Was it arrogant and presumptuous of Emily to turn round almost before she had finished the question, so sure was she of my acceptance? I thought it was, but it didn't stop me saying:

'Yespleasethankyouverymuch,' like an eleven-year-old who is on best behaviour in front of his friend's mum.

And so, at 12.15, armed with a bottle of wine hidden

in Daisy's buggy (I didn't want the neighbours to think it was an 'assignation') I knocked on Emily's door, and she greeted me still wearing her jodhpurs and looking as though she had just spent the last two hours fornicating with half a dozen stable boys. Perhaps she had.

'Sorry! I hope I don't smell! I've only just got back!'

'That's all right.'

'Do you mind if I have a quick shower?'

'You don't have to on my account.'

Emily raised a reasonably well-plucked eyebrow.

'Interesting,' she said, and then disappeared upstairs with a 'you know where everything is', which again was presumptuous, as by the time I found the corkscrew (under a pile of magazines next to the microwave), she had reappeared looking freshly showered and spruced, hair slicked back, and wearing not much more than a pair of skinny jeans and a V-neck. I passed her a glass of wine, and then we spoke about what we would feed Daisy, who was ensconced in the living room doing some puzzles. (She is obsessed with puzzles – I harbour optimistic suspicions that she is going to be a mathematician.)

'So then,' began Emily eventually, 'why are you looking so down?'

'I didn't realise I was.'

'C'mon, you've got one of those very expressive faces.'

'Have I?'

'YES! And now you're looking very quizzical!'

'I am?'

Emily snorted into her wine, and I could only join in the laughter. As I did so, instant guilt, because it occurred to me that Sally and I hadn't laughed like this in ages. In fact, I'm finding it hard to remember when we last had a good belly laugh, as good as the one I had with Emily. I know it's unrealistic to think that one should spend one's entire life cackling away, but even so.

After the giggles, I soon admitted that the reason I was down was because Sally was so against *WonderHubby*.

'But why?' asked Emily, sounding genuinely mystified.

I told her.

'That's not very entrepreneurial of her,' said Emily.

I didn't know how to take this comment – it felt uncomfortable having Emily (of all people) criticise Sally, but it was nevertheless true.

'Well,' I said, 'she's just not a risk taker, and I am. She doesn't get it at all. Thinks I should just be doing more consultancy work, and she doesn't see that if this works, then we're in clover.'

'Perhaps she doesn't want it to work.'

'Oh, she certainly doesn't.'

'How do you know?'

'She told me.'

Emily took a long draught of wine.

'Well,' she said, 'I think she's being terribly unfair.'

'So do I,' I replied, without thinking.

I felt even more guilty now. Not only was I having a laugh with Emily, I was now also being disloyal to Sally. I thought of her stuck in the office in London, the problems of the world on her shoulders, her job a matter of life and death, and here I was, slagging her off in front of the village bicycle, who I still suspected was saying all the right words to get into my pants.

Emily interrupted my guilt.

'Can't you just say that you're going to do it anyway, and that if it all goes tits up, then you can go back to consultancy?'

'Well, that's pretty much how I'm playing it. It just doesn't make for an easy time, that's all.'

'I can see that,' said Emily.

'You can?'

'That face again.'

I looked at her steadily, trying to seem impassive.

'Now that,' she said coquettishly, 'is a different sort of face.'

'What sort of face is it?'

'I'm not sure,' she smirked. 'But I don't mind it at all.'

Holy cow. I was quickly feeling out of my depth again, very reminiscent of THAT dinner. I tried moving the subject back to *WonderHubby*.

'Do you really think it's a good idea?' I asked.

Emily held my gaze.

'I think it's an excellent idea.'

She moved a little closer.

'Not too risky?'

'Life's no fun without risk.'

I nodded, telling myself that I could handle the situation.

'But what if doesn't work out?' I asked.

'I'm sure it will, and besides, if it doesn't, then I know you'll have had a lot of fun.'

Emily was really standing very close, and she looked up at me.

'So,' she said, 'why don't you just go for it?'

'You know,' I said, 'I think I will.'

Emily then reached up her left hand and started stroking the back of my head. Nearly every chemical that my brain was capable of producing surged through my system, chemicals that contradicted and fought against each other, some willing me to give in, some urging me to get the hell out of there as soon as possible, and some simply insisting that I was extremely dim-witted for not realising that she wasn't talking about *WonderHubby*. As the hormones waged their war, I stood paralysed, my body waiting for my decision. Meanwhile, Emily was pulling my head towards her, and standing on tiptoe as she strained to connect our mouths.

'Um.'

At first, that was pretty much all I managed to say. My head strained against Emily's grip, but still she pulled me towards her.

'Emily!'

'Come on Sam,' she whispered. 'Let's just go for it.'

'It's very nice that you want . . .'

75

'Sshhh!'

By now I could feel her breath on my lips.

'Emily! Stop it!'

I pushed away, this time rather too violently, causing Emily to spill her glass of wine down my front.

'Oops,' she went matter-of-factly.

'Sorry,' I said.

'It's all right, it didn't go over me.'

Emily edged back. I could feel my heart thumping, and I was glad that Daisy hadn't walked in when things were looking decidedly dodgy.

'Emily,' I said. 'I wish you wouldn't . . . you know . . .'

'Try to kiss you? Why not?'

She was so unabashed, it was extraordinary.

'Because I'm married and I love my wife, that's why.'

I tried not to sound pious, but I'm sure I did.

'Very moral of you.'

'Yes, well, I am very moral.'

'Really?'

'Yes. I don't like cheating – I don't think it's right.'

'But what if nobody knew?'

'That's not the point. And besides, they usually do.'

'Do they?'

'Yes. Come on Emily, how do you think we all know about what you got up to?'

'Got up to when?'

'Well – you know – on holiday in Greece.'

'What do you know about Greece?'

I could feel myself uncharacteristically blushing. Nevertheless, there was no going back.

76

'About you and those two fishermen in the beach hut.'

'Two fishermen in a beach hut?'

'That's what I heard.'

Emily scoffed at that.

'What a load of rubbish,' she said.

'Really?'

Silence.

'Yes. Really. It wasn't a beach hut, it was a hotel room thank you very much. And it wasn't two fishermen. It was three. Now then, what would you like for lunch? Do you like kebabs?'

Unsurprisingly, I didn't have much of an appetite.

Thursday 14 February

Valentine's Day today, and guess who forgot? Both of us. It wasn't until halfway through the afternoon that I remembered. So when Peter got back from school, we called Sally at the office. The children wished her happy Valentine's in unison, and then I got on the phone.

'I'm so sorry,' I said, 'I totally forgot. I haven't even got you a card or anything.'

Sally laughed.

'No problem. In fact, I have to confess that I forgot as well.'

'So we're both in the doghouse,' I said.

'Yup,' she said.

'Have you got people around?'

'Yup.'

'OK, love you loads.'

'Me too.'

I think we should just give up Valentine's Day from now on. It's such a bunch of crap, it really is. It's just an excuse for card companies to make a fortune selling their crappy wares, complete with naff rhymes and quilted pink covers. And it's a racket for restaurants as well. When Sally and I last went out on Valentine's night (a long time ago), we were treated like cattle, and sat mooning at each other as the wrong dishes arrived and the champagne was warm and the bill was £134.89 not including service and fuck that for a game of soldiers we said as we waited in the rain for a cab that didn't come because they were all being used by similar mugs who felt obliged to go out on Valentine's bloody night.

As an act of rebellion against all this, after supper, I got Peter and Daisy to make a couple of cards for Sally, which were actually pretty good. Peter's drawing skills are now almost as good as mine, and he drew Sally a lovely soldier killing some aliens. With a giraffe. Daisy sort of scribbled something pink, which she said was 'The Night Garden', so I believed her.

Although Sally got back late and tired, the cards certainly cheered her up. There's still a coldness in the air after our row about *WonderHubby*, which we have unspokenly (is there such a word?) agreed not to mention. She knows that I am too pig-headed not to give it a go, and I know that she will never agree to it. Therefore no point in arguing.

Something else which there was no point in telling

Sally about was Emily's behaviour the other day. It would only have ruined the couple of hours we had together before we went to bed, and I certainly didn't want to jeopardise any Valentine's night action. (I do sort of believe in Valentine's.)

Sunday 17 February

I do hate being in limbo. It's not that I'm expecting anything from Dom immediately, but I just want to know whether I'm going to spend the rest of my life as a freelance management consultant or a TV star.

Nevertheless, a nice weekend, and both Sally and I behaved ourselves. No arguments. No mention of *WonderHubby*/Emily/Work/Money/Jobs, all of which are topics that bring us both out in a row. Even the children behaved, sort of, although there was one hair-raising moment, when Peter thought it would be terribly good fun if he pushed his sister in her buggy into the river. I just managed to save her before she joined the ducks, although not without stepping in an enormous dog shit.

Sally and I were livid with Peter, and I came near to smacking him. I've smacked him before, and have always regretted it, because I had done it in anger – but then he had run into the road despite me yelling at him not to. However, I vowed never to do it again, and today was emphatically not going to be the day in which he felt a sharp thwack to his derrière, but instead we withdrew his normal Sunday night 'treat' TV watching.

(Sally thinks Peter and Daisy only watch TV at the weekends, a secret the children are miraculously keeping to themselves.) The removal of privilege engendered an enormous tantrum, which nearly did earn him a smack.

While he was at full pelt, Sally asked me, 'What would WonderHubby do in this situation?'

At least she was smiling about it. The truth was, I had no reply. There is nothing in the tenets of management consultancy that tells you how to deal with a client who is not allowed to watch TV. If *WonderHubby* ever happens, God knows how I'm going to wing it.

Tuesday 19 February
5 p.m.

Oh my God. I'm going to have to wing it. *WonderHubby* is happening! Well, a pilot is happening, at least. Dom has just this minute phoned me. He said that the TV station went mad for the idea, and said they loved the way it tied up all the elements of business (which is now sexy, he says) and childcare (which needs a televisual revamp apparently).

'It's incredible,' I said, 'that they've gone for it without even seeing me.'

'Well, I showed them some video of you.'

'What video?'

'Your spiel in our conference room the other day.'

'You were filming that?'

'Yes – didn't we tell you?'

'No!'

'Sorry about that,' said Dom, sounding as apologetic as Peter does when he's done something bad (i.e. utterly remorseless).

I was tempted to chew his ear off, but then thought better of it.

'What did they like about it?'

'I think they liked the way that it was so boring that it was funny.'

'Thanks.' I laughed a little, assuming this was some kind of joke. Dom's tone suggested that it might not have been.

'Don't worry,' said Dom. 'The fact is they love you and they love the programme. However, there are a couple of glitches.'

'Oh yes?'

'They want the pilot ready in a month.'

'That sounds like a long time.'

'Sam – you've much to learn. A month is fuck all. A nanosecond.'

'Oh. And what's the other glitch?'

'They've given us sod-all money, so I'm afraid we can't give you that much.'

'Oh.'

'Just a couple of grand I'm afraid.'

'Oh.'

'I know. But it doesn't matter, because when the series is commissioned, then the money will be decent, don't you worry. See it as an investment.'

'Oh.'

'Anyway, we'd better start as soon as we can. Can you come in tomorrow for a brainstorming at the channel? The commissioning editor really wants to meet you.'

'Sure!'

I'm thrilled, basically. Fucking thrilled. OK, so the money is rubbish, but I believe Dom when he says it's going to get better. Now all I have to do is to give Sally the hard sell. Oh joy.

11 p.m.

Sally is in the bath, and I'm sitting at my desk and there's a very bad odour in the air. I've told her about the pilot, and her first reaction was 'Oh God'. Her second reaction was to pour a glass of wine, and her third was to drain half of it in one gulp. (I know I joke that Sally is turning into a dipso, but I'm slightly worried about it.)

'I can't believe this is actually happening,' she said.

I tried to play everything down.

'It's just a pilot, sweetheart, and it probably won't come to anything.'

Raised eyebrow.

'You're really going to do it?'

'I'd really like to, yes.'

'And who's going to look after the children?'

'We'll have to get a nanny.'

Sally took a deep breath.

'This wasn't the idea.'

'I know, but we've been over this. It's not as though we're filming all the time.'

Sally drained the glass and then poured herself another.

'OK,' she said. 'You do it. But don't expect me to get involved.'

'Um . . .'

'What?'

'Well, I'm sure they'll want some shots of us as a family.'

'No way.'

'Please Sally, come on.'

'No way. Anyway I don't think work would be exactly thrilled about it.'

'It would only be for a few seconds.'

'In that case, they can manage without me.'

'It's not the same.'

'I'm sorry Sam, but I really don't think I have an option.'

I left it, and we prepared and ate supper almost in silence, both of us flicking through magazines.

I hate all this. I hate the rowing, the bickering, the constant feeling that we're on edge. Perhaps I should chuck in the whole *WonderHubby* thing. Perhaps Sally is right – it is just a waste of time, and could be seen as simply something to massage my ego. And if I chucked it in, would that put a smile on Sally's face? I doubt it. The damage has already been done, and besides, she's still having a rotten time at work.

And then again, why should I give it up? It IS a good idea, good enough for one TV station and one production company to spend time and money making it. How wrong can they be?

Wednesday 20 February

This time, I decided to leave the children at home, or rather with Emily. Despite her pass – and I'm sure there will be more – we're still on good terms. I think Emily probably makes passes at so many men that she's pretty unabashed about the whole thing. Mind you, I would have left the children with just about anybody, as, predictably enough, the train was delayed and overcrowded, and I couldn't face a repeat of our last little outing.

The channel was a pretty impressive place – huge marble atrium, trees, waterfalls etc., and the normal plethora of flatscreens and incredibly attractive women walking around. Why does the media attract such good-looking females? In all my years as a management consultant I came across about three women whom I found remotely appealing, and yet today I must have seen at least twenty in the space of three hours. Maybe my taste has declined as I have aged, but I'm not THAT old, and I like to think my standards are pretty high. After all, my wife has never had even the slightest tickle with the ugly stick.

The commissioning editor was called Dave Waldman, and he was one of these immensely enthusiastic people who must be infuriating to work with. His catchphrase was 'dig', which he said often, and was emphasised by clicking his fingers with a supple throw of the wrist. Also, he was bloody young – late twenties perhaps – and had I not known him to be in a position of authority, I would have taken him to be some sort of junior in the graphic design department.

He didn't really ask me many specific questions, but one thing he was concerned about was the families we were going to use.

'How are you going to get hold of them?' he asked.

I didn't have an answer to that, and I looked at Dom, who didn't seem particularly flustered.

'Shouldn't be a problem,' he said. 'We've already started looking for them. There are thousands of these oiks— I mean people, who are desperate to appear on shows like this.'

'Dig,' went Dave. 'And do you have a plan B, if the people aren't coming good?'

'Sure,' said Dom. 'The normal plan in these circumstances.'

'Dig,' said Dave, this time a little more conspiratorially.

'What's the normal plan?' I asked, doing my best not to sound like a naïve schoolboy.

Dom and Dave looked at each other with a little smirk.

'We like to call it "blending the truth",' said Dom.

'Dig,' said Dave.

'Blending the truth?' I queried.

Dom took a 'why do I have to explain this to you again?' breath.

'You know when you take notes of a conversation?' he began. 'Well, you don't write down all the ums and ahs and whatnot. You clean it up, in many ways, make the speaker appear more eloquent. You're doing them a favour. And that's all we do, except in a televisual way. Sometimes we'll ask people to say things again because we didn't capture it first time round, or they said it with too much swearing . . .'

'Or not enough!' interjected Dave.

'Dig,' said Dom somewhat greasily in imitation, although when he tried to click his fingers in the same way he merely succeeded in hurting his wrist, because he let out a slight wince.

'Anyway,' he continued. 'Sometimes we find people who are good for the programme, but we just find that they lack a certain something. So we get in others to recreate real events and conversations.'

'You mean you get in actors?' I asked. 'I know you said you made things up, but I didn't think things had got this bad.'

'It's accepted practice,' said Dom, looking at Dave.

'Dig,' he went. 'And we don't call it "making things up". We call it "reality enhancement". Anyway, we only use it as a plan B, and I'm sure we won't have any need for it. We're spending a lot of money making these reality programmes, and it'd be idiotic to rely on reality when we can manufacture reality so much better ourselves. Dig?'

'Dig,' I said, somewhat flabbergasted.

On the way back home, I wondered what I was getting

myself into. Despite my moaning about how long it was taking, it occurred to me that less than two months ago the whole thing had been a dinner-party joke, and already it was becoming a reality, or at least a reality of sorts. And, although I wasn't expecting to be in control of the whole thing, it was clear that Dom and Dave saw me as just another stooge. I'm curiously down about the whole thing. The truth about TV is that there is no truth. These are thoughts I won't be sharing with Sally.

Emily said the children had been very well behaved (wow) and that they had all got along together. Her twins had entertained Daisy, and had organised some teddy bears' picnic for her, which Daisy loved. While she was telling me all this, Emily detected that I looked a little pensive, and it annoyed me when I reflected that she seemed far more sensitive than my wife to my moods.

Thursday 21 February

Spent the whole of today trying to find a nanny. Sally said last night that finding a nanny would have to be my department as she a) didn't have the time and b) wasn't in agreement with it anyway. So much for marriage being about compromise.

Ideally, I'd just like to get an au pair, but according to the schedule that Dom has already sent me, my timetable is going to be packed. We have to have the pilot ready at the end of next month, and Dom tells me that I shall be needed full-time from 1st March onwards.

As au pairs aren't really allowed to work full-time, we have to have a nanny, which is a pain, and an expensive one at that. Any money I make will go straight into the nanny's pockets. I hate the poor woman already.

Friday 22 February

This nanny business is getting me down. Today I was told I could have an 'au pair plus', which at first I thought simply meant a fat au pair, but apparently they are au pairs who do more than 5 hours per day – around 7 hours. But I need an au pair who does at least 10 hours, and those sorts of au pairs are called nannies. There's no way round it.

11 p.m.

Oh yes there is. Just had a brainwave while Sally is in the bath. I shall hire TWO au pairs. It's a genius idea. The first one can do the morning shift, and the second one can do the afternoon. I've worked it all out, and between them, they'll have enough hours to cover the whole day. They'll have to share a bedroom, but I'm sure that will be fine.

I am almost rubbing my hands with glee. I'm sure Sally will see the logic in it.

Saturday 23rd February

Turns out she didn't.

'We are NOT having two au pairs,' she said to me over breakfast this morning.

'Why not?'

'Because there's not enough room in the house, and secondly, I know your real reason for wanting two au pairs.'

'What?'

Sally looked at me suspiciously and smiled a little.

'Oh come on, don't play the naïf with me.'

'Nice to hear correct use of naïf.'

'Don't change the subject.'

'What?' I went.

'You know,' she said.

Her coyness was a product of the fact that the children were tucking into their Rice Krispies.

'I have no idea what you are talking about.'

Lesbianism was of course the last thing on my mind. The very last thing indeed.

Sunday 24 February

At lunchtime, Peter asked why the parents of his friend Tom have two houses. (They have a holiday cottage down in Devon, the bastards. Still waiting for the invitation.)

'It's because they have lots of money,' said Sally.

My jealous side wouldn't allow this.

'I suspect it's because Tom's granny and grandpa gave it to them,' I said.

I looked at Sally.

'I can't believe that Tim earns enough to have bought it,' I said. 'And didn't Louise's parents snuff it last year? They're bound to have left them a load of dosh.'

'Charmingly put,' she replied. 'But it doesn't alter the fact that they still managed to buy it.'

'Ah, but it doesn't really count if they were left the money.'

Sally looked puzzled.

'What do you mean?'

'Well, I don't begrudge anybody inherited wealth,' I said. 'That's just luck of the draw, and good for them. But what I do resent is those who have earned it.'

'Surely it should be the other way round?'

'No. Those who earn pots of cash are invariably less talented and brilliant than I am, and therefore I resent the fact that they are richer than me.'

'But that's a bizarre way to think,' said Sally. 'So do you really think you should be the richest person in the world? Is there nobody more talented than you who deserves to be earning more money than you?'

'Um . . .'

Sally laughed. (Nice to see – we don't seem to laugh enough these days.)

'You're terrible,' she said. 'I just hope *WonderHubby* makes you millions of pounds, otherwise you'll spend the rest of your life as a bitter old man.'

'Mummy!' Peter piped up.

'Yes?'

'If Daddy doesn't have enough money, shall we get a new daddy?'

Much laughter from both Sally and me, although mine was rather hollow, and Sally's seemed rather fiendish.

'Not a bad idea,' she said, which made me smart, although after we had cleared away the plates she gave me a reassuring kiss and a hug. Peter and Daisy joined in at this point, hugging our legs, which was a Cute Moment.

'So do you support *WonderHubby*?' I asked.

Sally laughed.

'Not one little bit,' she said.

'Really?'

'Really.'

'Well, the whole thing will probably go tits up anyway if I can't find a nanny.'

'That would be most unfortunate,' said Sally.

'Hmmm. I can see that you really care about it.'

'What's that expression that you always use?'

'What? It'll be fine?'

'That's the one,' said Sally. 'I'm sure it'll be fine. Pudding?'

Tuesday 26 February

Nanny salvation has come, amazingly, from Sally. She brought home the good news this evening.

'There's a woman called Sue at work going on six months' maternity leave,' she told me, 'and she's decided that she doesn't need their nanny.'

'Why not? I'd have thought maternity leave would be the perfect time to have one.'

'Well, she's a little like me, and she doesn't particularly like having strangers around.'

Ouch.

'OK. And?'

'Well, because I'm lovely and helpful, I suggested that maybe we could take her on for a few months, IF your wretched programme goes ahead.'

'And?'

'Well, Sue is going to talk to her tonight. She said she'll let me know tomorrow.'

'And who is this nanny?'

'She's from Turkey, and she's called Halet apparently. The only reason why I'd consider her is because she's already been security-cleared.'

'Age?'

'I knew that would come soon. Fifty-four.'

My pathetic blokey heart sank. It was perhaps just as well.

'Waist–hip ratio?' I asked.

Sally aimed an imaginary pistol at me.

'By all accounts, it sounds as though her waist is wider than her hips.'

'Oh good.'

All this talking of measurements reminded me of our friend Clare, who worked out the Body Mass Indexes of all her potential au pairs, and ended up employing the one with the least flattering ratio. How Darwinian is that?

Thursday 28 February

Halet came to see us today, and I have to say, the children took to her immediately, and she to them. I liked her enormously as well – she's all Mumsy and cuddly and friendly and seems utterly reliable. She's been a nanny in Britain for some 16 years, and has two grown-up children of her own. I asked her whether they had gone back to Turkey, but she said that she didn't really come from Turkey, rather from somewhere utterly unpronounceable, and that it was easier just to say Turkey. Fair enough. Anyway, her two sons work over here, and she showed me some pictures of them, and a couple of bigger thugs you couldn't imagine, but I made all the right cooing noises about what strapping lads they were. Unfortunately, it transpires that Halet is a widow, and she took up nannying when her husband died. He was killed in a plane crash on the way back home, and I could see that she was still desperately sad about it.

Peter's first question to her was typically forward.

'Are you going to be our new granny?' he asked.

At first I was worried that Halet might be offended, but she ruffled his hair and said that she would love to be his new granny so long as his other grannies didn't mind, which I thought to be the perfect response.

Peter's second question was equally forward.

'Why is your skin so dark?'

Once again I closed my eyes in shame. Halet wasn't

that dark, but she definitely had the appearance of a much-cherished deep tan handbag.

'That's because I come from a long way away,' she said. 'Where there is lots of sun, and you know what the sun does, don't you?'

'It makes you warm,' said Peter.

'That's right,' said Halet. 'And it also makes your skin go dark.'

Peter chewed on this.

'You must have been in the sun a long time!' he said.

Halet and I laughed, and I bribed the children with some TV so she and I could talk business. The upshot is that I can't believe how perfect she is for us – she only lives 10 miles away, she has her own car, she's not too expensive, and she comes highly recommended. I told her that we could only employ her for three months at first, but hopefully, if my series paid off, she would be employed full-time. Again, she seemed remarkably relaxed. The only thing that seemed to cause her some confusion was the fact that I was the househusband, and Sally was the one with the job.

'Back home,' she said, 'this would never happen.'

'I'm sure,' I replied. 'It doesn't happen here very often either.'

'And now you're going to make a TV programme about how to look after kids, and yet you won't be looking after your own!'

Halet laughed at her own observation, and I did my best not to be peeved at her tactless recognition of the irony of the situation.

'Well,' I said, 'there are plenty of these so-called childcare gurus who do not even have children, so I feel more qualified than they are!'

'One day, I think I should like to make a programme,' she said.

Not a chance, I thought, shuddering at the thought of potential competition. I smiled weakly and went and summoned the children from the TV, which did not go well.

'OK, show Halet how you can turn the TV off,' I said.

'Don't want to!' shouted Peter. 'I'm watching *Bob the Builder*!'

'No!' shrieked Daisy, as if I had suggested that I dunk them both in ice-cold water.

'Come on, TV off!'

They didn't budge, much to my embarrassment. I was determined to show Halet just how authoritative I was, especially as she seemed somewhat sceptical about my forthcoming career.

'If you don't turn off the TV by the time I count to three, then . . .'

My voice trailed. The truth is, I never know what to threaten them with.

'One!' I began.

No movement.

'Two!'

My voice was louder and hopefully sterner now.

'Three!'

No movement.

Bob continued to do his thing with Wendy.

'Right!' I said. 'I'm going to turn it off myself!'

'No!' came an angry little chorus.

Suddenly, from over my shoulder, Halet spoke.

'Peter. Would you turn the television off please?'

Her voice was calm and authoritative – everything mine was not. Peter and Daisy looked at her with surprise, their cunning eyes scanning her face for signs of weakness. Evidently they could find none, because without any further argument both of them got up and made their way to the television, where they even had a brief contretemps about which one of them would turn it off. (Surprisingly, Daisy won – triumph of the will.)

I turned to Halet. I was both impressed and sheepish.

'Thanks,' I said croakily.

'Years of experience,' she replied.

'I think we could do with your years.'

Later, when I told all this to Sally, she struggled hard not to be delighted. After all, she didn't like the idea of a nanny, but she certainly liked the idea of the children receiving more discipline.

'Just think,' she said, 'you'll learn a lot, perhaps more than the children.'

'Gee. Thanks a bunch.'

Friday 29 February

Had a long chat with Dom today, and he told me that things were going really well. The format of the show has all been worked out (why wasn't I included in the discussions?) and it looks as though they've even found a family for me to do my consulting on.

'I can't tell you how dreadful these people are,' said Dom. 'We once tried using them for some partner-swap programme, but the people we were trying to swap them with refused so emphatically, they said they would take me to court for causing untold cruelty.'

'What's so bad about them?' I asked.

'Well, the dad, if he's ever around, once served two years for GBH. He's called Big Ted, by the way. Then there's the mum, Debbie, who looks like a bulldog licking piss off a thistle. Horrendous woman, all she seems to do is to smoke cheap fags and swear. Then there are the kids, Little Ted, who's fourteen, and Epernay, who's nine.'

'Epernay?'

'Yup. Epernay. They saw it on a bottle of champagne once.'

'Jesus,' I said. 'These people sound like chav central.'

'Indeed they are. And, get this.'

'What?'

'Little Ted has got his first ASBO.'

'Aaah,' we cooed together, as though we were marvelling at some charming kiddie moment.

Inwardly, I was shit-scared. These people sounded as though they might well kill me. I said as much to Dom.

'Don't worry about it,' he said. 'We'll have Eric on standby.'

'Eric?'

'Our friendly bouncer and skull-cracker. He's done

97

time for GBH too, so he should give Big Ted a run for his money if things turn nasty. Don't worry, you'll be in good hands.'

'But aren't this family a little extreme?' I asked. 'I mean, how the hell can I help them? My techniques only really work on nice middle-class families who've got slightly unruly kids who moan when they have to brush their teeth.'

'Extreme is what makes TV, amigo.'

I sighed.

'All right.'

'By the way,' said Dom, 'we need to film you all on Tuesday next week. Can your wife get the day off? You know the drill – we need to present you as the happy family, all perfect and cornflakes packet. Will make a nice contrast.'

I gulped.

'I'm sure that'll be fine,' I lied.

Sunday 2 March

Sally's first response was:

'I'm sorry, sweetheart, I'm not going to do it.'

Polite, calm, nice.

However, every time I needled her, she became more and more definitive.

'No. I've already said no.'

'There's really no point in you asking.'

'Sam!'

'Look. It's just not do-able with work.'

'You'll just have to manage without me.'

'For Pete's sake! No!'

'How many times do I have to bloody tell you?'

'I know what you're about to say – NO!'

'Fuck off!'

Honestly, you would have thought I was asking to do the thing we never do in bed. No matter how much I pleaded, how much I told her it was important, she was adamant. When I asked her what I was going to do without her, she just said that I should use an actress. Not a bad idea.

Monday 3 March
Noon

I suggested the idea to Dom, who said there was no time to get someone by tomorrow morning, and that I would just have to convince Sally, otherwise the whole shooting schedule would go out the window and there was no time for things to go out the window, because if that happened then the whole series would be in jeopardy and then where would we be?

Fuck. This is serious. There's NO WAY I'm going to be able to convince Sally. No way. Now what?

6.30 p.m.

The children are watching *The Night Garden*, and I'm feeling happy, because I think I have found a solution. It's not a perfect one, and it will have the most horrific consequences, I'm sure, but it's got me out of a hole. From this moment on, my TV wife will be Emily. I am going to be in so much trouble when Sally finds out, but I shall just have to say I had no choice. Which I don't, frankly. I'm also not going to tell Dom – I don't want him to think that Sally won't do as I ask. Emily's all up for playing the subterfuge, as I thought she might be.

Rest assured, she didn't need much convincing to take on this challenging new role. She's more excited than I am. 'Fame at last,' she kept saying. She's worse than me.

Tuesday 4 March

What a great big exhausting amusing educational disturbing scary fun day it's been. I can see why some of the actory-celebby types say their work is so demanding. I always thought that was complete bollocks, but now I'm a fully paid up member of the tellystocracy I can see why they always moan, despite their vast piles of cash.

The day started with me feeling a bit of a rat. As soon as Sally was out the door at 7.15, I phoned Emily to tell her to come over. (She was getting a neighbour to look after her children.) She did so promptly, and she was certainly dressed for the occasion – shortish and tight denim skirt, tastefully patterned tights, boots up to her knee, and a tight cream rollneck woollen top. There was no doubt that she was going for the yummy mummy look, and, to be fair to her, she had succeeded. Naturally, I felt absurdly guilty, almost as though I was having an affair, a feeling heightened by Emily's rather too affectionate kiss and flirtatious 'Hello new husband', which made her sound like that rabbit going 'Hello Mr Beaver' in that chocolate-bar ad from a lifetime ago.

'What's Emily doing here?' asked Peter.

Daisy kicked her little legs under the kitchen table – she loves Emily, and the feeling is mutual.

'Emily is here to help Daddy today,' I said.

'Oh,' said Peter, evidently unimpressed. He finds Emily a bit too forward, and kind of cowers when he sees her.

'I'm here to pretend to be your mummy,' said Emily.

'Why?' asked Peter.

'Well, there are some people coming to film us,' I explained. 'And because Mummy can't be here because she's at work, I've asked Emily to pretend to be our mummy for the people.'

'Oh,' said Peter. 'Is Emily going to be our mummy for ever now?'

'No!' I said, a little too emphatically. 'Just for today, that's all.'

'Good,' said Peter.

'Sorry,' I said to Emily, who was laughing.

'So all you need to do,' I said to Peter, 'is to make sure that you call Emily Mummy. OK?'

'But Emily's not my mummy.'

'I know, but we are pretending.'

'Like in the nativity play?'

'That's right.'

'Can I be Joseph?'

'What?'

'Can I be Joseph today? Joseph in the nativity play.'

'Well, we're not really doing a nativity play today. We're just having a normal day.'

'So when can I be Joseph?'

Mercifully I was saved by a knock on the door, which heralded the arrival of the 'crew', as us people in TV call them. This consisted of Dom, one of the Emmas, a cameraman, and a man with a microphone. I had expected more, but it was enough, as very quickly our small kitchen was packed with the crew and their kit, wires trailing everywhere.

I introduced Emily as 'Sally' to everybody, and I thought I detected a certain frisson between her and Dom, but that may have just been paranoia. After the pleasantries Dom invited us just to act normally, and to do our best to ignore the crew, who would just follow us around.

It was highly surreal. I made 'Sally' stay seated, as I didn't want it to be obvious that she had no idea where things like crockery and cutlery lived. She did her best to distract the children from just staring straight at the camera, but it was almost impossible.

'Don't worry too much about that,' said Dom. 'They'll get used to us.'

Dom then talked us through the shots we needed – me cleaning their teeth, me getting their coats on to go to school, me making Peter's packed lunch etc. Emily asked if Dom wanted her to do anything, but he told her that the whole point was that I was the one doing all the work, and shouldn't she be at work? Emily explained that she had taken the day off (as Dom requested), and Dom then suggested that we should do some shots of Emily kissing us all goodbye.

This wasn't great news, to put it mildly. The last thing I wanted enshrined on tape, for all the world to see – including my wife – was Emily giving me a kiss. But I could think of no way in which I could wriggle out of it.

'Why don't you get into your work clothes?' asked Dom. 'And then we'll do some shots of you going.'

'These are my work clothes,' said Emily quick-wittedly. I thanked God that we were spared the further hell of Sally seeing Emily kiss me while wearing one of her work suits. I think that would have meant instant divorce.

Emily grabbed a coat from the utility room, and then she bustled into the kitchen as if she had always lived here. I had to hand it to her, she put on a brilliant performance. The children, on the other hand, didn't, and Peter scowled when she kissed him, and Daisy said 'bye bye Emily', which luckily came out as 'aye aye ilee', and seemed to fool the assembled throng.

Then came the kiss goodbye.

'See you later, darling,' she said, her eyes locking on to mine, accompanied by her trademark smirk.

She then held my face in both her hands, and proceeded to give me a rather too passionate kiss for a wife who has said goodbye to her husband nearly every morning for seven years. It felt like utter treachery, but also thrilling treachery. Apart from the obvious reason of desiring sexual variety, I can see why people have affairs – it clearly feels SO naughty, and with that, an immense thrill that must only heighten the sex.

'Wow,' said Dom.

Emma gasped.

'I wish I got a kiss like that every morning,' said Dom. (To be honest, so do I.)

Emily smiled contentedly, clearly revelling in exhibiting her oscular prowess.

'However,' said Dom, 'I think it was a little too passionate. Can we try it again, and make it more husband and wifey?'

'Sure,' said Emily. 'No problem.'

Fuck, I said inwardly.

Emily came into the room again, said goodbye to the children, and then proceeded to give me yet another over-the-top smoocher.

'Again,' said Dom, giggling slightly.

Third take, and Emily once again over-egged it. I knew her game now – she was going to give me as many kisses as possible, wear me down with repetition. Well, I was determined not to let it work, and decided to make it feel as though she were kissing Hitler.

'Um,' said Dom, 'could you try and look slightly less revolted when your wife gives you a kiss please?'

By the eighth take we got it right, and I felt nauseous when I realised that it would be impossible to make the children keep it quiet. They both looked a little confused, especially Peter, who kept trying to ask what I was doing, and I kept pre-empting by telling him to eat his breakfast.

'Is there anything else you need me for?' Emily asked, clearly desperate to ensure a run on videotape.

'Um, I don't think so,' Dom replied.

'OK,' said Emily, her crest somewhat fallen.

'I suppose we could shoot you coming back home at the end of the day, but we need it to get darker for that. How about you come back at 4ish and we take some shots then?'

'Fine,' said Emily.

'You can have a day all to yourself, darling,' I said. 'You could go shopping or something. Have lunch with Kate maybe.'

Emily gave me a strange look. It was hardly surprising – Kate is a friend of Sally, and clearly not of Emily. Still, I had rather hoped that Emily wasn't going to be so dim.

'Kate?' she went.

'Yes, your friend Kate who lives in the next village. You know, Kate?'

'Aaah,' said Emily. 'Kate. Of course.'

She still looked blank, and I could tell that Dom and Emma were looking at us not so much with suspicion, but more out of confusion.

'Good idea,' Emily continued. 'I think I'll go and see Kate.'

'Send her my love,' I said.

'Will do.'

Phew. I really didn't want Dom to rumble that I was

using an impostor. Even though I knew that making up 'reality' was his stock-in-trade, there was no way I wanted him to think I was like him.

With Emily out the way, things were a bit more relaxed, and soon the three of us got accustomed to having the crew following us around. At one point Daisy asked if they wanted to watch her having a pee on her potty, but Dom and Emma thought that might be unnecessary. She looked most disappointed and ended up peeing on the floor, the result of which was captured on tape, along with my somewhat ineffectual attempts to clean it up. In the end, Emma had to show me how to do it.

'Dab it,' she said. 'Don't wipe it.'

I dimly recall Sally saying something like this to me once, but I tend to forget most domestic advice.

After I had done my best to clean it up, Dom asked if I could do it again.

'Do what again?'

'Clean up the pee,' he said.

'What?'

'The thing is, it didn't really look as though you knew what you were doing. You looked like any normal bloke trying to do it, and we want you to look like a complete expert. After all, nobody's going to take your advice seriously if you can't even clear up child's piss.'

This was a good point, but I didn't want to take it lying down. (I was in fact on my knees, which is no less submissive a position, perhaps even more so.)

'You really sure about this? I mean, it's not as though

I can get Daisy to pee at will. And I don't think it would be kind to make her drink lots just to make her pee.'

Dom held up his hand, laughing a little.

'Don't worry,' he said, 'we'll just use water.'

And so, a few seconds later, I was clearing water off our landing carpet. And then I did it again, and again, and during all this, Dom thought it a bright idea that I should clean the lavatory. So I had to scrub that repeatedly, and between each take we had to 'dirty' it with a little orange barley water and some chocolate, which looked surprisingly effective.

The rest of the morning largely featured me doing such chores, and talking to the camera, saying how all of this was part of a highly structured routine that had been born out of my years as a management consultant. Dom and Emma seemed delighted by what they rudely called my 'bullshit bingo', and said that it worked really well as I did the cooking etc. They even followed me taking the children to the supermarket after school, where I had to talk to the camera, explaining how the Holden Childcare Programme was useful in 'maximising the effectiveness of my grocery choice solutions', which again, Dom and Emma seemed to love.

By the end of the day, as I was filmed tucking the children into bed and giving them kisses good night (at least eight takes), I realised I was exhausted. The crew took a last few shots of me preparing dinner, and then they finally departed, leaving the house feeling exceptionally empty. When Sally came back I wanted to tell her all about it, but she said that she would speak to me tomorrow – too tired – and she fell asleep in the bath at 9.15. I almost had to carry her to bed.

I'm worried that our lives couldn't be more different. Is that good or bad? Now is perhaps not the time to answer questions like that. Bed for me as well.

Wednesday 5 March

Dom rang to say that the footage was great from yesterday, and said that I was very lucky to be married to someone like Emily, who not only kissed brilliantly, but also looked brilliant as well. I muttered appreciative noises about what a lucky bloke I am etc., and felt guilty. I am always feeling guilty these days. It can't be good for me.

Dom said that we would be starting the filming on Monday, although it might be held up, because Little Ted had to be at court that morning. Something to do with breaking his ASBO apparently. I'm terrified of these people, and told Dom as much.

'You'll be fine,' he said, sounding like me.

'I hope so,' I replied. 'At least I'll have Big Eric on my side.'

A silence.

'Yes,' said Dom eventually. 'About Big Eric.'

'Don't tell me he can't make it.'

'Not sure yet, I'm afraid.'

'Why, where is he?'

'He's got to go to court that morning as well.'

Great. What am I letting myself in for? By this time

next week I might be being stitched up in some grim Midlands hospital, the Holden Childcare Programme having seen its demise at the hands of a psychotic fourteen-year-old wielding a broken beer bottle.

Or you never know, the Programme might just work. In fact, I think I do know.

Thursday 6 March

Another call from the TV company, this time from an Emma, who wanted me to make some props for next week. Props? What sort of props?

'You know, management-consultant props – pie charts and easels and all that sort of stuff.'

'But we don't do props as management consultants,' I replied. 'We do PowerPoint presentations.'

'Well, can you put some of the PowerPoint stuff on old sort of stuff?'

'Old sort of stuff?'

'Yes – easels, flip charts.'

'But I'm telling you, that's not how it's done.'

There was a tone of mutual exasperation.

'Sam,' said Emma. 'You must understand that we need something large and visual.'

'Why?'

'Because that's how TV works, that's why. TV is not about subtlety, it's about black and white, making difficult things easy, and making easy things even easier.'

'Lowest common denominator, eh?'

'Whatever that means,' said Emma, thereby proving my point.

'OK,' I sighed. 'You'll have your flip charts and pie charts and stuff charts.'

What I find surprising is just how ad hoc everything is. Back at Musker Walsh and Sloss, projects would take weeks and months to come to fruition, whereas these people in TV are just kind of winging it and making it up as they go along.

They have a lot to learn.

Friday 7 March

Spent all day trying to make pie charts and flip charts and diagrams and whatnot. When the children were at school/playgroup I drove into a stationers in town and bought all the type of stuff that I suspected the Emma wanted, and then proceeded to draw out all my PowerPoint slides. In the end, I have to admit that they looked pretty good, although some of my pies looked like they had been baked by an amateur.

The children wanted to help when they got back, but I managed to stop them. It would have done no good having their squiggles all over my Domestic Evaluation Signifiers graph, or indeed my Activity Ratio Index pie chart.

Peter looked a bit winded when it became clear my refusal was absolute (rather a rare occurrence) and he folded his arms and asked, 'But what are they *for*, Daddy?'

'They're for the TV programme I am making.'

'Yes, but why?'

'It will show the family what to do.'

'What family?'

'The family I am trying to help,' I replied, keeping my patience.

'Why do they need help?'

'Because they are a bad family, and Daddy is going to make them into a good family.'

Peter gestured towards my charts.

'With these?' he asked, his little voice largely incredulous.

I looked at my handiwork.

'Of course,' I said, trying to sound more convincing than I felt.

'But you don't use these charts with us,' he observed.

'That's right.'

'Why?'

My first reaction was to say, 'Because they don't work', but instead I said, 'Because we are a good family, and you don't need this sort of help.'

'But Daddy . . .'

Peter paused. I could almost see the cogs in his head.

'Yes?'

'But Daddy, if you are going to help the bad family, who is going to help me and Daisy and Mummy?'

'I'm not going away for very long – just for a few days – and Halet will look after you.'

Peter looked a little sad.

'I don't want you to go away,' he said.

'It won't be for very long, and Halet is very nice.'

'No she's not!'

I bent down and gave Peter a hug. He was close to tears, which almost made me cry as well. Now I am really feeling guilty about everything.

Sunday 9 March

Right. I think I'm all set. I've got all my bags packed, Halet arrives at 7.30 tomorrow morning, and I'll be leaving at 9ish. We'll all go down to Peter's school together, and then I'll be off to the Midlands, where I shall either meet my doom, or enter into TV nirvana, or both. Perhaps I shall be killed on camera, and my entire life will be relegated to one of those comedy TV moments, forever to be repeated on some snuff website.

Sally picked up on my nerves over supper.

'It's not too late to pull out, you know,' she said.

'It is,' I replied, sucking up some spaghetti. 'I've signed a contract.'

'Oh, I didn't realise that.'

(Neither did I.)

'Yes, and besides, I don't want to let everybody down. Most of all myself. I really want to give this the best shot I can.'

Sally held my hand and looked into my eyes.

'Listen,' she said. 'I know I've been down on this whole thing from the start, but I don't want you to think that I don't support you.'

I didn't know what to make of this.

'So you do support it or not?' I asked, slightly too aggressively.

'I support you, but not the idea,' she said.

I smiled.

'Spoken like a true civil servant,' I replied.

'Spoken like a true wife. I want you to prove me wrong, I really do.'

'Don't you worry – I will. This thing is going to be an enormous success.'

Monday 10 March
11.30 p.m. Somewhere in the Midlands in a terrible hotel

Everything started so well. Halet turned up on time, we got the children to school OK, and my drive up here was fine. I met Dom and one of the Emmas and the rest of the crew at the hotel, and Dom explained that today would be all about watching how the family get on and how they behave, etc. – just observation. I'd need to stand around looking incredibly wise and jotting down notes on a shoddy *WonderHubby* clipboard that had been specially made. We'd stay with the family through to bed time (if there was such a thing), and then head off for a well-earned drink back at the hotel.

That was the plan, anyway. Things didn't go quite so smoothly as that.

The house, which was on a reasonably smart council estate, looked in pretty good nick. The grass was a little long, and one of the window panes was cracked, but that was about it. Perhaps they weren't such animals after all.

The only person who looked disappointed was Dom.

'What's the matter?' I asked.

'It's not what I wanted,' he said.

'Oh?'

'Not scruffy enough.'

He turned to Emma.

'Ems, could you sort out some rusty old bicycles and an old bath or something to put out the front here?'

Emma scribbled everything down on her pad, which I noticed didn't have '*WonderHubby*' emblazoned on it.

'But . . .' I started.

'I know what you're thinking,' interrupted Dom. 'But remember, the greater the difference before and after, the more chance we have of getting the series commissioned. You'll just have to trust me on this.'

'OK,' I sighed, wondering how well the natives would take it, and hoping that such liberties would only be taken with the pilot.

While Emma scampered off with one of the gofers (there seemed to be a hell of a lot of people attached to the crew), Dom rang the doorbell, and after a few seconds this enormously fat woman appeared at the door. It was impossible to place her age – it could have been anything between thirty-five and sixty-five.

'Yeah?'

'Hi there Debbie,' said Dom. 'How are you?'

'Are you trying to sell me something?'

'No! We're the TV people – the ones making the programme about you.'

'Which programme?'

Dom looked at the house number.

'This is number 23, right?'

'Yeah.'

'And you are Debbie Lampert?'

'Yeah.'

'Well, you must remember that we're filming you this week.'

'I know all that,' said Debbie, 'but which programme are you from?'

'*WonderHubby*,' Dom replied. 'The one in which we're going to try to help you look after the kids.'

'OK,' she said. 'That's good to know, cos we've also got a couple of other programmes coming sometime this week.'

Dom's eyes did the Tube logo thing.

'Which ones?'

Debbie wracked whatever brains she had.

'Well, there's *Pimp Your Lounge* for one, and the other one is *Bridgette Cassidy's Move That Arse.*'

'*Bridgette Cassidy's Move That Arse?*' we asked in unison.

'Yeah,' she smiled. 'Don't yer know it? It's on Sky. It's brilliant. Bridgette Cassidy comes along and gets rid of your arse.'

'How?'

Debbie shrugged – or rather wobbled – her shoulders.

'I dunno. Probably hipposuction or something.'

Dom and I tried not to laugh.

'So when are these programmes coming?' Dom asked.

'They said this week. Dunno when exactly.'

Just at that moment we heard a kerfuffle behind us, and we turned to see another TV crew trying to barge through ours.

'Oh look,' said Debbie. 'Here comes one of them right now.'

A bloke who looked a little like Dom (at least, they had the same rectangular glasses) came up to him and asked, 'Where you from?'

'Pantheon Productions,' said Dom. 'We're making *WonderHubby* and we've got them first. Where are you from?'

'The news,' said the lookalike, who then turned to Debbie.

'Hello Mrs Lampert,' he smiled. 'You OK?'

'Good thanks,' she replied, lighting a cigarette. 'What you here for this time, Bob?'

'Little Ted again, I'm afraid.'

'I thought he was in court,' she said. 'Big Ted took him there first thing.'

'Seems they never turned up,' said Bob. 'So we just wanted to see if they were here.'

'I expect Little Ted went to school instead,' said Debbie, at which point she broke out into a smoker's hacking cackle.

We all joined in the laughter, and Dom signalled to the crew that they should start filming, and then Bob did the same with his crew, and soon we entered into a very postmodern situation in which both sets of camera crews started filming each other.

'Do you all wanna come in for a cuppa?' asked Debbie, and so about 45 of us went into the house, which stank of fags and chip fat, and made our way through a tiny hall into a small kitchen where we found young Epernay, who was sitting at the table reading a copy of *A-Listers!* (The exclamation mark is not mine.) Amazingly, she just ignored us, and I noticed that she was listening to an iPod, which was causing her to draw out some annoying tattoo on the table at 250 beats per minute. Meanwhile, both crews continued filming. Bob kept asking questions about Big and Little Ted, and wondered how Debbie felt about the fact that they were earning a name for themselves as a father and son crime wave, all of which Debbie thought was rather amusing, as she manifested by her hacking laugh.

After half an hour the news crew left, and everything felt positively anticlimactic. We all sort of sat there in silence, until Epernay piped up.

'So what you doing then?'

'We're making a programme about your family,' I replied.

'What?'

'WE'RE MAKING A PROGRAMME ABOUT YOUR FAMILY,' I yelled over the headphones.

'No need to shout,' she said.

I studied Epernay's face. Although she was only nine, it was already showing signs of the unattractive features she would acquire after years of being exposed to fag smoke and saturated fats, and not being exposed to sun and exercise. She was pasty and chubby, and there seemed little hope. As I looked at her, I started wondering whether this programme could make a difference, and whether it was indeed possible for *WonderHubby* to do anything remotely positive. Or were we just here to take the piss out of poor people, like so many other TV crews, and then share our footage with other middle-class people for them to laugh at over their organic TV dinners? Probably. But then these people have a choice to be like this. They don't have to smoke all day. Fruit and vegetables are cheap. Exercise is free, as is fresh air. And it's not as though they are ignorant of the benefits of good food and exercise – it's just that they are lazy. And is there anything wrong with taking the piss out of lazy people? Probably. But I'm in too deep now.

'Why are you looking at me like that?' Epernay asked, pulling me out of my musings.

'Sorry,' I said, shaking my head. 'I was miles away.'

Suddenly a couple of shadows loomed behind me.

'Who the fuck are you lot?'

I turned to see who I could only assume was Big Ted. He was just as I imagined – a cross between a wrestler and another uglier wrestler. His hair was short, and below it was a face that was used to playing host to fists. He was wearing a tracksuit emblazoned with the name of the local football team, and even though he may have been as fat as his wife, he looked as fit as a prop forward.

Behind him peeked Little Ted, who was the thinnest member of the family by a ton. In fact, he was so thin he could have hidden behind one of his father's legs, which is basically what he was doing. He looked feral, and so unlike his parents that I began to doubt his parentage.

'Hello,' said Dom, holding out his hand. 'I'm Dom, and this is Sam, and we're making a programme called *WonderHubby*. Has Debbie not told you about it?'

Big Ted looked down at the hand, wondering what on earth it was doing there.

'No,' he said.

'I did tell yer,' said Debbie. 'Last week, when you came back from the pub on Tuesday morning.'

Big Ted shook his skull.

'I don't remember.'

'Think, Ted.'

'I remember,' piped up a weaselly voice that belonged to Little Ted.

'Yer see?' said Debbie. 'Anyway, where have you been?'

'To court,' said Big Ted, his eyes wide with innocence.

'That's not what the news said.'

'The news?'

'Bob came round here just now, saying that you never went.'

'We bloody did, didn't we son?'

'Yeah? And what happened?'

Debbie folded her arms as she squared up to her husband.

'Not much,' said Big Ted, and with that, he slouched off to his soon-to-be pimped lounge.

Little Ted remained in the room.

'Hi,' I said weakly.

'Hi,' he said moodily, his gold chain swinging from his scrawny neck.

I recognised his type. All mouth and no shell suit. The nasty little coward who would mug you from behind, even if you were a pensioner. The air filled with a mutually satisfying loathing. What was the posh twat doing in his house?

'So then,' I said. 'Did your mum tell you about the programme?'

'Not really.'

I noticed that the camera had started up again. I did my best not to feel self-conscious.

'Well, I'm the WonderHubby . . .'

A snort, the type of snort that suggested not only derision, but that the nose was the orifice through which Little Ted received the majority of his pharmaceutical sustenance.

'And I'm going to be using the techniques of management consultancy to show you how to run yourselves better as a family.'

'Management what?'

At this point Dom stepped in, ushering everyone to their feet.

'Right, let's do this properly. Let's set this up in the lounge, where Sam can show you how it's all going to work. Ems, fetch the flip charts and all that stuff.'

'But there's nothing wrong with our family,' said Little Ted, sniffing.

My presentation was a disaster. Finally, at around 12 o'clock, we managed to assemble the family in the lounge, which really did need to be pimped. The 'carpet' was purple, the walls were orange, and the sofas were a mixture of brown and grey. Along one wall stood a vast cupboard/display case thing, upon which were the naffest ornaments human beings have ever created, such as dolphins playing tennis and angels crying on toadstools. Unsurprisingly, the room was dominated by an enormous flatscreen television that somebody must have paid at least £2,000 for. I reflected that whoever had bought it must have been missing it.

Debbie seemed to take much exception to our moving the furniture around, and it took Dom to gently remind her that doubtless *Pimp Your Lounge* would be doing a lot worse, to make her shut up. Eventually, the Lamperts were squeezed onto one sofa, all of them – bar Epernay – dragging hungrily on their fags. The room was full of smoke, and as both the windows were permanently shut – 'There's a lot of stealing round here,' Big Ted explained – it was impossible to clear the air.

I set up all my presentation devices as planned, and began to talk to them about what I was going to do. I started by asking whether any of them knew what management consultancy was.

'Nah,' said Debbie, examining her yellowy fingernails.

'Fucked if I know,' said Epernay.

'Language!' hissed Big Ted.

'Management consultants are people who help managers run their companies,' I explained, doing my best not to adopt a primary school teacher voice.

'But,' interrupted Big Ted, 'if you need a management consultant to tell you how to manage your company, doesn't that mean you're a bit fucked?'

I closed my eyes momentarily. This was exactly the same question Sally's sister asked me a while back. Why does everybody think this?

'Do you think we're a bit fucked?' Big Ted asked. 'Cos if you do, you can fuck right off!'

'Language!' hissed Epernay.

'I don't think you're fucked at all,' I said.

'Language!' hissed Little Ted, at which point they all laughed.

'I just think,' I continued, 'like most families, you need to make some improvements. And that's what management consultants do with companies. They don't come in and run the company, but they show how to make everything a little bit better, and hopefully more profitable. Obviously, the notion of profit doesn't apply in a domestic-cum-familial scenario, although the underlying tenets of efficiency maximisation and yield-optimising techniques are identical in many ways.'

I realised they were looking at me as if I were a freak.

'You what?' said Little Ted.

'You're having a laugh,' said Debbie.

I looked at Dom and Emma out of the corner of my

eye, pleading with them to back me up, but they were smirking. As was the cameraman, the git.

I then proceeded to attempt to spell out in simple language what it was I was here to do. I did my best not to use too much jargon and business-speak, but that's the problem with management consultancy, you just have to use it, otherwise you're taking an age to explain every concept. The family looked slightly bored, and at one point Little Ted even turned on the television, which caused Debbie much annoyance.

'Don't be rude to our guest!'

This was accompanied by a slap round the head that would have felled a reasonable-sized tree.

After another fifteen minutes, I finally lost them. Little Ted and Epernay were playing with their mobiles, Debbie was reading a magazine called *Flick!* (once again, not my exclamation mark) and Big Ted was snoring.

'Shall I keep going?' I asked Dom.

'Of course!'

Arsehole, I thought. I didn't know who the programme was designed to humiliate more – the family or me.

We disappeared to the pub for a late lunch, and by the time we got back the family had disappeared. They returned about an hour later, armed with bags of shopping from the local supermarket, which we filmed them unpacking. I couldn't quite believe their contents, and neither could Dom. Out came beer, fags, crisps, frozen chips, ice cream, biscuits, frozen sausages, more frozen sausages and frozen sausage rolls. There was not one vegetable, piece of fruit, or anything that hadn't been processed in some way. No wonder they all looked so pallid.

Detecting our middle-class gasps, Debbie turned to me and said, 'Is there something the matter?'

Dom's eyes lit up at the potential confrontation.

'No,' I lied.

'Well what's the bloomin' face for then?'

'Well, don't you ever eat vegetables?'

'Nah. None of us like them.'

'Fruit?'

'Too much hassle.'

'Hassle?'

'Yeah, you know, having to deal with the skins and the pips and that.'

I have to confess I was speechless, and I resolved, in a nanny-state kind of way, that if *WonderHubby* did one thing with this lot this week, it would be to get them to eat something nutritious.

It was at this point, just as I was radiating the benevolent thoughts of a Victorian missionary, that Big Ted piped up.

'Listen pal, I'm not sure I like that look on your face.'

His eyes locked on to mine like some missile system in an Apache helicopter.

'I'm sorry,' I replied, all the time aware of the camera.

Big Ted allowed a finger to extend out of his permafists. He then pointed it at me as though it were a dagger.

'You come in here, all posh and southern and lah-dee-dah and you film us doing our normal things and then you take the piss. Am I right?'

'Er . . . no . . . not, not um, not at all.'

'Well, why are you here then? I mean, if you thought we was all OK, then you wouldn't bother, would yer?'

Big Ted's point was unassailable. I took a deep breath.

'Look, Ted, clearly there are some things that you might want to do better as a family. All I'm here to do – at Debbie's request – is to offer you some advice which you can take or leave.'

'I don't want your fucking advice!'

I'd had enough of this.

'So why did you agree to be on this programme then?'

'I didn't agree to be on this programme!'

'Oh?'

'No! She did!'

Big Ted stabbed his finger towards his wife.

'She didn't tell you?'

'No! Why? You gonna say I was lying next?'

By now Big Ted was standing very very close indeed, and I could smell his breath (boozy-cum-ciggy) and could see the blackheads that thickly peppered his red nose.

'Of course you're not lying.'

125

Ted's eyes narrowed as they continued in their relentless Apache-missile-lock mode.

'You know what I think?' he asked.

'What?'

'I think you're a tosser.'

'Well, I think you're a bit of a tosser as well.'

Oh dear. Why did I say that? What a stupid beta-male thing to have said. What did I possibly think I had to gain by standing up for myself? All I had to do was to turn away, ignore him, anything, but no, I called him a tosser.

Obviously I did not have time to reflect in this way, because within half a second Big Ted's fist had connected with my stomach, knocking the wind out of me. The next thing I did was to sort of crumple to the floor, attempting to catch my breath. It took me a few seconds to realise that I had actually been punched, something that hadn't happened in about thirty years, not since primary school. I thought I was going to pass out, and all I could remember was laughter, the word 'Ted!' being shouted, and repeated queries of 'Are you OK?'

After a minute or so, I stood up, holding on to Dom. I must have cut a pathetic sight, pathetic enough for the two Teds still to be laughing. Even Epernay was grinning, and Debbie merely looked embarrassed.

'I'm so sorry,' she said. 'I wish he wouldn't keep doing that to TV people. I think you're all right myself.'

'Thanks,' I croaked.

I tried looking steelily at Ted, but he just continued his low soft smoky cackle.

'So you think I'm a tosser do you?'

'No,' I replied, grinning sarcastically. 'I think you're a top bloke.'

'That's got that settled then! So then, now we know what's what, do you wanna continue?'

'Perhaps tomorrow,' Dom said.

Within five minutes we had gone. Dom was frantically apologetic and kept asking if I was OK, which I am. The only thing really wounded is my pride, and I'm not sure how quickly I can recover from that. Still, perhaps it's good to be punched. Perhaps I needed it to show me that what we are doing is insulting and condescending. Perhaps Sally is right, perhaps the whole thing is an absurd idea, and I'd be better off doing something sensible.

But something inside urges me not to give up. At least not yet.

Tuesday 11 March
8 a.m.

I didn't sleep well last night. I'm wondering whether to continue with all this. At around 4 in the morning I got up and just sat on the edge of the bed, considering what to do. I thought of Sally and the children, who would all be fast asleep, and it felt wrong to be so far away from them. Who am I doing all this for? Them or me? I'd like to think both, but I'm not sure if I'm being honest with myself. And although I like to think not, that punch took more out of me than wind. Hot air as well.

Knock on the door – that'll be Dom. I wish I could share his enthusiasm – last night he said that this was going to be commissioned, no sweat. Two days ago, I would have rejoiced. Today it depresses me. Knock, knock. All right, all right, I'm coming.

11 hours later

I've just spoken to Sally and the children, and they all sound very happy, which is more than can be said for me.

Peter was on extremely good form.

'Daddy,' he said. 'I love Halet.'

A pang of jealousy shot down my spine.

'Why's that?'

'Because we do lots and lots of things with her! Today we made some cakes *and* a spaceship! And Daisy made a magic crown!'

Guilt now. That's more than I've ever done with them.

'Wow!' I went. 'That sounds really cool! I'm glad you like her.'

'My spaceship goes all the way to Mars!'

'Wow!'

'And tomorrow Halet said we could make another spaceship after school and then we will be able to have a fight between the spaceships and mine will be the goodie spaceship and Daisy's will be the baddie spaceship and my spaceship will win because it is really fast and it has lots of guns and will be the winner.'

'Wow!'

'And then Halet said that if we are really good we can watch a little bit of TV but I don't want to watch TV because Halet is very good at telling stories and she does not have a book and they just come out of her head.'

'Wow!'

This was both brilliant and awful. What was Halet? Some kind of childcare genius? I thought I was supposed to be the genius, not her. Maybe she was right, maybe she should have her own TV programme.

After I said goodnight to Peter, Daisy came on the phone.

'Hello Daddy.'

'Hello little lady. How are you?'

'I did pee on the potty.'

'Wow!'

And I meant it. This was unbelievable. Could it be that Halet was already potty-training her? I had been kind of brushing this one under the carpet and hoping she'd just eventually copy Peter, after a fashion.

'Did you really?' I asked.

'Bye bye,' said Daisy, and with that she disappeared. She's a girl of very few words, my daughter. She would make a good soldier – only gives out need to know information and nothing more. If she had access to email, I'm sure today's would have been little more than:

Dear Daddy
Did a pee.
Love,
Daisy

Sally came to the phone. She was laughing.

'Did you get all that?' she asked.

'I did indeed, it's incredible. Halet seems to be a miracle worker. Not only has she weaned Peter off the box, but she also appears to be potty-training Daisy.'

'I know,' said Sally. 'Although I dimly recall you saying only last week that you were already potty-training Daisy.'

'Ah, yes. Well, we gave it a go and it didn't really work out for us.'

Sally didn't seem too worked up about it, and I heard a welcome warmth of tone in her voice.

'They seem very well,' I said.

'They are,' she replied.

It went unspoken that they sounded a bit too well.

'And how are you?' I asked.

'Not bad. Work is still pretty dire, but the situation seems to have calmed down a bit.'

'Good,' I said. 'Is that why you're back early?'

'It is, and to be honest, Mark told me that I looked shattered and thought I was burning the candle at both ends.'

'Sounds like the boss is right.'

'He is, it's just that . . .'

Sally's voice trailed off.

'What?' I asked.

'It's just that whenever he thinks people are looking tired, that's normally a prelude to moving them to Personnel or some other backwater.'

'I doubt that very much, and besides, is Personnel really such a backwater?'

'Comparatively. Anyway, how are you?'

I sighed.

'Not bad,' I said.

'That bad, huh?'

Sally knows full well that my 'not bad' is everybody else's 'fucking awful'. That's the funny thing about marriage (or at least one of them). No matter how well your partner knows you, you still persist with those little obfuscations that you would normally use with strangers. Why do I keep saying 'not bad' to Sally, when I should just be saying 'fucking awful'? What's the point in lying to someone who knows when you're lying?

'What's the matter?' she asked. 'Things not going well?'

'They could be better,' I started. 'Actually, they're shit.'

'Oh?'

'Well, yesterday I got punched, and today all that happened was that I got laughed at.'

'Punched? By who?'

I told her, and said that it was water under the bridge etc., and she wasn't to worry.

'But who was laughing at you?'

'The family, Dom, Emma, the cameraman, the rest of the crew, you name it. It seems that every time I open my mouth to try to suggest something constructive, they just find it all very funny.'

'But isn't it meant to be funny?'

131

'Well, I didn't think it was, but that's how it's turning out.'

'And what does Dom think?'

'So far, he seems delighted.'

'Well, that's OK then isn't it?'

'I suppose so.'

'You didn't really think that these people were going to sit there like clients and just take your advice and then play happy families happily ever after?'

I paused.

'A little bit I guess.'

Sally laughed.

'You're even more of a tyrant than some of the people we're dealing with in Ktyteklhdfistan.'

'Perhaps I should take the show over there.'

'Hmm . . . I'd strongly advise against it!'

After that, we said some night-nights. Dinner with Dom and Emma in a sec. I must get my head sorted.

Wednesday 12 March
6.30 a.m.

Another shit night's sleep. Nevertheless, last night's dinner was very productive. I expressed concerns to Dom and he reassured me that he'd got it all under control. He said that we needed this sort of footage to establish what monsters these people were, and that by the end of the week, we'd be able to show how I had transformed them into the perfect English family.

'But that's impossible,' I said.

I caught Dom and Emma smirking over our over-cooked plasticky steaks. Something told me that they were shagging. I'm normally pretty good at working out when people are doing so. It's usually assumed that it's about telltale intimacies, whereas in fact it's the very opposite. When you're at the pre-shag stage, you're full of little flirty remarks and touches and double entendres etc. But as soon as the secret shagging begins, all that ends. Not only is the tension between you broken, but you're also mindful that you don't want to look as though you're shagging, and so you drop all the flirting. In fact, you drop it to such an extent that you almost appear offhand with each other. This is an error, and if you want to appear undetected, then the thing to do is to keep up the flirtation.

In this instance, Dom and Emma exchanged the type of smirk that wasn't flirtatious, but intimate. It's the husband-and-wife dinner-party smile that tells each other that they're both thinking the same thing, that someone is being a prat and that they can't wait to talk about it later. I always find such smirks somewhat irksome, because usually I'm the prat who's being smirked about.

'Nothing's impossible,' said Dom.

'You're just going to pay them, aren't you?'

Dom reached into his pocket and brought out a thick wedge of notes.

'We call these "Reality Facilitator Tokens",' he said.

I couldn't help but laugh.

'How many Reality Facilitator Tokens is that?' I asked.

'Two thousand,' he said. 'A fucking fortune for these people.'

There was something very sneering about the way he went 'these people'. I would have been the same a few days ago, but I think my punch from Big Ted has given me a mixture of fear and respect for 'these people'.

10 p.m.

Money talks. It always does. I feel guilty that we are attempting to fool the Great British Public, but Dom keeps reassuring me that we are doing nothing wrong, and besides, everybody knows that programmes like this are made up. It's always been news to me, but then perhaps I'm naïve.

You should have seen Big Ted's eyes when Dom produced the cash. He didn't do so until we'd been there for a couple of hours, during which time Little Ted and Big Ted had had a (one-sided) fight, Epernay was caught stealing money out of Debbie's purse ('What do you want the money for anyway?' Answer: 'Fags.' 'I've told you, you've got to wait until you're ten!'), and Debbie had told me to fuck off after I had suggested that she might like to get Little Ted and Epernay involved in the cooking.

'Listen,' said Dom, as he took the envelope out of his pocket. 'I think we need to come to some arrangement.'

'Carry on,' said Big Ted, who was just about to go down to the pub.

'It's clear that our being here is proving to be a bit of

a strain,' Dom continued. 'And I think that it's only fair that we recompense you for all the hassle.'

'How much?' asked Big Ted, reaching out his right hand, which I hitherto had thought was permanently set as a fist.

Dom held up the envelope teasingly, which was pretty risky considering Big Ted's hand could easily transform back into its usual configuration.

'Two grand,' he said. 'But on one condition.'

'What?'

'That you follow the script.'

'Script? What script? I ain't learning no lines.'

'You don't need to learn any lines. All you need to do is to make it look as though Sam's techniques are working.'

'What so like we behave all hoity-toity?'

'Exactly.'

'For how long?'

'Just until end of play on Friday. Then we'll be out of your hair. OK?'

'Sooner the better mate.'

Dom prepared to hand over the cash, and just before he released it, he said, 'And we'll need to buy you some different clothes.'

'Whatever,' said Big Ted, his hand greedily shaking at its imminent reception of the cash.

'You promise to do as we say?' asked Dom.

'Of course I fucking do! I'm a man of me word. A promise is a fucking promise.'

Dom released the cash, and Big Ted snatched it away,

ripped open the envelope, counted out the one hundred crisp twenties, folded them, and then shoved them in his back pocket.

'Nice,' he smiled.

'What are you going to do with all that?' Debbie asked. 'Can we get a new kitchen? Come on Ted, I really want one.'

'Maybe,' he said. 'But I've got to go out now.'

'Where you going?'

'Out for a little shopping my love.'

'Where?'

'None of your business.'

'But Ted!'

'Shut it!'

And within thirty seconds he and Little Ted had gone, the screech of their departing tyres only matched in volume by Debbie shouting after them.

'TED!!!!'

'Will he come back?' asked a concerned-looking Dom.

'Oh yeah,' said Debbie, philosophically. 'He always does.'

'He's a softie at heart, is he?' I asked. 'Loves you more than he lets on?'

'Nah,' said Debbie. 'All his fags are here, that's why he comes back. He smuggled a vanload of Regals through Calais a few months back. He'll never leave 'em for the world.'

The Teds returned within half an hour, carrying an

enormous cardboard box with the name of an electronics manufacturer up the side.

'What the fuck have you got there?' asked Debbie.

'A new TV,' said Big Ted triumphantly, panting with its weight. 'Widescreen plasma – a real beauty.'

'But we've got a new fucking TV in the lounge. What's wrong with that one? I thought that was widescreeen plasma and all!'

'This one is bigger, and it's got a faster frame rate.'

Debbie shrugged her shoulders.

'So fucking what? Where are we going to put it?'

'Next to the old one.'

Ten minutes later the Teds had set up the new TV. The lounge was now utterly dominated by the two screens. It felt like an electrical retailer.

'Cushty,' said Big Ted. 'Now we can watch the snooker and the football at the same time.'

'And may I ask how much it cost?' said Debbie, her arms folded.

Big Ted reached into his back pocket and took out notes.

'Here you go love, a down payment for the new kitchen.'

Debbie counted out the notes and threw them to the floor.

'Fifty quid! Go fuck yourself Ted!'

'Language,' went Ted, and then he and little Ted sat down on the sofa, lit a fag each and proceeded to zone out to some daytime TV. Debbie stormed out the room in disgust.

'Nice TV,' said Dom, studying it. 'We've got the slightly older model in my office.'

And then he turned to me.

'At least we used to.'

After lunch, or rather, after chips, we took the Lamperts shopping for clothes. This was the first bit of fun we had, and we genuinely had a good time. We went to one of those God-awful malls where teenagers sit around smoking all day (indeed, Little Ted seemed to be quite the King of the Mall), and we kitted out the family in ridiculously preppy middle-class clothes.

Even Big Ted looked nice in a pair of chinos and a blue Oxford shirt. Sure, there was a touch of 'dressing for the magistrate', but there was no doubt that to a TV audience he would look as though he was being changed by me. We got Little Ted into the same rig, and, amazingly, he almost looked like a public schoolboy. Alongside Epernay and Debbie in floral print dresses, the family's transformation was astonishing.

'I'm liking this a LOT,' said Dom, 'this is a megamakeover!'

The fact that it was a load of invented crap didn't seem to bother him. And it didn't seem to bother our subjects as well, who went back home thinking that they'd just had the best day ever – which was fair enough considering they'd got a two-grand TV and a load of schmutter for doing sod all (i.e., their day jobs). And because I was the only person who seemed to be bothered, I did my best not to let it show.

When we got back, we decided to act out a scene in which Little Ted and Epernay actually ate with their parents, and what was more they actually had to eat something that looked as if it might put some colour in their cheeks. (Baaah! When I write things like that, I feel they should be said in an old-colonel-style voice.) The day before we had filmed what passed for a meal, which was more a case of the family wafting in and out of the kitchen to ping things in the microwave and eat them while smoking.

Today was different. We cooked them a shepherd's pie with peas and carrots on the side, and we served it on some brand-new crockery. (Naturally, all the shots showed Debbie taking the pie out the oven and doling it out, etc.) While they were eating, I was talking to the camera about how eating meals together was a way of enhancing 'intradependent family synergies'. Employees that ate together, I explained, worked well together. Companies in which everybody sits at their desks eating sandwiches and playing Minesweeper are companies that have low productive rates because their employees are not discovering methods of communication.

And then the fight broke out, just as I was saying: '. . . and the family that eats together, synergises together . . .'

Thwack!

'For fuck's sake!'

'Ted! Stop it!'

'Fuck you!'

'Language!'

I turned round to see dollops of shepherd's pie filling the air like soft shrapnel.

'Now then,' I said in schoolmasterly tones. 'Stop this at once!'

My commanding presence was not quite as commanding as I would have liked, and I soon found myself under a barrage of more dinner. Dom was cackling away, at least until the camera lens took a direct hit. We retreated to the lounge, where we knew we would be safe from assault because the TVs were the only things they wouldn't want damaged. (Although I'm sure Debbie cherishes her delightful ornaments.)

'What the fuck started that?' I asked.

'I have no idea. One minute they were eating peacefully, and the next minute – wham!'

After a few minutes we returned to find that the Teds had vanished, Epernay was up in her room, and Debbie was stubbing out a fag in the shepherd's pie. We looked at her quizzically.

'Ted was trying to shove his vegebatles on to Little Ted's plate, and Little Ted weren't having none of it and so they started throwing the stuff at each other and then me and little Epie and then – well you saw what happened.'

'So they had a fight because they didn't want to eat their greens?' I asked.

Debbie looked at me blankly.

'Greens?'

Later, in the hotel, we agreed that today had been a vast improvement, and Dom said that he had at least two minutes of footage which showed the family behaving in a nice genteel way. A huge result, apparently.

Thursday 13 March
8.30 a.m.

Just phoned the children, and spoke to Halet. She was tremendously reassuring, and said that they had eaten good breakfasts, and that she was just about to take them to school. I spoke briefly to Peter, who sounded on top form, and said that Halet had a really cool way of brushing his teeth, and that he now wanted to brush his teeth the whole time because the germs were baddy aliens and he wanted to kill all baddy aliens because he was a brave spaceman and yes I miss you very much as well.

11 p.m.

Can't possibly write about today as am too drained and emotionally wrecked, but suffice to say, it's a wrap, as us TV types call it. Will write about it all tomorrow.

Friday 14 March

Home at last. Not just any old home, but our clean and tidy home, with just its one reasonable-sized TV and its nice sofas and chairs and things that sort of coordinate.

Yesterday was unbelievable, and I still can't believe that Dom has enough footage, but he swears he has. Anyway, the day went something like this. I'm going to present it in appointment-diary form, as that seems easier.

8:       Turn up with crew. Knock on door repeatedly. No signs of life. We fear the family may have legged it.

8.15:   Still nothing. We try calling their number, but 'We're sorry, this telephone number is unavailable'.

8.30:   Eventually door is opened by a bleary-eyed Debbie. 'Sorry, got a bit pissed last night.' In we go. We explain that the children need to be on their best behaviour today, in order to show just how effective the Holden Childcare Programme has been.

8.35:   Ask Debbie and Little Ted if they can change into their nice clothes. Little Ted explains, quite matter-of-factly, that he's sold them down the pub, 'for a bit of whizz'. Gofer dispatched into town to buy more clothes.

8.45:   Big Ted emerges, says he's got to go to work today. 'Work?' we ask. We were rather counting on him being around. 'What sort of work?' Never you mind, we are told, but he should be back by lunch after 'the job is done'. Debbie asks if she'll get a new kitchen out of it. Ted explains that he was thinking of getting a nice new plasma for their bedroom. Debbie thinks he's joking. He's not.

8.48: Big Ted leaves. Little Ted asks if he can go. Big Ted says no, mutters something about 'health and safety'.

8.50: Big Ted returns. Goes upstairs and comes back down with a small toolbox. Grins at us and leaves again.

9.00: Film remaining three members of the family having an orderly breakfast. This time I manage to get in my 'a family that eats together, synergises together' without a fight breaking out.

9.30: Little Ted and Epernay help clean the kitchen, with much sulking and 'accidental' dropping of plates.

9.35: New clothes arrive. They're the same as the ones we bought yesterday, which causes much disappointment.

9.45: Debbie asks Little Ted to finish clearing up after breakfast, and he tells her to fuck off. She hits him over the head. He throws a plate at her; which just misses and smashes the (already cracked) kitchen window. During all this, we film Epernay stealing money from Debbie's purse.

9.50: I ask Dom why he did not stop Epernay. 'The observer should never react with the system,' he said. What crap. We've made up this system. 'Besides,' he adds, 'I can sell the out-takes of this to *Britain's Biggest Chavs* on Channel Six.' Dom is merciless.

Noon: A good morning's work, all in. We even bribe Little Ted with a packet of fags to make a Airfix Spitfire. Naturally he doesn't make it himself, and when it's finished he inserts a lit banger in its fuselage and throws it out the upstairs window. I have to admit, I rather share in the fun, although it feels a little treacherous blowing up a Spitfire and not a Focke-Wulf.

12.45: Big Ted stumbles back in, with cuts and bruises to his face and hands. He looks both terrified and angry.

'Get that fucking camera out my face!'

'Language!' hisses Debbie.

'Shut it fucking off!'

The cameraman drops it to his side, although I later learn he left it running.

'Where yer been?' shouts Debbie. ''Ave you been thieving again?'

'Mind your business,' hollers Big Ted as he heaves himself up stairs clutching his little toolbox. Little Ted runs up after him. Epernay just looks bored and sighs a lot. Debbie is fuming.

'What do you think he's been up to?' I whisper.

'Thieving, just like I said.'

'Thieving what?'

'Cars mostly.'

12:52: High drama! The Teds reappear. Both look white as sheets (although not their sheets).

'The law! It's here! Outside!'

They bolt to the back door, but there was the unmistakable silhouette of a policeman through the opaque glass.

'Fuck! Fuck!'

'Language!'

Both the front and back doors smash open.

'Are you getting all this?' Dom whispers to the cameraman, who winks.

In burst four policemen, and the place fills with a seething mass of fists, bodies, screams and expletives as the Teds try to wrestle with the many arms of the law.

After a few minutes, the Teds are in handcuffs.

'Edward Lampert?'

Big Ted grimaces.

'I'm arresting you for theft of a motor vehicle . . .'

'Oh Ted, for fucking idiot!' Debbie moans.

The policeman reads Big Ted his rights, and then turns to Little Ted.

'Edward Lampert?'

A surly nod.

'I'm arresting you for breaking the terms of your Anti-Social Behaviour Order . . .'

The policeman's words are interrupted by a gentle knock on what was left of the front door.

'Excuse me? Is this a bad time?'

13:02   Standing there is a ridiculous character in a purple velvet suit and a frilly shirt. His hair is luxuriantly long, and he sports a large rough trade moustache. Behind him stands a cameraman. All of us, including the police, are utterly nonplussed.

'My name is Rupert Steptoe,' he says. 'I'm here, to, um, Pimp Your Lounge . . .'

The rest of his sentence is drowned out by our laughter. Even Big Ted laughs.

14.00   We comfort Debbie and Epernay and decide to call it a wrap. Dom seems genuinely sincere in his offers to help. I make some noises as well, but know better than to make empty promises.

15.05   As we shake hands goodbye, I ask Dom if he really thinks we have a show.

'We've got plenty in the can,' he says. 'Remember, we've only got to fill 48 minutes – that's how long an hour of TV is because of the adverts. And some of that 48 minutes is intro and credits, and some more is that annoying reintro we've now got to do after each advert break, as people's memories are so shit. That'll bring us down to around 43 minutes. Twelve minutes of that will be introducing you and the concept, another 15 will be the family in nightmare mode, which leaves 16 minutes to show them getting better, and we've got more than enough of that.'

'Really?'

'Trust me.'

'Not a chance!'

Sunday 16 March

So the great embarrassment I've been enduring all weekend is that Peter and Daisy are SO MUCH BETTER behaved. Sally can't stop going on about it, especially at lunch today.

'I just can't BELIEVE that Daisy is almost pottytrained,' she said, as soon as I had sat down after cooking a magnificent leg of lamb.

'It's brilliant, isn't it?' I said. 'Halet obviously came at just the right time.'

Sally laughed as I carved.

'So you're saying she kind of came in at a late stage and took all the glory?'

'That's right. I did all the hard work, and she scooped up the prize.'

'You are joking aren't you?'

'Not at all.'

We looked at each other and smiled, although mine was through rather clenched teeth.

'OK, OK,' I said. 'I admit, it seems as though Halet has done a great job, and . . .'

At this point, Peter put his hand up.

'Yes?'

'Daddy, please may I interrupt?'

Blimey, I thought, what else had Halet achieved during the week? Normally Peter just shouts over the top of our conversation until we give way to him. I could see Sally was thinking the same thing as well.

'Yes Peter,' I said, my gob well and truly smacked. 'What would you like to say?'

'Ah, I just want to say that Halet is very nice.'

'I'm glad to hear it,' I said. 'Why is she so nice?'

'Halet nice,' echoed Daisy with an enormous smile.

'She's nice because we do lots of things with her and she is very funny and makes me laugh because she is very funny.'

'How is she funny?'

'She likes doing funny faces and funny voices.'

''unny 'oices'' went Daisy. (Lower labial-dentals are clearly an issue for her.)

'What sort of funny voices?' asked Sally.

Peter then made a growling noise and burbled in some unintelligible language. He and Daisy fell about laughing.

'What does that mean?' Sally asked.

'I don't know,' said Peter, 'but I think it is very funny.'

Sally and I looked at each other, a little mystified.

'I don't know about you,' I said, 'but I'm feeling a bit jealous.'

'So am I,' said Sally. 'Here's to your programme not

being commissioned so we don't feel jealous, and then again here's to your programme being commissioned so we benefit from more of the excellent Halet.'

I half-raised my glass.

Monday 17 March

I had a long chat with Halet this morning, and congratulated her on how well behaved the children are. I asked her about the secret of her success.

'Just good old-fashioned parenting,' she said. 'It's not magic.'

'It bloody seems that way.'

Halet laughed.

'Not at all. I use what you British call carrot and stick. It worked for my children, and it seems to work very well for yours. In my country we call it *fghddskjhf* and *asdhkksdfh*, but it is very hard to translate.'

'It sounds impossible.'

Halet laughed again. There was something serene about her, and it was infectious. Just being around her makes my shoulders slump slightly, and all my muscles relax.

'You know, they are lovely children you have, Mr Holden.'

'Call me Sam, please.'

'I prefer Mr Holden. I am a different generation to you and I like the formality. I am, after all, your employee.'

'But I call you Halet.'

'That is OK – I am your servant, you can call me what you wish.'

Gosh, I thought, I've got a servant. I'd never really thought of au pairs, nannies etc. as 'servants'. Somehow I imagine servants to be dressed in maids' costumes, the type of clothes I always want Sally to wear.

'Anyway,' I said. 'I'm glad you like Peter and Daisy. They seem to like you very much already. Sally – sorry, Mrs Holden – and I could not be happier with you.'

'Thank you, Mr Holden. I am happy that you are happy. And may I ask how your television programme went last week?'

'Extremely well thanks.'

'Oh good. I cannot wait to see it. Perhaps I shall learn a few tips?'

Wednesday 19 March

Dom rang to say that some of the material was better than he had hoped, and he wanted me to come in on Monday and Tuesday to do the voice-over. I'm going to be narrating the programme, apparently, which I'm happy about, because it makes me more of a star. Or something.

Sally back late again this evening. Once again she was shattered, and looked utterly depressed. She went straight upstairs, and she was up there for so long I thought she had fallen asleep. I went up to find her kneeling next to Peter's bed, stroking his sleeping head. I eventually dragged her back downstairs.

'Is there anything I can do?' I asked.

'Yes. Pour me a glass of wine, cook me a nice dinner and then a great shag.'

'In that order?'

'Hmmm. Wine, shag, dinner.'

It was a command I was happy to obey. After the second bit I tried to instigate a long chat about work, but Sally asked me not to ruin the evening. Fair enough, but I am still worried about her.

Thursday 21 March

I bumped into Emily today, who was her normal bouncy self. She was dying to hear about the filming, and she twisted my arm to go to her for lunch, and so, cravenly enough, I did.

She asked me how it went, and I told her it couldn't have gone worse. She fell about when she heard about the arrests and the arrival of the *Pimp Your Lounge* man. She then wondered if I had seen her scenes yet.

'I should see them on Monday,' I said, suddenly feeling uneasy. It wasn't that I had forgotten about THAT kiss, it's just that I'd put it to one side, and was kind of still hoping that it wouldn't get used.

'I can't wait to see it,' she replied, handing me a bottle of wine and a corkscrew. 'I did so enjoy filming it.'

Here we go again, I thought. Another one of Emily's thundering passes. What was she trying to do? Her flirting was as subtle as that of a drunk teenager.

I didn't really reply and just made a few 'hmmph' sounds, which she seemed to find amusing.

'What will Sally say when she sees it?' she asked.

'She will probably kill me,' I said. And I meant it.

Emily giggled and drained the penne.

'By the way, it's Ned Holland's fifth birthday party tomorrow. Has Peter been invited?'

'Of course – they're great mates. In fact, the whole family's been invited, as Sally's parents know Ned's grandparents.'

'Oh good,' she replied. 'It will be nice to see you again so soon.'

And she meant it.

Saturday 22 March

Sally still doesn't believe that something didn't happen. No matter how much I swear on all my relatives' graves, she is adamant that Emily and I did something on the wretched bouncy castle. It was at the end of the party, and we were all clearing up, and, horror of horrors, Emily and I found ourselves alone on the red and yellow rubber.

I could tell from the look in her eyes that she meant business. I could also tell that she was smashed, and even if she weren't standing on a bouncy castle, I expect she would have been just as unsteady on her feet. She sort of swayed/lurched/boinged towards me, and I swiftly fled but managed to corner myself beneath a turret.

'Emily!' I hissed. 'What are you doing?'

She let out a pissed giggle, her head slumped against her right shoulder in what she must have hoped was a coquettish way. In fact, it just made her look more drunk.

'There's no one here,' she slurred.

'They'll be back in a minute,' I replied. 'They're just putting the children in the car.'

I tried retreating further, but it was impossible. Red and yellow rubber walls stopped me – this really was a well-fortified castle.

Emily kept boinging towards me.

'C'mon,' she said. 'I want to bounce with you.'

'Um, er, er, I don't um think that this is the right time,' I stammered. 'Aren't we a little too big for bouncing?'

'The bigger the better.'

Until that moment I had doubted Emily's claim that it was three Greek fishermen, but now I could see it had to be true. In fact, the only part I now questioned was whether it was just three fishermen. Emily took my hands and started bouncing up and down. I did my best to stay still, but it was impossible. Her movements were causing the castle wall to thud against the back of my head, and I was in severe danger of losing my balance and toppling over on top of her.

'Bounce!' she insisted.

This was very bad. Sally and her parents were just outside. In a matter of seconds they would be witnessing their husband/son-in-law frolicking on a bouncy castle with a woman wearing a skirt that seemed to be working its way upwards with every b'doing.

'Bounce!'

I sort of lifted myself up on the balls of my feet.

'You can do better than that! C'mon, bounce!'

And then I had a genius idea. I would bounce, and bounce hard. With any luck it would cause Emily to let go and fall over, whereupon I could make my escape from the castle of marital death. I therefore jumped up as high as I could (which is not very high) and bounced.

'That's better!' said Emily.

After a few more bounces I had built up a pretty good momentum, and was causing Emily to stumble and wobble. I bounced harder and harder, and soon my head was clearing the top of the rubber ramparts. As I glanced over them, I could see Sally and Jane making their way to the front door of the hall. I had literally seconds in which to make my escape. I gave it one more huge bounce, and then . . .

POP!

Followed by a huge farting hiss.

Followed by rapid deflation of bouncy castle.

Followed by massive pissed giggles from Emily, who lost her balance and pulled me down with her. I was drowning, drowning under a tide of red and yellow rubber that reeked of children's feet and rancid cheap cocktail sausages. Soon we were both enveloped, and I found myself lying on top of Emily, whose arms were firmly clasped around me. In the dim latex gloom, our eyes met, and she gave me a look that would have attracted every Greek fisherman within 250 miles.

'Sam!'

I closed my eyes. It was Sally. Just behind her stood Jane, her arms folded like a sumo wrestler at the weigh-in. (If that's what sumo wrestlers do.)

'Sam! What are you doing?'

It seemed to take hours to extricate myself from the collapsed castle and the sprawling Emily. It didn't require much imagination to put myself in Sally's sensible shoes in order to see how bad this looked. I got to my feet and smoothed my hair in a pathetic attempt to seem dignified.

'Sorry darling,' I began, 'we were just, you know, bouncing.'

Sally held up a hand to stop me.

'I can see that,' she said.

A collapsed wall started to rustle behind me, and out of it emerged a pair of long legs, some knickers, and a skirt wrapped around a waist. A gasp from Jane.

'You're going to pay for this, Sam,' said Sally.

'What?' I asked. 'The castle? Of course I will pay for it.'

Daggers flew out of Sally's eyes.

'Not the bloody castle, you fool.'

It is now 10 p.m. and I'm in the spare room. I've never been in a bigger dog house, and no matter how much I plead my 100 per cent genuine innocence, the kennel just gets larger.

Bloody Emily. This is the last thing I needed. I really

felt Sally and I were turning a corner, and now this. How the hell do I get out of this one?

Sunday 23 March

I've been debating all day whether to tell Sally that Emily is my on-screen 'wife'.

The reasons for telling her now are:

1. She can't get any more angry;
2. It will look better if I tell her now than wait for her to see it on-screen;
3. It will bring the whole Emily thing to a head, we can have one final row about it, and then it will all be over.

The reasons for not telling her:

1. I'm a coward;
2. Not much else really.

Today has been as awful as I expected it would. Hardly any conversation, and refusals of small olive branches such as cups of tea etc. After the children went to bed I tried to have it out with her, but Sally said there was nothing to discuss, and that if I wanted to fool around with Emily, then I would have to take the consequences.

'I wasn't fooling around with her!' I said. 'And besides, what consequences?'

'I don't know,' she said ominously.

Of course, the first thing one thinks of when one's wife says things like that is the dreaded 'D' word, but surely not? But then again, maybe, just maybe. I mean, it's not as though we're much of a team at the moment, is it?

Perhaps this is paranoia talking. I just can't see Sally giving up on 'us' that easily. Aren't these troughs here to make one's marriage grow stronger? They had better.

Tuesday 25 March

The voice-over day did much to chase away my blues, and for a while I totally forgot about the disastrous bank holiday weekend.

Until I saw the footage of Emily kissing me.

The first thing I noticed is that I have a double chin, perhaps even a treble chin. In short, I look seriously ungood when I kiss. Naturally, I then thought what I might look like at more intimate moments (with Sally of course), and I suffered an immense feeling of self-revulsion. Some of our friends – Nigel and Clare particularly – video themselves having sex, but I just can't see the appeal. Unless it's well lit, you don't have an ounce of body fat, you have a great tan, and it's shot from side on, then home-made porn is a very bad idea. (I would have thought.) Otherwise, it's just grainy footage of one's hairy bum, and not even the most ardent hairy-bum fetishist would find a video of me in action a turn-on.

The next thing I noticed – or rather felt – was an acute sense of horror at what I was watching. It must have shown on my face, because Dom went, 'You've gone as white as a ghost. Are you OK?'

'I'm fine,' I lied.

We sat in silence as we watched the many takes.

'Does she normally kiss you like this?' Dom asked.

'No,' I said, which was true. 'She was clearly playing up to the camera.'

'You're telling me.'

'Do you think they're too, you know, passionate to use?' I asked hopefully.

'Not at all. I think the raunchier the better.'

Fuck, I went to myself. Not the answer I wanted to hear.

'Do you really think so?' I asked. 'I mean, viewers might think it a bit unlikely for your average morning kiss.'

'Let's face it, there's a lot in this programme that viewers may find a bit unlikely.'

He had a point, and I was stymied. I didn't want to admit that I had failed, and that I couldn't even persuade my wife to appear on my own television programme.

'And besides,' said Dom, 'if you don't mind me saying, Sally is really hot. It would be nice to get her more involved if and when we make the series.'

'Thanks,' I said. 'Yes, she, um, looks great.'

'You don't think so? Sounds like you've been married too long!'

'Not at all. No, I think she's great. Great tits and arse as well!'

Dom looked at me curiously. As soon as I had made that last observation, I knew that I had over-egged the pudding, or perhaps had even put in eggs that weren't required.

'Interesting thing to say about your wife,' said Dom.

'Well, you know, it's like, you know,' I blustered. 'I lust after my wife the same way as I did the day we met.'

Dom nodded slowly.

'Well, as you say, she looks great. And I think she could become a more integral part of the show.'

This was so not what I wanted to hear.

'How? I mean isn't the show meant to focus on me?'

'We'll work something out. Anyway, we should really get back to doing all the voice-over stuff.'

In the end we worked late, and I'm staying at Dom's house. Funny being in a bachelor pad, reminds me of all those years ago. Some of the similarities are eerie – the same heap of clothes next to the bed, the unwashed mugs, the high-tide mark around the bath, the scores of empty wine bottles waiting to be magically transported downstairs etc. etc. None of it is particularly scuzzy in that *Young Ones* kind of way, although the sheets on my bed don't look hotel smooth.

Called Sally, and she was brusque.

'Enjoying yourself up in London?' she asked.

The question was loaded with jealousy and accusation.

'I'm staying at Dom's – we worked late.'

'All right,' she said. 'I'll see you tomorrow I expect.'

She made my return sound as if I were an annoyance.

Wednesday 26 March

Finished off all the voice-over. It's amazing how quickly you get accustomed to hearing your own voice. Normally, whenever I hear it on home videos, I think I sound awful, but in fact it's not too bad. Dom thinks it works well because it's 'well spoken but classless'. I said that made it sound as though it were boring, which he denied rather too vigorously. Certainly some of the longer passages, especially the one about 'Harmonising the Context', sound a little dull, but Dom for some reason thinks they're great, as do the Emmas. One of them – I forget which – then said that I had the type of looks that would appeal to a 'certain type of housewife'. When I asked her to be more specific, she merely gave the other Emma a knowing stare.

When I got back home at 6ish, Halet was giving the children their supper.

'Daddy Daddy!' they both went, and then they asked Halet if they could get down so they could hug me.

Halet assented, and while I was being covered in kisses I couldn't help but think that I didn't want Peter and Daisy to be the type of children who needed to ask permission before hugging their mum or dad. That's the real price of having someone looking after them, I thought. It wasn't so much the not being with them, but the fact that they were being exposed to values that were not your own.

Halet said that they had been very good, and showed me what they had been up to since school/playgroup.

Peter had been practising his letters, and very good they looked as well (so long as you looked at them in a mirror), and Daisy had been drawing what she insisted were flowers. Once again, more wistfulness. I never felt like this when I was at work and Sally was at home, but now I do. I think it's because now I know what I am missing. It's what Sally feels, and she feels it very acutely.

Talking of Sally, when she got back she seemed to be in a better mood. As a result, we managed to discuss the Bouncy Castle Incident (hardly the stuff of a Robert Ludlum novel) in a sane manner over supper. She agreed that it was highly unlikely that I was trying anything on, and she took my word for it.

'But,' she said, 'that doesn't mean that *she* wasn't trying it on, and that you weren't deliberately exposing yourself to her.'

'Exposing myself? What, you mean flashing my willy?'

Sally laughed.

'No! I mean putting yourself in a vulnerable position. You know perfectly well what I mean.'

I did.

'Yes, but isn't this all rather similar to the Nick situation?' I asked. 'I seem to recall that you said you were entitled to see who you liked, and if Nick fancied you, then that was his problem, not yours.'

'True,' said Sally. 'But the difference between that and this is that I know Emily fancies you, whereas I knew that Nick was gay, and didn't fancy me.'

'But who else am I supposed to see?'

'There are plenty of people around – Lorna, Louisa, Lily.'

'Any who don't begin with an "L"?'

'Yes – Kate.'

'OK – Kate. OK, Kate. You're right, I should see more of Kate. But she probably thinks I'm a little too foul-mouthed.'

'Well, she'd be right,' said Sally. 'So don't be.'

'OK, OK – sorry! So there's Kate. Anyone else?'

'What do you think I am? A playdate agency for househusbands?'

'Now there's an idea!'

Sally playfully flicked a pea at me.

'And don't you go flirting with Kate,' she said. 'She's my best friend round here.'

'Honestly, who do you think I am?'

'A rogue who is making a ridiculous TV programme who I miraculously still love.'

'I love you too. And my TV programme is not ridiculous.'

'I bet it is,' said Sally. 'I can't wait to see it.'

Tick tick tick went the time bomb.

Thursday 27 March

Dom says that the editing is going really well and that they're bang on deadline to deliver by the end of the month. They'll bike a DVD down here on Monday so that I can 'curl up and watch it with that lovely wife of yours'. I made vague yippee noises.

Sunday 30 March

A really nice weekend ruined by the fact that Sally is going to kill me tomorrow night. I stupidly let slip that the DVD is coming, and she seemed very excited.

The children have been behaving impeccably, although there is rather too much singing of Halet's praises for our liking.

'Anybody would have thought I did bugger all when I was looking after them,' I said.

That earned a raised Sally eyebrow. She's going to raise a lot more than that tomorrow.

Tuesday 1 April

Why didn't I just hide the fucking DVD under the doormat? Aside from the obvious sodding reason that by doing so the door would be unopenable, why the hell didn't I? All I had to do was to chuck it in amongst all the unwatched DVDs. But no, sensible Sam decided that the best thing to do was to tackle the issue head on and just play the DVD and ride the bucking bronco of an argument. What a great big fat fucking error that was, as my present location testifies: Felicity's B & B down the road.

When I watched the DVD at around eleven this morning, it didn't seem so bad. Admittedly I was suffering from an enormous swelling of my ego that had been brought about by the opening credits, which features lots of images of yours truly doing his consulting with the Family From Hell. It seemed incredible that after years – decades – of watching television, there was finally a TV programme about me. I was elated, humbled, terrified, wary and excited. At some points I had to watch through my fingers, especially the part when we are introduced to 'Sally' (aka Emily of course).

Boy did Emily sashay for the camera, much more so than I realised at the time. And as for the kiss – well, it was pretty raunchy, but not too bad. The bit in which she fondled the back of my head looked a bit OTT, but it wasn't as though it was a full snog. And, as you could tell if you paused the DVD at just the right moment, I looked uneasy. I thought that would be enough to allay Sally. I thought wrong.

The rest of the programme was a triumph of 'reality enhancement'. What had been a week of violence, chaos, bad language, endless retakes and comedy, had been turned into an utterly convincing display of how one can use management consultancy to turn even the most unruly children – and their parents – into paragons of middle-class virtue. It was astonishing what Dom had achieved, and it was also disturbing. This was nothing less than a pack of lies, and it was being sold as the truth. Part of me wanted to trash the whole project, but I was in too deep. And besides, the greater part of me wanted the money and the attention.

I decided that my tactic to deal with Sally was that the whole thing was a load of bullshit, and that she had to see the use of Emily as just another untruth in the whole tapestry of deceit.

By the time she got home at 7.30 my heart was racing.

'Has the DVD arrived?' she asked.

Sally looked genuinely excited, and I told her as much.

'Well, it's not every day you see your husband's first TV programme, is it?'

'Quite. Anyway, I've got a takeaway curry so we can eat that and watch it.'

This was my other tactic – I thought that if Sally had her hands full dealing with nan breads, poppadoms, chutneys and whatnot, then it would be somehow harder for her to throw a complete wobbly. I don't know why I thought this, but again I thought wrong.

Sally got into her civvies, and I dished up the curry from the multiplicity of foil containers. Predictably, no matter how carefully I tried opening them, yellowy-orangey gloop splattered everywhere, along with microscopic specks of sag aloo. Nevertheless, within five minutes we were in the living room, beers opened, curry ready on the naff-but-useful coffee table, both of us on the sofa, me with the remote control, my thumb hovering over the play button, as if it were a detonator that would blow me to hell.

Sally found the opening credits and the first ninety seconds immensely enjoyable. She cackled away, constantly saying, through mouthfuls of curry, 'I can't believe this is really you.'

By now, I was rather wishing it weren't.

Then she saw the children, and made an 'aaaah' sound.

'Look! How funny to see them having breakfast!'

I closed my eyes and listened to my voice-over.

'And here's my wife Sally,' I could hear myself saying. 'It was thanks to Sally that I became a househusband in the first place. When I lost my job, she suggested that she should go back to . . .'

I opened my left eye to look at Sally.

She had stopped chewing.

She had certainly stopped smiling.

I think she might have even stopped breathing.

I looked at the screen. Emily was kissing me.

'I'm sorry,' I croaked. 'I forgot to tell you about this. Dom couldn't get an actress in time, and . . .'

Sally stared at me. Her expression was new to me. It was an expression of hate and loathing.

'You shit,' she said.

'Honestly, Dom was insistent, and as you wouldn't do it, I had to get somebody, and as Emily was on hand . . .'

There were tears in her eyes.

'I'm so sorry,' I said. 'I had no option.'

'In front of Peter and Daisy as well,' she stated. 'You total shit.'

'Please, Sally,' I begged. 'It wasn't my idea for her to give me a kiss. Look, I can rewind to it and show you that I was not enjoying it.'

'I'd rather not see it again, thanks.'

'But you must understand I had no choice.'

'Of course.'

It was clear that Sally was trying to keep her composure, but it was hard.

'Sweetheart,' I said. 'I know what you're thinking. And I promise you, 100 per cent, that there is nothing going on between Emily and me. She was the only person around . . .'

'So you keep saying.'

'Do you want to carry on watching?'

Dumb question Holden.

'I'm not too sure I want to carry on with you,' she said.

'What do you mean?'

'All you ever do is hurt me.'

A tear rolled down her cheek. I set down my curry and tried putting my arm round her.

'I'm sorry,' I said. 'I don't mean to. It's just that . . .'

'Ever since you lost your job, you've changed. You've become selfish. Opinionated. You don't care about my feelings at all . . .'

I kept trying to interrupt, but she was having none of it.

'And it's clear that you don't respect me at all. And what's also clear is that you have fallen for Emily, and as your childish little programme makes perfectly clear, you'd rather have her as your wife than me.'

'But that's just not true, sweetheart!'

I meant it, but there was no way I could convey my sincerity.

'I thought you were special,' Sally continued. 'But it's been clear over the past few weeks that you're just another normal bloke whose head is turned by the village tart. Well, you can have her, Sam, she's all yours. I don't care any more . . .'

'Please don't say things like that. You're overreacting, I promise you.'

'Well why don't you put yourself in my shoes?'

I didn't reply.

'Every day I wonder whether I am going to come back home to a little note that says "I've left you", and when I open the front door in the evening I wonder whether I'm going to find HER in this house, my house . . .'

'Please Sally!'

I hadn't realised how much Emily had eaten her up, I really hadn't.

'. . . and now she's on fucking film kissing you in front of our children! For the whole world to see! For all our friends to have a laugh at! Can't you see how humiliating it is? Can't you? Didn't you think before you got your little lover girl on film what effect it might have?'

'I'm sorry.'

My apology sounded pathetic. I even felt sick, physically sick. I hated myself at that point, hated my cowardice for not insisting that Dom hired an actress, hated myself for not realising quite how seriously Sally took the whole Emily situation.

'Sorry is not enough,' said Sally.

'Well what do you want me to do?'

'Get rid of that!' she shouted, waving at the screen.

I pressed stop on the remote.

'No, I mean get rid of it completely! Just give up the whole fucking thing. Ever since you started on it, you've changed, Sam! I thought maybe this was some bizarre midlife crisis, but it's not. You've just become a . . . a . . . I don't know. Something different.'

I stood up and started clearing up the curry.

'Can I get you anything?'

'Stop trying to sound so bloody calm! If you want to do something, you can just get out!'

'Out?'

'Yes – just go away! Go to your little girlfriend for all I care. See how long she stays faithful to you.'

'Sally, there is NOTHING going on between me and Emily.'

Sally threw a glass of beer over me.

'Don't treat me like a fucking idiot, Sam!'

'I'm NOT having an affair with her! Do you think if I was I would have allowed that to happen?'

'You may well have done! It wouldn't take that much bloody cunning, would it?'

'Oh for heaven's sake!'

I was starting to get angry now, and decided that despite my foolishness and my cowardice, I wanted to make it clear that I was not screwing Emily.

'Listen!' I shouted. 'One. I am not, repeat NOT, fucking Emily. I regret getting her involved in the programme, but it's done now. I apologise. If I'd realised you were so paranoid about her, then I would never have used her. Two. Of course I may have bloody changed, because my life has changed. What do you expect? You've changed too, in case you hadn't realised. You've become someone who just moans the whole time. If you hate your job so much, why don't you do another fucking job? You don't have to stay in any one job for the whole of your life, or has the civil service mindset set in?'

I'd never seen Sally so shocked. I wish I could have stopped myself, but my blood was up.

'And how dare you say things like "I don't want to carry on with you"? What's that supposed to mean? If you want to divorce me, just go and say it! Go on! I don't want to divorce you. But if you want to divorce me, then go ahead. On what grounds? Because I pretended to kiss someone in a TV programme? Because one of our neighbours fancies me? Because I've changed a bit? Because I'm making a TV programme you don't really want me to make? It's hardly unreasonable fucking behaviour, is it? It's not as though I shag around or beat you up or abuse you in any way. I try my fucking hardest, I do my fucking best, I know some of my ideas are a bit off the wall, but why can't they be? Where's the harm in them? Or do you just want me to stay in a box like a good little hausfrau?'

I was actually shaking with rage. My anger was such, that I went upstairs, packed my washbag and a change of clothes and stormed out the house.

Now what?

Wednesday 2 April

Up early and ravenously ate Felicity's cooked breakfast. She must have assumed that we had had a row, but she was too discreet to mention it. I expect rowing couples are her bread and butter, along with people who have broken down on the main road. I went back home at 6.45, and found Sally giving the children breakfast. She looked as though she had slept as badly as I did, and her eyes were red from crying.

'Daddy Daddy!' shouted Daisy in delight.

'Where have you been?' asked Peter.

'Daddy had to do some work last night,' I explained.

'What sort of work?'

'Um, important work. Very secret work.'

'Were you being a spy?'

I caught Sally's eye and we allowed ourselves an exchange of pale grins.

'No, I wasn't being a spy.'

'I think spies are really cool,' said Peter.

'Excellent!'

I sat down at the table, and Sally and I chit-chatted with the children. Even though there was the most God-awful atmosphere between us, it felt good just to be sitting down for breakfast as a family.

'Aren't you going to work today?' I asked.

'No,' said Sally. 'I'm going to pull a sickie. I deserve one. And I've told Halet not to come. I think we need to talk things through.'

I liked the sound of that, and after we had dropped

Peter at school and Daisy at playgroup (thank God we missed Emily at the drop-offs), we went for a long walk. We chatted for ages about us, basically. About what we were like before we had married, about what we were like now. We rarely do this, normally because we're too busy, and have never really had any reason to question the solidity of our relationship. We both accepted that we had allowed ourselves to drift apart, which I suppose is normal. We had so little time together, and when we were together, the focus was always on the children.

We apologised to each other, sincerely. That felt good, and I said so.

'We mustn't let ourselves get like this again,' said Sally, when we had reached the top of Tumble Hill.

'I agree,' I replied, feeling that it was more my fault that we were in this situation.

We gazed out over the countryside. It was a perfect English spring morning, and the view of the other hills was clearer than I had known. Down below, I could just about make out the roof of our house, nestling in amongst our neighbours. It seemed funny to think that all these momentous events – momentous to us, anyhow – happened under those few square feet of tiles.

'Now what?' I asked. 'How do we repair things?'

'I don't think it's a case of stitching,' Sally replied. 'I just think it's a question of making sure we don't cause any more wounds.'

'Agreed. The first thing I'll do when I get back home is to ring Dom and tell him that we can't use Emily.'

'Thank you.'

Sally turned to face me.

'Do you promise that you're not sleeping with her? Because if you are, tell me, and there's a chance I won't leave you. I shall do my best to understand. But if I find out later that you are, then I promise you I will leave you.'

I looked deep into her eyes, the same way as I did on our wedding day. Normally it feels absurd to hold someone's gaze for so long, but all those years ago, it felt natural. And it felt natural today as well. I also felt intense regret, regret that we've ended up as yet another couple who go on ruminative walks to talk about the state of their marriage.

'I promise you I am not sleeping with her.'

'Good.'

'And you must promise not to be paranoid. I know what it's like after everything with Nick, and it'll just eat you up. You must trust me. I have no intention of sleeping with anyone else. You're the only person I've wanted to be with ever since we met.'

We kissed and then walked back down the hill, hand in hand.

Friday 4 April

Dom phoned to say that Dave Waldman has the tape and that he's going to get back to us next week. We don't know when, so this could be an agonising wait.

Sunday 6 April

We had a really lovely weekend. Yesterday morning we went to Drewfort Castle, which the children loved. Afterwards we went for a pub lunch, an event which used to put fear down my spine, but now seems to be a pleasure, mainly because the children are well behaved at the table. I know this is thanks to Halet, and I feel grateful that she is working wonders, but I also feel guilty.

Today we had Nigel and Clare and all their lot round for lunch. That too went well, and they were showing tons of interest in *WonderHubby*. There was one awkward moment when Nigel asked if I had a DVD of the show, and I had to bluff it by saying that they hadn't delivered one yet. He didn't believe me, and started going through all my DVDs, but luckily – and I use the word loosely – the worst he found was a copy of *Asian Babes* that I had forgotten I had. This of course was passed around with much jollity (although carefully hidden from the children) and Sally gave me a fake bollocking, which made a pleasant change from a real bollocking.

I'm now as nervous as hell about whether *WonderHubby* is going to be commissioned. If it doesn't happen, well, I think it might be for the best, especially for our marriage. And, if it does, then I shall just have to make sure that I keep my feet firmly planted on the ground. Or they'll be taking many more long walks.

Monday 7 April

I'm going to be a star. Ohmygodohmygodohmygod. (Very teenage-girl thing to write.) I just can't believe it. Dave Waldman loved it, and wants a six-part series. We have to film it over the summer and it will be broadcast in the autumn as a 'flagship programme'. Wow!

Dom sounded as ecstatic as me – well, maybe not quite.

'I can't tell you how happy we are,' said Dom. 'I always knew this would be a winner as soon as I thought of it.'

(I let that one go. I seem to remember it was my idea, and looking back in the diary confirms this.)

'So what's the next stage?'

'Well, first of all we need to thrash out your contract and your fees. Can you come in tomorrow and do that?'

'Of course.'

I didn't want to sound desperate, and the idea of discussing money with Dom made me feel slightly uneasy. Besides, I didn't want to ruin the moment.

'And then we'll draw up a schedule,' Dom continued. 'We've got a fuck of a lot to do, not least to find six families who'll be willing to take part.'

'OK.'

'And there's one important thing that you need to do.'

'What's that?'

Dom took a deep breath.

My mind started to race. What could it possibly be?

Have a vasectomy? Dye my hair? Change my name to 'Ted Nobstein'?

'Dave thinks that you need to lose a little weight.'

'Oh?'

'Just a stone, maybe a little more.'

My feathers felt very ruffled.

'But I'm not fat,' I protested.

'Of course you're not,' said Dom in the type of voice that men use to tell their girlfriends that their bottoms do not look big in whatever it is.

'So why do I need to lose weight?'

'Because the TV always adds a stone to somebody, no matter how thin they are. So, in order to look even normal on TV, you've got to lose that stone.'

'All right,' I said, trying not to sound offended. 'Shouldn't be a problem.' Still, it might get rid of that extra chin or two.

After I had put the phone down, I punched the air in joy, and then pinched my stomach. OK, I thought, maybe losing a stone was a good thing, and a small price to pay for getting a TV series commissioned. And anyway, Sally was hardly likely to complain if there was less of me.

After about two more seconds of introspection, I called her.

'Guess what?' I said, as soon as she answered.

'Who's that?' came her reply.

'It's me! Your husband!'

'Sorry, my husband, your voice is about two octaves higher.'

'Sorry about that,' I growled manfully.

'So I guess you're excited because of what I suspect.'

'You got it,' I said. 'They've commissioned it.'

'That's brilliant, sweetheart!'

I've put that exclamation mark to indicate that Sally did sort of exclaim that sentence, but what that exclamation mark does not indicate is any sense of real delight. It was clear that there was a slight edge of disappointment. The last time I had heard such a tone was from myself, when I was congratulating Ed on becoming a partner.

'You don't have to pretend,' I said. 'I know your thoughts about it.'

'No,' said Sally. 'Seriously, I'm thrilled, I really am.'

'You sure?'

'I promise.'

After that I made a few more calls, to parents and friends, all of whom sounded really thrilled, and all of whom said, 'Will you remember me when you're famous?' and to all of whom I replied, 'Certainly not,' the irony of which was only lost on my mother. The one person I did not phone was Emily, who for obvious reasons I don't want to talk to at the moment.

When Sally got back, we opened a bottle of champagne and toasted the arrival of *WonderHubby*. She does seem to be enthusiastic, although she is determined to make sure it doesn't go to my head, unlike the champagne, which has made me feel quite pissed.

Ha ha! I'm going to be famous. People will recognise

me wherever I go, and will say to each other in hushed reverent tones – 'Gosh, isn't that . . . ?' And, 'Look, it's him off the telly,' etc. I've always wanted to be famous – let's face it, who doesn't – and now I'm going to be. I'm thinking, even now, of all those paparazzi shots of Sally and me going in and out of The Ivy.

But feet on ground, Holden, feet on ground.

Tuesday 7 April
7.30 p.m. Sitting on a delayed train back home

All that stuff about keeping feet on the ground? Forget it. What's the point? For Sam Holden, the WonderHubby himself, is being paid nothing less than £15,000 per episode, making a very sweet – thank you God, thank you – £90,000.

'Of course,' said Dom, as he was explaining the nuts and bolts, 'if it's repeated, you can expect half that again.'

I let out a cackle of sheer greed. I felt as if I had won the lottery – I had no idea quite how much money was in TV.

'And of course there's the potential book deal on top.'

'Book deal?'

'Sure! There's no such thing as a TV programme without a book these days. Look, you're being paid extremely well, and it's for a reason. Dave and I want to make *WonderHubby* the hot new child-raising brand. We want websites, books, interviews, mugs, T-shirts, pencils, baby bottles, romper suits, you name it, all to feature the *WonderHubby* brand.'

I swallowed.

'We want you to become Gina Ford, Dr Spock and Alan Sugar rolled into one.'

I swallowed again. This was heady stuff.

'Are you, um, quite sure?' I asked. 'I mean, isn't it better to start slowly, especially with a brand that hasn't been tried out?'

Dom batted the question aside.

'Not a chance, matey. There's no time to build brands slowly any more, not a spare second. It's got to be whump! Right out there, big, brash, coordinated and aggressive. And we've got a great brand, so why do it slowly?'

'Quite.'

I began to feel nervous about all this. What I had originally thought was going to be a couple of TV programmes on some obscure channel was now becoming a business that was going to rival Mothercare.

'You look worried,' said Dom.

'Well, I couldn't be more delighted,' I said.

'You don't sound it!'

I felt like Sally to Dom's Sam.

'I am delighted, honestly. I'm just a bit worried, you know.'

'You know what?'

'Well, you know, that it's, um, all completely made up.'

Dom literally waved it away.

'Who cares about the truth?'

'Some people do.'

'Leave truth to historians,' he said. 'All we should be interested in is making piles of cash and entertaining people.'

'I know that,' I said. 'And I'm as interested in cash as you are. But when it comes to telling people how to look after their children, don't you think we have a, you know, responsibility?'

'Responsibility?'

Dom started laughing.

'Responsibility?' he asked again, realising I was being serious.

'I don't want to sound naïve,' I said.

'Not at all – I think you're right to be conscientious about it. After all, Sam, children are very important people.'

Dom said that last sentence with the flippancy of the childless.

'Quite,' I said.

We paused, taking it all in.

'Still,' Dom said eventually. 'Let's not worry about stuff like that, eh?'

I was minded to agree, but there was one more issue I had to raise. The thorny question of Emily.

'Um, er,' I started confidently.

'Yes?'

'It's about my wife.'

Dom did the Tube-logo thing.

'Is there a problem?'

'Yes there is. You see the thing is, the woman who you think is Sally is not in fact Sally. It's somebody else. A neighbour called Emily. And the real Sally, my wife, has refused to be in the programme because it's not her thing, and that's why I had to get this Emily in at the last minute. However, when Sally saw Emily on the pilot she threw a bit of a wobbly, and says that she doesn't want the world to think I'm married to Emily, when in fact I'm married to Sally. Do you see?'

Dom didn't say anything.

Until: 'I see.'

He connected his fingertips together like a headmaster.

'So, basically,' I said, 'all I'm saying is that we need to get someone else, someone who isn't Emily.'

'But if your wife doesn't want to do it, why should she put the kibosh on Emily doing it? What harm does it do?'

'Because she thinks Emily has the hots for me, and thinks it's a way of Emily getting into my pants.'

'I see.'

A pause.

'The problem is that Dave Waldman likes Emily,' said Dom. 'Thinks she's got viewability.'

'Viewability?'

'Yes.'

'OK. You mean the viewers will like her?'

'Exactly.'

A pause.

'And there's another problem,' said Dom. He shifted in his chair. 'I'm, er, seeing her.'

'Who?'

'Emily. We're in a thing, you know.'

My flabber was gasted.

'But, but. . . .'

There were so many questions I wanted to ask. How long? How come? How?

'The problem is that I've kind of promised Emily that she can be part of the programme.'

Dom was wincing. He was clearly finding this as uncomfortable as I was.

'You've what?' I exclaimed. 'How do you mean promised her? If you thought she was my wife, why would you need to promise her?'

And then a light bulb shone furiously over my head, a light bulb that should have gone 'fring' ages ago.

'And if you thought she was my wife, why the hell were you fucking her?'

Dom scratched the back of his neck – this is a sure sign that someone is lying.

'But I know she's not your wife,' he protested.

'Oh come on! Tell me when you found out! Before this "thing" happened? Or after?'

'After, obviously,' said Dom. 'I mean before! Before!'

'Bollocks! You were happy to basically screw someone who you thought to be my wife behind my back, and all the time making out how well we worked together. You're just a fucking jackal, that's what you are!'

'You're in no position to throw your weight around!'

'Really?'

'Yes, really.'

'So where else are you going to find another WonderHubby? Come on, the programme's a dead duck without me.'

'I wouldn't be so sure.'

'Is that a threat?'

'Take it how you like. Listen, I don't have to defend myself here. I'm a single man, and all I've done is have sex with a single woman. Is that a crime?'

'Of course it's not. But you're being disingenuous. You know perfectly well why it might be of interest to me whether you thought she was Sally or Emily.'

Dom exhaled. He was clearly getting the message.

'Look, I'll be honest with you,' he said.

'Gee, thanks.'

'I found out before, or rather just after our first kiss.'

'Go on.'

'This is the truth, I promise you.'

'OK.'

'The day after we did the filming at your house, Emily got in touch with me.'

'How?'

'Fucking hell. Nobody expects the Spanish Inquisition.'

'How?'

'She phoned. She said she was coming up to town for 24 hours, and suggested that we met for an early evening drink, as she wanted to discuss you and the programme. At that point it just sounded like there was something important to discuss, maybe something important about you, and so I accepted.'

Dom stopped.

'Is that it?' I asked.

'No. Anyway, I met her at this hotel in the West End, and you know, we got talking. At first it was just normal chit-chat, you know. Anyway, after a few drinks, she started getting, well, a bit fresh.'

I could imagine.

'She started touching my knee whenever she made a point, which I always think is a sure sign that someone likes you.'

'I agree,' I said.

And I did, too. I always think women who touch you the whole time are real goers. Maybe that's bollocks, but in my (limited) field surveys of yore, my hunch has often been borne out. It was good to hear it confirmed by Dom.

'And then what?' I asked.

'Well, then she kissed me. You must understand that she didn't give me much option.'

'I can believe it.'

'And after she had kissed me, she said, "You don't know who I am, do you?" At which point I said, "Of course I do – you're Sally Holden". She then, um, told me that she was in fact Emily, and she told me how she was standing in for the real Sally.'

I studied Dom's face. I wanted to believe him, and I decided to give him the benefit of the doubt. I'm sure he would have slept with Emily even if he had thought she was Sally, but the fact is, he hasn't. I couldn't really blame him for that first kiss, and besides, if you're a bachelor and you've got a mildly pissed and flirtatious Emily perched precariously on a bar stool and laying it on thick, you're not really going to say no, are you?

'Emily is a force of nature,' I said.

'You're telling me,' said Dom, a slightly seedy grin on his face.

And then I felt a little jealous, and proprietorial of Emily. Which was wrong, but natural. I'd taken it for granted that she only flirted with me, whereas if I were being honest, I knew she was like that with everybody. My next comment was therefore a result of my jealousy, and I regretted saying it, because it sounded a little petty.

'You know she's got children, don't you?'

'Oh yeah,' said Dom. 'But I don't think I'm ever going to meet them. Emily sees me as a sort of London lover.'

I coughed. As opposed to her lovers in all the other cities in the land.

'Well, good luck with her,' I said.

I was extremely curious to know what Emily was like in bed, but I decided that it was none of my business, and that I didn't know Dom well enough.

'She's a great fucking shag, I can tell you,' said Dom.

I nodded disinterestedly, reflecting that I needn't have bothered with adhering to niceties.

'Does everything, if you know what I mean.'

I did. Everybody knows what 'everything' means. It means brown wings. Chocolate starfish. The brown tea-towel holder. It really came as no surprise that Emily put out in that way. Personally, I have no interest in using the sewer of the body as a playground, although most of my friends seem to hanker after it. Why, exactly? Are their wives' more conventional passages unsatisfying? And how many women genuinely like it? (Apart from Emily.) I think the whole anal thing is a way of establishing some sort of sexual superiority, something to suggest that you are so non-vanilla and adventurous. But the fact is that anal is now so commonplace that it's hardly the big deal it once was. I wonder what will be next? Will golden showers become the norm?

But I digress.

'Yes, her, uh, reputation precedes her.'

'I can imagine,' said Dom. 'She's absolute filth.'

We sat there in silence for a while.

'Anyway,' I said. 'It doesn't alter the fact that Sally will kill me if Emily is in the show.'

Dom sighed.

'There's no way you can talk her round?'

'Absolutely none. She'll walk out if Emily's in it.'

'Really?'

A rare expression of genuine surprise swept across Dom's face.

'Really.'

'Why, have you and Emily had a, um, you know, a thing?'

I shook my head.

'No. But Emily has made her intentions perfectly clear on numerous occasions.'

Dom nodded. No doubt he was dispelling any cute notions that Emily might be faithful.

'And so clear has she made her intentions,' I continued, 'that Sally's more than a little jealous. When she saw Emily was in the pilot, she went ape.'

'You didn't tell her before?'

'No.'

Dom let out a small laugh, which was fair enough.

'I see your problem,' he said.

Another silence.

'The thing is, I really do want to continue fucking her, and if I sack her from the show, then I suspect that'll be it.'

Charmingly put, I thought. Dom was really pretty mercenary. It was to be respected, in a way. He and Emily suited each other.

'And I really want to carry on with her,' he said. 'I haven't had such a cracking shag in ages, and . . .'

'All right,' I interrupted. I didn't want to hear much more. 'I've got a plan. Why don't I tell her the bad news? Why don't I say that I insisted on it, which is basically the truth, and that you were left with little choice? And when you're with her you can tell her whatever crap you like, but all I care about is making my wife happy, and that means getting rid of Emily.'

Dom thought about it.

'OK,' he said. 'You break her the bad news. Good idea. You can be the shit, and I can be the shoulder to cry on. That should work.'

I could see the cogs turning in his head, just as I can with Peter. It seemed incredible that his decision-making process was entirely governed by his groin, but there it was. We then spent another couple of hours thrashing things out, and afterwards we went for a few drinks. By the time I got on the train I felt a bit smashed, and it felt wonderful.

All in all, a good day. A fat pile of moolah on its way, and I'll definitely be in Sally's good books when she hears that I've got rid of Emily.

Hooray! This train has finally started to move.

Thursday 10 April

Last night Sally and I had a big chat about our professional futures. Now that we've got our personal and emotional selves back on track, I thought it was right to discuss money and her job. As soon as I brought up the topic, her response was:

'Not this again.'

'But don't you think we should talk about it?'

Sally theatrically slumped on to the table.

'Not really, no.'

'Will there ever be a right time to talk about it?'

'No.'

'So now is as bad a time as any?'

'Yup. So go ahead.'

I said nothing for a few seconds. Sally looked up.

'Well, go on,' she said.

'There seems little point if you're not going to listen.'

'I will,' she said, her head buried in her folded arms. 'I just feel that we've been over this.'

'But can't you see that the situation has changed? I'm going to be earning some seriously decent money now, and you really don't need to work. Or you can move to a less stressful job.'

Sally looked up.

'But can't you see that my job isn't about money or whether or not it's stressful? I know you laugh at the idea, but my job is important, Sam, really important. I'm not saying the fate of the world rests on my shoulders, but you must believe me when I say that what we are doing as a team is vital.'

'But do you really have to be a member of the team? Don't you think they could manage without you?'

'Of course they could. I'm not trying to make out I'm indispensable, I just don't want to let the side down. I don't think that's being arrogant, I just think that's showing a bit of pride in what I do.'

'I accept all that,' I said. 'But you can't deny that you're finding the job immensely tough and stressful. I've lost count of the number of times that you've come back absolutely wiped out.'

'I know, I know. It's just that it's been particularly tough recently, and some bad things have happened in our patch.'

I'm always curious about what goes on in Sally's patch. I know it's around Tdsflkjsdistan and that neck of the woods, but I don't know much more. Sometimes I scour the papers and the Web to see what has been happening over there, but I can never find much. Occasionally I read about the odd car bomb, and I wonder whether Sally was involved in some way. Did she and her team order the bomb? Or was it her agents who were being blown up by the other side, whoever they were? Or did it have nothing to do with her at all? I always know better than to ask, because the few times I have, she's given me pretty short shrift.

The more I think about it, it's actually incredible how so few people know what Sally really does. All our friends simply think she's a civil servant (which she is, technically) although I believe Clare has her suspicions. My parents are completely in the dark as well, but Jane, Sally's mother, has a very good idea, and I suspect she probably drops heavy hints at her witches'-circle coffee mornings.

'But don't bad things always happen in your line of work?' I asked. 'I mean, it's not as though people in that part of the world are suddenly going to be nice to each other.'

'Yes, but that's not a reason to give up. We've got to continue to make the area safer, and if we did nothing, then it would be complete chaos.'

'Really?'

'Really.'

Sally got up and poured herself a pint glass of water.

'And there's another thing,' she said.

'What's that?'

'One of us needs a proper job.'

'But I've got a proper job now.'

'No you haven't,' she replied, smiling. 'You don't get adverts for WonderHubbies in the backs of newspapers.'

'You don't for your job either.'

'True, but my job has security, stability, a pension, a monthly pay cheque – all the things we need.'

'And my sort-of job pays me a shitload of cash.'

'And what happens when your "job" ends? It could last twenty years, or until this time next year. Who knows? At least with my job, there'll always be a demand for it.'

'Why? Because nasty people in nasty parts of the world will always try to be nasty to us?'

'Precisely. A very accurate summation of the Central Asian situation.'

'I thank you,' I said, and did a mock bow.

I was relieved that this whole conversation was being conducted in a good-humoured way, and that we weren't having a row.

'You're not going to budge on this, are you?' I asked.

'Not for any money in the world.'

'Not even for me?'

Sally downed her water.

'Especially not for you!'

Friday 11 April

With the amount of flak I took from Emily today, I might as well have been married to her. Secretly I was rather hoping to be an ostrich about the whole sacking-Emily situation, but I knew that was impossible. I bumped into her at the village shop, and she was gushing about the programme. When I asked her how she had seen it, she went uncharacteristically coy before she eventually admitted that Dom had sent her a DVD. I did my best to look as neutral about that as possible. I then invited her round for a coffee, which took her by surprise, as it's normally her inviting me round.

While the children were upstairs playing, I decided to break the bad news. Gingerly I poured out the coffee from our cracked cafetière. (We seem to get through two cafetières a year.)

'Emily, there's something I need to tell you.'

Her eyes widened and she grinned a little, a grin that soon disappeared when she saw my expression.

'Yes?'

'Um, it's a little awkward, and there's no easy way to say it, but here it is.'

'You've fallen in love with me?'

Typical Emily. Nevertheless, I still spluttered and splattered.

'Um, er, no! No, it's nothing to do with anything, you know, like that.'

'Oh.'

'No, it's the show. *WonderHubby*. I'm afraid you won't be needed.'

'What?'

'Yes. We thought it was best that we hired an actress instead.'

'What?'

I had never seen Emily so angry, except perhaps for

the time when Sally and I declined her kind offer of a foursome with her and her ex-husband.

'I'm really sorry,' I continued, 'because I know how much you enjoyed yourself as my, um, "wife".'

'Oh I did, did I?'

'Well, it looked like it.'

'And what makes you so confident that I won't be needed?'

'Dom told me.'

'Did he now?'

Emily was doing her best to look as though she had an ace up her sleeve, so I decided to snatch it away before she could play it.

'He also told me that you and he are an item.'

She opened her mouth, but nothing came out.

'For what it's worth, he told me that you were a big hit with the channel.'

Emily frowned.

'So why is he getting rid of me?'

At this point I was mightily tempted to lie. I could have just said, 'I have no idea,' or that it had something to do with shooting schedules, but I knew that wouldn't cut much ice. And, absurdly enough, I thought I should be honest.

'The reason is because I want to get rid of you.'

As soon as I said it, I reflected that I could have put it more gently. Emily once again remained silent.

'It's basically to do with Sally,' I said. 'She doesn't think it's right that you should play my wife.'

'Oh really?'

'Really.'

'But she's happy for an actress to play your wife.'

I nodded.

'But not me?'

'Yes.'

'Why?'

'Oh come on, Emily! You must be able to work that one out for yourself.'

'I can't,' she insisted. 'Go on. I want you to tell me.'

'Emily! Come on. What's the point? You know perfectly well why.'

'Is it because Sally is a teeny-weeny bit jealous?'

Emily said that in a slightly babyish voice, which I found really condescending.

'Yes she is,' I said. 'Wouldn't you be?'

'No.'

'Well, you're different to Sally.'

'I'd say!'

'And she thinks that it isn't . . .'

'She thinks this. Sally thinks that. My wife says. Have you ever listened to yourself, Sam? All your opinions are entirely made up by her. Have you ever realised that? Have you? Do you actually have a mind of your own? Or has Sally completely emasculated you?'

'Come on Emily, that's crap.'

'Is it?'

'Yes. I'm as much my own man as the next man.'

'So that's why you're a househusband then, is it?'

'Yes it is. In a way, being a househusband requires more masculinity than sitting in an office all day.'

'Yeah right. Doing the laundry and ironing. Hmmm. So macho, Sam.'

'What the fuck is this?' I asked. 'You've got no right to accuse me of anything. How Sally and I conduct our marriage is none of your business. At least we've got a marriage.'

'Oo! Ouch! Right below the belt, Sam, nice one.'

'What is it you want?'

'What I want is for you to admit that you've been utterly spineless about all this, and that you've been entirely pussywhipped by your wife into getting me sacked from the show.'

'I'm not going to admit any of that, because it isn't true.'

'Of course.'

'And I don't see why I should have to justify my decision to you. It's my bloody show, my idea in the first place.'

'That's not what Dom says.'

'Well, Dom can say what he likes to you across the pillow. I know the truth.'

'Naturally.'

By now I was furious. This was a vicious, snide and nasty Emily, the Emily who didn't get her own way, the Emily who stamped and thcreamed and thcreamed until she was thick. At that moment I wanted her to get out, but I still retained a residue of utterly unnecessary politeness.

'It doesn't really matter what you say,' I said. 'Because my mind is made up, as is Dom's.'

'Hmm. So resolute. So determined the house-husband.'

'OK, OK, that's enough of that.'

'Mr Househusband has his own mind. Mr Big who does as his little wife tells him.'

'That's enough!'

'So commanding.'

'OK Emily, why don't you just fuck off?'

'All right, I will.'

As she got up she 'accidentally' knocked over her coffee, which spilled all over the table, and seeped over some of Peter and Daisy's drawings.

'Whoops,' she went.

'Just get out,' I said.

After she had slammed the door, I wanted to scream with rage. I'm sick of arguing with women, and hopefully that will be the last of it. My only fear is that Emily will do something to fuck up the whole *WonderHubby* thing, but I can't work out what. After all, she can't get me sacked.

Sunday 13 April

We had Jane and Derek round today. I had pleaded with Sally not to invite them, but she said we couldn't spend the rest of our lives avoiding her mother. I can't see why not, and just before they arrived I was tempted to pretend that I had been called up to London on urgent *WonderHubby* business, but I knew that would earn me the grandmother of all bollockings from Sally.

Jane was on her habitually fine form.

'So, Sam,' she said as she made a great play of carefully inspecting her morsel of lamb, 'Sally tells me that you are making a television programme.'

She said 'television programme' as though it were some kind of STD.

'That's right, Jane,' I said politely. 'It's all about bringing up children.'

Jane faux-choked on her morsel.

'Bringing up children?'

'That's right.'

'And what qualifications do you have?'

I glanced at Sally, who looked back at me in a way that said, 'Don't be rude, please don't be rude.'

'I don't have any qualifications, Jane. That's kind of the whole point.'

'I do wish you wouldn't keep calling me Jane like that. You make yourself sound like a salesman.'

'Sorry.'

'But if you don't have any qualifications, how are you qualified to make this programme?'

'Because I'll be bringing my experience of management consultancy to bear.'

Another little pretend choke.

'But what, pray, does management consultancy have to do with childcare?'

'There are lots of similarities, *Jane*, far too many to go into here.'

'How convenient. Besides, I thought you were a failed management consultant.'

I felt my fingers tighten their grip on the shaft of the carving knife. If the children hadn't been there, I'd have been enormously tempted to plunge it into the side of her neck and leave her to drip dry. I even imagined sitting down afterwards and eating lunch as normal. I don't think Derek would have minded too much, although I can imagine Sally might have been a bit upset, especially about the carpet.

'If you remember, Jane, I was offered my job back. The only reason I was sacked was because two of my colleagues were on the fiddle.'

Jane chewed her way through this.

'Anyway, I understand that you are *not* looking after your children during the filming of this "programme".'

'That's right, Jane. We've got this marvellous woman called Halet who comes in during the week.'

'We love Halet,' said Peter.

''alet! 'alet!' went Daisy.

Really, they were like Moonies about her.

'Well,' said Jane. 'She at least seems to know what she is doing. Peter and Daisy are far better behaved now than when they were under your "care".'

After that, I just got pissed.

Wednesday 16 April

Just got back from a very drunken lunch with Dave Waldman and Dom. Dave seems terrifically excited about the whole thing, just as Dom said he would be.

'Listen man,' he went. 'We are going to make you into a huge star.'

'I bet you say that to all the girls,' I said.

Thankfully, Dave found it funny.

'Dig, dig,' he said, clacking his fingers.

We spoke about some of the nuts and bolts of the programme, and Dom said they had already made great progress tracking down suitable families.

'Let's make sure we get a good mixture,' said Dave. 'We don't want them all to be chav scum like that last lot.'

'I agree,' said Dom, scratching under his collar. He had clearly been trawling for the most ghastly people he could find.

'The thing is, Domingo,' Dave continued, 'that we need some nice middle-class people in the mix. Dig? Otherwise it's just a pleb-hammerer like *Denaff Your Life.*'

'Dig,' said Dom. 'But we do need a few oiks though, don't we?'

'Sure. I loved the pilot's oiks. They were great. I might use them on another show.'

'Which one?' asked Dom.

'*Sell Your Kids.*'

'*Sell Your Kids?*'

'Yeah, it's great. We find families who've got some really frightful children, and then we find other families who need some children and then we auction them off.'

'But . . . but that's awful,' I said.

'Dig,' said Dave.

'Dig,' said Dom.

'It's completely awful,' said Dave. 'That's the whole point. We're really pushing the boundaries on this one. And the great thing about it is that we've got a premium-rate phone-in, in which viewers can bid live for one of the kids.'

'It's like slavery,' I said.

'Yep,' said Dave.

The waiter arrived.

'Any desserts?' he asked.

'Yes please,' I went.

Dom and Dave looked at me and then shook their fingers.

'Celebrities NEVER eat dessert,' said Dave.

'Dig,' said Dom.

And as a result, I had to watch them eat the most fantastic crème brûlées I had ever seen.

'But celebrities are allowed to order another bottle of wine?' I asked.

'Too fucking right. Let's get some shampoo.'

Friday 18 April

Had a long chat with Halet today. She says that she is really enjoying being Peter and Daisy's nanny, and reckons that they are the most fun children she has looked after. I asked her to work for us through to the end of the year, and she readily accepted. I gave her the afternoon off, and took the children to the park, where I spotted Emily. We sort of scowled at each other. This is going to be tedious if it carries on for the next few years. Either she'll have to move again, or we will. I'm sure there's nothing she can do to spoil the programme, but it irks me that she and Dom are intimate. God knows what sort of poison she will pour in his ear. Fuck her. She can do what she likes – without me, there is no *WonderHubby*. I am the WonderHubby.

Peter and Daisy seemed somewhat miffed that Halet was not looking after them this afternoon.

'But where is she?' Peter moaned.

'Where is 'alet?' Daisy asked.

'She's gone home,' I replied. 'I said that she could have the afternoon off so I could look after you.'

'But why do you want to look after us?' asked Peter.

'Because I haven't seen much of you for a bit, and I thought it would be nice.'

Peter stamped his right foot in a little huff.

'But I want to see Halet!'

'Peter! I won't have this sort of behaviour! Do you behave like this for Halet?'

'No,' he said.

'So why are you being like this for me?'

'Because I want to see Halet!'

(There was something very neat about Peter's logic.)

'I 'ant to see 'alet too,' said Daisy.

'Not you as well,' I sighed.

My irritation was quickly transmitted, and within a few seconds both Peter and Daisy were emitting a variety of moans, bleats and cries that their beloved nanny had abandoned them.

'If you're not quiet, you can both go to your rooms!'

This only made them more angry, and the volume and intensity of the moans, bleats and cries increased.

'Right! Up to your rooms!'

'No!' they shouted in unison.

Struggling to maintain my unlegendary sangfroid, I picked Daisy up and carried her to her room. This caused her to shriek, and when I closed the door on her I swear that what emanated from her mouth could have destroyed all the glass in a five-mile radius. Peter's hollering was no less violent, and after I had shut his door I could also hear the sound of toys being thrown around.

Thinking they would calm down in a couple of minutes, I retreated to the kitchen, where I turned on the kettle and anticipated a peaceful cuppa over the local rag. No such luck. If anything, the racket increased, and every time I shouted up the stairs for them to stop it, it just got louder. I was determined to win this particular battle.

In the end they were saved by the bell, or rather the phone. It was Sally, who was ringing to check in.

'What's that noise?' she asked. 'Have you got the TV on or something?'

'The children are bellowing in their rooms.'

'Christ, Sam, they sound as though they're in a Romanian orphanage! What are you doing to them?'

'I've shut them in their rooms because they were showing a distinct attitude problem.'

'Attitude problem?'

202

I explained what had happened.

'And so you've shut them in their rooms for that? Sam, shutting children in their rooms is a very harmful thing to do. You should only use it as the last resort.'

'Oh come on, my mother shut me in my room countless times. It never did me any harm.'

'That's debatable. And besides, I find that people who say "it never did me any harm" are damaged in some way.'

'Gee, thanks.'

The bellowing went up a few decibels.

'Jesus, Sam! Aren't you going to let them out?'

'Yes, yes. I just want to show them who's boss.'

'Where's Halet, anyway?'

'I gave her the afternoon off. I thought it would be nice for them to have some time with me instead.'

Sally laughed, darkly.

'OK, I'll let them out now. I'll see you later.'

It took at least half an hour of *Bob the Builder* to calm them down, and even by bathtime, they were still not exactly on great form. By the time I had tucked them up and started getting supper ready, I reflected that there was little 'wonder' in WonderHubby today. In fact, I was CrapBad-TemperedHubby. Shutting them in their rooms was too harsh, too Victorian dad, and I swore to myself that I'd make it up to them.

All this then gave me the fear about the whole programme, and whether I could possibly pull it off. I can't look after my own children properly, let alone those of other people.

Just how much bribery, editing and reality enhancement can Dom get away with? In some ways, this programme will have to be truly groundbreaking.

Monday 21 April

Another meeting with Dom in London. I wish he'd sometimes come down here to see me, but I don't think I'm quite ready to throw my weight around. The stretch limos will come, I've no doubt. Until then, I think it's best that I go for the low-key celeb approach. Not of course that I am a celeb. Not yet. And anyway, the country is too celeb obsessed, so in fact I don't really want to be a celeb, but if I end up being a celeb because the show is a hit, then celeb I'll just have to be.

Once again the meeting was nuts and bolts, and Dom told me that they'd made great progress finding willing families, some of whom seem normal.

'Wow,' I went.

'I know,' said Dom. 'If I had my way they'd all be a bunch of chavs and weirdoes, but Dave is insistent that we have relatively sane and decent people.'

'Perhaps it's about wanting viewers to identify with the families.'

'Balls to identification,' he said. 'If I wanted people to identify with the people in my shows, then I'd be making fucking gardening programmes. No, I like the freak-show element.'

'Fair enough. Well, there's room for a bit of both, isn't there?'

Dom opened a file and passed me a photograph.

'Meet the Sincocks,' he said.

The photograph showed a picture of a happy smiling middle-class family – one boy, around eight, one girl, around six, one plain brunette mother, mid thirties, and one slightly portly father, same age. They looked like something out of a gravy advert.

'They look all right,' I said.

'They look dull as you like,' said Dom. 'But if that's what Dave wants, that's what Dave gets. However, these people have a dirty little secret.'

'Oh?'

'He's a vicar.'

'A vicar? That's the first time I've heard being a member of the clergy described as a dirty little secret.'

'It is in my book.'

I tried to take that on board, and decided that I couldn't.

'But surely a vicar shouldn't have too many problems with his family? I mean I don't know many vicars, in fact none at all, but I always thought that their families would be more functional than most.'

'You would have thought. But apparently these children are nightmares. They have attention deficit hyperactivity disorder, which means that they fuck around all day.'

I'd heard of attention deficit disorder, but had never had it defined so succinctly.

'Isn't it, um, slightly bad taste to use people who've got a medical condition?'

'Come on, Sam. Can we drop all this "taste" schtick?'

He then opened a drawer and passed me a small piece of paper. It was a cheque. Made payable to yours truly. The amount: £30,000. I wanted to laugh out loud, but tried acting cool about it.

'Third now,' said Dom. 'Third on completion. Third on transmission. OK?'

'Great.'

'Now then, about taste. Can we stop worrying about that?'

I looked at the cheque and weighed up the pros and cons.

'No problem.'

'Good,' said Dom. 'Anyway, they're perfectly happy to appear, so long as we donate some moolah to the church. Keep its roof on, you know.'

'Fair enough.'

I looked again at the photograph.

'Sincock, eh?' I said. 'Great name for a vicar.'

Dom chuckled.

'We do know how to pick 'em. We'll be doing them next week.'

'Next week?'

'Yup. No time to waste.'

'Blimey. Yes. Fine. All right.'

We discussed more nuts and bolts, but what I really wanted to talk about was Emily. Dom had not said a word about her, and I was becoming increasingly anxious. Eventually, I decided just to blurt it out.

'Um, one thing – how is Emily? She took her, er, sacking pretty badly, you know.'

Dom took off his glasses and rubbed his eyes.

'She was pretty fucked off,' he said.

'What did she say?'

'Oh, Sam, let's not talk about it, OK?'

I wondered what he was trying to hide.

'All right,' I said. 'But I just want to make sure that you know that whatever she said about me and Sally was probably a load of bollocks.'

'Sure,' said Dom.

This was infuriating, and I said as much.

'Come on Dom, you're being unfair. I've got a right to know at least something.'

Dom put his glasses back on.

'Look, what goes on between me and Emily is private, OK? I know you're old friends with her, and are practically neighbours, but I don't see why I have to tell you everything that goes on between her and me.'

There was clearly no point in going any further, so I dropped it. But it's starting to eat me up. What the fuck is that bitch telling him?

Wednesday 23 April

Sally came back very very late last night – about 1 a.m. I had been asleep for two hours, and she woke me up as she came into the bedroom. I knew she was going to be late, but not that late.

'You OK?' I asked, my eyes squinting when she turned on the bedside lamp.

'I'll tell you in the morning,' she said. 'I'm sorry, I should have slept in the spare room.'

She looked absolutely exhausted, but I refrained from telling her so.

'No, it's OK,' I said. 'You can tell me now.'

Sally sat next to me on the bed and took her shoes off.

'There's been an almighty fuck-up at work,' she said.

'How much can you tell me?'

She sighed.

'Not much as usual, and it's not as though I know everything either. Basically, one of our most important networks has been compromised.'

'I'm assuming that euphemism means that a lot of people in your part of the world are being tortured as we speak.'

'You've got it.'

Sally lay down next to me.

'Do you know how it happened?'

'We don't. But everything seems to point to there being a leak.'

'What? You mean a mole? Like in John le Carré?'

'It's possible. It would explain a lot. It's not as though it hasn't happened before.'

'Are you sure? Isn't it a bit unlikely that someone at work is a traitor?'

'It's unlikely, but not impossible.'

'Christ. Why would anybody want to help one of those bastards?'

'Mice,' said Sally.

'Mice?'

'Money. Ideology. Compromise. Ego. The reasons why people betray.'

'Gotcha. I was thinking that some sort of rodent protection league was somehow involved.'

Sally sort of laughed and we lay there quietly.

'I can understand money and ideology,' I said. 'And ego. But what about compromise? I always thought compromise was about Russkis blackmailing people with pictures of them in bed with rent boys. But hasn't all that gone out with the Ark? I mean, everybody is allowed to be gay these days, so it's not such a big deal.'

'You're right up to a point,' Sally replied. 'But there are a lot of people around who have dirty little secrets.'

'I wonder what they are.'

'Oh, you know – mistresses, bizarre sexual peccadilloes, that sort of thing.'

'But even so.'

'I know, but a lot of the older types are vulnerable on this. They've grown up thinking all these things are shameful.'

I cast my mind back to Nick, Sally's ex, with whom I had been convinced she was having an affair the year before. I still inwardly winced at the memory of my following them up to London. Not one of my finest moments.

'I guess someone like Nick could have been a blackmail target,' I said.

'Nick?'

'Well, you know, him being secretly gay and all.'

Another sigh.

'You know what? If I were a cunning and low sort of person . . .'

'Aren't you meant to be?' I interrupted.

'True. Well, as I am a cunning and low sort of person, I'd suggest that you wanted to see Nick locked up for being a foul traitor.'

I playfully dug Sally in the ribs.

'Naturally,' I replied. 'And I'd want to see him hung, drawn and quartered.' I was relieved that we could make light of all this now.

'I don't see him as a traitor,' said Sally, in all seriousness.

'Really? I thought you people were supposed to be suspicious of everybody.'

'Yes, we are. And that's the worst thing about a suspected mole – it can paralyse an organisation, because everybody thinks everybody is guilty, and a lot of time is wasted on witch-hunts.'

'Well, you'd save yourselves a lot of bother if you just hauled Nick in and applied the old thumbscrews.'

Sally turned round and kissed me.

'I'm so glad you don't work where I work,' she said.

'Why? Because I'd be working with you?'

'That as well. But more because the safety of this country would be in grave peril.'

'Hmm! I think I'd make rather a good spy.'

'You'd be hopeless.'

'Why's that?'

I was slightly offended, but not much. At some point in their lives all men want to be spies, although I've now reached the stage where I've realised my talents lie elsewhere. Exactly where, I don't know.

'Because you love money and you have an enormous ego. All you'd require is a briefcase full of cash and a bit of flattery, and you'd spill the beans.'

I thought this over in my sleepyhead state.

'You make a good point,' I admitted.

Sally hugged me tight.

'It's nice being back home,' she said.

Thursday 24 April

It turns out that the Sincocks only live half an hour away, so I'll be able to come back home after each day of filming. Thank God. I hate staying in hotels on my own, no matter how nice they are. When I used to travel around a lot because of work, I stayed in some great places, but without someone to enjoy them with, they seemed pointless. Luxurious hotel rooms are for having lots of sex and room service, and whenever I'm in one on my own, I just feel a little depressed.

Saturday 26 April

Sally back v. late again last night. Says that things are a

little better at work, but that's only because people have got used to the idea of the crisis and are adapting. She was shattered, and I let her sleep in until 11 o'clock, when I decided that she might actually want to get up and see the children etc. She looked a million times better, but had to spend until lunch working at her laptop.

The day was rescued by the weather, and we went for a lovely spring walk along the river. Well, it was lovely until Daisy insisted on being carried after we had gone about four hundred yards.

''ummy 'ill u carry me?'

'No,' said Sally, 'you've got legs, you can walk.'

Daisy held her arms aloft, ignoring the answer.

'Carry me!' she whinged.

'No,' said Sally.

Daisy then transferred the request to me.

'Carry me Daddy!'

'No,' I said. 'You heard what Mummy said. You can walk.'

'But I tired.'

She then made a great show of rubbing her eyes. This was complete playacting, as she had slept well.

'Come on Daisy, you can walk.'

Daisy then went into full diva mode. She repeatedly screamed out that she was to be carried, and stamped her little green frog-eyed boots.

'Let's keep walking,' I suggested.

Sally looked uneasy at leaving her, but as the river is fenced off, and we were in the middle of a cow-free field, I told her that it wasn't a problem.

Now began a game of Willpower Roulette – fun for none of the family. The rules are simple and timeworn. The players are divided into two teams – parents and children. The opening gambit is for one of the children to throw a strop. The second move is played by the parents, who then walk away. The game real now begins. Who will give way first? The child, fearing permanent abandonment by parents? Or the parents, fearing the child may come to some bad end if left unattended?

After twenty seconds, Sally came close to breaking. She was walking backwards, which is technically a breach of the rules, but I wasn't about to tell her.

'Come on Daisy!' she shouted. 'We can't leave you there!'

'Turn round,' I said. 'Otherwise she'll win.'

'What do you mean, win?'

'She's got to learn that she can't always have her own way.'

'I quite agree, but abandoning her in the middle of a field is hardly going to teach her anything.'

'Trust the WonderHubby.'

'What? You are joking.'

I was, of course, but it did occur to me that 'Trust the WonderHubby' might make a great catchphrase for the show. Who knows? Perhaps it would become one of those comedy phrases that everybody repeats ad nauseam. 'You wouldn't let it lie.' 'Only me!' Etc. Yawn.

Meanwhile Daisy was still rooted to the spot, screaming loudly.

'Why are we leaving Daisy behind?' asked Peter, who looked genuinely concerned.

'Because she has to learn that she can't be carried,' I said. 'Come on, let's keep walking. She'll come along – you mark my words.'

Sally reluctantly took a few more steps.

'Sam, this is ridiculous.'

'It's not. This is the time when we need to fight these battles. The older she gets, the harder it'll be.'

'The expert speaks.'

'Trust the WonderHubby.'

'Please stop saying that.'

Daisy continued to cry out.

'Mummy! Mummy!'

'Sam, this is just cruel!'

'It's not cruel. And if it is cruel, it's because we're being cruel to be kind. Come on, let's keep walking.'

We did so, and Daisy's bellows grew more faint as we got around 50–60 yards down the field.

'Sam! This is miles away!'

'It's not! What's going to happen to her?'

'I'm just worried that she's frightened.'

'She's not frightened – she's just being wilfull.'

'Daddy?' asked Peter.

'Yes?'

'I am going to carry Daisy,' he said.

'That's very sweet of you,' I replied. 'But Daisy needs to learn that she can't be carried everywhere.'

'But she is only two.'

'Exactly. She is a big girl now.'

'Daddy?'

'Yes?'

'The other day you said I was a little boy and I am bigger than Daisy so how is Daisy a big girl now?'

It was an interesting point. Sally laughed, a little too loud.

'Touché,' she said.

I didn't know what to say, and mumbled something about size being relative.

Daisy was really roaring now, and Sally started to walk back to her.

'Don't!'

Sally ignored me and continued walking.

'Don't!'

'For heaven's sake, Sam!'

And then Daisy fell over. Not a massive tumble, but enough to cause Sally to run. (Is it just our children who fall over a lot?)

'She'll be fine!' I shouted.

Sally ran at warp speed, and within a few seconds she had picked Daisy up.

'Is Daisy OK?' asked Peter.

'Yes – she's just fallen over.'

'Maybe she would not have fallen over if she was with us.'

'Maybe not.'

Sally drew closer. I soon noticed that Daisy was covered in mud.

'I'm going back home,' Sally shouted. 'She fell in a cowpat.'

'Oh shit,' I went.

'Oh shit,' came a little echo down to my right.

'You mustn't say that,' I said.

'But you said it!'

'Daddy was naughty to say it.'

Sally didn't wait any longer, and shot off with a poo-splattered screaming Daisy. I don't know how to judge the result of that particular game of Willpower Roulette. A draw? The biggest loser will be me, because I will hear no end of this from Sally.

Sunday 27 April

I was right. No end to it at all. Comments included:

'She could have got hepatitis.'

'I should never have listened to you.'

'You should never leave children on their own.'

'Or lock them in their rooms for that matter.'

'I fear for those families you're going to look after.'

In fact, so do I. The Reverend Sincock and family beckon tomorrow. I've just been looking at ADHD on the Web – apparently there is no cure. Great. So what the hell am I supposed to do?

Trust the WonderHubby. Hmmmm.

Monday 28 April

I have neither the time or energy to write up what happened today.

Tuesday 29 April

Same.

Wednesday 30 April

And again. Suffice to say, it's been exhausting and bizarre. I shall write it all up at the end of the week.

Saturday 3 May

Where to begin? All I know is that this week has been one of the most eye-opening of my life. And that includes Richie's stag in Warsaw. Although Dom, typically, was delighted, as far as I was concerned the whole thing was an unmitigated disaster.

Naturally, it all started off well. The Sincocks were the model of middle-classness, and when we arrived Mrs Sincock (Ginny, naturally) offered us some tea and biscuits, which we ate in an immaculately clean kitchen, featuring no less than seven mug trees. The vicar – Norman – was charm itself, and for the first ten minutes the children were pretty well behaved (although they did seem to fidget quite a bit). The boy was called Michael and he was nine, and his sister Mary was six, and as they munched their Rich Tea biscuits, they seemed fine.

'How much do you know about ADHD?' Mrs Sincock asked.

'I've read about it on the Web,' I said, hoping my

look of sensitivity and concern appeared as sincere as I felt.

'How about you?' she asked Dom.

'Same,' he replied. 'Gather it means your children behave like sh— behave very badly.'

'Yes, well, there's a little bit more to it than that.'

'Can you tell us more?' I asked.

'Well, they're both what is called "predominantly hyperactive-impulsive".'

'Uh huh,' Dom and I went.

'Which means that they never seem to relax. They're always on the go – running around, jumping about, climbing up this and that, and they never stop talking.'

'They seem pretty mellow at the moment,' I said.

'That's because they're doing their best for you, aren't you, kids?'

The children nodded furiously. Nevertheless, their fidgeting was getting more pronounced, and the table was shaking as they constantly bashed into it with their swaying feet.

'It's as though they've got motors inside them,' said the Reverend Sincock. 'Out-of-control lawnmowers is what I call them!'

Initially I thought it slightly strange that the children should be spoken about as if they weren't present, but I was to get used to that during the week. By now the shaking of the table was growing acute, but the Sincocks didn't seem to notice or care. Again, I would later learn that this was small beer. Had this been Peter and Daisy doing it, they would have got a rocket, and quite possibly been sent to their rooms. This, however, was Michael and Mary's idea of keeping still.

'And, um, do you, you know . . .' I started.

'What?' asked Mrs Sincock.

'Give them medication?'

'Oh no!' said Mr Sincock.

'No?'

'We do not believe in drugs,' he stated, and folded his arms.

'What do you mean?' I asked. 'Do you not believe in them the same way as I don't believe in God?'

Cock. Fuck. Poo. Toss. Bugger. Balls. Wank. Shit. Cock again and a bit more fuck. Why did I say that? Was it the lack of dog collar? Or was it because God was on my mind, knowing that Sincock was a vicar, and in my conscious attempt to tread carefully and not mention God, my subconscious had rebelled and decided to have some fun? Yes, probably.

The Sincocks nodded. Dom looked skyward, or rather heavenward (if there is a heaven of course, which I don't believe, as should now be somewhat obvious).

'Christ,' I said. 'I'm so sorry.'

'Just because you are an atheist, Mr Holden, it does not give you the right to blaspheme.'

'Did I?'

'Yes. You just said "Christ".'

'Oh shit, I'm so sorry.'

Mr Sincock stood up. The children were now cackling away, and Mrs Sincock stared nervously into the endless brown pool of her tea.

'He said shit! He said shit!' shouted Michael.

'You're not allowed to say shit!' said Mary.

'Shit! Shit! Shit! Shit!' went Michael.

'Shit! Shit! Shit! Shit!' went Mary.

'Quiet!' shouted the good Rev.

They ignored him, and then the table-kicking got worse, and soon our tea was slopping out of our mugs.

'Keep still!' he shouted.

After a few more kicks the earthquake under us slowly died away, along with the 'shits'.

Sincock then turned his attention to me.

'Mr Holden,' he said. 'You have been invited into our home in order to help us. While you are here, I expect you to behave with respect to our beliefs and our feelings. Do I make myself clear?'

'Of course,' I said. 'And I sincerely apologise. I assure you that it will not happen again.'

Sincock studied my face.

'I pray – literally – that you are right.'

'Sorry.'

'Your apology is accepted,' he said, and I breathed out.

We spent the rest of the day observing and filming the children. I kept my mouth shut, although as the behaviour of Michael and Mary left me speechless, I hardly needed to adopt much self-control. I had never witnessed such scenes of childish Armageddon. Not a minute passed without the children:

a) shouting
b) screaming
c) running
d) climbing
e) knocking things over
f) fighting each other
g) fighting their mother
h) fighting their father (when he was around)
i) all of the above
j) oh yes, and throwing things

But there was worse. Not only did they behave – just as Sincock had indicated – like lawnmowers on the loose, but they also refused to listen to their mother. No matter what order she gave out, whether it was harshly put or gently put, they simply ignored it. When she asked them to come to the table they would lie on the floor feigning sleep, or they would lie on the floor having a tantrum.

By the middle of the afternoon, I was beginning to feel that my nerves were shot to pieces. The constant screaming and disobedience had got to me, and at one point I even joined one of the location assistants for a cigarette. That succeeded in making me feel light-headed, but I certainly felt a lot more mellow, too. God only knew, literally (although not literally if you're an atheist), how Mrs Sincock coped. It was either the power of prayer, or of a secret stash of Valium that she had hidden away from the vicar.

But teatime was the crunch. Teatime was the

nightmare. Mrs Sincock tried to make the children come to the table, but they refused. Instead they stayed in the playroom, doing one of the few things that kept them relatively peaceful.

'I wanna watch TV!' shouted Michael.

'I wanna watch TV!' shouted Mary.

'I'll take the TV away if you don't come to the table,' said Mrs Sincock.

Mary started screaming.

Michael started whining in the same way as Peter does, despite the fact that he is twice his age.

'I'll give you ten seconds!'

'No!'

'Ten!'

'Nine!'

'Eight!'

Still no movement from the playroom. Toby the cameraman poked his lens in, and as I could see from the VT later (notice how quickly I am picking up these TV words), the children just sat on their beanbags.

'Seven! Six! Five! Four! Three! Two!'

Nothing!

'One!'

Blast-off. Mrs Sincock, perhaps because the Valium was wearing off, stormed into the playroom and dragged the children away. They kicked and screamed, and then Mary took a savage, feral bite out of her mother's left forearm. Unsurprisingly Mrs Sincock cried out, and let go, at which point the children started laughing and ran back into the playroom.

It was tempting just to pick Mary and Michael up by their collars and help haul them out, but I heeded Dom's words that the observer should not react with the system. Funnily enough, Dom only follows this rule when things are going particularly badly.

I looked at Mrs Sincock's arm. The little beast had actually drawn blood.

'Are you all right?' I asked.

'I'm fine,' she said. 'It's not the first time. Can you see the scars?'

And sure enough, all the way up her forearms was a network of little white lines.

'Chri— Blimey,' I said. 'You should wear gauntlets!'

'I know!'

'But how do you manage to keep so calm?'

'I see it as a test,' she said.

'A test?'

'That's right. From the Lord. I know that he wants to test me, to see if I am worthy of his love.'

'Why you?'

'Who knows?' she said. 'As even you should know, the Lord moves in mysterious ways.'

I always thought this was a bit of a cop-out by the religious, a rather too easy way of explaining why crap has to happen. Naturally I refrained from expressing my thoughts.

'Quite,' I mumbled.

Eventually the children were sort of seated at the table. Mrs Sincock had cooked a nice-looking tea for them, and I was rather tempted to snaffle one of the sausages.

'I don't want this!' shouted Mary. 'This is poo!'

'It's not poo, dear,' Mrs Sincock replied. 'These are Fairtrade sausages and organic peas and potatoes.'

I must confess I'd never heard of Fairtrade sausages, but they looked bloody good. Michael thought so as well, although his method of eating them was positively Cro-Magnon, or perhaps Neanderthal, whichever is worse. He grabbed each sausage with his fist and just shoved it into his mouth. The peas, naturally, were flicked around, which Mrs Sincock ignored. I had thought that serving them peas was asking for trouble, but I suspect, like all good Christians, she wanted to give peas a chance.

Mary was eating nothing, and Mrs Sincock tried to feed her like a baby.

'I don't want it!'

Nevertheless her mother continued, despite the fact that each mouthful was spat out, or in the rare event of it being swallowed, was regurgitated in a semi-masticated lump back onto the table. I caught Dom's eye, and he gave me a covert thumbs-up, as I knew he would. He was merciless.

After a few more minutes the children simply got down from the table and ran back into the playroom. Mrs Sincock chased after them, and gave them an almighty rocket. My attention, however, was caught by the deliciously plump sausage that Mary had left on her plate. Reckoning that it would only be going to waste, and motivated by greed, I removed it and started chewing it.

'You can't do that!' hissed Dom. 'You're on a diet!'

I noticed that he had no moral problem with my small act of larceny.

'Shh!' I went. 'I'm bloody starved.'

The sausage tasted delicious, and I was delighted that Mary had left it.

'I'm definitely going to get some of these Fairtrade bangers,' I said. 'Damn good!'

Of course, that was the moment that Mrs Sincock walked into the room.

'I give up,' she said.

I tried stuffing the sausage into my mouth as quickly as possible.

'What are you eating?' she asked.

'Nothing,' I lied, my mouth clearly full.

'Is that . . . is that a sausage?'

'Er, yes.'

'Where from?'

'Um, from Mary's plate. I thought she had finished.'

Mrs Sincock looked stunned. (It's just occurred to me that I've been referring to her as 'Mrs Sincock' throughout. It just feels right – some people don't need first names.)

'You took food from my child's plate?'

'Um, I didn't want it to go to waste.'

'But that's outrageous!'

'I'm, er, terribly sorry,' I said abjectly. 'Just a terrible misunderstanding. It's kind of what I do at home, you know, when the children have finished their food. I was feeling a bit peckish and just thought, you know . . .'

'No I do not! And how did you know my children had finished?'

'Well, they, um, got down.'

I sensed Dom was brewing the most massive 'church laugh', and his whole body was shaking as he tried to control that paroxysm of giggles that was surely about to break out.

'Just because they had got down, Mr Holden, does not mean that they have finished eating.'

'I see. I'm sorry.'

I felt like a schoolboy being chastised by head matron. Mrs Sincock must only have been a few years older than me, but I might as well have been nine. Blimey, I thought, it was only a poxy sausage, which her daughter would have spat out anyway. She looked at me, no doubt evaluating some sort of punishment. What was it to be? Sent to my room? A talking-to from Father? Six of the best?

'Mr Holden, the whole idea of inviting you into our home was for you to help us with the difficult task of disciplining our children. I cannot see what hope we have if you yourself require that same discipline.'

Dom's shaking was getting worse, and it was infectious. Toby the cameraman was shaking as well, and soon I found myself starting to make bizarre snorting noises in my throat. There was something so absurd about being lectured by this woman about my pinching a sausage, when the children had spent the entire day behaving like tearaways. On reflection, there was no doubt that she was venting all her frustration on me, but at the time I was too dim – and a little petrified – to appreciate that.

'I'm, er, terribly sorry,' I repeated.

I could see her weighing up her options. Would she throw us out for sausage pilfering? If she did that, there would be no money for the church roof, which would be a disaster. On the other hand, why should she have to endure these sniggering thirtysomethings, who were hardly helping make her children behave better?

'Apology accepted,' she finally said, albeit with marked reluctance.

'Thank you,' I said.

Then, out of the playroom:

'Fuckity poo fuck!'

'FUUUUUUCK!!!'

It was inevitable that this high-octane outburst of childish swearing would cause the release of our church laughs, and out they came, our stomachs aching as we doubled up with mirth.

'I don't see what's so funny!' said Mrs Sincock.

'I'm sorry . . .' I started to say, but it was impossible. I laughed so hard I felt as if I might rupture a stomach muscle (that's if I have any).

'I think it's best if you just leave,' said Mrs Sincock. 'I don't see why I have to put up with this!'

We pleaded. We begged forgiveness. We almost got down on our knees, but it was no use. I even found myself saying 'We promise to behave,' but it was no good. Mrs Sincock wanted us out, and within ten minutes we indeed were. As soon as we were outside by the car, Dom left me in no doubt whose fault it was.

'For fuck's sake,' he said. 'That's gone and totally fucked our schedule.'

'So it's all my fault, is it?'

'Yes it is. First of all you announce you're an atheist. Then you blaspheme. Then you actually steal food from the mouth of their daughter. And, finally, you laugh at her.'

'We all laughed at her!'

'I admit that, but by then you had dug us in too deep.'

Dom had a point. In fact, he had some points. I decided that there was no possibility of defending this particular flank, and it would be easier simply to attack him back.

'Anyway, they were a totally inappropriate family to use,' I said. 'Those children need a psychiatrist and medication, not a TV crew to take the piss out of them.'

Dom held up his hands and then let them fall in histrionic despair.

'Holy fuck,' he said. 'I thought we had been through all this taste shit.'

'Yes, but now I'm faced with the reality of the situation, and I don't like it.'

'But you always knew what the reality of the fucking situation was. I bloody told you!'

'I know, but I've got my doubts.'

'You're a bit bloody late for doubts. About ninety bloody grand late! If you don't want to do this programme you can simply give me the money back, and I can find someone else.'

'Oh yeah? Who?'

'Any number of failed management consultants.'

This enraged me.

'So you're calling me a failure?' I asked.

'Well, generally people who are out of work tend to be failures.'

'I decided not to go back to work. It was a matter of choice.'

'That's not what I'd heard,' said Dom.

'Really? From who?'

I paused.

'In fact,' I continued, 'you don't need to answer that. Why don't you go and fuck yourself, and then fuck Emily, in that order. Fuck you both.'

Dom didn't say anything. Instead, he was pointing over my shoulder, and had the look of a man who had been pointing over my shoulder for a while. I turned round.

'Hello Mr Holden,' said Mr Sincock.

In the end, Dom sorted it. He promised another grand for the church roof, and said that I would be on my best behaviour. Mrs Sincock didn't like it, but her husband apparently gave her a lecture on forgiveness, as well as on water damage in thirteenth-century churches. When we turned up the next morning it was as if nothing had happened, although I was suitably apologetic, up to the point at which Mrs Sincock said there was really little need to go on about it, and that everything was forgotten.

We then spent most of that Tuesday morning watching the children run wild once again, and Dom was delighted with the footage we were getting. As I watched, I decided that the only way to handle the Sincock episode was to treat the whole thing incredibly seriously. These children were unstable, and it was clear to me that Mrs Sincock was not applying the same sort of discipline to them as she had done to me. She had given up ages ago, and when she was confronted by my naughtiness she had really let rip, knowing that I was a (relatively) sane human being, who responds to reason. (Sometimes. Sally would dispute this.)

At lunchtime Dom, one of the Emmas and I went off for a meeting to discuss how to handle this family. Much of the air from the day before had been cleared, and as we sat in the pub enjoying a couple of pints and not enjoying the food, I told them that I didn't want to be seen as taking the piss out of a couple of children whose behaviour was a function of a condition rather than of poor upbringing.

'Nobody is asking you to take the piss,' said Dom.

'All we want you to be is yourself,' said Emma.

I supped my pint. As you do. (You never sip pints, you always 'sup' them.)

'That's the problem,' I said. 'I think that being myself inherently takes the piss.'

'Out of whom?' asked Emma.

'Out of them, of course,' I replied. 'The family.'

Emma nodded.

'I wouldn't worry about that,' she said.

'Exactly,' said Dom.

'You really sure about that?' I asked.

'Absolutely.'

Another sup.

'Anyway, what's your management plan with the Sincocks?'

'I've been thinking about that,' I said, which indeed I had. 'I want to create a system of proxy incentivisations and disincentivisations.'

'You mean like carrots and sticks?' Emma asked.

'Not quite. Carrots and sticks are actual incentivisations and disincentivisations. What I'm looking to create is a system of representational incentivisations and disincentivisations.'

'I see,' said Emma.

'You mean sort of pretend incentivisations and disincentivisations?' asked Dom.

'Exactly,' I said. 'Pretend incentivisations and disincentivisations.'

'What good would they do?'

'Encourage them to behave, of course.'

'I see.'

'I'm a little lost,' said Emma.

'Why's that?' I asked.

'Well, I'm not too sure what poxy incentivisations and disincentivisations really are.'

'Proxy incentivisations and disincentivisations,' I corrected.

'Fine, but what exactly are they?'

'Proxy incentivisations and disincentivisations?'

'Yes.'

'Well, they're the function of a strategy for implementing a system of non-financial rewards and penalties. In this way, employee performance can be ascertained and improved within the same co-current holistic process, resulting in a potential maximisation of human resources.'

'Right,' said Emma, who now looked as if she had been awake for two days.

'Clear as day,' said Dom. 'Another pint?'

'Why not?'

Dom went up to the bar. I turned to Emma.

'I'll need a chart,' I said.

'A chart? What sort of chart?'

'One for the incentivisation and disincentivisation strategy.'

'But what do they look like?'

I took out a pen and paper from my laptop bag and drew two 2 × 10 grids, one marked 'Incentivisation Totems' and the other marked 'Disincentivisation Totems'.

'Whenever Michael or Mary do something good, we want to further incentivise them to carry on doing good. Therefore we apply a cross on the incentivisation chart. If they do something bad, we want to disincentivise them from doing more bad, and we put a cross on the disincentivisation chart. One crucial element of the two charts is that their products are mutually inclusive.'

'What?'

'They, um, cancel each other out.'

'Aaaah, now I've got it!' said Emma.

'Excellent!'

'We used to have this at my primary school.'

'Really? That must have been a very advanced school. These charts represent the cutting edge of management-consultant thinking.'

'Not at all. We just called them blacks and golds.'

'Blacks and golds?'

'Yes. You got a black if you were bad, and a gold if you were good. The blacks cancelled the golds, and whoever got the most golds at the end of the term won a prize. Isn't that basically the same as your system?'

'Er, yes.'

'So why does it have be called disincentivathing-ummyadoodah?'

'Because that's what it's called. But it's more than just your blacks and golds.'

'Really? How?'

'It's structured.'

'Right.'

I decided that I didn't want to listen to any more of Emma's questions. Sometimes it's hard to defend management consultancy. To the outsider it looks like a load of crapola management speak, but really, it's not. I was cynical at first, deeply cynical, but when I saw how well management consultancy worked on some of our clients, my doubts were swept away. The systems and the strategies that we put in place would reap huge dividends, and would sometimes make our clients some money as well.

However, I didn't want to go into all this with Emma, so instead I just said, 'If I explained it all in detail, you'd be very very bored.'

Emma smiled and took my grids from me.

'I'll get Ted to make some nice charts for you this afternoon.'

Mr Sincock was around that afternoon, and as a result the children were slightly better behaved. This is not to claim that they were well-behaved, as there was still an enormous amount of disobedience and breaking things. After teatime I tried to explain the purpose of the incentivisation and disincentivisation strategy, and the family looked blankly at me.

'This sounds like pluses and minuses,' said Sincock after I had shown them my presentation.

'Quite,' said Mrs Sincock. 'We used to call them merits and demerits when I was at school.'

'I'm glad you're aware of the principle,' I said through gritted teeth.

'What's this shit anyway?' said Michael. 'It sounds like BOLLOCKS!'

'Bollocks!' said Mary. 'You're bollocks!'

'Quiet you two!' went Sincock. 'That's quite enough of that language. You shall go to your rooms if you use it again!'

'Aha!' I went, slightly too triumphantly. 'This represents an excellent opportunity to introduce the charts. Clearly we wish to disincentivise bad language, don't we, so now we should award a disincentivisation totem to each of them.'

I then took out my red marker pen and filled in a disincentivisation box on each of their charts, which brandished spankingly smart *WonderHubby* logos.

'There,' I said, admiring my handiwork. I think I might have even put my hands on my hips, as though I were surveying a drystone wall I had just spent several hours making.

Everybody looked at the two little red squares, transfixed. For a moment or three, silence did actually reign.

'What a load of bollocks!' said Michael.

'BOLLOCKS!' shouted Mary.

Sincock started to open his mouth, but I beat him to it.

'Ah! Ah! Not so fast!'

I grabbed my red pen again, and filled in two more disincentivisation squares on their charts.

'You see?' I said to Mary and Michael. 'Every time you say bollocks, you get another square!'

'But you just said bollocks!' shouted Michael.

'Bollocks! Bollocks! Bollocks!' screamed Mary.

'Yes, but that was an accident!' I insisted.

I looked at the parents, hoping they would see the funny side, but alas no. Instead, they looked on grimly, unimpressed so far with my exciting new method. I then addressed the children.

'But do you see how it works?'

They nodded.

'Every time we say bollocks you draw a red square,' said Mary.

'That's right,' I said. 'But don't say it again, or I'll have to give you another red square. And that goes for any other rude words or bad behaviour.'

'What sort of rude words?' asked Michael.

'You know which ones,' I said.

'Shit is a rude word,' said Mary, straight-facedly.

That earned another red square.

'So is crap!' said Michael.

That earned Michael square number three.

'Poo!'

'Willy!'

'Turd!'

'Piss!'

'Cock!'

'Fuck!'

'Right!' said Sincock. 'To your rooms, now!'

'Please,' I said, as I struggled to match the squares to the language. 'Please just give my system a chance!'

'Can't you see that it's encouraging them?'

'There will of course be an initial excitement scenario, which will dissipate when the full reality of the chart sinks in.'

'How, exactly?'

'Just you watch – it will take some time, but the yields are surprisingly high.'

By the end of the day Michael had earned 24 disincentivisation points, and Mary 26. Miraculously, they had earned 3 incentivisation points, all of which were for turning off the TV (although it should never have been switched on in the first place).

All I could say to the Sincocks was that 'it will be fine'.

It wasn't. By the end of Wednesday Michael and Mary had earned 87 disincentivisation points between them, and no more incentivisation points. I had told Mrs Sincock that we had to stick with it, and that she was not to worry, because the system was bound to work.

'These are not normal children,' she said, close to tears.

I caught Dom's eye over her shoulder. He was rotating his hand to indicate that the conversation should continue. Gormlessly, I couldn't work out why, and frowned back.

'They're perfectly normal children,' I said. 'They're just a little high-spirited, that's all.'

'You mean you don't believe in ADHD?'

'Not really.'

'Well, it's real, and if my children haven't got that, they must have got something else.'

Dom scribbled something on a sheet of paper and held it up behind her.

MAKE SURE SHE CRIES

I couldn't quite believe what I had just read.

'No,' I mouthed.

Dom's eyes did the Tube-logo thing. He then underlined the words, and made throat-cutting actions.

I weighed my options quickly. I would go to hell if I followed Dom's order, but then as I didn't believe in hell . . .

I turned back to Mrs Sincock. I put a gentle hand on her shoulder.

'I'm so sorry,' I said. 'But you must remember that underneath all that naughtiness are the tender souls of God's children.'

Mrs Sincock started to blub. Massive thumbs-up from Dom.

'Because,' I said, 'I can tell that they are, in their little hearts, the sweetest and most affectionate children there could be. I've no doubt that they will grow out of it.'

'Oh dear Lord, I hope so!'

Mrs Sincock then started to cry properly. Not full on howling and wailing at the wall, but enough to put a huge smile on Dom's face. I felt disgusted with him, and disgusted with myself. What made me feel worse was when Dom leaned forward and asked, in the most sensitive tone he could muster, 'Mrs Sincock? Would you like us to stop filming now?'

'Yes please,' she nodded.

'I totally understand,' he said, and then looked at Toby to turn off the camera.

Until I found out the truth, I thought a miracle had happened. The change started in the early afternoon. Mrs Sincock was taking the children out for a walk, and they actually behaved decently. They didn't swear that much, and instead of running around they walked obediently alongside her, as if they were well-trained Labradors.

By the time we got back Mrs Sincock looked both delighted and stunned.

'Well,' she said. 'You've both been very well behaved!'

'I agree,' I added. 'You certainly deserve some squares on the incentivisation chart!'

As I coloured, I couldn't quite believe what had happened. When we had been on a walk the day before, they had all but murdered each other, and had even beaten their mother with some elder branches.

'Mum,' said Michael. 'Please can we watch the TV?'

Mrs Sincock looked as if she'd had a turn.

'What was that?' she asked.

'Please may we watch the TV?'

'Um, no darling, it's not time yet.'

'All right then.'

I checked to see whether the camera had caught this historic moment in the life of the Sincock household, and indeed of the Holden Childcare Programme. Surely, I thought, this was the defining moment, the moment in which the programme went from being some sort of joke to raise a cheap laugh, to becoming an actual system that people could use throughout the world to take control of their offspring. I felt immensely proud.

Michael and Mary sat down in their playroom and started to look through some books.

'This is incredible,' said Mrs Sincock. 'I don't know if

there's ever been a time in which they've just sat down and read of their own accord.'

It was indeed incredible. Dom also looked impressed, and gave a little thumbs up. Mrs Sincock then cooked the children their tea, and while she did so they continued to either read or play quietly. For the first time in days we could hear the hum of the fridge and the sound of the fan in the oven.

'I don't know whether it's your programme, Mr Holden,' said Mrs Sincock, 'or whether it's a miracle, but this is the longest time I've ever known them to be quiet.'

'Can you say that again please, Mrs Holden?' asked Dom. 'I don't think we quite picked it up.'

Mrs Sincock looked happy to do so, and Dom just grinned and grinned. And, when the children were at the table, they ate nicely – barring the odd fish-finger regurgitation – and even had to be told that they could get down. When their father appeared just towards the end, he too was dumbfounded.

'Well, well, well,' he said. 'The Lord be praised. I've been praying for this for many years, and finally he has answered. I see this as a true test of faith.'

He then turned to me. Frankly, I was a bit shagged off that God was getting all the credit.

'Thank you, Mr Holden,' he said, and he sounded sincere. 'If you are indeed sent by the Lord, he does indeed move in mysterious ways!'

I didn't know what to make of that, so I just smiled inanely.

'My pleasure,' I said. 'But let's not count our chickens just yet!'

'Quite! If they're like this tomorrow, then I'll know that you have succeeded.'

Dom was insistent that we turned up before breakfast, which I found pointless, but he said he wanted to catch the 'little buggers at their worst'. I said that they would now be fine, but he had his doubts, and wondered whether it had all been a fluke. Sadly, he was right, and it looked as though the 'miracle' had worn off. Michael and Mary were back to their appalling selves, and throughout breakfast they repeatedly threw their food at each other, their parents and even the camera. Dom didn't seem to mind, and just stood there with his quotidian voyeuristic grin.

'I'm sorry,' I said to the Sincocks.

'Don't be,' said Mrs Sincock.

'It looks as though the Lord is testing us still,' said the Rev.

Nevertheless, I continued with awarding them disincentivisation points, although after they had earned no less than 24 in the space of 15 minutes I was wondering whether Sincock was not in fact right, and that it was merely encouraging their bad behaviour.

However, about half an hour after breakfast, their mood changed, and once again Mary and Michael sat down in their playroom and started reading and playing with their toys.

'Another miracle,' I said to Mrs Sincock.

'You know, I think you may be right,' she said.

'What I find strange is the delay.'

'I know what you mean. It's as though the lessons of the charts take a short while to sink in.'

I watched while the Reverend kissed his children goodbye. They actually reciprocated the affection, and I could tell that he was deeply touched.

'Do you have time to say a few words?' asked Dom.

'What sort of words?' Sincock enquired.

'Well, just a few sentences about what you think of the programme, and how it's gone.'

'Of course.'

Dom and Toby then discussed the best place to film the parents, and they plumped for the conservatory, with the children playing quietly at their feet. I was sitting alongside them, and the comments they made were addressed to me directly. It all felt very staged and scripted, which in fact it was.

'At the beginning of the week,' said Sincock, 'I had my doubts about your programme. I thought it was all management speak and highfalutin language, but now I realise that it really did mean something.'

'Thanks,' I said. 'Michael and Mary were certainly a challenge for any system of childcare.'

'But with your management strategies,' said Mrs Sincock, 'you have made a world of difference. Michael and Mary are so much better behaved.'

'Yes,' said Sincock. 'With your incentivisation and dis-incentivisation charts, our children are now functioning as high-value members of our family.'

'I'm so glad,' I said. 'It goes to show that with any turn-round solution, constant reapplication of strategy is key for a successful result.'

'I couldn't agree more,' said Mrs Sincock. 'We shall certainly be rolling out your solutions from now on.'

'Excellent,' I said. 'But there are two people whose opinions count most of all, and they are of course Michael and Mary.'

I leaned down with a fixed smile, and felt like the evil Child-Catcher from *Chitty Chitty Bang Bang*.

'So what do you think of the programme, eh?'

'Bollocks!' shouted Michael.

'Cut!' shouted Dom.

I tried not to laugh.

'Shall we film that again?' I asked.

Dom and Emma exchanged glances.

'Nah,' he said. 'I think we've got enough. You can pack up, Toby.'

'Pack up for this interview?' I asked.

'No, for the whole thing,' he said. 'We've got more than enough.'

'But I thought we were meant to be here until tomorrow.'

'So did I,' said Mrs Sincock.

'No need,' said Dom. 'It's clear that the programme has worked wonders already. We can all award ourselves an early weekend.'

I pointed at Michael.

'But he just said bollocks!'

'So what?' said Dom. 'The occasional bollocks isn't going to hurt.'

'Bollocks!' said Mary.

'And now she's saying it!'

Dom ignored me and walked over to the Sincocks.

'Mr and Mrs Sincock,' he gushed, 'it's been an absolute privilege being allowed into your home over the past few days. I am extremely grateful.'

'Not at all,' said Sincock. 'It seems as though your programme has worked wonders, which is not a word I use lightly.'

'Bollocks!' went Michael.

'I expect there will be a little of that left,' said Dom. 'But as Sam will doubtless tell you, keep applying the programme, and I'm sure you'll reap the benefits.'

'Er yes,' I went, 'keep applying the programme.'

Much to everyone's confusion, including mine, we were out the house in about five minutes. When we got to the car, I asked Dom why we had to leave so suddenly.

'I was worried that the children were going to start behaving badly again,' he said.

'But we could have continued to apply the programme, it was really starting to work.'

Dom looked at me.

'Do you really think so?'

'Yes! The proof of the pudding was in the eating. There was no doubt that they were beginning to change.'

'In the eating,' Dom repeated. 'Funny you should mention that.'

'Why?'

He reached into his pocket and passed me a small plastic tube. There was no doubt what it was.

'Oh fucking hell,' I said. 'You . . . you . . . actually drugged them?'

'Yup,' said Dom.

'But that's . . . that's criminal!'

'To my mind, it was more criminal of the Sincocks to refuse their children medication.'

'But you can't just give them . . . how the hell did you give it to them?'

'Powdered up the tablets and put them in their food.'

'So that's why you wanted to make it before breakfast this morning.'

'Exactamundo.'

'I don't believe this,' I said. 'You actually spiked some pre-pubescents in order to make a TV programme?'

'Yup.'

He seemed utterly unashamed.

'What I can't believe is that you really thought your chart was the thing that was doing it.'

'What else was I supposed to think?' I asked.

Dom just shrugged his shoulders.

'I was worried that it was a bit too obvious. Yesterday I thought I had OD'd them – they were almost comatose.'

'Jesus! You know, one of them could have had a reaction. They might have died or something!'

'Well, they didn't.'

'How were you to know?'

'I didn't. But look, these drugs are pretty bloody safe. Millions of children are on these things. They're fine. I wasn't going to bloody kill them. And besides, I've done them a favour. They had a few hours of peace didn't they?'

I didn't know how to respond. And I certainly didn't know what I should do. What had I got myself into? This was more than just 'enhancing reality', this was illegal.

'Look,' I said. 'I really need to think about this.'

'Think about what?'

'What do you fucking think?' I said.

'Oh please spare me the sanctimoniousness,' said Dom. 'Emily said you were a bit of a vicar.'

'Oh yeah? Why? Because I'm not a wife-swapper and because I don't spike children's food? Is that all that's required to be a vicar these days?'

'This is boring,' said Dom.

At which point I got into my car and drove back home.

I haven't spoken about this to Sally yet, but I will do tonight.

Sunday 4 May

Sally thinks I should pay the money back and get the hell out. Dom has crossed a line, she says, and there's no reason why he should drag me over with him. I'm minded to agree, but what the hell can I do? The truth is, I can't pay him back, because I've already spent most of the money paying off credit-card bills incurred from the Great Flood. (Insurance is never fully comprehensive, as I should have well known.) It would be great to take some principled stand, but I simply can't afford to. Sally sees the brutal reality of that situation.

Meanwhile, Peter and Daisy continue to prosper. This evening I helped Peter with his homework. His teacher had given him a load of words on little pieces of paper that he had to identify. They were reasonably tricky ones as well, and he got 18 out of 20 right.

'I'm very clever, aren't I Daddy?'

'Yes you are,' I replied, laughing at his lack of modesty.

That's one of the great things about being four. You can show off, but not sound arrogant. I, on the other hand, can sound arrogant even when I'm not showing off. I need to make sure that Peter is different from me in many ways.

Nevertheless, it felt good to have a weekend with my proper, decent, functional, kind and loving family, doing the simple things like Sunday lunch and homework. It makes me realise how lucky I am to have a life like this.

Tuesday 6 May

I called Dom first thing after the bank holiday in order to clear the air. According to his assistant, he couldn't come to the phone right now but could he ring me back? I spent the best part of the morning fretting, and even went down to the supermarket just to take my mind off it. We were supposed to be shooting the next episode later in the week, and so far I had heard nothing about where it was, who it was, etc.

Of course, going to the supermarket did not help, and neither did bumping into Emily by the deli counter.

'Hello,' she said.

'Hello,' I said.

'How are you?' she asked.

'Well,' I replied. 'And you?'

'Well,' she replied.

And so on – a meaningless vacuous exchange, in which both parties were thinking the foulest thoughts about each other. (By foul, I do not mean dirty. I mean foul.) I constantly pictured Emily and Dom lying in bed, laughing about my supposed prurience. Fuck them, I thought. She's only belittling me because I've rejected her (frequent) advances, and now she wants to cut me down so the rejection doesn't seem so bad. Well, *dummkopf*, I thought, the smaller you make me in your mind, the more bitter you'll feel, because isn't being rejected by someone supposedly less impressive even worse? We parted with much faux amicability, and then we walked off. I annoyed myself by turning to see if she was looking back at me, which she was, whereupon she flashed me a fake smile.

Dom had left a message.

'Listen Sam, we need to have a serious talk. Bye.'

I dialled him back immediately. If I were a sensible sort of person I would have taken a deep breath and mentally laid out my stall, but instead I just charged in.

'Hi Dom it's Sam.'

'Hi.'

'Listen,' we both said simultaneously.

We both laughed a little, which helped.

'You first,' said Dom, which was frustrating, because he had got the magnanimity in first. Wanker.

'Look, I know that I'm new to all this, but there are some things that have really surprised me. I think I can handle the reality enhancement, but as far as I'm concerned, giving children drugs without their or their parents' knowledge is just way out of line. I hate to say that I'm speaking as a father here, but I am. If I found out that someone had given Peter or Daisy some medication without telling Sally or me, I wouldn't be responsible for my actions. This is not about being a prude or anything like that, it's simply about being a decent human being.'

'You finished?' said Dom.

Grrr. He was going from magnanimous to condescending.

'Yes I have. Your turn.'

'All right,' he said. 'I admit that dosing up those kids wasn't exactly the done thing, but it did the trick. But besides, that's not the point. The point is, every time I do something that you find objectionable in your moral universe, you bleat about it.'

The word 'bleat' really annoyed me.

'And can't you see,' Dom continued, 'that if you've taken the money, you've agreed to play the game? I'm sorry that TV isn't as trustworthy as people like to believe, but there we go. The fact is, people want more and more outrageous reality-based programmes, and reality is simply not exciting enough to pull in the viewers. OK, sometimes we overstep the mark, but most of the time we get it right, and give the polloi what it wants.'

'I know all that,' I said. 'And I'm not worried about it. But I still think it is absolutely outrageous what you did. I think you should tell them. These are people's lives you are dealing with, Dom, not pixels on your latest flatscreen.'

'Tell them? You've got to be kidding, right?'

'Not at all. They should know. And if you don't tell them, then I will.'

A pause.

'Are you being quite serious about this?' he asked.

No pause.

'Yes,' I said.

'Great. So now we'll have one fucked series, one court case and the end of both our careers, simply because you're prattling on about some wayward kids.'

'It'll be better than when they suss something is up, then run a toxicology test.'

'Christ, you make it sound like *CSI*.'

I said nothing.

'All right,' said Dom. 'Here's what I'm going to do – nothing. And that's what you're going to do as well. Because if you do something, then I will simply . . .'

(I was expecting him to say 'sack you', but this was far far worse.)

'. . . tell Sally about your little fling with Emily a while back.'

'WHAT?'

'You heard.'

'I've never had a fling with Emily! In her fucking dreams. For fuck's sake, is that what she told you?'

'Yup.'

'And you believe it?'

'Yup.'

'Well it is 100 per cent complete and utter bollocks. I have never done anything with her.'

'Is that so?'

'Yes it bloody well is! How dare she go around spreading those sorts of lies, and how dare you blackmail me!'

'How can I be blackmailing you if it's not true?'

'Because you know perfectly well that Sally would be more than likely to believe the accusation because of her feelings about Emily. For fuck's sake, Dom! Why do we have to go down this nasty little path? All I was saying is that it was wrong of you to have spiked those children's food, and now you come out with this threat.'

'Calm down,' he said.

'No,' I replied.

'Look, just think it over.'

I put the phone down and screamed.

'Is everything all right, Mr Holden?'

The voice gave me a shock at first. It was Halet, who was calling up the stairs.

'Fine thanks,' I shouted back down. 'Just a little work problem!'

'You are sure?'

'Of course.'

Or rather, of course not. The worst thing about this is that I can't really confide in Sally, as she'll think it's some weaselly way of pre-empting some 'revelation'. I'm minded to have it out with Emily, but I don't think that's going to achieve anything, apart from making her more bitter.

On reflection, I am just going to have to swallow my pride and my decency (whatever I have left of both) and carry on with the programme. £90,000 is a lot of money, and will make an enormous amount of difference to us. And who knows what other money might come in?

Wednesday 7 May

Well, I've spoken to Dom, and we've agreed to a kind of stalemate. I won't say anything about the medication, and he won't bring up the so-called 'Emily situation'. I also told him, half jokingly, that he was never to be trusted, and he told me that he would make sure he was on his best behaviour from now on.

Sally has noticed that I've been a bit quiet over the past few days. I told her that I was fine, just a little tired etc. I asked her how it was going at work. She said it had 'stabilised', although everybody was still deeply worried, and that there almost certainly was some kind of leak. I asked if they had arrested Nick yet, and put him in an iron maiden, but that earned me a playful punch to the stomach, which Sally mistimed and ended up slightly winding me.

Friday 9 May

I've spent much of this week refining some of the Holden Childcare Programme. I'm aware that I've been winging it somewhat with the first two families. Us management consultants actually call this 'situational adaptability', and even though I've been doing all right, I want the next 'consultancy sessions' to have more structure. Up to this point, I realise that I've been far too nervous and self-conscious of the camera, but now I need to act like the Master of the Universe us management consultants really are.

I have now distilled my methodology down to a few easy-to-remember phrases. Enter Confidently. Seize The Initiative. Dominate the Proceedings. Rebuff all Countermeasures. Roll out the Victory. Retire with Reward. I had rather hoped that this might make a good acronym: ECSIDPRCRVRR. However as this is largely unpronounceable, it may just have to be an abbreviation.

On second thoughts, it does sound like 'exit prick rover', but then that sounds like you're trying to stop your dog shagging a hole in the beanbag. My talents lie elsewhere.

Monday 12 May
11 p.m. Somewhere in the south-west in the inevitable
Travellers' Rest

This time Dom has chosen a single mother with four children from four different fathers. She's called Suzie, and her children have remarkably normal names – no Kylies and Chantals, but Jamie, Mark, Jonathan and David. They range in age from eight to two, and although the children are no worse behaved than ours (or rather no worse than before Halet), it's clear from Suzie's face that they're a handful. She's thirty-four apparently, but she looks about fifty-four. The bags under her eyes are so large they could line wheelie bins, and her hair is prematurely grey. I told Dom that she should be on a makeover programme, as underneath she looked quite attractive. He told me that he was working on it. Obviously.

It was clear that Suzie was rather overawed by being on TV, and was convinced that I was famous.

'I'm so pleased to meet you,' she said.

'Thanks so much for having us here.'

I felt a little like a politician as I looked around her house, as if I were evaluating the state of one of my constituents. It was small, but she managed to keep it tidy, and what furniture she had was in reasonable condition. The children were in reasonable condition as well, and when we were introduced to them they all seemed very polite.

'I can't quite work out why we're here,' I told Suzie.

'You seem to have everything under control.'

'Thank you,' she said. 'I do my best, but one can always do better! I think your management idea sounds excellent. If I ever had the time, I'd want to be a management consultant.'

'Really? Where do you work at the moment?'

'I'm the number two at a leisure centre in town. It's quite full-on, especially as the boss has been sick for a few months.'

'So you run a leisure centre and four children?'

'That's right! My mum helps a bit, but she's got a bad hip and has been waiting ages for an operation, and it makes it hard for her to get around.'

'Blimey,' I said, and meant it.

A little later, I spoke to Dom.

'I have really no idea what I'm going to do with her,' I said.

'I know what you mean,' he said. 'She's a fucking saint. When the researcher said four kids, four fathers, I thought perfect. I even checked the postcode on our market-research database, and that said this area was all chav heaven, so I just assumed from the researcher's notes that she'd be a real Waynetta. But she's not!'

'Too right – she's more of a Sophie or a Charlotte.'

'She's quite fit as well.'

'I thought that too.'

'I've an idea for a programme.'

'What?'

'*Make Me A Sloane.* She'd be ideal!'

'You're right,' I said. 'Give her an Alice band and a pony between her legs, and you're there.'

Dom scribbled down a note, and I had no doubt that *Make Me A Sloane* would appear on our screens within the next 24 months.

'This still doesn't solve our problem,' I said.

Dom chewed the end of his pen.

'I know what you're thinking,' I said.

'What?'

'You're wondering where the nearest chemist is, aren't you? You're thinking that if you can get hold of something that can make this lot hyperactive, we can have a show on our hands.'

Dom laughed a little too hard.

'I wasn't actually, but I was thinking of ways in which we could make them behave worse.'

'And?' I asked.

'And I couldn't think of any. Come on – you're the dad, surely you must know of something we can do?'

'The thing is, one spends most of one's time thinking up ways of making one's children behave better, not worse. This is quite a novel situation.'

'Hmm,' went Dom.

'Hmm,' went I.

Then I had an idea.

'Why not just feed them to the gills with fizzy drinks and E-numbers?'

'Not bad,' said Dom. 'But she'd never allow it. She seems far too sensible, and besides, you can't slip that

256

sort of thing into their food quite so subtly as pharmaceuticals.'

'OK,' I said. 'Perhaps we could just ask her. We could say, "Look, this programme is about children who behave like brats, and your children are not brats, so could you make them appear to be brats and then we've got a programme."'

'Honesty, eh?'

'Well . . . I thought it might be worth a try.'

We carried on thinking.

'Or we could create some sort of disaster at her work,' I suggested. 'So she's forced to take her eye off the ball on the domestic front and the children go a little haywire.'

'This is sounding good,' said Dom.

'Perhaps somebody could drown in the pool,' I said.

'Wow! You're getting worse than me!'

'All right, maybe not that extreme, but you know what I mean. And then we can get the granny in with her dodgy hip to look after the children. Lots of sympathy, and the programme will show that even a lame old dear can look after four children with WonderHubby's techniques.'

Dom gave me a high five, or rather he attempted to give me a high five. Unfortunately I'm not terribly good at high fives, and I missed. We tried again, and we sort of clipped each other's little fingers, which was somewhat painful.

'OK,' said Dom. 'This is great. All we need to do is

engineer a disaster at the leisure centre, and we should be on.'

'What are you going to do?'

Dom smirked.

'Don't you worry. I'll think of something.'

'But please,' I said. 'No deaths.'

'I promise.'

Tuesday 13 May

When we arrived a little after eight o'clock, Suzie was on the phone. She looked ashen-faced, as the tabloids would say.

'Legionnaires' disease? Are you quite sure?'

Dom winked at me. At first I thought he really had killed somebody, until:

'And are they going to be all right? They are? Thank God for that.'

We listened patiently to the rest of her side of the conversation. Toby started setting up his camera, but Dom made him put it down, which was cunningly sensitive.

'So where are they now? . . . Still in hospital? . . . Do you think I should see them? . . . No? OK . . . What do we have to do? . . . You're joking! For how long? . . . A week? But Mr Thompson will be so angry . . . I know it can't be helped . . . Drain the pool? . . . Oh God, this is terrible . . . Anything else? . . . Just drain the pool and decontaminate the gym and the toilets and the changing rooms . . . And the kitchen? . . . Right . . . I'll be in as soon as I can . . . I'll try and get my mum to take the kids to school . . . OK, Ian, thanks . . . Yup . . . see you in a mo.'

'What's happened?' asked Dom.

'Something terrible,' she replied. 'A couple of people have contracted legionnaires' disease, and the Health and Safety people think that it's from our pool.'

'I'm so sorry,' said Dom.

'Me too,' I said, but I really meant it, because Suzie looked genuinely upset.

'I've got to get over there right now,' she said. 'But I've also got to get the kids to school, and then get David to his playgroup.'

'Normally we don't like to offer any practical help,' said Dom, 'but in this case I think we should make an exception. Perhaps we could pick up your mother?'

'Would you really?' she asked. 'She could take David down to the playgroup. You sure you're sure? That would be wonderful.'

'I'm sure,' said Dom. 'Perhaps Sam and I could get her – I expect we'll be seeing a lot more of her this week, and maybe it would be a good idea if she and Sam bonded a little bit.'

'I don't know how to thank you! This is a complete nightmare.'

Within five minutes Dom and I were in the car on our way to Suzie's mother, who we now knew to was called Maureen.

'Legionnaires' disease?' I said to Dom. 'Really?'

Dom chuckled contentedly.

259

'Not really. But at the moment we've got two researchers giving a very good impression of it.'

'But it'll cost the leisure centre a fortune having to drain the pool and disinfect the whole place.'

'They'll be insured, and besides these places can normally do with a clean, can't they?'

Dom had a point. Our local pool seems to breed more bacteria than the average hospital ward. Dip the children in the water and hey presto! A fun new skin disease called molloscum! An exciting new cough!

'But maybe Suzie will be sacked?'

'She won't,' said Dom. 'People never get sacked these days.'

'Really? I did.'

Dom didn't say anything. For once, he looked genuinely sheepish.

Maureen was in a worse state than we had expected. The poor woman could barely walk, and it took about five minutes just to get her into the car.

'Are you sure you're OK?' I said.

'I'll be fine, dear,' she replied. 'But who are you two anyway?'

We briefly explained who we were.

'So am I going to be on the telly?'

'You are indeed,' said Dom. 'I suspect you will be the star of the show.'

'In that case, I think I shall buy one.'

'Buy what?' asked Dom.

'A telly, of course.'

Dom's eyes, Tube logo.

'You mean you actually don't have a TV?' he asked

'That's right. I never saw the point. There's so much to be getting on with besides the telly. I have friends who watch the bloody thing all day and it rots their brains, I can tell you. From what I've heard, it's just full of programmes about doing up houses. That, or doing up people. You would have thought some people could get a life.'

Dom went silent. I allowed myself a covert smile. I looked in the rear-view mirror and studied our passenger. She must have been in her late sixties, and shared her daughter's good features. Occasionally those features would contort as a bolt of pain from her hip shot up her body. It was painful even to watch.

'Do you need anything?' I asked. 'Perhaps we could stop at a chemist?'

'No it's all right, dear. I'm drugged up to the eyeballs as it is.'

'OK, well, just let us know.'

We arrived back at Suzie's just as she was leaving to take the three children to school. Toby was filming her, and as she looked stressed and flustered, it was making great TV in Dom's eyes. Once again I thought it an abuse, but I felt even worse than after what had happened with the Sincocks because it was basically my idea. We waved Suzie goodbye, and wished her luck, and then we turned our attention to Maureen and little David.

'So how do you normally get him to the playgroup?' I asked.

'Well, obviously I walk him down there.'

'And how far is it?'

'It's about half a mile.'

'Half a mile? How long does it take you?'

'Depends on the old hip. Sometimes ten minutes, sometimes the best part of thirty minutes.'

She let out a wince of pain.

'Well I don't think you should be walking anywhere today,' I said. 'We'll give you a lift down.'

'Honestly love, that's very sweet, but I'm fine.'

She didn't look it.

'I really think we should,' I said.

At this point Dom pulled me aside.

'Perhaps we should let her try,' he said. 'Just to get some footage.'

'Really?' I asked. 'But she looks in terrible pain.'

Dom went and spoke to her.

'Do you think you might be able to manage a little walk?' he asked in that condescendingly high-pitched voice that people use with old people. (Not that Maureen is that old.)

'Of course I can manage!' she said. 'Honestly, all this fuss!'

'OK,' said Dom.

Once more I reflected on a spectacular display of faux sensitivity by Dom. It was excruciating to watch Maureen take little David by the hand and walk down the road. In fact, he was the faster of the two, and it was more a case of him leading her.

'Hurry up Nan!' said David mercilessly.

She did her best, but it was clear that the going was too tough. Bone was rubbing against bone, and although that doesn't sound as though it should be painful, I'm told that it is.

'Come on Dom,' I hissed after she had struggled for about thirty yards, 'that's got to be enough.'

'Let's just give it another ten yards.'

'For fuck's sake! How much more do we need?'

I could see another bolt tear through her body.

'Right, that's enough,' I said, and ran forward. I could hear Dom tutting, but I just ignored it. I reached Maureen and David, and told her that she really didn't need to continue.

'But I must take David to his playgroup,' she insisted.

'But we can help you,' I said. 'I can give you a lift. You're clearly in a lot of pain, and I really don't want you to suffer on our account.'

Her eyes were wet, and she was struggling hard not to cry.

'Come on Maureen, I insist.'

'But I must do it,' she said. 'I really must. I don't want to let Susan down.'

'I know,' I said. 'And you won't be.'

The pride was easy to understand. This was a woman who didn't watch TV, and was therefore presumably pretty active, or at least used to be. Clearly the idea of not being able to do something as simple as walking her grandson to his playgroup was more emotionally painful than the physical pain of trying to do so.

'It just makes me so angry,' she said. 'I've been

waiting two years for a hip, and the bloody health service keeps letting me down. Two operations cancelled, all at the last bloody minute, and every time it's cancelled it's another four-month bloody wait.'

She paused to wince again.

'OK,' I said. 'Here's a plan. We'll drive up to the playgroup, we'll take some shots of your dropping David off, and then we'll drive back to Suzie's and have a cuppa.'

'Whisky?' she asked.

'A cup of whisky?'

She smiled.

'Fooled you there!'

I laughed. I liked her enormously, and if she had really meant it about the whisky I wouldn't have blamed her.

Suzie rang a little later to tell us the news.

'Well, it wasn't legionnaires' in the end,' she said.

'Thank God for that,' I said.

'It was all a bit strange – the two patients just discharged themselves from hospital. They said they were feeling a lot better and just left.'

'So does that mean that you guys are off the hook?'

Suzie sighed.

'I wish! Health and Safety are still making us drain the pool and get the whole place disinfected.'

'How long is that going to take?'

'Until Friday, and it'll mean working late. I really don't know how much of a help I'm going to be with your programme, I'm so sorry.'

'Not at all,' I said.

'Perhaps we can make it another week.'

'No need,' I said, 'we've decided to focus on your mum instead.'

'My mum?'

'That's right. Is that OK?'

'Er, I guess, if she's OK with it? But you must remember her hip is really bad, and she won't be able to do very much. Normally I just ask her to fetch the children from school and give them their tea if I'm running late.'

'Well we can do all that.'

'But I thought the programme was all about watching how I did it and then advising me?'

'We can do that with both you and your mum.'

'You sure?'

'Absolutely.'

After I put the phone down Dom took me to one side.

'This wasn't the idea at all,' he said.

'Oh?'

'The idea was that we were just going to let granny get on with it, and watch the chaos that ensued.'

'But she's not capable of doing anything!'

'That's not our fault. What if we weren't here? What would happen then?'

'But the reason why she's here at all is because of us!'

'How do you mean?' Dom asked.

'Because of the cock and bull story about the leisure centre, of course.'

'All right, all right, but we've got to get some fuck-ups on cam. These people are too normal, and you're being too nice to them.'

'Compromise?'

'What?'

'We help them out today, and then tomorrow we let it play its natural course.'

Dom scratched his stubble, and then he grinned.

'I've got it,' he said. 'We put up some cameras around the house, and then make her wear a "GrannyCam", which will show her point of view. I'll then say we've got to be off filming something else, and we can just watch what happens remotely.'

'Very Big Brother,' I said.

'Well, why not cross formats once in a while?'

'Why not indeed.'

We hardly did any filming after that. I picked the children up from school in the car, although the edit will make it look as though Maureen did it. We cooked the tea, and the four children ate it all up, and even said their pleases and thank-yous, annoyingly enough. While all this was going on the crew were rigging up the house with cameras everywhere barring the lavatory. Then they showed Maureen how to attach her GrannyCam. (That's probably also the name of a website I don't want to look at.) We left when Suzie got back, which was at 6.30. We told her what was happening tomorrow, and although she looked unsure, Dom insisted that Maureen would be fine, and that a researcher would be watching it from our hotel, and if there was a problem, we could pop round and sort it out.

Suzie still looked doubtful, as did I.

Wednesday 14 May

It felt immensely voyeuristic to sit and watch somebody get on with their life, but that's what we've done all day. Well, nearly all day.

We dropped Maureen off first thing in the morning, and from then on we sat back to watch the 'show' in a mini-studio that Dom had set up in his hotel room. Because GrannyCam was streaming over the Internet the quality was a bit jerky, but we got a good idea of what was going on. At times we got far too good an idea, as Maureen kept forgetting to turn off the GrannyCam when she went to the lavatory. Although this wasn't as visually disconcerting as it might have been, it was more aurally offensive.

We watched everything – Suzie supervising the kids brushing their teeth, Suzie repeatedly asking whether her mother was going to be all right, Suzie leaving for work, Maureen getting their coats on, Maureen hobbling to school. This was particularly painful to watch, and although she said that she had taken some industrial-strength painkillers, we could still hear her wincing as she walked. However, when she looked after David she managed brilliantly – taking him to the swings, feeding the ducks, all the cliché granny things.

At three o'clock she hobbled back to school to pick up the children. By this point Dom was desperate for things to go pear-shaped.

'C'mon you little beauties,' he said. 'One of you pick a fight. Or fall over. Something naughty, please.'

Instead, the walk back home went without incident.

As did much of the afternoon.

As did teatime.

By then Dom was literally tearing his hair out. I thought people only did that in cartoons, but Dom really was.

'For fuck's sake!' he shouted at the screens. 'Can one of you bloody kids just piss around!'

'Are you sure you haven't drugged them?' I asked.

Dom took this badly.

'No of course I haven't!'

'Joke! Joke!'

'I'm going to kill the fucking researcher who found this lot. Who was it, Emma?'

'I think it was Nicola,' said Emma.

'Didn't she ever meet these fucking people? Didn't she realise they were saints?'

'I don't think she did.'

'Why the fuck not?'

'Because you wouldn't give her any petrol allowance to drive down here, remember?'

'Oh.'

It was always nice to watch Dom being skewered by his own actions.

We carried on watching, and then, just as the children were finishing their tea, Maureen let out an enormous scream of pain.

'My hip! My hip!' she kept crying.

The GrannyCam then went all sort of skewy, and when we cut to the kitchen cam we could see that she had fallen. The two younger children started laughing, whereupon the older two laid into them.

'Don't laugh at Nan!' said Jamie (I think).

And then, much to Dom's delight, a fight broke out. Plates, cutlery, cups – all were thrown, some of which landed on Granny, who moaned as every new missile impacted.

'This is perfect,' said Dom, 'just perfect.'

I shook my head in disbelief.

'The poor woman's in agony, and you think this is perfect?'

'She'll be OK, she's just fallen over. Where are you going, anyway?'

I had stood up and was feeling for my car keys in my pocket.

'I'm going to help her, Dom. That's what people do when they see other people in trouble.'

'She's fine! She'll get up in a sec and take another painkiller.'

I opened my mouth, but nothing came out.

I drove round as quickly as I could, only to find that the door was locked. I knocked on it furiously, and although I could hear the children running riot inside, they couldn't hear me (or chose not to). I then decided that as it would take too long to knock on neighbours' doors to see if they had any keys, I would just have to break the door down.

Easier said than done. At first I tried it with my shoulder, but all that did was hurt. I then remembered that the best thing to do was to actually kick the door in, which I tried next. I kicked hard, the door didn't open, and then, because I had been bracing myself to go forward, I lost my balance and fell arse over tit. Nice one, Holden. Thank God I wasn't an SAS trooper at the Iranian Embassy siege.

'What are you doing?' asked a neighbour. She had a hairnet, but not a rolling pin.

'I'm trying to break in.'

'Why? Are you a burglar?'

'No! But do you know Suzie's mum Maureen? She's had a nasty fall and she's trapped inside with the children. Do you have a key?'

'No. And how do you know she's had a fall?'

'Because I saw it on film.'

'You saw it on a film?'

'Never mind,' I said, whereupon I stepped back and gave the door an almighty kick. Kerpang! Thank God for that, I thought, not just for the sake of Maureen, but also for my dignity.

I rushed in. The children looked startled, and little David was crying. Some paternal instinct made me want to pick him up and give him a quick cuddle, but I thought it best to attend to Maureen first. She looked in a bad way. Not about-to-be-dead bad, but bad in a should-be-in-bed-and-not-looking-after-four-small-children way. She was moaning gently, and repeating, 'My hip, my hip'.

'It's OK Maureen, I'm here now. Do you think you could get up?'

'I don't know, love. Can you help me?'

I noticed that her clothes were covered in food that the children had thrown at her. That made me think of Dom, and then made me uncomfortably aware that I was being filmed. I tried lifting Maureen up, and each time I did so she moaned in agony. The situation was clearly getting worse, and the children had finally realised that Nan was not playing.

'Listen,' I said. 'I'm going to call an ambulance.'

'Don't do that!' she snapped. 'I'm perfectly OK. I just need a little time.'

'Maureen, I don't think that you are. I reckon you may have hurt yourself more than you realise. If you're feeling this much pain through the painkillers, you ought to be in a hospital.'

'I've fallen over before,' she said. 'I just need a few minutes. I don't want to waste anyone's time.'

'You won't be,' I said.

The ambulance arrived in ten minutes, and within five minutes she was in the back of it. ('Broken hip I suspect,' said one of the paramedics.)

'Is Nan dead?' asked one of the children.

'No, she's just hurt her leg.'

'I thought when people go to hospital they die.'

271

'No they don't,' I said. 'Some people do, but not your granny, because she's very strong.'

'What's a granny?'

This was not the time to explain that one, so I turned on the TV and sat them in front of it. I then called the leisure centre, and within ten minutes Suzie was back at home.

'How did it happen?' she asked.

I told her, and she started to cry.

'Poor Mum,' she went. 'It's all my fault, I should never have asked her.'

'It's not your fault,' I said. 'You had no choice.'

'Maybe I could have asked a friend. I should have asked my neighbour Dawn, that's who.'

More tears.

I put an arm round her gently.

'It's not your fault,' I said. 'It's our fault, it's this bloody TV programme.'

'That's kind of you to say, but it is my responsibility.'

She picked up the phone and called Dawn, who came round ten minutes later. I decided that I was intruding, and, after checking that I wasn't needed, I left.

When I got back to the hotel Dom gave me a high five, which I neglected to return.

'That was great!' he said. 'WonderHubby to the rescue!'

'Oh cut it out,' I said. 'That woman's got a broken hip because of us.'

'It'll heal. But you should see the footage! We've even got the camera in the hall showing you kicking in the door! It's like some cop show. Brilliant! And then the stuff of you trying to lift her up, and then the ambulance turning up – we can dub in some nice sirens – all great, just great.'

'I think I'm going to go home,' I said.

'No problemo,' he said. 'I think this one's in the can.'

'But we can't have got a show out of this.'

'Wanna bet? We can make a show out of anything.'

Friday 16 May

I rang Suzie today to see how her mother was. Her hip was indeed broken, but it was a blessing of sorts, as they had to operate then and there. Unbelievably, we had done her a good turn. I then asked how the leisure centre was.

'It looks great! And the pool has never been so clean. In fact, the whole place feels brand new! I think we're going to get a lot more members.'

'Wow. Kind of a cloud with a silver lining then.'

'Exactly! I don't know what it is about you, but you brought both disasters and miracles.'

'Well, the Chinese ideogram for crisis is the same as the one for opportunity,' I said.

'That sounds very clever,' she said. 'Where did you learn that?'

'I wish I could say to you, "Oh, I just happen to speak Chinese" but I'm afraid not.'

'So how then?'

'Er . . . Trivial Pursuit, I think.'

273

Saturday 17 May

Sally was appalled by what had happened and made her feelings very clear. She said that it was amazing that nobody had died. I agreed. I said that if the series continues like this, Dom and I would be in prison for manslaughter. Perhaps I need to take out some form of insurance.

Monday 19 May

Dom has emailed a schedule of the remaining shoots. It looks exhausting, and it's going to take me all the way through to July. God knows how many more lives we will wreck. I emailed back:

> Dom
> thanks for the schedule. It certainly looks exhausting! I just hope that we manage to get through it without being sued. I'm being serious about this. It's bloody lucky that Suzie and her mum haven't done us for what happened. Or the Sincocks. So far we must have committed around a dozen offences, all of which could have seen us in prison. When I signed up for this, I knew that I would have to take some scales off my eyes, but I didn't realise that I would have to become a criminal.
> I really need your assurance that we're going to play it straight from now on.
> Best
> Sam

His reply came back about ten minutes later.

> Sam
> No prob
> Dom

This hardly inspires me, but what else can I do? I'm in so deep, the money's spent, and all I can console myself with is the fact that nobody's been actually killed.

Monday 26 May

Just back from filming up in Scotland. For once, and probably never to be repeated, it genuinely WENT WELL. Amazing! The family were a nice bunch, but just naughty enough for Dom, and, incredibly, they actually reacted well to some of my HCP techniques. The incentivisation and disincentivisation charts worked really well, and by the end of the week there was a distinct improvement. What was also gratifying was that nobody was killed or wounded.

The only thing that was strange was that Dom kept having bad-tempered conversations with someone on the telephone. He was quite careful not to let anybody earwig, but I did manage to catch the end of one of them.

'Well, I can't help it . . . It's just the way I am . . . I know, I know . . . but I thought you would understand . . . OK . . . OK . . . Yes, I agree, best not to talk about it on the phone . . . all right . . . see ya.'

All very mysterious.

Thursday 29 May

Why do I always keep bumping into Emily in the wretched supermarket? She actually seemed slightly more friendly, but I refused to engage her in conversation. I think she's got a guilty conscience.

Sunday 1 June

Last night was our wedding anniversary, and we went to Rookster Hall for dinner. It's our nearest country house hotel, and as such, it should do some good food. But it doesn't. In fact, it is dismal, stuffy, overpriced and just shit, frankly.

The first warning sign was when they made me put on a tie. I couldn't believe it. It wasn't as if I was wearing jeans, and I had on a stylish (I thought) royal blue linen jacket and a white linen shirt. Sally looked lovely, and before we went out we congratulated each other on how glam we were.

But not the right sort of glam for one David Bird, who said that I could either wear a tie or we could eat in the bar, which wasn't exactly the idea. So I wore the fucking thing, and it looked utterly absurd with the linen shirt, which was clearly not designed to take a piece of neckwear, especially polyester neckwear. I just don't get it, this obsession with ties – I looked far far worse wearing it than without.

Bad sign number two was that our gin and tonics were execrable. They were warm, the tonic was flat, and a miserable piece of old peel floated on each. When I complained the barman looked at me as if I were an out-and-out tosser, despite the fact that I complained politely. I felt like telling him he was a fucking hick, but fights and wedding anniversaries seldom mix. Oh yes, and the crisps were stale.

The next bad sign was the emptiness of the dining room. Despite it being a Saturday night, the only people there were a middle-aged couple, an elderly couple and a man about my age reading a trashy WWII thriller by someone called Guy Walters. We weren't expecting a room full of the young and the beautiful, but we were expecting a little more liveliness.

Then came the menus – enormous things, full of overly complicated dishes that you just knew couldn't be cooked there and then. And if they couldn't be cooked there and then, that could only mean one thing – they were basically all ready meals, ready to be pinged in the microwave, and ready to be met with the derision they deserved. Eventually we both opted for soup, and Sally went for some monkfish and I for steak. How would sir like it cooked? What an irrelevant bloody question that was. Whatever you answer, it will always come back well done.

The soup was fine, but our main courses were terrible. The plates had been microwaved along with the food, and although I have no objections to microwaves for heating things up, they are not ovens. They do not cook things. They simply make things hot. Thus our food was hot and not cooked and it was expensively revolting. We didn't bother with pudding, neither did we go back to the bar for a coffee or a whisky. We just wanted to get out.

The price for all this? £150. Fuck knows how. But there you go. The middle-class curse: paying far too much money for shit food because we don't have high ceilings at home. Madness.

Wednesday 4 June

This week we're up in London with a family called the Desmonds. Again, it seems to be going well. Children are normally bad, and the mother, Sarah, I reckon suffers from depression and lets them watch far too much TV. The Holden Childcare Programme simply involves minimising the TV watching, after which everything has sort of fallen into place. Of course, I've made it seem far more in-depth than that, and I think she's fallen for it.

It feels good to have been in London, and I've spent most evenings getting smashed with old friends. This has meant hangovers during filming, but nobody seems to notice.

Friday 6 June

Today I overheard another mysterious Dom phone call, or at least the first bit of it.

'. . . I'm sure you can get used to it . . . it's not as if it's that strange . . . don't be like that . . .'

And then he noticed that I was near and moved off. I wonder what it's about?

Monday 9 June

I know now. Oh boy do I know now. Hahahahahahaha! Who would have thought it? Anyway, to begin at the beginning.

Once again I bumped into you-know-who at the supermarket. But this time she looked really upset, and even more keen to talk to me. Because I'm a complete softie, and because I'm so nosy, I asked her what the matter was.

'I've split up with Dom,' she said, clutching her shopping list.

'I'm, er, sorry to hear that,' I lied.

'I know you're not.'

'All right, I'm not.'

It was tempting to play the hard cold fish (if such a role can be played), but I couldn't find it in me. In fact, I'm old enough to know that it's not actually in me at all, so there's no real point in looking for it.

'But I guess I'm sorry for you,' I continued. 'I thought things were going well.'

'I thought so too,' she said.

'So why did it end?'

Emily looked around.

'I don't think I can really talk about it here.'

'Fair enough.'

'Can you come over after you've unpacked your shopping?'

I thought about this hard, I really did. This woman has caused me no end of fucking grief with her lies and flirtatiousness, so why did I owe her any of my time? A reasonable response would have been, 'Fuck you Emily, I owe you nothing', but the actual response was:

'Of course.'

And so at 11.35 I found myself knocking on her door, and her asking whether it was too early for a glass of white and me saying of course not because if you've split up with someone a glass of wine at coffee time is just what you need and besides who cares.

'So why did you split up?'

'Do you swear not to tell anyone else, not even Sally?'

Again, this is another thing about myself that I have given up trying to improve. I am incapable of keeping secrets. So when people ask me that question, I now always say 'No,' except for today when I went, 'Yes.'

Emily took a big big swig of wine.

'It's because he's weird in bed.'

'Weird in bed?'

'Yes.'

'What sort of weird?'

'Very weird.'

By now I was actually rubbing my thighs in glee.

'Come on!' I went.

'I don't know if I should tell you. Perhaps I'm being unfair on him. After all, he can't help it.'

Jesus, I thought, how bad could this be? If it was too

racy for Emily, it must have been immensely bloody racy.

'Stop teasing me!'

Emily took another swig.

'All right,' she said. 'But you promise promise promise?'

'Yes, yes, yes!'

'He's got a fetish.'

'Yes?'

'It's a strange one.'

'Well, we've probably all got one of those.'

'Yes, but this isn't like asking your girlfriend to dress up as a maid, or spank you, or tie you to the bed, or wear rubber or high heels or anything like that.'

(That all sounded rather good, I thought.)

'OK?'

'This one's REALLY strange.'

'What is it?'

'He likes to dress as a baby.'

'WHAT?'

'That's right, and he even has to wear a nappy.'

'A nappy!'

'And a dummy. And he insists on making these goo goo noises and asking to suck milk from my tits.'

'MILK!'

By now I was shrieking like a teenage girl who was listening to her best friend describe giving her first blow job. (I'm so imagining that. Maybe such conversations take place in an atmosphere of respect and reverence for the male member, but I'm guessing not.)

'And he wears a bonnet!'

'A BONNET? You've got to be fucking kidding.'

'I wish I was.'

'But . . . but . . . but . . .'

So many questions, but which one first?

'But . . . but . . . but what . . . what does he actually do?'

'Well, he insists on lying on the bed dressed like that – and he has a teddy bear by the way – and I have to talk to him as if I were his mother, you know, sing him nursery rhymes and things like that.'

'Holy cow. But why did you agree to do it?'

Emily chewed her bottom lip, and then drained her glass. I quickly refilled it, hoping it would make her even more indiscreet, although as this was the most indiscreet conversation that has ever taken place, more alcohol hardly seemed necessary. She thought for a bit longer and then:

'Well, I think everybody has their "thing", you know?'

'I do.'

I briefly thought about my 'thing'.

'And I think one should be tolerant of people's things. Because people's things are important parts of their sexuality, and so long as it's not illegal and doesn't involve shit, then I'm pretty much game. I had one boyfriend who liked to be spanked with sausages.'

'Raw or cooked?'

'Gosh, what a strange question. Um, raw. He liked them in a string, you know.'

'And did you eat them afterwards?'

'God no!'

'It's only because I have a thing for sausages as well,' I said.

Emily studied my face.

'You're taking the piss, aren't you?'

'Of course!'

'Fuck! I totally believed you for a second.'

'Anyway, you were talking about "things".'

Another mouthful of wine. She was really putting it away.

'Well,' she said, 'I really respected him for telling me what his thing was. It can't have been easy. So I went along with it, partly out of curiosity. But the problem was, after we had done our first session with him as a baby, I just couldn't take him seriously at all. All I could see was this gangly figure on the bed, wearing his nappy – God knows where he got that from – and with his bonnet and dummy and teddy bear and making all these goo goo noises.'

'And would you . . . you know?'

'What? Have sex?'

'Er, yes.'

'Yes we would. I had to go on top and he would go goo goo as we did it.'

'Jesus.'

We both took glugs of wine. This was huge news.

'But what I don't understand,' I said, 'was what made you split up? I mean, it sounds as though you'd taken it all on board.'

Emily looked me in the eye.

'Are you sure you want to hear this?'

'Probably not.'

(I was trying to sound cool about it. Yeah, right.)

'Well, it was about our third or fourth baby session, and about halfway through, before we got to the actual sex bit, he asks if I can change his nappy.'

'What? Had he wet it? Ha ha! How rank!'

But Emily had gone quite solemn.

'Worse than that.'

Cogs whirred in my brain. They didn't have to whir that much.

'YOU'RE JOKING!'

'I wish I was, I can't tell you how utterly disgusting it was. He kept going, "Mummy, change nappy," and the smell was something else.'

I started to feel physically sick. Unfortunately, I am very good at visualising things, and the sense of nausea was very real. I took another swig of wine to try to mask the virtual stench that was wafting over my olfactory nerves.

'You didn't change it, did you?'

'Fuck no! I walked straight out there and then! It was the grossest thing I'd ever seen!'

'That's saying something.'

'What do you mean?'

'Sorry, sort of came out the wrong way.'

Emily let it go.

'Anyway, I told him the following day that was that, and he pleaded and grovelled and begged. You know what you men are like. But as I said, I don't do shit, and what really annoyed me is that he KNEW that, because I told him before we had our "what's your thing" conversation.'

'Jolly rude of him.'

Emily giggled.

'Stop it. It's not that funny, you know.'

I tried not to laugh, but I couldn't, and soon we were both in hysterics. After we recovered, Emily swiftly became somewhat maudlin.

'So now I'm single again.'

Uh-oh, I thought.

'And,' she continued, 'I said some beastly things about you.'

I got up from the chair.

'Yes you did,' I said. 'And despite all this laughter about Dom, I'm really angry with you for telling him a pack of lies. You know he tried to blackmail me with them?'

'I do, yes.'

'Well, it was fucking unpleasant.'

'Believe me Sam, I'm so terribly sorry. I really am. It was foul of me to have said those things. I guess I was annoyed at not being on the programme, and a whole load of other things as well.'

'What other things?'

'Oh, they're not important.'

'No go on, what other things?'

Emily got up and fetched her handbag, out of which she extracted a packet of cigarettes.

'Would you like one?'

'Go on then.'

We lit our cigarettes and remained standing. Emily started picking at a scab on her arm.

'Other things,' she said gently under her breath.

'I'm all ears.'

I knew what she was going to say.

'Oh godammit Sam, are you really so thick? Can't you guess what it is?'

'I think I can,' I said. 'But if it's what I'm thinking, then it would feel somewhat arrogant to assume it.'

'In that case you're thinking the right thing.'

'I am?'

Emily's eyes looked watery as she stared at me.

'Yes you are, because you must already know that I love you very much.'

My hand shook as I took a drag of my cigarette. I was totally blindsided by this. Even though I had no intention of acting upon Emily's declaration (how Jane Austen that sounds) it still felt like a big moment. Here was somebody declaring their love for me. (To think that I just thought that she fancied me.) The last person who had done that was Sally, and that was many moons ago. (I'm not referring to all the subsequent I Love Yous, I'm talking about the first one, the really BIG one which feels like such a risk when you say it, because there's always that little bit of you that worries whether a rather big bit of them doesn't really love you that much, and that the whole thing has just been about fondness and sex.) I didn't know what to say. Normal procedure is to say 'I love you' back, but this was not normal, and neither would I have been telling the truth.

'So,' she said. 'There it is. I love you, Sam Holden. I have for a long time, because you are a wonderful man. You're kind and thoughtful and funny and not bad-looking at all . . . and I really really want to know what your thing is.'

I laughed nervously.

Another drag of my cigarette. More wine. It felt like the type of talk one should be having twelve hours later, not in the middle of the day. And, funnily enough, now that the air was cleared, there seemed very little to say. It almost felt anticlimactic.

'You must understand, Emily, that I love Sally. Only Sally. You do realise that?'

She nodded.

'And I'm one of those boringly monogamous types, as you've probably worked out.'

'More's the pity.'

I know what she wanted to ask me. Just because I loved Sally, that didn't mean I couldn't love someone else. But the fact is, even though I think you can love two people, I just don't love Emily. But I thought the kindest thing to do was to lie.

'And I'm also one of those people who can only love one person at a time.'

Emily nodded ruefully.

'You don't even love me just a teensy bit?'

I shook my head.

'I'm sorry,' I said. 'Perhaps it would be different if I were single or in another life, you know. But this is who

I am, and I love Sally. That's not to say that I don't think that you're great fun and that you're attractive . . .'

'But you just don't love me. I'd rather you found me boring and ugly and yet loved me. Do you get that?'

'Yes I do.'

(No I didn't. Because I'm a man probably.)

I flicked my cigarette into the fireplace, where it smouldered. I watched the smoke curl up, and I tried to attach some symbolism to it, but I couldn't be arsed.

'Well, there it is,' said Emily.

She looked at the fireplace.

'Yes, there it is,' I agreed

'I love you and you don't love me. And I shall just have to get on with it. As you can probably guess, I'm somewhat used to getting my own way in this department, and I'm not very good at coping with rejection.'

'But Emily, it's not really rejection. That kind of says I'm throwing you away. You should think of it as, I don't know, running into some kind of force-field or barrier. There's a point you can't get past. But that point is not throwing you back. You can stay at that point for as long as you need, and if you choose to walk away, that's your choice.'

'OK.'

'Do you see?'

'I think so. But what I want to know is this. How close is that point, this force field or whatever, how close is that to your heart? I know that sounds very soppy, but I need to know for sure.'

I looked at her directly. I wanted her to be convinced that my response was completely sincere.

'Emily, that point is miles away from my heart. Do you understand?'

Her eyes looked puffy, and she wiped them with the back of her hand.

'Yes,' she whispered.

'I'm sorry.'

And I felt it. I felt really sorry for her. Sorry because she had been so honest. Sorry because she was now feeling hurt. Sorry because she had nothing to look forward to. And sorry because I felt protective of her, some sort of skewed paternal thing when confronted with a woman crying.

Normal procedure at this point is to put a comforting arm around the woman in this position. This is a massive error, and can only result in exploratory, tender tear-salted kisses, which then leads on to absolutely amazing sex, and then a declaration of love from the man, and then him regretting it twenty-four hours later, and then being too cowardly to ring her and say that it was a mistake, and her (rightly) feeling that he has just used her.

So I didn't do that.

Instead, I drained my glass and said, 'I think I should go.'

'You don't want to stay for lunch? I got us some nice pâté, you know the salmon one you like.'

'Got us'. There was something touchingly assumptive about those two words, something very uxorious. It's the little combinations of small words like that which I expect you would miss if you were divorced. Her thoughtfulness about the pâté seemed almost contrived, an attempt to woo me. But the 'got us' suggested a partnership, a very man-and-wifey partnership. Sally and I must say it to each other the whole time, and I never think about it. Why should I? I assume the 'us' in my life. Everything is about 'us'.

'I mustn't,' I said. 'And I won't give you some bull that I've got things to do. It's just that I don't think it's fair on you if I stick around and drink wine and smoke fags and have a jolly time. I want you to know that when I walk out that door, it's me saying that I can't return your love, and I can't place myself in situations in which lovers might find themselves.'

'OK, you're beginning to sound a bit pompous now.'

'That was the idea.'

(It wasn't.)

'You'd better go before you get any worse.'

We then made our predictably awkward goodbyes.

So now what? A LOT to think about. Do I tell Sally? I wish somebody could help me with this, but who? Nigel? He'd only tell Clare, and then it would go round everyone. Matt? He'd just laugh, and then say I should poke her. No, I think I've just got to deal with this one on my own. God knows how I'm going to sleep tonight. All I can see when I close my eyes is Dom in his nappy.

Tuesday 15 July

I've been immensely slack with my diary, and the reason for this is simple. Hard bloody work. It's a bit of a shock to the system, frankly. So what have I been up to? Well, because I'm a management consultant at heart, I'm going to bullet-point it:

- Family first: Sally's job keeps reaching new lows. There's no doubt that the information leak is just that, and they're sure that there's a mole in the department. Despite my repeated (and sometimes sincere) protestations that they should give Nick a 'thorough debriefing', Sally is convinced that the traitor is not Nick, and she is getting a little tired of me saying so. The one person who never comes up in conversation is Emily. I decided very quickly that there was no need for Sally to know that Emily was in love with me. Although I really do think that there should be no secrets between husbands and wives, because exchanging secrets is a great way of enhancing trust, I cannot see how telling my wife that another woman – a SEXUAL PREDATOR, no less – has fallen for me will help our marriage. These things happen, one has to be big about them, and even though I am pretty bad at being big, I am doing my best to steer the wisest course.
- Peter and Daisy continue to thrive under Halet, which is good and bad. Good because they are now well disciplined, polite, have got into a good

routine and have progressed well at school and playgroup this term. Bad because, er, this shows up my efforts. And bad because they seem to be amazingly fond of Halet, which makes Sally and me feel jealous. And bad because she won't be with us for ever. I also can't believe how quickly they are growing up. I know this is such a parent cliché, but it's true. Daisy is now a proper little girl, and her talking is quite brilliant (as far as Sally and I are concerned). She is a proper little madam as well, despite Halet's best efforts, and she is very insistent that everything goes just as she likes it. Example: she still drinks out of one of those Doidy cup things, and if the spout isn't exactly 90 degrees to the handles, and therefore directly in line with the Little Mermaid motif, she has a fit. And not just a little tantrum, but a full-on fit. Toast must be cut into triangles, she must have two baths a day, and woe betide anybody who tries to make her wear something that isn't red. Hmmm. I just can't wait for the teenage years. Peter is a lot more laid-back, although like many boys he seems to have a new craze every day. At the moment it is Daleks, and he is insistent that we allow him to watch *Doctor Who*.repeats. This is refused, as it is too scary even for Sally. Protests that best friend Phil is allowed to watch it are given short shrift, although I do not explain that Phil's parents are pretty chavvy, and play computer games the whole time.

- *WonderHubby*: We've finally finished filming! And,

miraculously, nobody got killed or wounded. There were a couple of near misses, however. The worst was when a family of six capsized on a boating lake and the mother (who couldn't swim) nearly drowned. Despite the fact she hated water, Dom had insisted that he wanted them in the boat, as this would make a nice cheesy end-of-programme shot. We finally decided to use the segment with dramatic footage of me running into the lake in an attempt to save her. Please note the word 'attempt', as I did not actually manage to save her. I got bogged down in mud after four yards, and had to be rescued myself. All I succeeded in doing was ruining the contents of my wallet, and discovering that our household insurance does not cover iPods in the event of jumping into lakes, even if it is to save a life. The second near miss was when the Holden Childcare Programme decided that the children should spend a day looking after the parents. (We call this Role Transalignment Bonding.) It started well, and the parents even got breakfast in bed, but when it came to allowing six-year-olds to do the ironing, it ended badly. Thankfully, nobody got burned, but Dom had to cough up for a new living-room carpet and seven new shirts for the dad.

- Now that the series is in the can, Dom and Emma are going to spend the next few weeks editing. I've asked if I can help, but they've decided that it's best, for the sake of the deadline, that they go it alone. The series airs at the beginning of September, and they need to get preview DVDs out as soon as possible.

- The Dom situation: Although he knows that I know that he has split up from Emily, he doesn't know that I know about his 'thing'. And what a 'thing'. However, I think he suspects that I may know something, and as a result, I've found him to be a lot less domineering. And whenever he does try to get arsey with me, I just imagine him crapping himself in his nappy, and then a smile of utter superiority crosses my face. I still can't get over it, and naturally I've told Sally, Nigel, Clare, Victoria, Paddy, Ian, Ed, Adrian, Sam, Rick. Of course, I've sworn them all to secrecy. The one who found it the most hysterical was Sally's sister, who has known Dom for ages, and says that this revelation 'explains a lot'. Apparently he's never really had a serious girlfriend. I can now see why. The only way he's going to find a woman who's willing to indulge his taste is to pay her, and that sort of woman isn't the sort you really want to stay with for ever. I almost feel sorry for the guy, and it makes me realise that I am lucky that my 'thing' is very tame indeed.

- This brings me on to the Emily situation. Since her great DECLARATION, I have kept my distance, for the same reason as when I walked out of her house all those weeks ago. We bump into each other, which is inevitable, and we keep up an air of warm civility. The children like playing with each other, it's just that the adults don't. Or at least one of them knows that he shouldn't. Whenever I drop Peter round for a playdate, she always invites me in for a coffee or a glass of wine. I always politely decline, and her expression is usually a mixture of hurt and annoyance. Perhaps I should accept one of these days. The more I refuse, the more it looks as if I'm trying to steer myself away from temptation, which I'm not. Honest. There is no temptation.

And now we're going to go on holiday. I can't wait. With all our massive *WonderHubby* wealth we've hired this amazing villa in Chiantishire, and we're having a week with just the four of us, and then the second week we're being invaded by Nigel and Clare and all their mob. It's going to be such fun – and, best of all worlds, Halet has agreed to come and help look after the children during the second week. I feel like a millionaire. Sally was reluctant at first, thinking it would be an invasion of our privacy, but I said that I was sure that Halet was enough of a woman of the world to avert her eyes when drunken thirtysomethings decide that skinny-dipping is just the best fun in the world.

Monday 4 August

Holiday was exactly as I had hoped – see separate photo diary for details. The children behaved and the adults misbehaved, which is just as it should be. I now have a tan, and I have restored all the weight lost for and during the filming. What's more, thanks to Halet being around, Sally and I managed to have lots of sex, which made us feel like a couple again. If you don't get round to having sex, or fall out of the habit, then you can end up feeling like just good friends who are bringing up children together. Highlight of the holiday was Nigel appearing in a makeshift nappy after one drunken supper, whereupon Clare ripped it off and chased him round the garden until he fell into the pool. I think you had to be there. I'm just glad the children weren't awake.

Tuesday 5 August

Have just got back from London from seeing the final edits of the programme. I'm both astonished and appalled. Astonished, because they have truly made silk purses out of sows' ears. Appalled, because the level of deceit that the viewer is being exposed to is almost criminal.

'Wouldn't it have been easier to just hire actors?' I asked Dom. 'And then got them to sign non-disclosure agreements?'

'We could have done, but I like to think that we make quality programmes.'

'Ah.'

(I wondered what could possibly be inferior, but then I don't have satellite TV.)

'And you can also just tell when actors are acting,' he continued. 'Let's face it, the only actors we could afford are ones that nobody would recognise, and there's often a good reason why an actor is not recognised.'

'Because he's crap?'

'Exactamundo. So, cheaper to use real people, as we don't have to pay them, and when they moan that the editing has made them look bad, everybody ignores it because people always moan about the editing.'

'Cunning.'

'Extremely.'

(The image of Dom in his nappy crossed my mind, but I did my best to get rid of it.)

'What I find amazing,' I said, 'is that it actually looks as if the Holden Childcare Programme really works.'

Dom chuckled.

'I know. Because let's face it, it's a bunch of bollocks, isn't it?'

I honestly didn't know what to make of that, and I still don't. The truth is I'm increasingly undecided about the whole Holden Childcare Programme. Yes, yes, yes, I know deep down that it's probably a load of – sorry, a bunch of – bollocks, but at the same time I still think there is something in it. There's no doubt that the way we bring up our children is entirely haphazard, slap-dash, make-do, on the wing, random. None of us really think it out and plan how we're going to do it. These creatures arrive, and then we just muddle through from day to day, and kid ourselves that we know what we're doing and that we're completely in control.

The fact is, we're not. The children are in control. Not in the sense that they're telling us what to do, but because our lives are entirely based around them. There's nothing wrong with that – in fact, it's just as it should be – but isn't it ridiculous that we don't have a system in place that enables us to be in command of childcare in the same way as a good CEO is in command of his company? It's not that I want my children to behave like cowed employees, but I just want the whole thing to run itself smoothly, and to have a programme that enables that.

Hence the HCP. I think, besides all the management speak, it really has potential. The only problem has been the way it's been applied. I haven't done it successfully at home, and with our six families the whole thing had been hopeless, frankly. Utterly unscientific, and completely chaotic. So much for the observer not reacting with the system. I'm convinced that with at least two or three of the families, a properly established HCP might have yielded some results, perhaps even positive ones.

I pretty much said all this to Dom, who nodded.

'Well, I'm glad you think that,' he said. 'Because you're going to need to be saying that sort of stuff over and over again for the next few months.'

'Really?'

'Oh yes. Have you not seen Emma yet about your media schedule?'

'No.'

So I did. And when I saw her, I was amazed. She read out a long list of magazines, newspapers, TV and radio shows, some of which I had even heard of.

'You're very much in demand,' she said. 'And this is before the preview DVDs go out. We're extremely excited Sam. We think this could be bigger than *Make 'Em Work!*'

'*Make 'Em Work?*'

'Didn't you see it? It was our biggest hit. It was all about getting your kids to do your job for a week. The coalmining one was a hoot.'

'I must have been out or something.'

'Anyway, we think this is going to go far far bigger than that.'

'Wow.'

'Wow indeed. Look – here's a provisional timetable.'

She passed me three sheets of A4.

'You'll see that the first interview is on Monday with Julia Stocks on BBC9. Can you do that?'

'Course I can.'

'Great! Because from now on, these interviews are your 100 per cent priority, OK? No excuses!'

'Who is Julia Stocks anyway?'

'You've never heard of her?'

'Nope.'

'She's an agony aunt-cum–shrink type. You must know her – fat and annoying.'

'I tend not to mix with such people.'

Emma laughed.

'Anyway, she's one of the original feminists. I think she was even there when Emilia Pankhurst chained herself to that horse back in the 1960s.'

There were too many errors in that sentence to even

bother correcting, so I just let it go. Having worked with TV people all these months, I'm used to the staggeringly bad grip that they have on history, or 'facts' in general. In truth, TV people just don't care about the truth. Truth is boring and static, and it shouldn't be obeyed. There's nothing sexy about truth whatsoever.

'Julia has this theory that the whole househusband thing is a load of crap.'

'Does she now?'

'Oh yes! She told me on the phone that it was just a myth put about by men in order to make it look as though feminism had succeeded.'

'Sigh,' I said. 'Will these people never be happy?'

'Of course not! Take away their war, and you take away their reason for living. But you must promise to behave, do you understand? You must be nice to her, or she'll tear you apart.'

'Hah! Tear me apart? Some old braless dungaree-wearer with a crap haircut? Not a chance!'

'Hmm,' went Emma. 'You see, that's the old-fashioned attitude that you need to keep hidden. And please never admit you vote Conservative.'

'Why?'

'Because it's TV death.'

'Really?'

'Yes. Do you remember all those stars in the 1980s who used to make pop records for Maggie at election time?'

'No.'

'My point exactly. They're the same ones who also said they were going to leave the country when Labour got in, and somehow they never got round to it.'

'Interesting, but I don't see why being right wing is TV death. After all, aren't most people in this country pretty right wing?'

'Of course they are! But they're not Conservatives. There's a huge difference. Being right wing is pretty much OK, but being a Tory is a total no-no. Got that?'

'OK, OK, got it, but please don't tell me what to say or think,' I said. 'I react very badly to it.'

'Perhaps we should cancel Julia,' said Emma as she looked down the list.

'Certainly not!' I said. 'Bring her on! I shall answer her questions sensibly and with the intelligence she and her listeners deserve.'

Emma raised an eyebrow.

'I really think we should cancel.'

'I really think we shouldn't.'

Thursday 7 August

We should have cancelled.

The interview was, to put it mildly, a complete and utter fucking disaster. Thank God the BBC9 audience is only in the tens of thousands.

Of course, I took an instant dislike to *Ms* Stocks. And she took an instant dislike to me. It was like the first time chalk and cheese had ever met, and they both knew that their differences were going to be the stuff of metaphor. By the end of our half-hour together, I was tempted to find out whether hitmen listed themselves in Yellow Pages.

The first ten minutes was suitably banal, and I felt at ease plugging the show, and telling her how the childcare programme worked. Of course, had I realised it at the time, I wouldn't have relaxed quite so much, and on reflection, her tactic was to make me drop my guard. The first tricky question was a simple one, but it was loaded with subtext.

'What I find interesting about all this,' she said, 'is the tacit assumption that men are better at just about everything. Your programme seems to strip away centuries of female-led childcare with a kind of "let the man do it" attitude.'

'Do you think so?' I replied.

'I don't know,' she said. 'I was wondering whether you thought it, that's all.'

'You mean if I think men are better at doing things than women?'

'Yes. But with regard to childcare.'

'I don't think we're better, I just think we're different.'

(So far, so good.)

'How?' she asked.

'Well, I think we're different in our approach to childcare in the way that men are different in their approach to lots of things. I think we're much more interested in systems and order than women are. I think we look at a task and try to implement a very logical set of structures in order to complete it. Women, on the other hand, tend to feel their way round a problem, and it's a more instinctive process.'

'And you think that's the case with the way women raise children?'

'Generally speaking, yes.'

(At this point, I knew I was well out of my depth.)

'So you think women are illogical in the way they handle children?'

'No. They're just a little more instinctive. It's a question of emphasis, that's all.'

'But your so-called programme is more than a question of emphasis, isn't it?' she asked. 'I mean, your approach seems to suggest to women, "Come on girls, you've been doing it wrong all this time, here, let a man step in, he'll sort it." '

I sort of laughed.

'I don't think that's what I'm saying at all, Ms Stocks.'

'Really?'

'Yes. All the Holden Childcare Programme is saying is that there is another way of bringing up children.'

'A man's way?'

'My programme could have easily been invented by a woman.'

'But women are more instinctive, you say. They don't use programmes or systems or logic.'

'You're somewhat polarising my position. All I said is that it's a question of emphasis.'

'But there's no way that your programme is just a little bit of emphasis, or a subtle nudge or anything like that. It's a completely revolutionary approach to childcare.'

'Thank you,' I said. 'I'm glad you think so.'

'A male approach to childcare.'

'Not necessarily.'

'Then why is it called *WonderHubby*?'

Again, I sort of laughed – the bitch had me.

'Well, you know, it's just a nice light-hearted title for the show.'

'Yes, but it's all about how a man is going into a woman's world and telling her how to do things.'

'You make it sound like I'm ordering them around.'

'Well you do, don't you?'

'Not at all. It's a consultative process. That's the whole point of management consultancy, as I said at the beginning. The word "consult" is absolutely key.'

'It's a strange kind of consultancy that involves going into people's houses and sticking incomprehensible charts on walls with very long words and then giving them precise instructions about what they should and shouldn't be doing.'

'Well, obviously for the sake of the show we've had to distil many aspects of the Holden Childcare Programme into a short space of time, so it probably makes me look bossier than I am!'

'OK,' she said. 'I can see that we're not getting anywhere here. But I would like to ask you this. You say your wife works, is that right?'

'Quite so.'

'And that you're a househusband.'

'That's correct.'

'Except you're not really, are you? You're making this programme. So what I want to know is this: who looks after your children on a day-to-day basis?'

Fucking bitch, I thought. Why the hell did she have it in for me so badly? Would anybody actually enjoy listening to these nasty little chippy left-wing questions? Nevertheless, I thought it best to be honest.

'We have a nanny,' I said.

'A male nanny?'

'No, a female nanny.'

'Why do you have a female nanny?'

'It's of no consequence whether our nanny is male or female. It just so happens that ours is female. Most are, you know.'

'I do indeed.'

I had rather hoped that would be the end of that thread, but it so wasn't.

'And does your female nanny use the Holden Childcare Programme?'

I should have seen that one coming a mile off.

'I'm afraid not,' I said. 'I'm afraid you can't teach an old dog new tricks!'

Fuckfuckfuckfuckfuckfuckfuck, I thought.

'You're calling your nanny an old dog?'

'No! It's just a figure of speech!'

'Rather an offensive one, wouldn't you say?'

I didn't reply.

'But your "old dog" doesn't use your system?'

'No.'

'Why not?'

'Because she has her own way of doing things.'

'Ways that you approve of?'

'Absolutely.'

'And she's a woman?'

'Yes.'

'So a woman's way can be the right way, yes?'

'Yes of course.'

'So what's the point of your programme?'

'As I keep saying, it's a question of emphasis. And besides, people don't have to use my programme. It's just another way of doing things.'

'So perhaps I should be interviewing your nanny instead of you?'

'Perhaps you should. But you asked *me*, didn't you?'

'We did indeed,' said Ms Stocks, her tone indicating that she wanted to throttle her producer.

We paused momentarily.

'Another thing confuses me,' she said.

'What?' I asked bad-temperedly.

'You say that you're a househusband, and yet you have made a TV programme. Do you think it's really fair to describe yourself as such?'

'Yes. If I hadn't been a househusband, then the show would have never come about.'

'Maybe, but how long were you a househusband for?'

'It's not a question of "were", I still am.'

'How can you be if you have a nanny?'

'The nanny is a temporary measure while I make and promote the show. When this is over, the nanny will go.

If I were a cook promoting a cookbook, you wouldn't turn round and say that I was no longer a cook because I wasn't spending every waking hour in the kitchen. It's absurd to suggest otherwise.'

'Thank you for that,' she replied. 'But let's face facts here. There's no such thing as a househusband. It's just a myth. Aren't the men who describe themselves as househusbands just being ironic, because they either don't need the money, or they've got some lucrative part-time job they can do at home?'

'Not at all,' I said. 'I've met plenty of househusbands, and they are all genuine.'

'Genuine?'

I thought of all those prats I met at the zoo the year before last, when I tried to bond with the 'HouseBands' – Tet and Spilby and all those stupid crusties. The truth was that they were a bunch of arrogant alternative wankers, who were as prescriptive about their lifestyle as they claimed people like me were about mine.

'Yes, genuine,' I said. 'Most househusbands are the primary carers of their children, and although a few have some part-time work, so do many housewives, and yet they are still described as such.'

'Do you describe people as housewives?'

'Yes of course.'

'And you don't think calling them that is in some way derogatory?'

'No, it's a statement of fact. And don't give me any politically correct crap that they should be called homemakers.'

307

'I wasn't going to.'

'Good.'

'I just wondered whether the term "househusband" is in fact offensive to women, more so than housewife.'

'For heaven's sake, why?'

'Because the word "househusband" is always used ironically, as if to suggest that the role is some kind of cultural joke or anomaly. While the female equivalent "housewife" is used matter-of-factly, it also carries those same negative connotations, and it will never lose them unless the word "househusband" is used seriously.'

'Well that sounds like utter bunkum, Miss Stocks.'

(I used the 'Miss' deliberately, and I could see her seethe.)

'Hardly the most sophisticated argument, Mr Holden.'

'Your point of view doesn't require sophistication. You have got it into your fat head that men just spend their time laughing about housewives all day, whereas in fact they don't. Your militancy is just perpetuating a difference that no longer needs to be there.'

'I'd ask you to retract that I am fat.'

'I didn't say you were fat.'

'You said I had a fat *head*.'

'Jesus! "Fat head", in case you haven't heard, is another figure of speech that denotes that someone's thinking is somewhat clouded.'

'So the word "fat" carries a negative connotation?'

'Of course. What is this? Some kind of mid-1990s campfire debate at a shit American university? I suppose you call yourself "differently sized", whereas in fact you are simply fat.'

'I find you remarkably offensive.'

'Well, you are fat, aren't you?'

In fact, she was probably clinically obese.

'And even if I were, what would be the problem with that?'

'Um, where shall I begin? Increased risk of heart disease, increased risk of cancer, increased risk of strokes, excessive pressure on your ligaments and bones – any more you would like me to mention? People like you create an all too literal burden on the health service because you are incapable of self-discipline. As a result of your inability to control yourself, you look for other parts of your life that you can control. With you, I'm afraid it's other people and the way they live their lives.'

'Have you quite finished?'

'No. I've come on to your programme in a spirit of good will, and all you have done is insult me and make snide remarks. People like you are so out of touch with ordinary people's lives, and yet you are totally unwilling to accept that. You can fuck off back to Greenham Common, frankly.'

'I think we should end it now.'

'Why? Have we run out of time?'

'I'm afraid so, Mr Holden.'

'Well, it's not live, so why don't we continue?'

'I'm afraid it is live.'

'Oh fuck.'

Friday 8 August

I can't actually believe that my interview has made the papers, but it has. In a big way. Perhaps it's because it's the silly season and there's bugger all else to write about.

> Page five of the *Herald*: WONDERHUBBY TELLS SUPERFEMMY TO F.O.!
> Page five of the *Bugle*: F-WORD WONDERHUBBY SHAME!
> Page eleven of the *Clarion*: NEW CHILDCARE GURU IN SPAT WITH LEADING FEMINIST
> Page six of the *Daily News*: WONDERHUBBY SOCKS IT TO JULIA
> Page nine of the *Gleaner*: F*** OFF TO GREENHAM, SAYS WONDERHUBBY

'This is all fucking brilliant,' said Dom when he phoned at 8.20 this morning. 'You're a fucking PR genius. Great stunt, mate. Emma didn't tell me you were going to do all that. How sweet of you to keep it a surprise! I'm touched, mate, I really am.'

'Er, it wasn't exactly planned as such.'

'What? It was all spur-of-the-moment stuff? You're kidding!'

'I'm afraid it was.'

'Doesn't matter. What matters is that we've got the *WonderHubby* brand out there, all over the place. Red tops and broadsheets. Waldman is going to really dig this, you wait.'

I did wait, and not for long. Waldman phoned at 8.50.

'Sam, dig!'

'Thanks Dave. I was a bit worried . . .'

'Don't be! Everybody hates that lefty old bitch. You certainly showed her where to stick it. Fuck off to Greenham, brilliant!'

'Thanks!'

'However, let's not have too much more of that, OK? I don't want you making a name for yourself as some rude cunt, all right?'

'I promise not to be a rude cunt.'

'Dig!'

And with that, Waldman put the phone down.

Since then, I've been taking stock. At the beginning of the year, I was just an anonymous bloke living in an anonymous village in an anonymous county who didn't have a job and just looked after the children. Now I'm slowly turning into some sort of media figure, and the TV programme hasn't even aired yet.

I shared all this with Sally over supper.

'Please don't let it go to your head,' she said.

'I'm not. In fact, I'm finding the whole thing rather humbling. More than that, I confess it's a little bit scary.'

'How?'

'Because when you become a public figure, you have to give yourself to everybody. And not everybody is going to like you, and they're going to say nasty things. Suddenly you don't have control of your self-image any more, and I find that a little frightening.'

'But I thought you were desperate to be famous.'

'I was,' I admitted. 'But now I'm about to become famous, I'm finding it's not quite what I thought it was. You become a cartoon figure, two-dimensional. Like some painting in a gallery that anybody is free to come along and do whatever they like to. They can spray on me, shred me, whatever.'

'Draw a funny moustache and spectacles on you . . .'

I laughed.

'You're right,' I said. 'I'm being a bit too serious.'

Saturday 9 August

Normally I wouldn't be at my desk at 11 o'clock on a Saturday morning, but I've just been asked to write an article for the *Sunday Advertiser*. I've never written an article before, so I'm a bit nervous, especially as the *Advertiser* is the largest-selling mid-market paper. The article is going to be headlined something like: WHY A MAN'S PLACE IS IN THE HOME. The commissioning editor, some bloke called Toby Andrews, said that I shouldn't worry too much about style etc., as he would probably rewrite the whole thing anyway. Charming. Anyway, as he's paying me £1,500, I'm hardly in a position to complain! They're even going to send a photographer round to take shots of me in the kitchen with the children – great publicity.

Sunday 10 August

Lots of calls regarding the article, which was an entire

double page. Friends, family, Dom, Dave, you name it. They all seem to love it. Dave sent a text which simply went: U ON A ROLL. DIG! Incidentally, I now know that the correct word to use for an article is 'piece'. And you don't say 'double page'. You say 'spread'. I shall remember this to make myself sound more media savvy over the coming weeks. From now on, my piece will cover a spread. Ooer.

Wednesday 13 August

So far – and it's still three and a bit weeks to go until transmission – this week has been nuts. For some reason my piece touched a nerve, and I've had no end of obscure TV and radio programmes ringing me up for interviews. These are the ones in addition to those that Emma has already lined up. Emma said they can't cope with it in-house any more, and they've had to hire a PR firm, who I must see tomorrow for lunch with her, Dom and Dave. And guess where we're going? Of all places, the Clarendon Hotel. The very same place where I fainted the year before last, having stalked my own wife in a fit of jealous rage. It will be nice to associate the place now with something a little more positive.

Friday 15 August

Fuck I love my job, if you can strictly speaking call it a job. Yesterday was all about eating well, getting smashed, and not having to pay for it. I can barely remember a thing. What I do recall is that somewhat squarely, I wore a tie. My last visit to the Clarendon involved the management making me wear some sort of 1980s pink monstrosity round my neck, and I wasn't going to have that. Of course, when I rocked up into the dining room this time round, I found that I was the only person wearing one. I looked like an accountant, so I subtly whipped it off, although I later realised that it had been hanging out of my jacket pocket all afternoon, which must have looked as gauche as hell.

The PR woman was called Laura Raynor, and she knew her stuff. She also looked the business, which I guess is why she is in PR. Married man or not, she could sell me anything. Not only did she look great, she was also bubbly without being idiotic, and sassy without being overly knowing. A rare combination, rare enough for me to look at her left hand to see if she was wearing a wedding ring. (She was.) I hated myself for doing this, felt icky and disloyal, and mentally flagellated myself with a cat-o'nine-tails. (Clearly to have literally done this would have created a scene in the Clarendon that would have surpassed my last visit.)

The conversation was then basically all about me, which was sort of wonderful really. I remember there being lots of talk about not peaking too early, and how I had already built up a really good brand that we needed to utilise and to build on, and all sorts of stuff like that. To be honest, marketing and PR is totally over my roof, and so I just nodded away inanely, pathetically grateful that I was in this position. I was so grateful I decided that many toasts were in order, and so, every seven or eight minutes, the party had to endure my increasingly bibulous expressions of affection for all the hard work, and 'how great you guys are' etc.

Thankfully, I stopped just short of embarrassing myself (I think), although there was one awful Freudian moment when I was toasting Dom.

'I jusht want to shay,' I slurred, 'how NAPPY I am to have Dom as my producer.'

'Nappy?' went Laura.

'Nappy?' I went. 'What's a nappy got to do with anything?'

'Nothing, I hope,' said Laura. 'It's just that you said how "nappy" you were to have Dom as your producer.'

I must have gone white, because I certainly bloody felt it.

'Did I?'

I struggled not to make eye contact with Dom, although the farthest corners of my peepers were telling me that he had gone slightly off colour as well. At that point, he must have realised that I knew. Maybe he knew before – could he have really trusted Emily not to have spilled the beans?

'I must have nappies on the brain,' I continued. 'That's what comes of being a househusband! In fact, I'm trying to potty-train Daisy at the moment, so I'm kind of obsessed with getting rid of the things.'

This of course was a lie, as Halet had sorted all that out months ago. Even though I thought I explaineth too much, I think I got away with it, as Basil Fawlty might have said.

The rest of the meal passed in a haze of burgundy and champagne. I dimly recall leaving, I remember a taxi at some point, I even remember a train, and then I woke up this morning at 5 a.m., still in my suit, spread-eagled on the spare bed. Sally explained just before she left that Halet had filled her in on my return, which was disgraceful but not appalling. Had I offended her, I wondered? Apparently not, despite the fact that she is a good Muslim. Good old Halet. I owe her.

Now I've just got to get rid of this God-awful hangover. I don't suppose Halet knows too many hangover cures.

Sunday 17 August

Today we took the children to one of those country park places that feature a small steam train and all that jazz. Being summer, it was heaving with the most unspeakable people. I try not to be a ferocious snob, but it's pretty hard not to when one is presented with the so-called Great British Public.

On an individual level the average Brit is all right, but when you put us all together, we're a horrid fusion of excessive flesh and uncouthness. We don't seem to care that we're badly dressed, that we shout at each other, that our children behave appallingly, and that we all insist on getting sunburned. You can see why other Europeans hate us when we go over there, because, quite frankly, we lower the tone. And, to rub salt into the insult, we're proud of it. I don't get it. What's there to be proud of? What's so great about shouting 'Kylie, eat yer chips!' the whole time? Why would you want to wear clothes that exacerbate your rotundity?

I moaned as such as we walked round.

'Stop being such a terrible snob,' Sally hissed. 'After all, these people will soon be your viewers.'

'I don't know whether that's good or bad.'

'It's good. Who knows, perhaps the Holden Childcare Programme will help to make their children behave better?'

'That's right,' I said, utterly unconvinced. 'In ten years' time, thanks to the great HCP, British society will be revolutionised. I wish.'

'Well, you never know.'

'Oh, I do.'

'Why?' asked Sally. 'Do you not believe in your programme any more?'

I told her pretty much what I told Dom.

'The thing is,' I said, 'I'm in so deep, I can't express my doubts publicly. I mean, if it were properly done, then I really think it could work, but it hasn't been properly done. It's been very badly done, and then fudged to make it look as if it's as effective as a boot camp.'

'You're right there,' said Sally. 'It looks extremely convincing from the DVDs.'

'All the wonders of editing.'

'You're telling me.'

We walked along holding hands. The children were running ahead of us, playing hide-and-seek along a sandy path that led through some pines. Because we had walked away from the main area for more than five minutes, we pretty much had the place to ourselves.

'What do you think?' I asked.

'Think about what? Life in general?'

'I was just thinking about the whole *WonderHubby* thing.'

Sally clutched my hand hard.

'I think it's both great and awful.'

'Tell me the awful bit first.'

'I think it's awful for all the reasons you were talking about the other day – becoming a public figure, and all those people having some sort of hold on you, or some opinion about you. I'm worried that you could get hurt. And I'm worried that we'll all get dragged into it in some way. I think you're much more sensitive than you make out, and I worry how much abuse you can take.'

'I think that's fair,' I said.

'But who knows? All that may not happen.'

'Hmmm. And the great bit?'

'Well, I know I had my doubts, but I think that it's great fun. Lots of people want to be on TV, and you're actually doing it, and you're being paid well, bloody well. And you may even make *more* money. I can't deny that I like the money very much!'

'Aha! The gold-digger is finally revealed!'

'Oh yes,' she said, hugging me tighter.

We stopped and kissed.

'Eeeeurgh!' shouted Peter. 'Look Daisy! Mummy and Daddy are kissing! Yuck!'

We broke off.

'It's not yuck,' I said. 'It's what mummies and daddies do.'

'You are always kissing,' said Peter.

'I wish we were,' I said.

'I could do with another holiday,' said Sally.

'Now that would be nice. What say you we plonk these two in front of the box when we get back and have a little siesta?'

'A very fine idea. Sometimes I utterly approve of TV.'

Wednesday 20 August

Dave phoned late afternoon to say that everything was scheduled for Friday 5 September at 8.30 p.m.

'Dig that mate, prime fucking time.'

'I most certainly am digging it.'

'Ha! I love the way you say digging!'

And with that he was gone, perhaps with another 'dig'.

Friday 22 August

Toby Andrews has commissioned me again. He said that his editor loved my last piece (note correct use of journo-lingo) and he wanted something else about men being good at activities that are normally associated with women.

319

'I'm a bit worried I might be seen as a chauvinist,' I said. 'After my fight with Julia Stocks and that last piece, I could end up looking like a complete old fart.'

'I don't think that'll happen,' he said smoothly.

'Perhaps I should talk to my PR.'

Andrews kind of harrumphed down the phone.

'I'd really prefer it if a PR didn't get involved.'

'Oh?'

'They just put honey in the gearbox. It all tastes nice and sweet, but it also clogs everything up. PRs always want to justify their position, and I hate having to deal with them.'

'I'm sorry, I didn't realise. I'm a bit new to this.'

I cursed myself for admitting my neophyte status.

'Not at all,' said Andrews. 'Who is your PR anyway?'

'Laura Raynor.'

'Laura Raynor? Bugger me! You've got her?'

'Yes. Why? Is there something wrong with her?'

'Far from it! She's about the foxiest PR in the world.'

'Yes, I'd noticed. But is she any good?'

'Of course she is. She's sensational, but she's still a PR. Anyway, look, do you want to do another piece or not? I'll pay you two grand.'

I thought about it. For about two seconds.

'What do you want it on?'

'Why not a piece on how women are crap at cooking, and in fact it's men who are the true geniuses in the kitchen.'

'Done,' I said. 'When do you want it?'

'First thing tomorrow morning.'

'Gosh, that's quite soon. Can I have any longer?'

'No.'

And then he put the phone down. Fair enough I suppose. If you're going to earn £1.33 per word, then you've got to do it when the man says.

Sunday 24 August

People were divided into two camps about the piece. There was the camp that liked it, which consisted of me, and the camp that hated it, which consisted of everybody else. The person who hated it most was Laura, who rang up at 8.30 this morning and gave me an earful while I was still in bed.

'Have you forgotten everything we said about positioning?'

'No. Not at all.'

(I had forgotten everything we had said about positioning. In fact, at that point in the morning, I couldn't even think what positioning meant.)

'Well, in that case, you'll remember that we wanted to position your brand as the sensitive new man, yet someone who is strong and knows his own mind. What we have here is a man who has strong opinions, but they are very much of the old-man variety.'

'Oh come on, they weren't that bad!'

'Really?'

I heard a rustle of newspaper down the phone.

'Try this,' said Laura. ' "The truth is, women can't really cook. All they can do is cater, and there's a big difference. The only people who can actually cook on this planet are men, even the ones who only cook once a year when their wife or girlfriend is ill." '

'So?'

'So?! Can't you see how sexist and old-fashioned that sounds?'

'Well, you know, I kind of exaggerated it for effect.'

'You weren't shy of doing so, were you? How about this? "Women are useless at following instructions, in this case recipes." And "Why does my wife always forget some essential part of the meal?" I could go on, Sam.'

I sat up in bed. Something in me snapped.

'Hang on a minute,' I said. 'I'm entitled to express my own opinions, no matter how objectionable you find them. You can't tell me what I can and cannot write!'

'Yes I can.'

'Why?'

'Because this TV programme isn't just about you, Sam Holden. In fact, you're just one little bit of it. Don't you see how much time and money has been put into it? This is about people's jobs, not just about your ego. Lots of people are counting on this show being a success, and they don't want it fucked up by you turning yourself into the most unattractive figure you can create. Do you understand that?'

'Of course I do, but I really didn't think it was that bad.'

'It is that bad. It's one thing telling a joke figure like Julia Stocks to fuck off back to Greenham, but another to tell all your potential viewers that they're complete fuckwits in the kitchen. In fact, perhaps Stocks had a point.'

'OK, OK, you've made your point.'

'I've got another one as well. Why didn't this go through me? I specifically told you at lunch that everything you did, every word you said to any media outlet, every word you wrote for every newspaper, all had to go through me. Do you remember that?'

'Of course!'

(Of course I didn't. I was too pissed.)

'Then why didn't you let me know you were doing the piece?'

'Because I just didn't think I had to, all right? Look, I'm new to all this, so just cut me some slack, would you? Christ! Without me, this bloody programme wouldn't have even existed.'

'That's utterly irrelevant. The fact is, you're now locked in with people who depend on you, and you need to depend upon them. You can't just be a loose cannon, do you understand?'

'Yes, yes.'

'Good. Fine. Right. Enjoy the rest of your weekend.'

'I'll try.'

I put the phone down. (Or rather, pressed the red button, which is a far less satisfyingly emphatic way of ending a bad-tempered call.)

'Who the hell was that?' Sally demanded from under the duvet.

'Laura, the PR woman.'

'What was it about?'

Sam Holden

I crashed back on to the pillow.

'Me becoming owned.'

The rest of the day felt somewhat sour. I kept trying to justify my actions to myself, but deep down, I knew that Laura was right. It wasn't all about me. Nothing ever is.

Tuesday 26 August

Sally put my PR problems (never thought I'd have such a problem) into perspective by telling me that things at work were reaching crisis point. It looked as though they might just have to roll up everything and get out. Nearly every asset had been compromised (I think that is the technical term), and the future was looking very very bleak for the whole section.

'Does this mean your job is on the line?' I asked.

'Yes. And before you start pleading with me to chuck it in, I'm not going to.'

I am surrounded by strong women. Or at least women who are stronger than me.

Wednesday 27 August

Laura phoned to tell me three things. First, that she hadn't forgiven me for not keeping her 'in loop' regarding the *Sunday Advertiser* piece. However, she sounded somewhat better-tempered about it. I decided not to apologise, because I already had. The second piece of news was that having sent out preview DVDs 'we

324

are getting great feedback' from the TV reviewers. Nothing specific, but they all seemed to like it, and it would certainly get a lot of review coverage, which is both great and terrifying. And, more exciting still, she's booked the Harpo Club for a launch party next Friday. Excellent! Now I can truly call myself a fully fledged member of the tellystocracy.

An actual party. I can't remember the last time I went to one of those, probably some dull management-consultancy affair. I expect the one at the Harpo will be very different. Better-looking people, for starters. And a lot more cocaine.

Friday 29 August

Today was the big interview day, which was spent in a suite in one of those trendy little boutique hotels in a part of London you never knew existed until you found yourself having to give interviews in a suite in a trendy little boutique hotel. Laura was fantastically efficient, and had lined up no less than twenty-three people to interview me. I was astonished – an emotion I am experiencing more often these days.

Normally I quite like the sound of my voice, but by the end of the day I hated it. Of course, I don't want to sound blasé, but there's nothing more tedious than repeatedly answering the same questions. How did you become a househusband? Where did you get the idea for the programme? What was it like to make? Why are your children not on the Holden Childcare

Programme? (They had clearly listened to my interview with Stocks, which I see has become a bit of a hit on the Web.) Will you go back and visit the families you helped on the show? (Er . . . no, but I said yes. Nobody is to know that we aren't planning to.)

What irked me was that Laura sat through all the interviews. I told her it really wasn't necessary, and that I was perfectly capable of answering questions all by myself. Laura said that was the problem. Now I know why celebrities say they feel like caged animals. You're there to perform, and although your cage is very opulent there's no doubt that if you don't perform just how the zoo-keeper and the public want, then you're thrown back into the wild. Naïvely, I thought that spending a whole day in a suite talking about myself to pretty female feature writers would be almost the stuff of a wank fantasy, but it wasn't. At one point, when the umpteenth journalist asked me how I had become a househusband, I felt like shouting, 'Read the fucking press release you thick twat!' and then storming out. It's amazing how quickly you become a prima donna.

What also annoyed me was that Laura forbade me to have anything to drink, by which I mean booze.

'Why not?' I asked.

'Because you'll only get pissed and start insulting everybody.'

She was perfectly charming about it, but I could tell that she was as serious as a post-coital female Black Widow.

'You just don't trust me at all, do you?'

'Not one little bit.'

This brought out the rebel in me, and I vowed that I would help myself to something in the minibar when she went to the loo. Eventually, at some point in the mid afternoon, she disappeared, and I seized my chance. I dashed over to the fridge and opened it up, wondering what absurdly overpriced little something was going to end up down my neck. A little bottle of whisky? A quick cheeky beer? Perhaps even one of those cans of ready-mixed gin and tonic? I felt like a complete alkie.

I couldn't believe it. I was in the one hotel suite in the whole of London that couldn't provide an alcoholic drink. What was this, some kind of Mormon boutique hotel? And then it occurred to me – Laura must have taken it. She is as sly as she is beautiful. I was so put out, I challenged her about it.

'Did you take all the drinks out the minibar?'

'Yes.'

'OK.'

And that was that.

When the interviews were over, I went down to the nearest pub and necked two pints of bitter before you could say 'positioning'.

Sunday 31 August

This afternoon, Sally and I had a great time working out who should come to the launch party at the Harpo. Naturally, both sets of parents, various siblings, and old muckers such as Nigel and Clare, etc. By the end of it we had thirty names, and it was pretty tough keeping it that short.

'Will you be inviting the families in the show?' Sally asked.

'Good idea,' I said. 'After all, they were the ones who put in the real work.'

Monday 1 September

Laura's first words were:

'You've got to be kidding.'

Her second set of words were:

'Are you mad?'

And her third:

'We don't want them anywhere near.'

'But they're the ones who really made the programme,' I said. 'They're the ones who gave up their time, took their children out of school, made big sacrifices. The least we can do is ask them to have a drink. Where's the harm in that?'

'One. Launch parties are not for the subjects of the show. They are for the people who are going to write about it and publicise it. If the journalists actually found out the truth about how these programmes were made, then we'd be sunk before we even set sail. We can't have some of those people actually talking to journalists! Have you no idea?'

'None whatsoever,' I said wearily. 'Anyway, was there a second reason? You began by saying "one".'

'Yes. The sort of people featured in the show would

massively bring down the tone of the party. They're the
cooee brigade, the type of people who've won a trip for
two to the West End to meet the stars of some crap
musical. Betty and Derek from Blackpool. No thanks.'

Blimey, I thought. Laura was even more of a snob
than me. That took some doing.

'Don't you think that's just a little unfair?'

'No. They were never promised a party, and besides,
these people's real thrill is appearing on TV. That's
reward enough for them.'

It was clear that I wasn't going to win this one. So the
next exchange came as no surprise.

'I'd like to email you a list of some people I want to
invite. Don't worry, they're friends and family, not the
cooee brigade.'

'OK. How many?'

'I've got thirty.'

'Thirty?'

'Why, is that too many?'

'WAY too many. Can you get it down to six?'

'SIX? But that's nothing.'

'I'm sorry, Sam, but there's not much room for
friends. You could do eight, at a pinch. Sorry, but that's
the way it is.'

'Gee, thanks a bunch.'

'There's nothing stopping you having your own
party.'

The logic of that was perfectly unassailable, but it
wasn't really the point. And besides, holding parties in
clubs in London is not cheap.

'Right,' I said. 'I'll get it down to eight.'

'Great,' she said. 'And remember your wife counts as one of those eight, OK?'

Somehow that didn't surprise me. I can't believe I was so easily charmed by her at the Clarendon. I can see why she's a good PR now. In a way, I should count myself lucky that I have such a tough cookie on my side. I hope she doesn't rub up journalists in the same way. I doubt it – I expect she's in full seductress mode for them. It's only people like me, the poor old fool who came up with the idea for the programme, and who actually stars in the bloody thing, who get treated like crap.

Wednesday 3 September

I saw Emily – where else? – in the supermarket. Today our accidental meeting-place was near the household-cleaning products, glamorously enough. We did the normal hellos, and then Emily said, 'I expect I won't be seeing much of you soon.'

'Why's that? Are you moving?'

'No. But soon you are going to be so rich and famous you won't bother coming to the supermarket, you'll have slaves to do it for you.'

'Too right,' I said. 'And a punkah-wallah to cool me down in the summer.'

'What's that?'

'One of those chaps out in the Raj who used to pull a rope all day attached to a sail-like fan that kept the room cool.'

'I could do with one of those,' she said. 'It's far too hot at the moment.'

I didn't know what else to say. This is always a problem when you know someone is in love with you (the expert speaks) because the only thing on your mind is the great unspoken.

'Kate tells me that you're having some kind of party on Friday up in London.'

Oh shit, I thought, somebody is angling for an invitation. I've invited Kate and her husband, because they are new best friends, and I want to cement our friendship.

'That's right,' I said.

Never apologise, never explain, I said to myself.

'I'm sorry not to invite you, but the numbers are limited,' I told Emily.

'Honestly, I wasn't expecting to be invited,' she replied. 'I doubt Sally would want me there.'

I smiled weakly.

'Probably not.'

We said perfunctory goodbyes. As I trolleyed away, I reflected that Emily had changed radically. Her spark had died, fizzled out in a muddy pool. She seemed depressed, gloomy. The flirtation had gone, and there was an edge of chippy bitterness to her. If I'm being harsh, I'd say all this was her own doing, all down to her giving into her sexual incontinence. But then isn't the definition of incontinence suggestive of a lack of control? How can you be blamed for something you can't control? What makes Emily so special that she feels she can cheat on her husband, and get other women's husbands to cheat on their wives?

I'm worried that Emily is going to turn sour, like forgotten milk in the back of the fridge. If I could, I would help her, but I know I'm part of the problem, and I also know that sympathy friendships always end badly. I shall just have to keep an eye on her, and be as nice as possible, from a distance mind you.

Thursday 4 September

Halet said that she was very excited about my programme.

'I've told all my friends to tune in tomorrow night,' she said.

'Excellent,' I said. 'The more viewers the merrier. I expect you will find it a bit silly though.'

Halet flicked that aside.

'It's TV, isn't it? It's all silly.'

Why hadn't I known that?

I'm getting really nervous about tomorrow night now. I've decided that I'm not going to drink, as I'll only get mullered and make a fool of myself. Laura tells me that all the newspaper and magazine TV editors will be there, and it will be quite a bash. When I told her that I was intending to stay dry for the night, she sounded as pleased as I do when Daisy tells me that she has been to the loo all by herself.

Peter asked me a funny question during teatime.

'Daddy? Are you going to be famous?'

'A little bit, yes.'

'Cool!'

'Well, I don't know if it's cool.'

'It's really cool. Josh's mummy told Josh that she had seen you on the TV! Are you going to be on the TV again?'

Josh's mummy must have seen one of the trailers. I hadn't seen one yet. Oh God, I thought, it's really happening.

'I will be, yes.'

'Cool! And will you be really rich?'

'Erm, no. I shall have a bit more money, yes.'

Now it was Daisy's turn to pipe up.

'I like money,' she said.

I had to laugh.

'Why do you like money?' I asked her.

'Because it is shiny,' she said.

'I like money too!' Peter announced.

'And why do you like it?'

'Because money buys lots of toys,' said Peter.

'That's right, but you have to have lots of money to buy lots of toys.'

'I will have lots of money one day. Enough to fill the whole world, and I will buy all the toys in world.'

'And where are you going to get all the money from?'

'From being famous and being on TV like you.'

The sad thing is that I pretty much thought like that too a few months ago.

Saturday 6 September
6 p.m. Back home

Still hung-over, but I don't care, because I'm on a high. The party went well, the reviews in this morning's papers are mostly excellent, and the initial viewing figures are looking really positive. Perhaps all that PR bollocks was worth it after all, although I'm pretty sure that the whole success of *WonderHubby* is down to me. After all, it was my idea, and what's the point of having a trumpet if you can't blow it?

The one thing I found strange about the party was that even though it was notionally in my honour, I barely knew anybody there. It rather seemed to be an excuse for journalists to get drunk at someone else's expense, which is fair enough I suppose. Most of those who had interviewed me came along, but they showed more interest in talking to each other. Perhaps I had bored them. Anyway, it didn't matter, because Sally and I had a great time talking to Kate and Nigel and Clare, etc., which Laura moaned about until I told her that I had tried talking to the hacks, but they weren't interested.

However, I did make a short speech, which went down well, as most people appeared to be listening. Just as one would expect, I thanked everybody who needed to be thanked, and then I made a great point of thanking the poor buggers who had appeared in the programme, and expressed regret that they couldn't attend. That earned a somewhat muted clap.

At one point, Dom and Dave collared me. There was a lot of 'dig' and backslapping and clumsy high fives, and then the invitation to have some 'yayo'.

'I think it's about time, now that you're a telly star, that you enjoyed all the trappings of your new status,' said Dom.

'Dig,' said Dave, who was sniffing as though he had a bad cold.

'I'm, er, not sure . . .'

'C'mon mate! Just a celebratory line!'

Drugs. I've always had an ambivalent attitude towards them. Of course, like 99 per cent of people in their thirties, I've tried them, but nothing serious. All just felt a bit pointless, really.

'That's ever so kind of you,' I said to Dom. 'But I'll leave it, thanks.'

'Sure? This is excellent Bolivian, you should really try it.'

'Bolivian, eh? This isn't just normal cocaine, this is Bolivian cocaine,' I said, imitating that woman's sultry voice in the well-known supermarket ad. 'You'll be saying that it's Fairtrade next.'

Dom laughed.

'I doubt it, but I do know that it's organic.'

'You're joking!'

'Not at all. My man told me it was.'

'And you believed him?'

'Of course. I trust my drug dealer implicitly!'

With that, Dom and Dave disappeared to powder their noses. I was slightly jealous because it seemed like fun, but I was paranoid enough not to be tempted, and besides, one of the journalists might have seen me. And what about Laura? If she didn't like me drinking, what would she say to WONDERHUBBY IN COCAINE SHAME all over the tabloids? Quite a lot, I would imagine.

As the party dwindled at around ten o'clock, Laura came up to me.

'A few of us are going on to Cooper's,' she said. 'Do you and Sally fancy joining us?'

My reply was instantaneous.

'No thanks,' I said. 'I've got a table for me and my friends. Sorry, if I'd known . . .'

I didn't have a table. I just couldn't face hanging out with media people any more. I wanted to be with my wife and my friends. As it was we did well, and although it was probably the worst restaurant in the whole of Soho, the Greasy Kukri, or whatever it was called, did us proud. I must have drunk every variety of sub-continental lager they had, and even Sally was keeping up.

'To WonderHubby!' said Nigel at one point, and I responded by toasting them. It seems a bit cheesy and sentimental now, but at the time it felt just right. It was good to know that I would always have these people around, as the Doms and Daves and Emmas and Lauras will no doubt flitter off as soon as a more nectar-laden flower blossoms into view.

We caught the last train home, and I just had time to buy every first edition of the newspapers in order to read the reviews. Sally and I drunkenly spread them out over our table, and read them aloud to each other. Our fellow passengers must have thought we were partly insane, but I didn't care.

In the main, they were pretty good. The best was in the *Daily Advertiser*, which read:

WonderHubby *is a bizarre mixture of management programme and childcare, and more bizarrely still, it does the trick. It works not only as a system for raising your children – the results appear to be impressive – but also as a TV programme. The presenter and inventor of the eponymous system is Sam Holden, a former management consultant who decided to apply the principles of his old job to raising his children. He makes an engaging host, and although he sometimes bedazzles the viewer with his vocabulary, he radiates much warmth and decency, all too rare qualities on our screens these days. I predict that this series is going to go a long way, and I wouldn't be surprised to see Sam Holden becoming the new childcare guru of our times. Move over Gina!*

All I could to say to that was, 'Wow!'

All Sally could say was, 'Please make sure your head doesn't get too big.' But I could tell she was proud, and she gave me a massive kiss.

The more downmarket *Herald* loved it as well.

WonderHubby *is the best reality TV to hit our screens since* Gay Up Your Kitchen. *Host Sam Holden, the inventor of a whacky new childcare system which seems to involve lots of long words, shows families how to look after their kids by using the techniques of business folk. Judging by last night's show, it really seems to work! He stops short of putting the kids in pinstripe suits, but there is method in his crazy bizspeak! Look out for this next week, it's a must!*

And even the normally rather snooty *Clarion* gave it the thumbs up:

There are many of us who are sick of reality TV, childcare TV, and 'Business is Sexy' TV, and it took a brave commissioning editor to go ahead and order six episodes of WonderHubby, *which mixes all three. Nevertheless, this combination of stale ingredients produces a highly digestible dish, which blends much good sense, situational humour and surprisingly useful advice. The presenter, Sam Holden, does a good job in holding it all together, and this reviewer would not be surprised if* WonderHubby *has a great future.*

The only mixed review was from the *Gleaner*.

It's hard to think of a bigger mess of formats, and although WonderHubby *has its comic moments, they are presented at the expense of the participants, who are mainly from low-income families. The supposed childcare system is the brainchild of the show's host, Sam Holden, a former management consultant, who seems to think that by chanting bullshit business mantras at the harassed families, their children will somehow behave better. I wasn't convinced it worked, and I suspect* WonderHubby *is more a triumph of editing. I'd be interested to see what the families really thought off camera, and would welcome an update in a year's time, to see if the Holden Childcare Programme really matched the hype.*

Funnily enough, that one didn't get me down at all, because I pretty much agreed with it. In fact, I was more surprised that only one of the reviewers had seen through it, but then maybe the rest chose not to, no doubt not wanting to jeopardise their free evenings at places like the Harpo.

As if to ensure that my feet stay rooted in the soil, Peter and Daisy have been uncharacteristically foul today. For some reason, they've just been whingeing at the slightest thing, and my and Sally's patience – never particularly long with hangovers – has been painfully tested. Still, I can't complain about anything at the moment. It's all feeling a little too good to be true.

Monday 8 September

And it gets better. Laura phoned me at 8 o'clock to say that a car would be here at midday to take me to London. I was to be interviewed on nothing less than *Joseph and Mary*, which is THE daytime chat show to appear on. Unreal, utterly wonderfully unreal. And the car was no ordinary car either, but some massive top-of-the-range Audi, complete with all of today's papers neatly laid out on the back seat, and even a TV set with a DVD player.

The interview went well, partly because Laura wasn't

able to sit next to me telling me what to say. It seemed as though both Joseph and Mary were genuine fans of the show, and they asked me a load of piss-easy questions.

'I wish we had brought up our children with the Holden Childcare Programme,' said Joseph.

I glowed with a very sheepish pride.

'So do I,' said Mary. 'We had all that Dr Spock nonsense. Your system seems a lot better.'

'We just threw Spock away, didn't we darling?'

'I remember throwing it out the window one night,' said Mary.

'Well, I hope that doesn't happen to my advice,' I said, and they laughed a bit too much.

As soon as we were off air, Mary asked me whether I wanted to come on again.

'We need someone like you in the mix,' she said.

'A younger man, eh, darling?' said Joseph.

'Oh shut it!'

'I'd be delighted,' I said.

'Do you think you could do a weekly slot?'

'I'd love to, although I'd better check with the TV company to see if they're happy.'

'I'm sure they will be,' said Mary. 'Who's your agent by the way?'

'Agent?'

'You mean you don't have one?'

'Er, no.'

'You're joking! You must have an agent! Joseph, did you hear that? Young Sam here doesn't have an agent.'

'Lucky him,' he said. 'If you can get away with it, don't bother.'

'But nobody will take him seriously without an agent,' said Mary.

'I'm not sure they take me seriously anyway,' I said.

Mary scribbled a number down on a piece of paper.

'This is our agent,' she said, handing it to me. 'Give her a call, and she can negotiate a fee with our producer.'

So, two hours later, I had not only an agent called Cat, but also a weekly slot on *Joseph and Mary* that will net me £1,000 per week. Fuck me.

Tuesday 9 September
2 p.m.

Better still. I've just had a call from Toby Andrews at the *Sunday Advertiser*. They need a new weekly columnist in their lifestyle section, and how would I feel if it were me? I told him I'd feel delighted. He said that they would pay me £1,500 per column. I almost fainted. In the past twenty-four hours, I've become £130,000 per year richer. This is on top of the £90,000 TV money. Bloody hell. This is a lot better than being a management consultant. This is better than winning the lottery, because it sort of means something.

2.30 p.m.

Just phoned Sally to tell her. It was clear she was having

a(nother) shit day at work, but she more than registered her astonishment.

'But that's amazing,' she whispered. '£1,500 per week? Really?'

'Really!'

'I knew I was right to encourage you to do this,' she said.

'Hey!' I went.

'I must go,' she said. 'Let's celebrate later.'

'I won't need much persuading.'

4 p.m.

Dom has just phoned me.

'Mate, are you sitting down?'

'No. Should I be?'

'Yes.'

'Has someone died?'

'Nope. Even better than that.'

'Go on.'

'You know we were talking about getting a book out of this?'

'Oh yes.'

'Well,' he said, 'we've had a few offers.'

'Really? From whom?'

'Publishers, you twat!'

'OK, sorry, yes, not quite with it. Carry on.'

'Three are not worth considering, two are OK, but there are another three which are not bad at all.'

'OK.'

'MacIntosh Tanner have come in with £150K. Nesbit are at £140K. And Artemis are in at £175K.'

'Fucking hell!'

'Obviously, these are just the opening offers. And remember, these get split fifty-fifty as per our contract. Our literary agent should be able to beef those up to well over £250K. She says she wants best bids by 5.30 today, so stand by your phone.'

'I will, don't you worry.'

Holy smoke, Batman. I won't phone Sally. I think I'll present it as an afterthought later.

5.35 p.m.

It's gone to Nesbit for £285,000. Half of that is mine. Oh my God. For once, I am speechless. It's looking like a £300,000 year. And that's not counting a second series. This is almost too easy. No, not almost, it really is too easy. I have this idiot permagrin on my face, and I just don't want to tell Halet about it, because it seems vulgar. Heading to the off-licence in a jiffy to buy a lot of champagne.

Wednesday 10 September

Sally was more than a little happy. I needn't go into detail here, because I'm not likely to forget. Suffice to say, at one point we actually held hands and jumped up and down. And then I fell over and things got more champagney and amorous.

My feelings now are 'finally, finally'. I sort of feel, and I would only dare admit this to my diary, that I deserve all this, that I deserve lots of money and success. It's how I'm wired, how I've been brought up. And what's so nice about it is that I don't have to be some chippy bloke in my mid forties who watches all his friends get richer and buy big houses and cars, etc., because I'll be one of them. At this rate, I'll be the richest of the lot.

Friday 12 September

Sally and I had a long chat last night about her stopping work. I know this has been my refrain all year, but surely now is the time for her to stop torturing herself? Her response was just as I had feared.

'Now would not be a good time to give up,' she replied. 'I know that you are going to be earning tons and tons, but who knows how long it will last?'

'I have no idea,' I said. 'But even if it all fizzles out after a couple of years, I'll have made enough money for us to really think about what we want.'

'Maybe,' she said.

'We'll have the freedom to choose. We could pay off the mortgage and stay here, and sort of live the good life. Or we could push ourselves and buy a bigger house. Or we could sell up and move to the South of France where we could buy an enormous chateau with a pool.'

'Who do we know in the South of France?'

'Nobody. But who cares? It's mainly British anyway. We'd find friends, no problem.'

'But they'd all be retired.'

'Hmm . . . I gather quite a few young people are moving out there these days.'

'Rubbish,' she said.

'OK, you're probably right. But you get the gist. We're free to choose. All that's holding us up is your job.'

'But my job is secure, Sam.'

'It doesn't sound it. The last thing you told me was that it looked as though it was on the line.'

'Well, things are looking up in that department.'

'Oh?'

'I'm sorry, I just haven't had a chance to tell you in amongst all your good news. They think it may not be a mole, but possibly a hacker, or some sort of communication intercept. Whatever it is, it looks more likely to be something electronic at fault rather than some human.'

'Blame the IT department?'

'Exactly! Even in my world IT always takes the rap!'

'My point still stands, though,' I said. 'I wish you would give it up. Would you give it some serious thought?'

'Of course,' said Sally.

'You promise?'

'I promise,' she said. 'But don't forget, it wasn't that long ago that you agreed to be a househusband, and now look at you. You only did it for five minutes. And if you're asking me to give up work, you're asking me to become a housewife again.'

'Was it really that bad?'

'I don't find it as fulfilling as some women do.'

'Fair enough,' I said. 'But by next September the children will both be at school, and so you'll be able to do something part-time.'

'Maybe, but it never quite works out like that, does it?'

'Doesn't it?'

'Tons of women who say they're going to go back to work once the children are at school never do.'

'Yes, but you're different from them.'

'Perhaps, but with your vast income, maybe I won't have the imperative to work. That's probably why I'm sticking with the Ministry, because the imperative is not about money.'

'So what's it about then? Making the world a better place?'

Sally nodded.

'Yes, frankly.'

I couldn't really argue with that.

Anyway, I'd better stop writing now, because episode two is about to come on. It'll be cool to watch it air across the country, in amongst the adverts for soap powder and tampons.

Saturday 13 September

Lots and lots of phone calls today from people saying they loved part two. It was the one featuring Suzie and Maureen, and many people thought I was quite the action hero busting the door down. Luckily there was no footage of me bruising my shoulder at the first attempt. That would have taken the *Wonder* out of *WonderHubby* and somehow *Hubby* doesn't quite cut the mustard as a TV programme. Sounds like some interminable Israeli soap opera. Set on a kibbutz.

I spent this afternoon writing my column. (That's a nice sentence to have written.) Toby said it was great, although when he emailed it back to me an hour later it was unrecognisable.

'It was great,' he said again when I called him, as though great were the lowest form of praise. 'We've just got to get you to write in our house style, and then it'll be fine.'

'So is "fine" better than "great"?' I asked.

'Much better,' he said. 'If your piece is fine, then you've almost won a press award.'

'Is there anything better than fine?'

'I once told someone that their piece was really quite nice.'

'Wow, high praise indeed. Who was that?'

'Martin Amis.'

Monday 15 September

Oh fuck. I think I have a stalker. Just as I suspected, Emily's begun to go off, badly off. I now know that all those 'chance' meetings in the supermarket were entirely deliberate. How do I know this? Because I saw her in her car in the supermarket car park waiting for me.

I turned up at around 9.30 a.m., my usual time, and I noticed her just sitting in her green Peugeot estate. However, she hadn't seen me, and I parked a few spaces behind her and waited. And waited. And waited. In all, I waited for twenty minutes, and still she sat there. Then I decided to drive round in front of her car, and pretended not to see her as I got out and walked to the entrance. When I got there, I hid behind the *Postman Pat* kiddy ride-on van and watched her walk in.

I then followed her into the supermarket at as great a distance as I could manage. Sally would have been impressed by my sleuthing skills. Strangely, however, Emily wasn't putting anything into her trolley, and instead she seemed to be looking around. I knew what she was searching for: me. Was I being paranoid? I don't think so. Nobody sits in a supermarket car park for twenty minutes, and the fact that she got out only after she had seen me was suspicious as hell. And now, here she was, wandering around the store with an empty trolley, patently looking for something other than fruit and bog roll.

I followed her for a few minutes, and then decided to surprise her.

'Hello Emily,' I said, tapping her on the shoulder.

She jumped a little.

'Hi! Gosh, you gave me a fright there!'

'We always seem to be bumping into each other here,' I said. 'What a coincidence!'

'Quite! Well, I always find Monday morning a good time to go shopping.'

348

I looked down at her trolley.

'Nothing that takes your fancy?'

'What?'

She looked extremely distracted and somewhat frazzled. Not only that, her hair was greasy and unkempt, and she had bags under her eyes. In fact, she looked like a poster warning teenagers of the dangers of drugs.

'Your trolley, it's empty.'

'Yes, I've only just got here.'

I knew this was bullshit, and she must have known, because we were two-thirds of the way round the shop. I, on the other hand, had been cunning, and had put things in my trolley, into which Emily was now looking.

'I didn't know you had a dog,' she said.

'I don't.'

'So why have you got dog food in there?'

I looked down, and there it was. Perhaps my cover was not so watertight after all. Sally would not be signing me up as a spook any time soon.

'It's for Rachel next door,' I said, after a probably not very convincing pause.

'Oh,' she went, because let's face it, there's only so much conversational mileage you can get out of discussing a neighbour's canine's dietary requirements.

'Did you see my programme on Friday?' I asked.

'No, I'm afraid I missed it,' she said. 'I was out.'

She was scratching the back of her neck, which we all know means that someone is lying. Why was she lying? Was she trying to make out that she wasn't interested?

Answer: Yes. Why? Answer: Because she's trying to make me hungry for her, pay more attention to her. Will it work? Answer: No.

'Well, you can catch me on *Joseph and Mary* this afternoon,' I said.

'OK,' she said, trying to sound uninterested, but I could tell she was feeling the opposite.

The conversation petered out, and although we came across each other once or twice as we trundled round, that was pretty much the extent of the meeting. I was so distracted I actually bought the dog food in the end. I must go round and give it to Rachel.

Wednesday 17 September

Woken up at 2 in the morning by a silent caller. It had to be Emily, although the number was withheld, so I couldn't be sure. Then I couldn't get back to sleep, not until five o'clock, by which time it was broad daylight. I slept badly for about half an hour and finally gave in and got up to go for a walk. It was a beautiful morning, but I was too tired to enjoy it properly.

'Who was that last night?' asked Sally.

'Must have been a wrong number.'

'Bloody odd time for a wrong number.'

Thursday 18 September

This time the call came at 3.

'Look,' I said, 'who the hell is this?'

I clamped my ear to the phone, trying to pick up any sort of clue. I thought I could make out a slight sobbing noise, like a small child in pain. In the middle of the night, it sounded positively creepy.

'Whoever you are, please stop it.'

I didn't want to say the word 'Emily', because as far as Sally is concerned, there is no Emily situation. I listened hard, but still that faint sobbing sound.

'Can I listen?' asked Sally.

I passed her the phone. I could just about discern her troubled expression as she held it to her ear.

'The person's hung up,' she said.

It had to be Emily, I thought.

'I'm going to call the phone company first thing,' said Sally.

'Don't worry,' I said. 'I'll do it.'

This was a little pork pie. The last thing I wanted Sally to discover was the identity of our midnight telephonic stalker.

'They should be able to tell us who it is,' she said.

'It's probably some nut who's seen me on TV. I bet this happens a lot.'

'It could be,' she said. 'But we're ex-directory, so how would they have got the number?'

'Maybe it's Nick,' I said.

'Stop that! It's not funny.'

'Sorry.'

'If the phone company don't tell us,' said Sally, 'then I'll just have to do it the naughty way.'

'Via work?'

'Yup. One of the intercept guys owes me a favour.'

'Sometimes your job has its advantages,' I said.

'I know,' said Sally. 'You see, I would be mad to chuck it in.'

We both lay awake for a few minutes, and then thought that if we were awake, we might as well be frisky. We started off well, but my equipment was not interested. I was too preoccupied by that strange sobbing noise, and it had a remarkably detumescent effect, although I hadn't really tumesced in the first place.

I didn't call the phone company, because I knew there was no point. Instead, after the school/playgroup drop-off, I went straight round to Emily's. When she answered the door, she looked startled.

'Hi!' she said. 'What a surprise!'

She looked wraithlike, a shadow of her former self. In fact she looked as though she had been up all night crying, and making crank calls. Very Princess Diana.

'Do you mind if I come in?' I asked.

'Not at all.'

The house was a mess. It was never clean, but it was now sluttishly dirty, too dirty even for a bachelor Sam Holden.

'Jesus,' I said. 'Have you given up tidying?'

She tried to laugh.

'Sorry, it's a bit of a tip. I was about to give it a good going-over.'

She lit a cigarette and then stood there, picking the scab on her arm as she had done when she made her 'declaration'. The scab looked kind of bad, the type of scab that your mum tells you to stop picking.

'Would you like one?' she asked.

'No thanks.'

We stood in silence. I decided I would get straight to the point.

'Listen, Emily, I know it's you.'

She made a great play of furrowing her brow.

'What are you talking about?'

'You know full well.'

She shook her head. So far, so theatrical.

'What?' she asked. 'What?'

'Emily! Please don't do this!'

'Do what for fuck's sake?'

It was rare for Emily to swear, and the word jolted me a little.

'The phone calls, Emily.'

'What phone calls?'

'The ones in the middle of the night.'

She took a drag of her cigarette.

'Hang on,' she said. 'Sorry if I'm being a bit slow here, but what exactly are you accusing me of?'

'Calling me up in the middle of the night two nights in a row.'

'Er . . . no.'

She seemed convincing. In fact, she was such a good actress, I began to feel small shards of doubt lancing me. I had to take a punt and call her bluff.

'Emily, please don't deny it. The phone company have told me it was your number.'

'But they wouldn't have done that.'

'That sounds like an admission,' I said.

Emily said nothing, but instead walked to the kitchen and went to the fridge. She scrabbled around inside it, and then slammed it shut.

'Fuck!' she exclaimed.

'What?'

'I thought I had some wine left.'

'It's a bit early for wine, isn't it?'

'Never too early,' she said, and then she cackled, in a slightly unhinged way I thought.

'Come on Emily,' I said. 'You've got to stop this. I know what else you've been doing as well.'

'Go on then, I'm all ears. What else can you accuse me of this fine morning?'

As she was talking, she was rummaging through the cupboards, no doubt on the hunt for some booze. She was in a bad bad way, and I didn't want to break a butterfly upon a wheel.

'Well, I know that you follow me to the supermarket.'

This was met by an OTT snorting sound.

'Now why, Mr Holden, would I do something like that?'

I didn't want to respond to that, because we both knew the answer. There was also something pathetic about her continued denial, and I didn't want to play her game.

'I saw you waiting in the car,' I said.

'When?'

'On Monday.'

'I was making a call.'

'No you weren't.'

'How do you know?'

'Because I could see you.'

'I have a hands-free.'

'No you don't.'

'How do you know?'

'Because it's just not something you would have. Shall I go outside and check?'

Emily slumped down on a kitchen chair. I thought she was going to collapse, pass out, but instead she just sat there, looking emptily at the bottom of the fridge, the fridge that had so cruelly cheated her of alcohol.

'My life is fucked,' she declared.

'No it's not.'

'Yes it is.'

'Why is it fucked? You have three lovely children, you have a nice house, you look good, I don't see the problem. All right, I know that you are still upset about me, but surely not enough to say that your life is fucked.'

'Externals, Sam. Is that all you're interested in?'

'No, but . . .'

'Because you don't know what happens up here, do you?'

She tapped the side of her head.

'No, of course not. But I can guess. I can guess that you're upset because you've got divorced. You're stuck in the middle of the countryside with three children and you're on your own. Your last lover was a shit-loving-nappy-wearing pervert, and the man I think you still love doesn't love you back, and does in fact live in a state of marital bliss, which makes your own situation feel worse. I can guess that you are desperately worried about the future, about whether you'll ever find another husband, or at the very least a decent boyfriend who can be a father to your children, and you're worried that if you don't, you're going to end up lonely. And I can guess that the more you think about these things, the more they eat you up, and you become more and more preoccupied, until you realise that you are not doing your job as a mother. And I guess that in turn eats you up, and from then on it's a vicious circle of self-doubt and self-loathing. And then, one final guess, the great healer is of course the bottle. Except it's not really, is it? When you wake up, you hate yourself for doing it, and so the loathing gets worse. And so on.'

Emily started clapping, the type of sarcastic clap that crap playwrights insist on putting in their plays, and the kind of clap that nobody does in real life.

'Well done, Dr Freud,' she said.

I didn't reply. I slightly regretted putting on such a long spiel.

'Be as sarcastic as you like Emily, I still think you need help.'

'No I don't,' she said. 'I'm fine. It'll be fine, you'll see.'

'How can it be?'

'Because I'll get over you, that's how. It shouldn't take too long. You're not that special.'

I laughed.

'That's the attitude,' I said.

'But you think you're special, don't you?'

Uh-oh, I thought. Here comes the sourness.

'No,' I lied.

'Yes, you do. Oooh. Did you see me on Friday night? No? OK then, well you can catch me on *Joseph and Mary*. Oh yah, the party in London was such fun. So sorry I couldn't invite you. Numbers, eh? Wretched PR girl, you know what it's like. By the way, sorry that we had to sack you from the programme. Wife too jealous. Oooh. Did I tell you I'm now a columnist for the *Advertiser*? Make sure you get it! Looks like there'll be a book as well. Should be fun, don't you think?'

'Come off it,' I said. 'I'm not that much of a show-off.'

'Pah! You've become unbearable.'

'That's not fair!'

Emily lit another cigarette. This time she didn't offer me one. Her face contorted into a pinched, suddenly somewhat haggard, expression of pointed malice.

'You just think people like me and other people in this village are the little people.'

She jabbed her finger into my chest every time she said 'you'. It actually started to hurt.

'You just can't wait to get out and go and live in your old rectory or whatever it is. We're just stepping stones for you, aren't we? And I expect you find it all jolly fun that the village bicycle has declared her love for you, and I bet you laugh about me behind my back, and share jokes about me with all your London friends.'

'Jesus, Emily! Where is all this coming from? I haven't mentioned a word of what you said the other day. I haven't even told Sally. And that's the truth! God, this is eating you up. This isn't good for you, Emily, or your children. You should see someone professional. A psychiatrist even. Please.'

'I don't need a fucking shrink!'

'OK, OK. But you need a rest, or at least somebody neutral you can talk about all this to. That's what psychiatrists are for . . .'

'I don't need a fucking psychiatrist. Didn't you hear?'

'All right. But isn't there someone you can just talk to?'

'No. And besides, I don't need someone to talk to. The person with the problems is you, don't you see that?'

'Me?'

'Yes, you! You're the one who's losing touch with it all. You're the one who's lost their balance. You're the one who should see a fucking shrink!'

'I find that a little hard to take from someone who looks through their fridge for a bottle of wine at 10 in the morning.'

'And so fucking pompous as well.'

'Emily, please stop being like this.'

Watching her was soul-destroying. I wished I had told Sally about Emily now, then at least I could ask for her help. She'd know exactly what to do in this situation.

'No! It's YOU who needs the help. It's you who needs to be brought down. All that *WonderHubby* thing is just

358

shit. It's not you. It's all a pack of lies and crap. You must give it up Sam. Save yourself!'

This was all sounding far too dramatic.

'Have you been taking something?' I asked.

'Fuck off.'

'Have you?'

'No! Can't you see I'm angry with you? Can't you see that you're living a lie?'

'No. What's a lie?'

'Everything!' she shouted. 'The TV! The newspapers! The magazines! I've read all of it, and it's just shit! It's a load of lies. And your marriage to that woman, that's a lie as well.'

'Take that back,' I said.

'No. Because it's the truth, Sam. You know that you want to be with me, and you just won't admit it to yourself. And you'll never admit it if you stay with her.'

'But Emily, I don't want to be with you! I love Sally, and that's that.'

'You love me as well, I know it.'

'You're wrong.'

'No I'm not,' she insisted. 'No I'm not. You need to be brought back down to earth. All this *WonderHubby* shit has got to end, then you'll see who really counts, me or her! Let's face it, Sam, she's only with you because you're a success. And when you're no longer a success, then you'll see.'

Although she had a valid point that *WonderHubby* was probably the greatest deceit played upon the British public since the discovery of Piltdown Man, she had alienated me still further by bringing Sally's feelings into this. She knew nothing about how wonderful Sally really is. I felt indignation rise in my gut.

'How dare you speak about her like that? Can't you see that you're just jealous, Emily? You're jealous because Sally and I have everything you've ever wanted. But dragging us down isn't going to make you feel better. It'll just create more pain and resentment, and you'll be hurting people who haven't even touched you. Please Emily, I beg you, just leave it alone. Forget about me.'

'That's what you'd love, isn't it? For me to forget about you, and for you to forget about me. Mad old Emily. Remember her? Well, I'm not mad, and you're not going to forget about me.'

'There's no chance of that.'

She Dutch-fucked another cigarette.

'OK,' she said, hazily waving the fag in my direction. 'Here's a plan.'

'What?'

I was doing my best not to sound irritated.

'A plan,' she repeated.

'OK.'

'I want you to leave your wife for me.'

'No.'

'Ah! Ah! Patience. I haven't finished.'

I said nothing. Most of my being wanted to stand up, tell her to eff off, and be done with it. However, some sense of – what? Cowardice? Decency? Middle-class politeness? Sympathy? Whatever it was, I heard her out.

'And if you don't leave your wife, then I'll tell the newspapers that *WonderHubby* and the WHOLE Holden Childcare Programme is a pack of lies. You have until Monday. If I don't hear anything by then, I shall go to the press.'

'You can have your answer now,' I said.

'Oh yes?'

'You can stick it up your arse! How dare you black-mail me?'

'It's the only way, Sam. It's the only way to make you do what's right. And that's to be with me, and not her.'

'No, Emily, no. This is so fucked. So wrong. You're . . . you're mad. You should be fucking sectioned!'

'You're the mad one, Sam.'

'No I'm not, and yes you are.'

'You have until Monday.'

She clearly didn't want to accept my answer.

'I've already told you, Emily. Fuck you, and fuck off. Tell the papers what you like. They'll never believe you anyway, because they'll see you for the drunk little conniving bitch that you really are.'

'They'll probably like me, then. I thought all journalists were conniving little bitches. The women too. Hah!'

'Goodbye Emily. I came here to help you, and now I've been blackmailed. Well go on, do your worst. Then you'll see how much I love my wife.'

I walked out, and made sure not to slam the front door. That would have given her a victory of sorts.

I'm now eaten up by this. What can I do? I feel like phoning Laura and saying there's a madwoman on the loose, but what can she do? If Emily does go to the press, what she'll tell them is true. And it won't take them much to substantiate it. All they'll need to do is to phone the families and then that's it. We're sunk.

Just when it was going so well. I can see why people commit murder now.

Friday 19 September

I haven't told Sally the truth. I will, but not yet. Instead, I said that the phone company has traced the mysterious calls to somewhere in the West Midlands, and that they have barred it from calling us. As we know nobody in that part of the world, Sally is satisfied that my theory that it's some deranged fan is the right one. She was a little confused about how they could have got hold of our number, but I said that she must know that the phone companies are riddled with people who sell ex-directory numbers.

It was programme number three this evening, and I just felt sick watching it. All I could think about was Emily and her insane threat. I can see all my recent fortune disappearing as quickly as it came, just because a madwoman in a small village is obsessed with me. Perhaps I should tell Sally, and she could get some heavies from the Ministry round to put the frighteners on Emily. It's not really Sally's style though.

But what can I do? Nothing. Clearly I'm not going to

leave Sally. What was Emily thinking? She has utterly lost the plot.

Sunday 21 September

Sally kept asking me if I was OK. I told her that I was a little stressed out, but I was sure I would get into a routine. I have to spend Saturday morning writing my column, and Sunday afternoon preparing my slot on *Joseph and Mary* on Monday. Even though they're both quite straightforward, I want to get them right. Sally says our weekends are getting somewhat scuppered, but all I said was '130 grand'. No argument.

But of course the real reason why I'm stressed out is Emily. Fucking bloody Emily. I just feel so impotent.

Tuesday 23 September

Yesterday was a day of truly historic proportions. I'm not kidding. It will go down in the history of espionage, although I suspect that it will be a history that will not be released for seventy-five years. Peter will be eighty by then. I really hope he will still be around, because he, undoubtedly, was the unwitting star of the whole event.

It all started with an innocuous comment he made at breakfast, before Halet arrived. Sally had already left for work, and the three of us were having a relatively laid-back breakfast, despite the fact that it was a school morning. Somehow they were both dressed correctly, their packed lunches ready, and we were just eating our toast. I was keeping one ear on the radio, and the other on the usual surreal conversation that Daisy and Peter like to indulge in. Yesterday morning's was about Daleks and poo, I recall.

The radio news was talking about laptops, and about how there was some project to send them to the Third World. I couldn't quite work out what starving people would do with laptops, and I was listening intently to the rationale. As a result, I didn't really hear Peter's question until he shouted it at me.

'Daddy! I asked you a question!'

'What?' I responded irritably.

'What's a laptop?'

'Oh, a laptop is a computer that looks like a book. You know, like the one I have in my study.'

'Why are they called laptops?'

'Because they sit on your lap.'

'But yours sits on your desk.'

'I know. They can sit on your desk as well as your lap. They can sit anywhere that's flat.'

Peter munched his toast, and I returned to the radio.

'Mummy has a laptop, doesn't she?'

'Mummy ha' a 'aptop,' said Daisy.

'Yes, yes,' I said.

'Why does Mummy have a laptop?' Peter asked.

'What?'

'Why does Mummy have a laptop?'

'Because she uses it for work.'

'OK,' said Peter.

He carried on munching. I noticed that he had spilt

some milk on the table, and I went to get some kitchen roll. Meanwhile I carried on tuning in to the radio item. Then came Peter's key statement.

'Daddy?'

'Yes.'

'Halet uses Mummy's laptop.'

I literally felt the hairs on the back of my neck lift up. As did the ones on my arms. I felt cold and almost sick. It was the most peculiar sensation I have ever experienced. It was rather like one's first orgasm.

'What was that?' I asked.

'Halet uses Mummy's laptop.'

'When was this?'

'Lots of times. She uses it when Mummy is having a shower in the morning and you are still in bed. Halet says you are a lazy bones!'

He grinned at his indiscretion. I squatted down so we were at head height.

'Peter,' I said. 'Daddy is being very serious now. Did you really say that Halet uses Mummy's laptop?'

Sensing my tone, he looked at me solemnly.

'Yes. Sometimes she plugs a little phone into it.'

The sensation grew stronger, and my heart suddenly started pounding.

'You are absolutely sure about that?'

'Of course!'

'Does she say anything when she is doing this?'

'No. She just does it.'

'When did you last see this?'

'I can't remember.'

That was hardly surprising. Children of Peter's age have no concept of time. Christmas could have been last week for all he knows.

I rushed to the phone and tried Sally's mobile. It rang straight through to the answerphone, which meant she was probably on the Tube. I left a message, and then left a message on her work voicemail. I tried not to sound panicky, but I was. I kept trying to work out some innocent explanation, but I could think of none.

A key in the front door. Halet.

'Listen,' I said to Peter. 'Don't talk about the laptop. Understand?'

Peter could tell I was being deadly serious – an expression he probably hadn't seen since I threatened to leave him at the next station on the train to London.

'Good morning!' said Halet.

'Morning Halet!' we all went.

Don't be strange, I said to myself. Be your normal slightly bleary-eyed and useless self.

'I'm making some coffee,' I said. 'Do you want some?'

'Yes please,' she said.

I switched on the kettle and thought quickly. I had to make sure that I kept Halet just where I wanted her, and the best thing to do was for me to take the children to school and leave her in the house.

'Halet, I'm going to take Peter and Daisy to school this morning. I need to see Peter's teacher.'

'No problem,' she said. 'I'll clear up the breakfast things if you want.'

'Thanks so much. I don't know what we'd do without you!'

I looked at the kitchen clock. Half past eight. I would have to leave in fifteen minutes. Fifteen minutes in which to keep the children quiet, and for me to continue to act normally.

'Right you lot,' I said, 'upstairs to brush teeth.'

'It's OK, Mr Holden, I shall do it.'

'No, it's fine. Sally said it was about time I pulled my weight in the mornings.'

(She says this often.)

I hurried the children upstairs to brush their teeth and comb their hair.

'Daddy,' said Peter. 'Why isn't Halet taking us to school this morning? Is it because of the laptop?'

I put my hand over his mouth so hard I feared I might bruise him. I then held a finger to my lips and silently went 'Ssh!' He got the message, as did Daisy, who looked most perturbed.

'I've got to see Mrs Eyres,' I said. 'She wants to talk to me about a dinner Daddy is giving a speech at.'

This was nearly true.

'What's a speech?'

I was relieved to be on this non-laptop topic of conversation, and I kept it going for as long as I could. After ten minutes Peter had a working knowledge of demagoguery that far outshone that of any other five-year-old on the planet.

'OK, Halet, see you in a bit! If Sally rings, can you tell her I'm on my mobile?'

'Of course, Mr Holden.'

It was hard to reconcile my suspicions with Halet's friendly face.

'Say goodbye to Halet,' I said to the children. I knew even then that they would never see her again.

'Bye-bye Halet,' said Peter. 'See you later!'

'See u 'ater,' chimed Daisy.

'See you in a sec,' I said casually.

As we walked the four hundred yards to school, I tried Sally's mobile every few seconds. It constantly went to answerphone, and I left messages indicating that she should not try home, but call me on the mobile.

We reached the school, and I dropped Peter off at his classroom before making my way to the Portakabin that houses Daisy's playgroup. Still no call from Sally. Perhaps the Tube was stuck, or her mobile was out of battery. This was maddening.

When she did ring, it was just as I was delivering Daisy to Simone. I all but bundled Daisy towards her with a brusque 'bye-bye sweetheart', and Simone looked most put out. I mouthed a 'sorry' to her, but it clearly wasn't enough. Oh well, I thought, I would explain later.

'What the hell is it?' asked Sally. 'You've left about six messages. Is it the children?'

I dashed away from the Portakabin so I was out of earshot.

'No, it's not the children,' I said. 'It's Halet.'

'What about her? Is she sick? I thought she may have been coming down with a cold last week, so perhaps . . .'

'No! Nothing like that. Listen to me!'

'Jesus, Sam!'

'Halet has been looking at your laptop.'

Silence. I could hear street sounds down the line. Taxi horns, buses, a noisy thoroughfare.

'Are you there?' I asked.

'Yes. Say it again.'

'Halet has been looking at your laptop.'

'How do you know? When?'

'Peter told me. He says that she's looked at it lots of times. And, sometimes she attaches a mobile to it.'

'Fuck.'

'It looks bad, doesn't it?'

'Fuck! Fuck!'

'What are you going to do?' I asked.

'I'm going to activate something called Blue Switch.'

'What the hell is that?'

'You'll soon find out. Listen, Sam, this is what you must do. Get back home. Now. Act normally. Chat. Drink tea. Whatever you do, keep her in the house. Have you got that?'

'Yes, but what's going to happen?'

'You'll see in about twelve minutes. It'll be noisy and a bit frightening, but you'll be fine.'

'Twelve minutes?'

'It's never taken longer.'

We ended the call. As well as being absurdly nervous, at the top of my mind was: fuck, my wife has a cool job.

I walked back home quickly, but not ridiculously so. I was excited and scared, and the adrenalin made everything seem hyper-real. How the hell was I going to act normally? By the time I got back, two minutes had passed. There was just ten minutes until Blue Switch, whatever the hell that was.

'Hi, Halet,' I said breezily.

'Hello, Mr Holden.'

'Thanks so much for clearing the breakfast things.'

'Not at all. You were quick!'

'Oh yes – Mrs Eyres was off for some reason.'

I stood gormlessly in the kitchen. By my reckoning things would start happening at 9.18. I looked at the clock. It had just turned 9.09.

'I think I'm going to have another coffee,' I said. 'Do you want another?'

'No thanks! I've still got this one on the go!'

Once again, I switched the kettle on.

'Are you all right, Mr Holden?'

'Me? Oh yes, I'm fine. Absolutely fine.'

'You seem a little nervous.'

Sally was right – I would have made a crap spy.

'Do I? Oh, it's because I've got the *Joseph and Mary* show today. Have you seen me on it?'

'Oh yes,' she said. 'I thought you were wonderful! Very funny. Mind you, I don't care much for Mary, but he is almost as handsome as you!'

'You're too kind!'

The kettle switched off. I poured myself a thick cup of instant, realising that it was highly unlikely I was going to drink it.

9.11.

I looked into the garden. Everything seemed peaceful

and normal. I noticed the bird table had fallen over, and had sent a load of nuts and seeds all over the terrace. I would have to clear that up, I thought. I couldn't quite believe that Blue Switch, whatever it was, would be here in seven minutes.

At twelve past nine, I heard a dim thudding sound.

'What's that noise?' Halet asked.

'What noise?'

'Listen,' she said. 'That one. That sort of bdbd-bdbdbbbdr . . .'

I stayed still, pretending to strain my ears.

'Oh yes,' I said. 'I dunno.'

I did know.

It was a helicopter.

'It sounds like a helicopter,' said Halet.

'Do you think so? I think it could be some sort of funny car on the main road. Maybe it's a combine.'

'A combine?'

'You know, a combine harvester. Gathers up the crops. It's harvest time, so it's probably one of those. They're huge noisy buggers.'

'I don't think it's one of those,' said Halet.

I pretended to listen again.

There was no doubt that it was a helicopter, but what the hell was it going to do? It couldn't land here – we were in the middle of the village.

'No,' said Halet, her mind very much made up. 'It is a helicopter.'

'Yes,' I said. 'I think you're right. Probably the air ambulance.'

'The air ambulance?'

'Yes. Have you not seen it before? Sometimes, when there's a bad crash on the main road, it takes the injured people back to hospital.'

'I see,' said Halet.

She looked very ill at ease. And then she did something that scared the shit out of me. She reached into her handbag. Oh fuck, I thought, she's getting her gun. She's going to take me hostage and I'm going to die. This was it, I kept thinking, my last day on the planet.

She pulled out a small bag, from which she removed a little compact mirror. What was this? Poison? Was she about to commit suicide?

'You are staring at me, Mr Holden! Have you never seen a lady check her make-up?'

I laughed awkwardly.

'Sorry, I've got the morning stares.'

'Ah yes – my late husband used to have those.'

9.15.

Three minutes.

The helicopter was right overhead now, and it was making a fearsome racket.

'Perhaps there has been a crash in the village?' Halet asked.

'Maybe,' I said.

'We should go and look! We could help. I used to be a nurse, you know.'

I knew it was imperative that Halet should stay in the house. I had to delay her.

9.16.

'A nurse?' I said. 'Well I never knew that! How long were you a nurse for?'

'Fifteen years,' she said. 'Back in my home country. But never mind that! We should go and see what the helicopter is doing.'

The helicopter was so loud now we could barely hear each other. Something was about to happen, I just knew it, or at least my body knew it, because my heart was going nuts.

'Your home country,' I said. 'Remind me what it's called again? I can never remember how to pronounce it!'

Halet gave me a quizzical look. Why was this crazy Englishman asking questions like this when there was a helicopter buzzing about a hundred feet above the house?

She opened her mouth.

I won't ever know what she was about to say, because at that moment our front door exploded. Then, if I've got the sequence of events right, I heard the words 'Armed police! Do not move! I repeat do not move!'

At the same time, the entire kitchen filled with this acrid white smoke that stung my eyes as if bottles of shampoo had been poured into them. My throat tried to turn itself inside out, and I threw up my breakfast.

I was aware of black figures, torch lights, and Halet screaming, as well she might. Strong arms picked me up and took me through the back door out into the cool fresh air, where I gulped lungfuls of the stuff. It tasted so nice compared to the puke and what I now know was tear gas.

'Are you all right, Mr Holden?'

I nodded, and then squinted at the questioner. He was wearing a balaclava and was in the process of removing his gas mask. He looked the fucking business, and I desperately wanted his job there and then. In his right hand he held a black pistol that looked unspeakably cool, and so unlike the type of shitty thing you see in a film.

'I'm fine, thanks.'

'Hey, I know you!' he said. 'You're that chap off the telly! What's your name?'

'Sam Holden,' I hacked.

'You're that bloke who tells people how to look after their kids!'

'That's right!'

'Can I have your autograph?'

'With pleasure. But listen mate, you've got this all wrong.'

'How do you mean?'

Fuck, my eyes stung.

'You're not meant to be in awe of me, I'm meant to be in awe of you. Which I am!' I broke off, a hacking cough grasping my breath.

The policeman laughed and patted my back.

'Nasty stuff, eh? I'm sorry about that.'

'That's OK, I understand. Where's she gone, anyway?'

He looked up into the sky.

'She'll be halfway to some spook house by now.'

Another policeman joined us. He was dressed as awesomely as his colleague.

'There's a car here for you, sir.'

'For me? Am I being taken in as well?'

'No! He says he's from the *Joseph and Mary* show. He's to take you up to town.'

It should come as no surprise that I had quite forgotten.

'Could you tell him to wait ten minutes?'

'Of course!'

One has to be a pro about these things, I thought. Even if you've just been tear-gassed in your own kitchen and had your nanny choppered out to some interrogation centre, the show must go on.

Wednesday 24 September

Lots of fallout from Monday. Obviously it never made the papers, and the official line for the village – for those who didn't see Halet being bundled off – was that the police had made a cock-up. They thought a local drug dealer had taken refuge in our house, but they had been given the wrong intelligence. Most of them seemed to swallow that.

More importantly, Halet was indeed a spy. I still can't believe this, but Sally told me she buckled under interrogation. Apparently she had turned against the West when her husband had been killed in an American airstrike some years back, and she had been recruited by her country's intelligence service to come over here and inveigle herself into British society. She had been amazingly lucky to get work with Sally's colleague, and then even luckier to get work with us, because being more senior, Sally had access to far more sensitive information. It was Halet's spying that had blown all the department's networks. It seems incredible to think that while she was looking after Peter and Daisy so brilliantly and so kindly, she was simultaneously responsible for the deaths of dozens of people.

As was to be expected, Sally was severely reprimanded for poor security with her laptop. I thought she would have been sacked, but she had defended herself by saying that Halet had been given security clearance in order to work with Sally's colleague.

Peter and Daisy are very sad about what has happened to Halet, and the official line as far as they are concerned is that she had to rush back home in order to see her sick mother. 'When is she coming back?' Peter keeps asking, and Daisy provides her usual refrain. When I tell them she might not come back, there are lots of tears. They miss her so much and, to be honest, so do I.

Friday 26 September

Although we're still in a state of shock, I've been trying to get things back to normal. As we no longer have any childcare, I've resumed my househusband duties. It's fun being back in the saddle, and it's putting money where my *WonderHubby* mouth is. I got special dispensation to take the children out of school, and I took them shopping for toys. We bought the most disgusting amount, and I further spoiled them rotten by taking them for a pizza.

'Can we do this every day?' Peter asked.

'I'd love to,' I said. 'But I think if you bought toys all the time you'd get a bit bored.'

'I wouldn't be bored,' he said.

All this talk about toys made me worry about Emily. Obviously, with the drama of Halet's arrest, she had been firmly dispatched to the back of my mind, but toys had reminded me about money (toys always remind me about money) and that in turn made me dwell on Emily's threat. Would she really carry it out? And would anybody believe the drunken drawlings of a mad dipso from the Shires?

Yes they would, probably.

So I've resolved to see her once more. I'll go round tomorrow morning and try and sweet talk her. It's my only option.

Saturday 27 September
7.30 p.m.

Today has been even more dramatic than Halet's arrest day. An utter rollercoaster. I'm in dire need of the stiffest of drinks, but first I want to get everything down. It needs to be recorded for posterity, if that doesn't sound too self-important.

I went round to Emily's house just after nine o'clock, having told Sally that I was going to the ironmongers to get some handles, knobs etc. for the front door. (The police said they would pay for the damage, but so far no joy. The kitchen also stinks of tear gas, which keeps making me want to throw up.)

At first I thought all was well, because the car was in the drive and one of the upstairs windows was open. I knocked and waited, and then I knocked again.

'Hello!' I shouted through the letter box.

Still nothing.

I peered through. The place was even more of a tip than it was last week.

'Hello!'

Silence.

For some reason – a logical one, probably – I decided to walk round the house to see if everything was OK. As I did so, I looked through the ground-floor windows, which revealed scuzz everywhere – unwashed crockery, leftover food, toys scattered, laundry piled up on the kitchen floor. It was like a dosshouse, but somehow worse, because I knew children had to live in it. (We used to have a neighbour who lived like this, and it constantly amazed me that her children were able to emerge unscathed without some sort of deadly bacillus.)

I reached the back door and knocked.

'Hello?'

I tried the handle. It turned. Should I go in?

'Hello?'

Why did I keep saying that?

I walked into the kitchen, and was struck by the smell of the unwashed laundry and the dirty dishes, an olfactory combination that took me straight back to bachelorhood. Aaah – carefree, hygiene-free days.

'Emily?'

I made my way up the stairs. I could hear nothing, but the smell was getting worse.

I couldn't remember which one was her bedroom, so I tried the first door I came to. It was a child's room, festooned with toys and clothes. The second door was another child's room, a little tidier than the first, probably because it was a girl's room.

'Emily?'

It was becoming obvious that there was no one here. They must have all been picked up by someone and taken away for the weekend. There was one more door to try, which had to be her room. I gently pushed it open.

I was met by darkness and a smell of vomit. Jesus, I thought, this was getting out of hand.

'Emily?'

No reply. My eyes grew accustomed to the gloom.

'Emily?'

A figure on the bed.

'Oh my God!' I shouted.

I rushed in, my brain struggling to cope with what my eyes were relaying to it. Emily was sprawled on the bed, her body messily arranged like a rag doll.

'Emily?'

A bottle of vodka lay empty by the bed, and her hair was matted in a pool of half-dried sick. God knows how many hours she'd been like this. Then a flood of panic came over me as I realised she might not be breathing – she could have choked on her vomit.

'Oh God no!'

I slapped her face. Nothing.

'Emily! Wake up!'

A stir. A very weak mumble. She heaved and I jumped back, fearing she'd be sick again. She briefly opened her eyes and then they lolled back up in her head again. I thanked a non-existent god that she wasn't dead. I couldn't believe things had got so out of control. Why hadn't I realised how depressed she was? I shouldn't have left. I should have helped more. Silent tears rolled down my cheeks as I shifted her into the recovery position, away from the sick. The stench was making me gag.

And then I spotted the pills, or rather the empty bottle of pills, neatly placed on the bedside table. I felt my heart skip, a lump of guilt and despair rising in my throat.

'Oh shit oh shit,' I think I went.

Medically, I had no idea what to do, so I covered her up with the duvet, recalling that warmth was always important in these scenarios.

'Phone,' I shouted to myself, 'where's the fucking phone?'

I looked around the bedroom. No phone.

I raced downstairs, nearly tripping over.

'Come on! Where the fuck is it?'

I scrabbled through the mess in the drawing-room. No phone. Into the kitchen, and after what seemed like decades, I found it under a cereal packet. I pressed 999. Nothing. I looked at the screen. Blank. The wretched battery was not charged up!

'Must be a normal phone! Come on! Give me a normal fucking phone!'

I ran around the house, panicking. I knew that panicking would achieve nothing, and I made myself calm down. I went back to the drawing-room, and tore it right up. No phone.

No phone in the dining-room, but just off the dining-room was a small door, which I all but kicked in. A study! There had to be a phone in here, there just had to be.

And there was. And it was a normal, batteryless phone.

I dialled 999, reflecting that the only land-based emergency service I had yet to encounter this week was the fire brigade.

'Which service do you require?'

'Ambulance please!'

After an age, I was routed through to some control centre in Djibouti.

'She's had an overdose,' I shouted. 'Please come quickly.'

I ran back upstairs, back into Emily's bedroom, and checked on her. I became angry and upset, feeling that this was somehow all my fault, and yet knowing that it really wasn't. Emily was in a far worse state than I – or perhaps anyone else – had imagined.

'You stupid girl,' I said. 'You stupid bloody girl.'

Once again, that strange feeling of paternalism. I felt like she was my daughter, and that I had to do my best to protect her. At that moment I felt a very real and deep love for Emily, the love of a father for a child.

When the ambulance came I felt a sense of relief, but also a sense of loneliness. I needed someone here, and that could only be one person.

Sally clutched my hand reassuringly while we watched Emily being loaded into the ambulance. When the police arrived Sally carried on holding my hand as they satisfied themselves that I wasn't some failed murderer. Afterwards, as I sat numbly at Emily's kitchen table, remembering happier times when we had shared glasses of late-morning wine and chatted about the children, Sally went about cleaning Emily's bedroom and the general carnage. What a woman.

Then we left, grateful to return to our warm, happy home. It still amazes me that Sally asked no questions. We both knew that what had happened had gone beyond jealousy and marital tiffs.

After leaving Peter and Daisy with Kate, we went to see Emily in the hospital. I couldn't believe that Sally wanted to come, but she insisted.

'The woman's ill, Sam,' she said. 'She needs our help. I'm not going to let the fact that she is in love with you stand in the way of that.'

'Thank you,' I said.

We arrived at her bedside, where we found Jim, her ex-husband. He looked terrified.

'How is she?' I asked.

'She'll make it,' he said. 'I expect her liver will be a bit ropy from now on.'

'No more booze for her,' I said.

'Quite.'

We all stared down at her in silence. She was asleep, and she looked peaceful. There was some colour in her cheeks, and, strangely, she looked better than she had done in weeks. It was as if all the vomiting had purged her of her demons. Jim looked up and caught my eye.

'I gather you found her,' he said.

'That's right.'

'Thank you,' he said simply.

He looked down again at his ex-wife. He had both love and tears in his eyes.

'Do you think she wanted to die?' he asked.

I paused.

'No,' I said confidently. 'I think it was a cry for help.'

'I hope so,' he said.

'She's not been well,' I continued. 'You know she's been . . .'

'I do,' Jim said immediately. 'That's why I've just been awarded custody of the children.'

Sally and I exchanged glances.

'I hadn't realised,' I said.

'She only found out yesterday. I convinced the courts

that she was no longer fit to be a mother. Too much drinking. Too much, you know, *running around*.'

I knew what the euphemism meant.

'But it's created a vicious circle,' he said. 'Made her worse.'

Jim's bottom lip started quaking. Sally walked over and put an arm round him. I stood there hopelessly while he wept.

'Would you like a cup of tea?' I asked.

'How brilliantly British,' said Jim through his tears. 'And do you know what, yes I bloody well would. A good cup of thick black English builders' tea.'

I went off, knowing that the chances of finding a decent cup of tea were minimal.

As I walked down the corridors, vainly searching for a vending machine, my mobile rang. I cursed that I had forgotten to turn it off, but I nevertheless answered it.

'Hello?'

'Hi Sam, it's Toby Andrews here.'

'Oh hello.'

This was the crunch time. This was when they were ringing me to get my response to all of Emily's allegations. The fact that it was Toby doing it annoyed me, because of all the media people I had been dealing with, he's the only one I've got any time for.

'Where's your bloody column?' he asked.

'My column?'

'Yes. I was rather hoping to have had it by now.'

'I'm sorry, I'm in a hospital at the moment. A good friend has just had a terrible accident.'

'Does this mean you can't do it?'

I literally scratched my head.

'I was kind of thinking . . .' I began.

'What?'

'I was thinking that you wouldn't want a column from me any more.'

'Why?' Toby sounded perplexed.

'Um, haven't you been approached by someone about my programme?'

'Yes.'

'Emily Taylor?'

'That's the one,' said Toby.

'And, aren't you going to be doing something about what she said?'

'Hold on a sec.'

I heard Toby issuing some instructions to an underling.

'Sorry about that,' he said. 'Where were we?'

'Emily Taylor,' I said. 'Apparently she came to see you with a story about me. I was wondering if you were going to be writing about what she told you.'

'No.'

My heart skipped.

'No?'

'That's right.'

'But why not?'

'Three reasons. First, she's a honey-nut fruit loop. Second, there's no mileage in stories about reality TV being bollocks. We all know it is, and frankly, everybody knows your show is a comedy. No one believes your system really works. And thirdly, we are loyal to our columnists.'

'So you're not going to run anything?'

'That's what I said. Now when can you give me your bloody copy? If I don't get it by four, I'll be tempted to go with Emily.'

'I'll do it right away,' I said.

'Good stuff. Hope your friend gets better and all that.'

'I'm sure she will, thanks.'

I put the phone back in my pocket. I walked along, dumbfounded. I literally jumped up and clicked my heels together, and then realised too late that I am not very good at jumping in the air and clicking my heels together, and fell over.

SAM ON A SUNDAY

Yesterday I had one of those experiences that has reminded me what's important in life. You need these experiences pretty regularly, otherwise it's too easy to forget about who you really are, and who you really are to other people, especially those you love and care for.

I don't know what time my friend took too many pills, but I do know that when I got there, she was in a bad way. I'll spare you the details, but she was very ill indeed. Not being a medical man, all I could do was to roll her into the recovery position and dial 999. While I waited for the ambulance, I thought she might die, because what she had taken could have felled a horse.

The good news is that she pulled through. Her death would not just have been a tragedy to her ex-husband, who I know still loves her very much, but especially tragic for her three beautiful children to whom my friend is a brilliant mum.

The bad news is that the pills and the alcohol will have damaged her insides, although the doctors say it is too early to establish quite how badly. But the crucial thing is that she is alive.

So why did my friend take an overdose? As is usual, there are lots of reasons, some of them simple, some of them complicated. The simplest one is the fact that she had fallen in love with someone who didn't love her back. Another simple one is that she was clinically depressed, and I am now kicking myself not to have insisted that she sought some help. I think that the overdose was not so much a suicide attempt, more a desperate call for attention.

Not so long ago, my friend was a vivacious, fun-loving woman. She was a bit of a flirt, frankly. Parties without her were just not the same, even if wives no longer had to keep an eye on their husbands! But it was all just a bit of fun for her, and she wasn't some kind of man-snatching monster.

But recently, eaten away by the depression and the unrequited love, she began to change. She became bitter and increasingly poisonous. She no longer took any care of herself, and her house began to resemble a squat. Things got so bad that her ex-husband was granted custody of the children. Although this was right and necessary, it was a deep blow.

She knew, deep down, that this sort of behaviour was not right, but she was unable to change it. She knew she was starting to mutate into a quite different person, and there was nothing she could do.

Or she felt there was nothing she could do. She could have sought help, but a part of her was revelling in her new self. I think she enjoyed being nasty, and found it liberating. It was only when she was sober that she realised quite how horrific the mutation was becoming.

The gap between her two selves soon became so great that she could no longer function. The more extreme the two selves, the worse she became. At some point she had to snap, and that's what must have happened on that lonely Friday night.

Her actions have made me think of a conversation I had with her a short while ago. I was telling her that she was starting to lose it, but she was insistent that it was me who had the problems, that it was me who was living the lie, not her.

At the time I dismissed it, but now I think she was right.

As you know, over the past three weeks my programme WonderHubby *has been airing. It's all about how I try to help families by using the techniques of management consultancy.*

It's quite fun, I like to think, and has already earned me a column in this great newspaper, as well as a regular slot on Joseph and Mary. *The programme has had some great reviews and healthy viewing figures. There's already talk of another series in the wings, and, before I forget to mention it, I'm writing a book.*

To put it mildly, it's been quite a change from my old life as a househusband, in which I looked after my children Peter and Daisy.

And that's the point, it's been a change. But has it been a change for the better? Sure, I'm earning a lot more money than before (in fact, I was earning none), but is there a gap between the old Sam and the new Sam?

I think there is, and the reason is this. I've become a liar. WonderHubby is the biggest pack of lies that has ever invaded your living room. What you see on the screen has NO bearing at all on reality, and yet you are being told that it's one hundred per cent true.

Well, let me tell you now. It's not. It's a load of crap, frankly. And I'm responsible for it. What started off as a bit of fun has now become deadly serious, and I've heard that there are some people who really want to use my system to bring up their children.

My advice to them is this: Don't. I tried it with my kids and it doesn't work. The Venn diagram which shows Management Consultancy and Childcare has no bit that meets in the middle, not even a crumb.

What my friend did has made me aware that being two people is just not a possibility. And I don't like the lying person I'm becoming.

So, TV producers and agents and PR people, you can keep all your deals and exciting offers. I just want to stay the same old Sam. He may not be terribly rich, and he's probably a bit of a fogeyish fart, but at least I like him. And so do my family.

All right. That's it. I'm off.

Diary of a Hapless Househusband

Sam Holden

One man's encounter with domesticity . . .

When father-of-two Sam loses his job, he (reluctantly) agrees to stay at home while his wife returns to work. Secretly thinking this whole parenthood thing a breeze of leisurely jaunts to the park, reading the paper while the children play quietly and occasionally attending a civilised play date or two, Sam quickly realises just what exactly it means to be a stay-at-home parent.

Inevitably, domestic mayhem ensues. Just trying to get dressed in the morning and out of the house without going to A&E is a feat, as is managing the children's complicated play-date schedule while fending off the unwelcome advances of Jodhpur Mum at the playground. And Sam's foolproof 72-step Childcare Programme doesn't seem remotely up to the task.

Desperate to get his life back on track, Sam seizes upon a variety of mad schemes, but just as things look like they're beginning to fall into place, he makes a very surprising discovery . . .

'A very, very funny and often touching account of one man's struggle to try and run Planet Home.'
Allison Pearson, author of *I Don't Know How She Does It*

arrow books

The Playground Mafia

Sarah Tucker

Meet Caroline Gray: divorcee and newly-single mother. Firmly closing the door on her acrimonious divorce, Caroline and son Ben have moved to the trendy town of Frencham where they join Caroline's long-time best friends, Heather and Eva. Settling into their new life is easy, but nothing has prepared Caroline for the demands of motherhood at The Sycamore, the school the trio's beloved offspring attend. Forget classroom bullies, forget trips to the head's office, this is full-scale adult playground politics. This is battle with the mothers who won't take no for an answer – the Playground Mafia.

Amidst the four-wheel drives, Ben's complicated afterschool play-date schedule and her friends' perilous extra-marital affairs, Caroline tries to keep a low and very single profile. But it's not long before she too finds herself under the mafia's scandal-radar, and her life takes an unexpected turn . . .

arrow books

ALSO AVAILABLE IN ARROW

The Battle for Big School

Sarah Tucker

There are 50 places at The Oaks, the best grammar school in the area, and 1,000 children applying. Competition is fierce and parents are prepared to do everything and anything to get their child one of the coveted spaces. Absolutely anything . . .

Close friends Lily, Julie, Karen and Paul aren't overly concerned. After all, aren't their children are bright and sociable enough? But they're quickly shaken out of their complacency when enrolment time approaches and turns out to be little more than a rigged lottery, where only the most ruthless hold the cards. Marriages and friendships crumble under the pressure, fake addresses abound and tutors rates soar. And, of course, money passes hands like water, between estate agents, local councillors and City fundraisers, all of whom hold the purse strings for school funding.

As measures get extreme (well, down-right ridiculous really), the four quickly rally their troops and throw themselves into the battle for big school. Initially wary to be in competition with each other, they realise that the only way of out-smarting the rest of the pack is by coming up with a plan. Because getting their kids into The Oaks will demand determination and strategy akin to Mission Impossible . . .

arrow books

School's Out

Sarah Tucker

In school playgrounds across the country parents huddle in worried packs, desperately putting together their final plans to survive the summer weeks of mayhem – school is officially out!

For once, Amanda has a simple, cheap and fail-safe plan to make it through the summer holidays with her three overexcited offspring. But a last-minute addition of fellow-mum Suzanne and her perfect son Orlando quickly shatters Amanda's vision of the quintessential bucket-and-spade summer adventure.

In fact, before she even makes it to the picture-perfect Cornish idyll that is home to her one-time playground comrade Skyler, Amanda has to endure tantrums, floods, and an eerie B&B, all with three ratty kids and a carsick dog in tow. When they finally arrive, dishevelled and exhausted, she discovers that not only must she endure Suzanne at close quarters in a cramped cottage, but also that Skyler's business is in dire need of a helping hand.

In the weeks that ensue, Amanda discovers there is only one way to survive the summer holidays, and that's with a stiff drink, a pair of wellies and a bucket-full of bonhomie!

arrow books

The Secret Life of a Slummy Mummy

Fiona Neill

For Lucy Sweeney, motherhood isn't all astanga yoga and Cath Kidston prints. It's been years since the dirty laundry pile was less than a metre high, months since Lucy remembered to have sex with her husband, and a week since she last did the school run wearing pyjamas.

Motherhood, it seems, has more pitfalls than she might have expected. Caught between perfectionist Yummy Mummy No 1 and hypercompetitive Alpha Mum, Lucy is in danger of losing the parenting plot. And worst of all, she's alarmingly distracted by Sexy Domesticated Dad. It's only a matter of time before the dirty laundry quite literally blows up in her face . . .

'This slice of angst and affluenza is several cuts above the rest . . . witty, observant and supremely intelligent.' *The Times*

'There is something of Bridget Jones's hopeless-but-adorable quality about Lucy . . . Neill's hilarious depiction of the manifold daily perils of stay-at-home motherhood is so convincing that it soon looks like the most challenging job in the world – and Lucy is all the more sympathetic simply for staying afloat.'
Daily Telegraph

arrow books